THE

RESENTMENT

THE
RESENTMENT

A THRILLER

T. O. PAINE

DARK
SWALLOW
BOOKS

Published by Dark Swallow Books
www.darkswallowbooks.com

Library of Congress Control Number: 2021924723

Paperback ISBN-13: 978-0-9992183-5-8
Hardcover ISBN-13: 978-0-9992183-6-5
eBook ISBN-13: 978-0-9992183-7-2

For those who have it in their hearts to forgive.
For those who live and let live.

CHAPTER ONE

LAUREN

My husband's life flashes before my eyes. He hangs from the Cedar River bridge, grasping my wrists, and I've got to pull him up. I've got to save him, but—

I close my eyes and pull.

He's thin as ever but still too heavy for me.

His life—our life—our history won't stop flashing before my eyes.

I see him leaning against a keg at the college party where we first met. Tall, skinny, British geek. Mr. William Kaine. He wasn't my type, but he became my everything. Oh, God. Without him, I have nothing. Tonight's our twenty-second wedding anniversary, and he's going to die.

He squeezes my wrists. I squeeze back. He dangles above the raging torrent.

Darkness hides the rain, but I feel it on my face.

Fear grips me. I can't focus. Too many memories. My anger swells, but I push it away.

Our wedding day rushes into my head. The insidious Ryan Kaine, my brother-in-law, is there. He raises a wine glass, makes a toast, and stumbles off the stage.

Focus.

I've got to pull William up. Save him, but I can't. He's going to fall. He's going to die and make me a widow, and Mason—Mason's only sixteen. Mason needs his father.

I try to open my eyes, but the stress of holding onto William is unbearable.

I pull.

The rain falls.

William.

I see myself sitting in a bathtub surrounded by flowers. Yellow petals float on the surface, clinging to the edges of the tub. William poured the bath for me a few weeks after Mason was born. He did it so I could have a break. So I could relax. It was maybe the last time I relaxed, and—this can't be happening.

What do they want? Why were they chasing us?

I open my eyes.

The look of terror on William's face ignites my rage. He never learned to swim.

I can't let go.

I won't let go.

His wrists begin to slip through my fingers. I lean farther over the concrete barrier and pull with both hands, but gravity is winning. The river rushes through the darkness below, but I won't let it take him. I teeter on my toes. I let go with one hand and brace myself against the barrier.

I pull.

His wrist slides free, I lean over the edge, and our fingertips catch long enough for me to grasp his forearm with both hands.

He kicks his legs.

I hang onto him with everything I have.

He's my world.

Help.

Looking over my shoulder, I strain to see if anyone has come to help, but there's only the sedan that chased us. It sits mangled against the bridge abutment. The passenger side headlight is destroyed, but the driver's side headlight comes on, sending shivers down my spine. Steam pours over the crumpled hood, obscuring the windshield. Someone's in there. The bridge didn't budge when the car slammed into it, and William barely escaped being crushed by leaping over the edge.

I waste precious energy scanning the riverbanks below for someone. Anyone. It's so dark down there. Lights from the apartments across the way penetrate the trees, but there's no movement. The units are too far away. No one can hear my screams. The rain runs into my eyes, making it hard to see, but I won't wipe it away. I won't let go. I sniff, and I struggle, and the smell of motor oil sullies my senses.

I'm losing my breath.

There's a clicking behind me.

The car's headlight turns off, then on again. It flickers. The engine turns over, sputters, then stalls. The dome light comes on for a split-second, but I can't see who's inside.

"Are they coming?" William asks. His eyes are gray in the darkness, his free arm flailing over his head, his shoulders twisting.

"No, I don't think so." Steam obscures the car's windshield.

"They want the card," William says. "They're after me for

the card."

He slips.

I lunge forward and grab his shirt with my left hand. I manage to lock my other hand around his wrist. "Pull. I've got you."

"The card," he says. "They want the card. It's in St. Croix."

"Pull!"

"St. Croix!"

The engine turns over, bursting to life.

I startle and lose my grip.

William reaches for me, grasps at my fingers.

My feet slip off the ground, and I lose hold of his shirt.

He strips the wedding ring off my finger as he falls, backstroking through the night air. The drop is short, but the raging river pulls him under, and he is gone.

Instinct says jump in after him, but my rage takes over.

Everything turns red.

I race to the driver's side window and beat my fists against the glass. The engine revs. One strike after another, I pound. My knuckles bleed, and I scream, but everything sounds far away like I'm trapped in a tunnel.

The engine whines.

The gears grind.

Tinted black glass, black paint, black tires, black hubcaps. I plant my palms on the window, trying to see inside. Steam pours over the hood, burns my cheek. Blood from my knuckles runs down the glass.

Hot tears course down my face.

The driver—nothing but a shadow—leans away from me, grips the steering wheel, and jerks his knee up and down, pumping the gas. He shifts the car in and out of gear, over and over. The transmission howls. I can't see his face.

"Open the door, you bastard. I'm going to kill you!"

The rear wheels spin.

I jerk back.

The car reverses, and the front-end swings out wildly, then rocks to a stop.

The license plate—torn and twisted—dangles from the bumper.

It's unreadable, but the trunk lid has five rings and an A8 emblem.

The driver guns the engine, and I stand there, helpless, watching the taillights vanish into the night.

CHAPTER TWO

RYAN

Ryan Kaine settles into his office chair with his lucky blanket wrapped around his shoulders, his cup of coffee on his desk, and the heat turned all the way down. His computer hums like a defiant child. He has all evening to make the code compile, and if he can do it, he can move on to chapter four, "Conditionals and Control Flow."

Ryan presses the F5 key, but an error message bursts onto the screen.

java.lang.NullPointerException on line 19.

Line nineteen?

The file with the error message has thirty-two lines of code, and this null pointer exception isn't the only error. Other errors stack, one on top of another, filling the output window.

Ryan scoots back from the monitor and puts his Java programming book down. He gazes at his HTML book—*Web Design with HTML*. Creating web pages with HTML is far simpler than learning to write code. When a web page is messed up, it just looks bad. It doesn't rattle off meaningless error messages. How frustrating.

What a way to spend a Saturday night, but it's better than getting drunk.

The blanket slips off his shoulders, and the draft from the window hits him in the back of the neck. His landlord said the window couldn't be sealed—something about the wooden frame not butting up against the sixty-year-old bricks correctly. It costs a fortune to run the heater, and it barely works. The building owners refuse to replace anything. In fact, they've threatened to raise the rent, and if that happens, his salary as a truck driver won't cut it.

Downtown Seattle must have less expensive places to live, but he's entrenched here, trapped by his own circumstance. He sobered up a few blocks away, and everyone here knows him. They know his past, and it keeps him honest. Living near his homegroup meeting keeps him honest. And sober.

Thank God he's sober.

A chill hits him, and he shivers. He should be grateful for what he has, but gratitude doesn't make the studio apartment any warmer. Top computer programmers live in four-bedroom lofts. If Ryan could learn to write code, he would settle for a two-bedroom condo. No. He'd settle for one bedroom with a big furnace.

But he'll never have a better place if he can't make this damn program compile.

He punches the F5 key again, and the error reappears. He flips through the Java book and reads about object references. Everything points to something. Everything must point to something, or it's null. But this object isn't null. It can't be.

He's checked every line of code, and it matches the example in the book.

Screw this.

He opens Firefox and navigates to a real estate website and searches for apartments near his. The rents have gone up. Bored, he browses to a job website and types in *Java Programmer*. The starting salaries are three times what he makes. He could easily afford to move if he could just learn how to program this damn—his pocket vibrates. It's a call from Juan, his sponsee.

Between work and AA, Ryan never has enough time to learn computer programming. Sure, he's sober. Sure, he's got his eight-year chip—one of the most dangerous years, the year most people get complacent and relapse—but he deserves a break.

No.

He can't get complacent. Like the *Big Book* says, he can't rest on his laurels.

He's made it this far because he's worked the program, sponsoring alcoholics like Juan. Yet, things aren't getting better. He's sitting here freezing, trying to save a few bucks on his electric bill, wrapped in his lucky blanket like old times. Like he's homeless again.

His phone vibrates.

"Hello?"

"I'm at the Squire, man. I don't know what I'm doing here. I—"

"I know what you're doing there. Come on, Juan. We both know what you're doing."

"Hey, I haven't been drinking, man. Honest."

"I'm glad you called, but the question is . . . what's next?"

"I went inside, man. I just wanted to say hey to the guys,

you know? But I—"

"Are you still inside?"

"No. I'm in the parking lot. I—I think I'm going to be alright. I shouldn't have called."

Beneath Juan's smooth, nothing-much-matters tone swims a trembling forgetter. Ryan can hear it plain as day. Juan has forgotten the misery that brought him to AA. The misery of waking each day, wishing for serenity, but finding nothing but a craving.

Ryan swivels in his chair, presses the phone to his ear, and gazes at the crooked window beyond his ragged brown couch. It's cold in here, but it's colder outside. If the rent goes higher, he'll be forced to move, and then he remembers what it was like living on the streets with nothing but his lucky blanket. His reindeer blanket. The silver, deer eyes staring up at him each night in the park. The golden ribbons tying the deer together as they bound off rooftops, unifying them for some purpose, holding them together while the world tries to tear them apart by selling mini shooters for ninety-nine cents and throwing them in jail as if they were evil. As if they didn't suffer from a disease.

It's cold, but life's not so bad. Ryan has a desk and a computer and a future.

"I'm going to get off the phone now, man," Juan says. "I got to go."

"Hold on, Juan. You didn't answer my question." His keys lie next to his HTML book, and he picks them up. Ryan is grateful he owns a car and never lost his license. He's not only allowed to drive, but SPD Delivery trusts him with an expensive truck. Most alcoholics aren't as fortunate. Most don't have a chance.

But his sponsee, Juan . . . he has a chance. He came into

AA on his own, out of desperation. He hit bottom, but there is always lower to go. His next binge could kill him.

We alcoholics are not cats. We don't have nine lives.

"Juan, you didn't answer me. The question is . . . what's next?"

Silence.

"I'll understand if you want to go back inside, get drunk, and start all over, but you know where that will lead, right? You've been there before."

"No, man. I'm not going back in. I'm off that shit, for good. I just thought, you know, I thought I should call you. *No importa.*"

"The Squire? Over there on Fourth Avenue?"

"Yeah, but don't worry, *güey.* I—hold on. I'm getting a call. It's my girl. I gotta go."

It's a lie. No one's calling Juan's cell phone. His girl stopped speaking to him months ago. "Call her back later. I need you to stay on the line, okay?"

"No, man. I—"

"Juan, listen. Things have gotten better since you stopped, right?" Ryan grabs his jacket and rushes into the hall, pulling the door closed behind him.

"Yeah, man. But—"

"Don't throw it away. Don't let your forgetter take over." Ryan stops and looks at the cracked paint in the hallway. He goes back, rams his key into the deadbolt, and locks it. The corridor smells like rotten leaves. "Life's gotten better, right? Do you want to throw it all away?"

"I know. I know." Juan breathes into the phone. Ryan can almost smell the alcohol. "And I know what you're doing, man. Don't worry. I'm not going back in there."

Ryan runs down the hall, wondering if he should use his

honesty speech. No one can stay dry if they can't be honest, but telling Juan life will continue to get better in sobriety is a lie. Ryan's been sober in this hell-hole apartment for the last eight years.

Sober and cold.

"What are you doing, man?" Juan asks.

"Are you still outside the bar?" Ryan hits the stairs.

"Yeah."

"Okay. I'll be there in fifteen minutes."

Ryan can get there in ten if his old Civic doesn't break down.

"You don't have to come, man."

"I know."

CHAPTER THREE

LAUREN

Last night was our twenty-second wedding anniversary. Our last wedding anniversary.

William drowned in the river.

His voice comes from his office, but he's not in there. These hallucinations have been happening all day. He's not in his office because he's gone.

Because he drowned.

William Kaine drowned.

My everything drowned.

Now he's nothing but a figment of our daily routine. I hear him putting on his shoes, getting ready to go to work, brewing a pot of coffee. It's not even a workday. It's not even morning. It's Saturday night, and I'm standing motionless in the kitchen, my mind wandering. My thoughts haven't been straight since leaving the hospital this morning. Since the police rudely interrogated me, wanting to know about William.

No, that's not fair.

They weren't rude. They were just doing their job.

And William was perfect, by the way. He was driven, intelligent, and proud of his profession. Work was his life. He was making the world a better place by stopping computer hackers. He was brilliant. Al Gore may have invented the internet, but William's work at TriamSys was revolutionizing it. He had so much to live for.

What's the world going to do without him?

What am I going to do without him?

They want the card. It's in St. Croix.

There's an empty bowl on the counter. I've been staring at it for a while. Why did I come into the kitchen?

Mason.

I came to get my sixteen-year-old a bowl of ice cream. He hasn't eaten all day. Actually, he's hardly eaten since he started high school. Now that his father is gone, he might wither away completely. He—

The tears come.

I go to the freezer and take out a box of vanilla ice cream. From the refrigerator, I snatch a carton of strawberries.

A few neighbors and my good friend—my only friend—Olivia, brought us bereavement baskets and casseroles earlier, but strawberries and ice cream are Mason's favorite. I hope he'll eat. I hope he'll open up. After I told him the news, he shut himself in his room. He's been in there all day.

It's rained all day. The clouds won't go away.

I place the ice cream container and the berries next to the bowl and take out a spoon. I need to focus on dishing this up, but the image of the black car and the bridge . . . William falling into the river . . .

Every time I think of it, my anger swells.

William never learned to swim. When the search and rescue team found his body, the police opened an investigation. I hope to hear something soon, but I'm not holding my breath. The car—that black car . . . it just drove away.

I need to know who drove that car.

But Mason needs to eat.

And he needs to leave his room.

What if he becomes a total recluse? Sitting in bed, glued to the internet twenty-four-seven. William and I hoped that would change when he got older, but it didn't. When he turned sixteen last summer, we offered him a car, but he wasn't interested. All his friends are online, not that he has many friends.

We should never have bought him that laptop.

I scoop the ice cream into the bowl and listen. Sometimes he makes noise, moving around upstairs, but not tonight. He might have fallen asleep. I pull a knife out of the butcher's block, place a strawberry on the cutting board, and line up the blade.

I slice the strawberries into halves.

Focus on the blade.

The black car . . . the Audi . . . it just drove away.

I got mad last night. Really mad. My anger returned. I hadn't seen red like that in years.

The knife slips, and I narrowly miss cutting my thumb.

My mind is wandering again.

Focus. Mason needs to eat.

The strawberries bleed onto the cutting board.

Someone killed my husband.

My hands tremble.

Someone almost killed me.

William said they wanted *the card*, but I don't know what that means. He never told me about a card, but it must be related to his work at TriamSys.

My anger swells. I need to stay calm.

I need to focus.

William always put his work ahead of me, and now he's dead.

Damn TriamSys.

Tinges of red skirt my vision, and I nick my thumb.

Ignore the pain and focus.

Swiftly, I slice the strawberries, splitting each one in two, watching the red juice seep from the centers. The syrup runs off the cutting board onto the counter, and I'm reminded of the blood from my knuckles last night, streaming down the car window as I pounded my fists against the tinted glass, demanding the driver get out.

Demanding to know why he murdered my William.

The back of my neck heats up. My hands quake. I lose my grip on the knife, and it falls onto the marble countertop with a *clang*. I close my eyes and picture the black car. The chase— William and I running, hand-in-hand. I've replayed it a thousand times, but I can never see who is behind the wheel. The license plate was mangled. Unreadable.

I put my hands on the counter and take a deep breath.

No one heard me scream last night, but someone must have seen me. The police arrived too fast not to have received a call from someone. *Hello? Is this the police? Yes, there's a car stopped on the bridge, and a crazy woman is attacking it with her fists.*

How embarrassing.

But I couldn't help it. I saw red, just like old times. Just like when Mason was kidnapped. My anger issues were so bad back then, William sent me to a specialist. She diagnosed me with IED. Intermittent Explosive Disorder. A chronic condition resulting in spontaneous episodes of violent behavior, but the diagnosis was wrong. It only happened a few times. I found help online and calmed down without the specialist. The flare-ups, seeing red, losing control—it mostly went away . . . until last night.

I put the strawberries into Mason's bowl, dropping them on the mountain of ice cream, one by one. Calmly, I grab a paper towel and wipe the juice off the countertop. I attempt to arrange the strawberries, spacing them evenly, but they roll off the creamy mound and cling to the bowl's edges. It's not where I want them. It's infuriating.

Keep calm.

Focus.

The strawberries won't stay on top of the ice cream, and William couldn't swim. Why didn't he mention the card sooner? Thinking back, he *was* edgy this week. Someone at his work was fired, and it was his fault, but . . . he didn't say anything else. When the police asked if I was planning on taking a trip outside Seattle, I became edgy. I was angry. I told them to screw-off and left for the hospital. What a nightmare. The flashing lights, the dull green scrubs, those blank, expressionless faces—those stone-cold callous faces. I stood in the basement where they keep the dead, still wanting to save William, but I couldn't.

And I can't make the strawberries stay on top of this damn ice cream. One rolls down, hits the edge, and bounces onto the countertop.

I chuckle like a mad scientist from a bad sci-fi flick.

William's fall from the bridge wasn't far, but the river was quick. They found him wedged between a log and the shore less than a mile away.

I should call Olivia and tell her about the chase, the card—the black car. The five silver rings and the A8 emblem on the trunk. I should ask if she's seen an expensive Audi lately, but that's ridiculous. William and I were in Renton, miles from where we live on Mercer Island. Besides, I don't want to bother her. She doesn't need to know I got angry again.

I shove a spoon into the ice cream and pick up the bowl. William used to dish up ice cream for Mason. He used to make sure the dishes were put away before bed. He used to take care of us.

Breathe.

If I can get through this first night, I'll be okay. I just need to focus.

I missed a spot of strawberry juice on the counter, so I dab it with my finger and take a taste. It's not as sweet as I'd hoped, and . . . William is dead.

My God—he's dead.

He's really dead.

My anger builds, and I try to remember the breathing exercises the specialist taught me. She gave me mantras, but that was so long ago. Thirteen years. What did I chant to escape the hate—the seething, the fury, the wrath—when Mason was kidnapped?

He was only three when he was taken, but I got him back.

William is gone forever.

The kitchen turns red.

The rage comes.

I must calm down.

I can't remember my mantras, but I can—what can I do? Journal?

No.

Meditate?

No.

Scream.

Yes.

That's it. The screaming exercise.

But I can't. The neighbors will hear me. They'll call the police.

Using both hands, I pick up the bowl of ice cream. I can't hold it steady.

The room darkens. Turns crimson.

I must calm down.

I put the bowl down.

My lower lip hurts because I'm pinching it. Hard.

Old habits die hard.

Fury is knocking at my door. Where is my seahorse?

I pull my hand away from my lip and rush across the kitchen.

The sliding glass door to the backyard is closed.

I unlock it. Burst outside.

Nature. Peace. Serenity. There must be something serene out here. The gardener didn't come this week. The weeds are overgrown. There is no serenity. No solace in the pool, the hot tub, the deck, the chairs . . .

The back fence is far away—the neighbors are farther—but I have a loud voice, and my lungs are on fire. We purchased this place because of the lot size, and—why can't I stop thinking in terms of *we*? There is no more *we*.

There is only Mason and me.

With my hands pressed tight over my mouth, I scream. I scream until my head spins, and I find my way back inside, stumbling.

I sit at the kitchen table and rest my face on a bereavement basket of soap, shampoo, potpourri, and essential oils.

Thank you, Olivia.

I exhale.

The air leaves my lungs, and the release comes.

Ahh.

The release is good.

The bath and body scents are comforting.

Mason needs his ice cream.

I need to find the driver of that car.

CHAPTER FOUR

MASON

Mason keeps his eyes closed to avoid the setting sun. The rays slip through the blinds in his bedroom window like ninjas bursting out of the shadows. He rolls over and fumbles for his cell phone. He's shirtless. The covers are piled on the floor again, and the air is cold. His cell phone shows no messages, and there's only one percent battery left. The fucking thing won't hold a charge through the day anymore. His dad needs to buy him a new one, but that's never going to happen.

His dad died last night.

Mason sits up in bed and listens to his mother moving around in the kitchen downstairs.

She's making too much noise.

It's Saturday night, his dad is gone forever, his phone is dead, and she's making too much noise.

He throws his phone against the wall, the case flies off, and it falls to the floor.

His room is dim.

His life is dimmer.

He wants to hide under the covers, but something isn't

right with his bookshelf. It's off. His books stand up straight, but it's as if he's never seen them before—*Death Note, Honto Yajuu,* a few volumes of *Dragon Ball, Fairy Tale,* and his favorite manga, *Ten Count.* But they're not right. Something's not right. If he were to pick one to read right now, it would be *Ten Count,* but he can't. It's like he's in a foreign country where everything is backward.

Goosebumps form on his arms. The air feels frigid on his bare skin, except it's probably not cold in here. He considers pulling the covers off the floor and wrapping them around his shoulders, but it's probably not necessary. He health class teacher, Mr. Jackson, would say the air only feels cold because of Mason's low BMI. Because he's too skinny. It's okay. Mr. Jackson is one of the few good teachers at Mullen High, even if health class is too much about birth control and not enough about sex.

Mason shivers, crosses the room to his dresser, and opens the top drawer to get a T-shirt. A chill hits him, and he puts his hands on his chest while avoiding his reflection in the mirror. He wishes he had some muscle. Some pecs. But bench presses suck. Push-ups suck. Going anywhere near the gym at school, anywhere near all those jocks . . . sucks. Working out alone in the basement is pathetic. Maybe he'd look better if he dyed his brown hair a bright emo blue. That's something he could do. Maybe this weekend. He might as well.

No one can stop him now.

His dad can't tell him not to color his hair—not that his dad ever did.

Mason shoves the T-shirts aside and pulls out a bottle of cologne. The nozzle smells like burnt chocolate. He sprays the cologne, waving it back and forth near the mirror. With his eyes closed, he breathes it in and slowly exhales. Sticky beads form on the mirror's surface. A memory of walking in the park with his dad creeps into his mind. Tears threaten to come, but he doesn't let them.

With his father gone, he's got no one. His mom doesn't understand him. Always squeezing her lip and flying into fits of rage over the stupidest things. What he needs is to find someone he can be with.

He hides the cologne under his shirts and slowly closes the drawer.

What he needs is to get laid. *As if that's ever going to happen.*

The manga books catch his attention again, and he realizes why they're wrong. The Japanese totally got it right when they chose to print the pages starting at the back. It's funny when some American opens one up and reads it from the front. Spoiler alert, asshole; you just read the ending.

Actually, it's a matter of perspective. Manga books aren't printed backward. American books are. Books should be read top-to-bottom, right-to-left, back-to-front. Manga books aren't backward. Everyone else is.

His books stand on the shelves in perfect order, alphabetically, by volume number, beginning at the top left. For manga, this *is* backward. It's wrong. His *Berserk* series should be on the bottom with Volume 1 all the way to the right, followed by his *Black Butler* series. He doesn't have any books starting with *A*, or they would start there. He can't believe he never noticed how out of place his books were until now. It's not that he's one of those pathetic Westerners obsessed with Japanese culture—a weeaboo—but he does respect everything Japanese.

Mason plops down on the thick carpet next to the shelf and begins rearranging his collection, making it conform to Japanese wisdom.

Tears stream down his face. His cheeks heat up, but his back remains cold.

His dad would have flipped out if he saw Mason rearranging the books, but that's because his dad didn't understand how manga books worked. He was such a computer geek. Computers must have everything in order, and so did his dad. Everything has an order, and right now, these books are out of order, but Mason can fix this. He's going to fix everything. No one understands. Manga aren't comic books. His dad *thought* they were comic books, but his dad was wrong. He was—

He is—dead.

Mucous from the tears collects in Mason's throat, choking him and forcing him to swallow. He blinks, wipes his eyes, violently coughs, and bumps the bookcase. Half the *Black Butler* series falls off the top shelf and hits him in the head. The corners of the books jab his scalp, and one bounces off his shoulder. He winces and recalls his dad telling him to buy real books. Books on history and science and philosophy. Once, his dad had asked him why manga were printed backward. *I don't know, Dad. Why do you drive on the right side of the road? Why did grandma and grandpa drive on the left? Were they backward, or was it just you? Don't you think you're backward, Dad?*

He grabs the second volume of *Ten Count* and throws it across the room.

Just because his dad believed one way, it doesn't mean other ways are backward. These books aren't backward. Mason isn't *backward*. Fuck his dad for dying and leaving. Now, at least, Mason doesn't have to hear about how, when his father was sixteen, he had a job, or how Mason's last haircut was too long in the front, or how reading comic books—dammit, they're not comic books—is something

Mason should grow out of.

At least now, Mason doesn't have to hear about his father's opinion on gays in the military. He doesn't have to see his father's disappointed face when Mason finally summons the courage to come out.

To tell everyone he is gay.

To tell everyone they're just going to have to deal with it.

Mason doesn't have to hear anything from his father anymore, because—because William Kaine is dead.

The air *is* cold.

Mason wraps his arms around his knees and pulls them to his chest. He rocks back and forth.

William Kaine is dead, and that makes one less person who will judge Mason. One less person who will act weird around him. William Kaine will never know Mason is gay because he'll never *get* to know because—dammit. Mason will never get to tell him.

Mason rocks harder, hits the bookcase again, and more books fall.

He's got to tell someone.

He'll have to tell his mother.

Someday, he'll have to tell everyone.

Someday, he'll have to come out because, if he doesn't

. . .

He'll freeze to death.

CHAPTER FIVE

RYAN

Ryan drives past the Squire Tavern because all the parking spots in front are taken. There's no place for him at the bar tonight. Not this Saturday night, nor any night. Nor at any bar, ever. Any night.

He parks his dented Civic on the street and walks down the sidewalk, passing a teriyaki restaurant. The sick-sweet smell mixes with the grungy odor rising from the gutter. Seattle is the city of rain, but it never rains hard enough to clean the streets. The neon light from the Squire's sign hangs lopsided, shedding a red glow across the soaked asphalt.

Ryan walks across the parking lot toward the door, scanning for Juan's motorcycle, but it's not there. What a waste of time. He could have stayed home, written computer code, and updated his LinkedIn profile.

The cars in the lot match the tavern—faded, scratched, and not from this century. All except for a stunning black Audi A8. Someday, when his computer cooperates, and he has an office job writing code, he'll own a luxury car like this one. Not exactly like this one, but something close. Something that isn't dented and rusted and old.

A broken red brick holds the door to the tavern open. From outside, he hears pool balls smack, men yell, women giggle, men jeering at TVs, clanking glasses. A jittery light spills into the parking lot, showing Ryan the way inside. He leans in the doorway, glances at the bar, and doesn't see Juan. Even if Ryan had left the moment Juan called for help, he wouldn't have made it in time. More than likely, Juan is already at another bar.

Alcoholism is a sucking force, a broken promise. A death sentence.

Ryan takes another look inside, then turns away. He walks past the Audi and crosses to the other side of the building, heading for the alley. No reason to stay any longer than necessary, and definitely no reason to walk by the door again. He enters the passageway, intending to walk behind the teriyaki restaurant and back to his car, but stops when he sees a man sitting next to a dumpster, holding a cell phone.

Juan.

His sponsee's imposing body casts an oval shadow on the dumpster. He holds his head in his hands, and—that's strange. He's traded in his white t-shirt, leather vest, and denim blue jeans for something professional. A dark business suit. Perhaps it's not Juan, but few men are this large, and as Ryan approaches, he recognizes the motorcycle boots. The ones with the skulls and daggers.

"How much did you have?" Ryan asks.

Juan raises his head. "*Nada.*" His goatee is trimmed, and his hair is slicked back.

"Are you sure?"

"If I was drinking, man, would I have called you?"

"Maybe not. Come on, get up." Ryan grasps Juan's elbow.

"Let's take a walk."

Juan's right. He probably wouldn't have called if he'd started drinking again. Juan is a binge drinker, and once a binge drinker gets started, days turn into weeks. Looking at his round face and childlike eyes, Ryan knows better than to believe him. Maybe Juan is drunk, and maybe he's not. It doesn't matter because he will always be an alcoholic.

"I'm alright, man."

Juan's suit and tie clash with the tattoo of his mother's face on his neck, but he looks great. Night and day from when he first came to AA. Juan came in on his own, sick and tired of being sick and tired. Truly desperate. This gave him a chance. Having hit bottom, he looked the part—puffy eyelids, red nose, a gut the size of a buoy. He played the part too— angry, despondent, confused, arrogant. Not the man standing here tonight.

"You want to go to Denny's?" Ryan asks. "Get some coffee?"

"No, man. No Denny's." Juan ambles toward the parking lot, drifting to the left.

"We should talk." Ryan follows. "There's one up the street."

"Let's go somewhere else. I'll drive."

An old red Ford Mustang pulls to the parking lot's edge, brakes, then accelerates onto the street. The teriyaki smell next door makes Ryan realize he hasn't eaten since noon. "Drive what? Where's your motorcycle?"

"I got a car." Juan motions toward the Audi.

"How'd that happen?"

"I got a job driving these business dudes around."

"That's great, Juan. See? Things do get better. Let's get some coffee, and you can tell me about it."

"No, let's go to Murphy's downtown." Juan steps onto the sidewalk in front of the Squire and falters. "I'll drive."

"C'mon. Let's just walk to Denny's. It's not far. The rain stopped."

Juan pulls out a set of keys and hits a button. The Audi beeps in response. He gazes at the Squire's door. The wide-open door. "No, I'm tired. Never mind. I think I'll go home."

"Are you sure? It's only a couple blocks away. I'll buy the coffee."

"No, man. I'm going home. I'm alright now, really. I'll be alright."

Tension builds in Ryan's neck. To let Juan go is to let him die. Ryan has attended too many funerals to let someone with so much potential go. It might not happen tonight, but it could. Juan could drink and drive—crash and die. And if not tonight, then soon. If he drinks, he will die. That's a certainty. Ryan's last sponsee contracted pancreatic cancer. Three months later, Paul O was dead. It's not always the liver that loses the war.

Right now, Juan is losing.

Death *will* happen.

The big man turns his back on Ryan and steps off the curb next to the Audi.

Ryan reaches up and grabs Juan's collar. "Don't go."

"Get off me."

Ryan reaches for the keys, tries to grab Juan's wrists, but misses.

Juan puts his hands on Ryan's shoulders, and Ryan goes down. His butt slams onto the concrete.

"Leave me alone." Juan's cheeks shake, and his eyes glimmer, flooding with pain. "I said . . . I'm . . . alright." His two-ton chest heaves, and he puts his hand on the door handle. "Leave me alone, *pandejo*."

Ryan stands. His right palm is scraped. Scratched. It burns. "I'm not going anywhere."

Juan shakes his head and opens the car door.

"Would you leave me alone if I relapsed?"

Juan pauses.

"Would you just let me die?" Ryan steps forward.

"I told you, man. I didn't drink. I—"

"Juan?"

"I got to work in the morning, man. Leave me alone."

"Yeah, you have to work in the morning. Why is that?" Ryan closes in. "How is it you have a job? You didn't have a job a few months ago, but now you do. How did that happen? Huh? And now that things are better, you're going to go home, relax, and have a few *cervezas*, aren't you? Tell me, Juan, how did that work out for you last time? Huh?"

Juan lowers his head.

"Where did you wake up last time? How many days were you drunk?"

"Don't, man." Juan closes his eyes. "Don't say it."

"You woke up in jail, Juan. Hell, why don't you just go straight to county so you can visit your papa again."

"Don't."

"Do you think they'll let you share a cell?"

Juan puts a hand on Ryan's shoulder and stares into his eyes. Juan's pupils shake like pebbles in an earthquake. "I . . . didn't . . . drink."

"You don't have to drink to be drunk." Ryan pushes Juan's hand away. "You're thinking stinks. You're headed the wrong way."

"I'm not going to jail."

"Maybe not. Maybe you'll die first. Maybe you'll never see

your papa again. Jail would be a blessing compared to where you're headed." That's enough. Ryan turns toward the teriyaki place and walks away with his hands in his pockets.

"Wait," Juan says.

"It's your choice," Ryan shouts. "Death or Denny's. I'll be at Denny's."

"I'm not drunk!"

Ryan turns around, points his finger. "You can lie to me. You can lie to yourself. You can get into that car and forget about how bad things were when you came in. You can go to hell, literally, because that's where you're headed, Juan. To hell."

Rain begins to fall, splashing onto the Audi's windshield. Spots appear on Juan's suit, and his hair takes on a brilliant sheen. He's already dressed for his casket. "You can go to hell, or you can come with me and get some coffee. Your choice." Ryan turns away and puts his hand back in his pocket. "I could use someone to talk to if you decide to come. Even if it's all lies."

"I'm not lying, man."

"I smelled the beer when you pushed me down, Juan. You ought to be more careful." The rain soothes the back of Ryan's neck. "If I smelled it, the cops will smell it. All you have to do is get pulled over."

"No. Wait."

Ryan stops. "What was it tonight, Bud Light?"

Without a doubt, Juan got drunk on beer.

Juan doesn't respond.

Ryan turns and marches up to the big man.

Juan averts his eyes and nods yes.

Ryan holds out his hand, palm up.

The rain pours down.

Juan stares at a puddle forming on the pavement. "I don't know what I was thinking, man. Sorry I pushed you."

Ryan juts his palm into Juan's line of sight.

Juan jerks his head away, then looks back at Ryan. He wipes the rain off his face and raises the keys above Ryan's hand, but he doesn't let them go.

The Audi's key fob glows in the Squire's neon light.

Ryan motions for Juan to drop the keys.

They fall into Ryan's palm. "Okay. Let's go get some coffee."

CHAPTER SIX

LAUREN

I reach the top of the stairs carrying Mason's ice cream. He needs to eat. The bowl tips in my hand, and a strawberry falls onto the carpet. It's going to leave a stain, but I don't care. I'll clean it later. This late at night, the walls are dark, and the floor is darker, but I don't need the hall light to see my way.

The scent of William's cologne greets me outside Mason's room. Burnt chocolate. I swear I smell it, but it can't be real. William is dead.

"Mom? Is that you?"

My heart skips. I was so intent on getting something into Mason's stomach, I didn't think about what to say, so I freeze.

The ice cream melts.

I shouldn't be here.

Sobbing comes from his room, and I picture him flipping through a comic book, his tears smudging the drawings. I want to go to him, wrap my arms around him, and make everything better, but I'm afraid I'll make everything worse.

I don't know what to say.

An image of the steam rolling over the Audi's hood

comes to me. Heat courses up my neck. I want to run down the stairs, jump in my SUV, and race to the police station. I want to know everything they know. I want the driver dead. My son is withering away, and this ice cream isn't going to fix anything.

The bowl shakes in my hand.

He weeps. Then he moans. It's like listening to puppies drown.

He needs closure.

We need the funeral.

I wish it could be tomorrow, but the arrangements must be planned around William's egocentric parents. The glorious Nigel and Evelyn Kaine of Westport, Connecticut, simply must have time to travel and prepare themselves. So they can be proper. So they can sip their tea, on their schedule, and arrive in Mercer Island whenever they feel like it.

It makes me seethe.

I need to stay calm, and—yes.

My calming mantra comes to me.

Breathe. This too shall pass.

I close my eyes.

Breathe. This too shall pass . . . this too shall pass.

I lean against the door frame.

"Mom? Is that you?"

The scent of William's cologne is strong, and it's for real. It's not my imagination.

"Mom, are you out there?"

"I've brought you something to eat. Can I come in?"

"No. Just leave it and go, okay?"

I open his door.

"Mom!"

Mason sits on the floor next to his bookshelf. His window

shades are drawn, and his comic books are everywhere. He's rocking back and forth, and he's not wearing a shirt. I can see his ribs. His face is red from crying, or anger, or both.

"Here, honey." I extend the bowl as I step inside.

Something crunches under my foot. It's his cell phone. What was once a clear window into the internet is now a colorful mosaic of cracked glass.

"What are you doing?" he says. "Get. Out."

"You need to eat."

He looks away. "Did you break it?"

I shove his dirty clothes off the dresser and put the bowl down. "Why was your phone on the floor?"

"I—it went dead. It's worthless."

I pick up the case and try to put it back on the phone. "Worthless? Did you get angry and throw it?"

"Yeah. So?"

"Mason, that's the fourth phone this year. You can't keep breaking them."

He looks up at me. "Please, don't get mad."

"Mad? I'm not mad." I resist the urge to pinch my lip. "I'm not the one throwing things." His dragon poster—rainbow scales, flaring nostrils—catches my eye. Fire flows from the dragon's mouth in bright red flames, and I know how the beast feels. I know rage, but I'm okay. This phone thing isn't a big deal, and . . . I've got my mantra back.

I breathe. "You need to watch your anger." I pick up the ice cream. "Here, have some."

"I'm not hungry. " He shoves the bowl away, making the pink cream slosh onto the floor, staining the carpet.

"Honey, you need to eat."

He turns away.

"Do you want to talk about what happened? About your

father?"

His chest caves in. He folds his arms and rocks back and forth. I'm reminded of these suicide prevention ads that keep popping up on the internet.

"No," he says. "You wouldn't understand."

"Try me."

He stops rocking. Says nothing.

My boy is in pain, and I could cry, but if I do, he'll think I'm weak. I need to be strong and show him what confidence looks like, but at the same time, I want to hold him. "You're right. I don't understand. Why don't you tell me what I don't understand? Why did you throw your phone? Is it because your father—"

"It's not about Dad, okay? It's about someone at school. And now—now I can't text them."

"Who?"

"Just somebody."

"Who? Tell me—wait . . . is it someone you like?"

A sheepish grin flashes across his face.

He's not distraught over his father.

No. He *is* distraught over his father, but there's more. He's got other problems.

He's in love.

"What's her name?" I ask. "Does she go to your school?"

Silence.

"Well," I put the ice cream back down. "I bet she's beautiful."

CHAPTER SEVEN

RYAN

Ryan sits alone in a booth for four, sipping his coffee and watching Juan talk on his cell phone. Juan paces up and down outside Denny's, staying under the awning to avoid the rain. Occasionally, he glances inside as if he's making sure Ryan hasn't left. Or maybe he's hoping Ryan will leave so he can grab a beer.

Ryan isn't going anywhere.

"Refill?" asks the waitress. She hovers a carafe over Ryan's cup.

"Yes, thank you."

"Did you want to order something?"

"No, not yet. Maybe later."

The waitress sighs, then strides toward the entryway just as Juan steps inside. He brushes the rain from his suit, and the waitress makes a wide berth around him, stops, and looks up at his kind round face. She asks if he needs a seat, and Juan shakes his head, pointing in Ryan's direction. It's late, but only half the booths are filled. This place will be packed after the bars close.

Ryan pulls the table toward himself to make room for Juan to slide in. "Who were you talking to?"

"My girl."

"I thought you were over months ago."

"We were." Juan gazes toward the window. "Mostly."

"What happened today?"

"Okay, man. I'm sorry I didn't tell you, but she made me a deal when she dumped my ass. If I got clean and got a job, she told me I could call her."

"This was before you came to AA?"

"Yeah, man. I should have told you."

"I thought you came because you were sick and tired of being sick and tired."

"I did, man. I did. But we had this deal—"

"So you stopped drinking for a couple months, then you got a job and called her?" Ryan sits back in the booth and raises his hands. "Why didn't you tell me?"

"I'm okay."

"Did you call her before or after you started drinking today?"

Juan lowers his chin. "Before."

"I could have helped. You should have told me."

"I didn't mean to keep it from you, man. Really. Everything was good, so I called, but she sounded funny, you know, like something was up. Then her friend got on, told me to leave her alone—said she's been seeing some *pandejo*." He grips the table with both hands. His forearms bulge. The ketchup bottle dances on the tabletop. "The next thing I know, man, I'm sitting in my car with a six-pack, and it's half gone. I don't know where I got it."

Ryan clasps his hands together. "Strange mental blank spot."

"What?"

"From now on, you've got to be honest and tell me everything. We need to get back to working the steps."

The waitress walks up and puts a cup down in front of Juan. "Coffee?"

He pushes the cup aside. "No. I'm good."

She looks at Ryan. "How about you? Are you ready to order now?"

"Give us a minute, please."

"Okay. I'll be back."

Juan says, "I'm not feeling good, man. I think I'm going to go." He glances at his cell phone. "Thanks for the walk, but—"

"I went in and out of AA for five years before it stuck. The last time, before I sobered up for good, I went to thirty-two meetings in thirty-two days, and I drank between each one. The booze just kept magically showing up, day after day. I could never remember how, where, or when I got it, but I did. Day after day. That's the strange mental blank spot the book talks about, but it doesn't have to be that way."

Juan's cheeks redden. "She cheated on me, man. She broke the deal." He grabs the table with both hands again, looks at the coffee cup, and the ketchup bottle shimmies. "It's bad. It's her fault."

"Relax." Ryan puts his hand on Juan's. "I understand. I blamed my sister-in-law for my drinking, but I was lying to myself. It wasn't her fault. She rightfully put a restraining order against me. I was so resentful. She kept me from seeing my brother and my nephew, and I cursed her name every day. Lauren. Then I'd blank out and get drunk."

"Why'd she do it, man?"

"She had a good reason, believe me, but my point is,

resentment kills. I didn't drink because of the restraining order. I drank because I liked the effect produced by alcohol. You didn't drink because your girl was seeing someone else. You drank because—"

"I don't know, man." He leans back. "Kristen, man. I thought she loved me." He glances at the windows over Ryan's shoulder and licks his lips. "It doesn't matter now. She never wants to see me again."

"You don't have to use her as an excuse to drink."

"I'm sorry for lying. The only reason I went to AA was to get her back, and now—"

"It's okay, Juan. We're all liars. It's part of the disease, but look at what's happened since you came in. Look at everything you have now. Look at your suit. You look great, and you've got a job and a car, and—you've got two months clean. No one can take those two months away from you."

"I'm scared, man." He looks at his phone, then at the windows. "You're right, but I don't think I can stop, you know? Not after what I did today." His face scrunches. "I'm going to lose my job. I'm going to lose everything." He bumps the table as he reaches into his pocket, and the ketchup bottle falls over.

"It's going to be okay." Ryan sets the ketchup bottle back up. "We'll just have to take this one day at a time."

"Here." Juan slaps his silver sobriety chip onto the Formica surface. "That thing didn't work for me."

"I can't argue that. Just a second." Ryan reaches into this pocket, pulls out a rock, and places it next to Juan's chip. "My sponsor gave me this eight years ago, and I've carried it with me ever since. Do you see anything special about it?"

"No."

Ryan picks up the rock. "This side is smooth as glass, and

this side is rough as hell. I always put it in my pocket with the rough side out."

"Why?"

"So I'm reminded of the way I want my life to go. I want it to be smooth, Juan." Ryan runs his thumb over the rock. "Every day, every hour, every minute, I have a choice to make. I can either choose the rough side and drink or the smooth side and let life happen. Life's going to happen whether I like it or not, but it doesn't have to be rough. I never have to drink."

"What about the blank spot? I swear, after her friend got on the phone, I lost it. I don't know what happened."

"Here. Take it." Ryan holds out the rock.

Juan leans away and puts his hands up. "No, man. That's yours."

"It's yours now, Juan. You need it more than I do."

Juan takes the rock, gazes at the two sides, turning it back and forth.

"Remember. It's up to you which side you choose. Pray for help from God, work the steps, do whatever, but remember, when the blank spot comes, you still have a choice."

Juan slips the rock into his jacket pocket. "*Gracias.*"

Ryan takes the sobriety chip off the table. "You know what you have to do next, don't you?"

Juan's shoulders drop. "Raise my hand?"

"Yes. You'll get another one of these chips at the meeting, but only if you come in and raise your hand."

Near the kitchen, a waiter drops a pile of dishes, and everyone in the place applauds. The waitress stops to help her coworker, and Juan gazes out the window.

"Look, it's important," Ryan says. "You shouldn't feel

ashamed. Trust me. We don't shoot the wounded. You'll be welcomed back."

"I don't know, man."

"You should come tomorrow. Don't give yourself time to forget."

"I've got to work during the meeting tomorrow. I'm taking some dude to the airport."

"So, you're like a chauffeur now?"

"No, man. It's not like that. They call me at random times, and I go pick up rides, but it's not Uber. You know. It's different people all the time, but it's good. I tried Uber, but they checked my history."

"DUI?"

"Yeah." He smirks. "I have a couple of those, but these dudes don't care. They said for me to drive and not ask questions. It pays a lot."

"Sounds sketchy. Are you sure it's on the up and up?"

"What else am I supposed to do, man? Look at me. The only other job I can get is as a bouncer, and, you know I shouldn't be hanging out in bars."

"I'm happy for you, Juan. Really. Just be careful."

An older man in a baseball cap argues with the waitress near the entryway. Filth clings to his tattered clothes. Ryan can't hear what they're saying over the bustle, but it's probably about food. Juan doesn't realize just how close he is to becoming that man. If Juan starts drinking again, he could end up begging for leftovers by the end of the week.

"It's ironic," Ryan says.

"What?"

"We've both had problems drinking and driving, and now we're both delivery drivers. I deliver packages, and you deliver people. Otherwise, there's no difference. We've just got to stay sober."

Juan nods.

"We're in this together."

"Thanks, man. I can't go to the meeting tomorrow, but I promise. I'll go and raise my hand Monday night. Deal?"

"It's your choice."

The older man storms out of the restaurant, and the waitress catches Ryan looking at her. She approaches the table. "Can I get you something now?"

"Could I get a side of bacon and some pancakes?" Ryan says.

"And you?"

Juan slides out of the booth. "Sorry, no. I've got to go."

"Wait—"

"No, no. I'm not hungry. I'll see you Monday."

Juan isn't hungry. He's thirsty. Ryan knows that look. In the blink of an eye, Juan is off to the races, but he has the rock now, and if he put it in his pocket wrong, maybe it will rub. There's still hope. Maybe Juan will feel the rough side and remember he has a choice before it's too late.

"Stay safe, Juan. See you Monday."

The waitress saunters toward the kitchen.

Juan follows close behind her, then dashes out the door.

Ryan did all he could do, but if Juan doesn't stay sober, this will have been a waste of time. Time Ryan could have spent learning to program computers.

He looks around the restaurant. If he spends all his time delivering packages and helping alcoholics, he'll only ever eat in places like this. He pictures his brother, William, seated at a long dining table, using silverware made of real silver, and eating filet mignon, washing it down with a glass of Cabernet.

Cabernet was Ryan's favorite wine.

He wonders if it has been long enough. Has his sister-in-law Lauren had time to find forgiveness? Are thirteen years long enough? The computer courses haven't helped, the coding examples in the tutorials never work, but his brother, William—he knows how to write code. If William could forgive Ryan, he could teach Ryan. It would be like tenth-grade science again.

Ryan takes a long drink of his coffee.

It would be like they were brothers again.

He swallows and puts his cup on the table next to the ketchup bottle.

Ryan pictures his nephew Mason all grown up. A teenager now.

He puts his hand in his pocket and wraps his fingers around Juan's keys.

Outside, the rain comes down hard, and the old man passes by the window, homeless and hungry.

Are thirteen years long enough?

Could Lauren ever forgive him for kidnapping Mason?

CHAPTER EIGHT

LAUREN

The rain pours over the grocery store parking lot in waves, splashing off the cars and beating on the roof of my Lexus. I search for an empty spot to park. Across town, Mason's school is about to let out. It's already Monday. He promised to come with me to the store if we made it home before any kids could see him.

I had to get him out of the house. He's staying home from school this week because of his father's death, but he's going back next week.

I won't allow him to become a recluse.

His head rests against the passenger side window. His eyes are closed, and he's listening to his earbuds.

It's only been three days since William died. An eternity in some ways, and a flash in others. I need to take it easier on Mason. Maybe let him stay home another week. The problem is, I'm like my father. I have to push Mason's recovery. I have to accelerate the inevitable.

I park next to a glistening Porsche, step out, and wait for Mason to join me under my umbrella. An old man smoking a cigarette stands near the store's entrance. I've seen him somewhere before. He's wearing a yellow baseball cap with a black hoodie pulled over it and sunglasses. The wind gusts, blowing his long, gray beard to the side, and he's just standing there, staring at the lot. It's not unusual to see people like him in Seattle, but out here in the suburbs? The homeless usually don't stray this far from the freeway onto Mercer Island.

He's peculiar. It's strange how he stands in the downpour, smoking his cigarette, unaffected. The rain beats on his shoulders, but he just stands there, smoking. Staring in our direction.

The wind blows rain against my back, chilling my bones. We near the entrance and pass by the old man. Winter is on its way. Mason and I head straight for the coffee kiosk. As a rule, I don't drink coffee after one o'clock in the afternoon, but today, it's too cold not to.

We order, and the barista works on our drinks. I chose a white mocha for myself and a hot chocolate for Mason. He stands in the entryway, slouching with his hands in his pockets instead of on his phone. Poor guy. Too bad his phone is broken. I'm sure he's dying to text that girl.

Across the way, rain streams down the charcoal tinted windows. The beep-beep of scanners, and the chitter-chatter of checkers babbling about the weather and God-knows-what-else, blends into a cacophony of white noise behind me.

Outside, the bearded man in the yellow baseball cap stands there, smoking. He's facing the store now, gazing inside. Looking in my direction. He can't possibly see me through those sunglasses, through the windows and the rain, but I swear he's looking right at me. Where have I seen him before?

I walk over to Mason. "Do you see that man out there?"

"Yeah. What about him?"

"I don't know. Doesn't it seem odd he's not coming inside?"

"He's probably waiting for someone. There's no smoking in here." Mason glances toward the checkout lanes. "How long is this going to take? I want to text Abigail."

"Oh, is that her name?"

"No. Abigail's just a friend."

"Lauren," the barista shouts, "I have a white mocha and hot chocolate for Lauren."

"We won't be here long." I put my hand on his shoulder. "We'll go to the phone store right after this so you can text her. I promise."

We pick up our drinks and head for the carts. I look over my shoulder, and the old man is still out there, staring in through the windows. I remember him. I *think* I remember him. When I left the hospital Saturday morning, a man was standing right outside the door, puffing on a cigarette. Had I not been rushing home to Mason, I would have demanded he read the sign and move away from the doors. Twenty-five feet. That's the law.

I don't remember if the man outside the hospital wore sunglasses, but he did have a beard. And he *was* smoking.

Mason follows me to the carts. I pull on the strap to my handbag and tighten it against my shoulder. William gave me this bag. The red leather clashes with everything, but I don't care. It's a Gucci with fourteen-carat clasps. My first car cost less, but I take it with me everywhere I go.

I love this red bag.

More now than ever.

We walk down the laundry aisle toward the dairy section. I need to get eggs and English muffins and—wait. No, I don't.

William is the only one who will eat English muffins, but he doesn't need them anymore. He doesn't need anything anymore, and he won't be waiting at home to help me unload the groceries. Not anymore.

There's a crack in the first egg I check. The second carton has a gray egg. It's not to be trusted. The third carton looks good.

"Hey, Mom," Mason says. "There's your friend."

At the far end of the laundry aisle, the bearded man peruses the detergents. Bleach. What would he need bleach for? He can't possibly own a washing machine. At least he's not looking our way, but . . . he followed us.

He must be following us.

He followed me home from the hospital and then to the store.

And now to the dairy section.

Is he stalking me?

For a moment, I'm sent back in time. Back to when I grabbed Mason's hand and pulled him out of that hotel. Back to when the police arrested his uncle Ryan for kidnapping him. Back to when I saw red and didn't care. Mason was only three years old—my baby—and I pulled on his arm, and I rescued him from that worthless alcoholic.

Ryan Kaine.

I hate Ryan Kaine.

Breathe.

Now, I'm standing in the grocery store, and Mason is sixteen, and my anger has returned. I want to confront that old man. My nerves shiver, and my skin heats up. The fury comes on like old times, but I know what to do. I close my eyes.

Breathe. This too shall pass. Breathe. This too—.

Someone's cart rams into me. My hip erupts in pain, and I step sideways to catch my balance. The agony forces me to squeeze the egg carton, and an egg slips out. I try, but I can't keep it from falling and exploding on the floor. A gaunt woman in a cheap T-shirt and ripped sweatpants pulls her cart away. She's holding a cell phone.

"I'm sorry," she says. "I didn't see you there."

The old, bearded man is gone. I wanted to confront him, but now he's gone.

Mason glances at me, concerned.

I turn to the woman.

She stands in a crimson halo, unaware of my wrath. My condition. The venomous hostility inside my heart is not my fault. My hip hurts, and she is to blame. She has no idea what it's like for me to lose control. It's not that I want to explode, but she taps on her phone with her thumb and says, "These ads won't go away. They're so distracting. I'm sorry I ran into you."

We make eye contact.

She lowers her phone and gapes at me.

The carton shakes in my hand. The eggshells pulsate in their pods. I tighten my grip.

"Mom?" Mason puts his hand on my arm. "Mom. You're pinching your lip."

I step toward the woman.

"Mom, don't."

The woman's face is ashen. She's speechless, but I'm not.

"What's the matter with you?" I raise the eggs. "Are you so addicted to your phone that—do you think it's okay to text and walk? To crash into people?" She has a twelve-pack of beer buried in her cart beneath a bag of celery. "Are you drunk? Do you think it's okay to drink and text and drive and slam into people? You—you alcoholic!"

"I—"

"Do you think it's okay to hurt people? To hurt everyone around you? Don't you know what you're—do you think? Are you capable of thinking?"

"I'm sorry, I—" She raises her hands as if under arrest.

I grab my cart with my free hand and swing it wide, slamming it into hers. My mocha goes flying out of the basket. Her cart teeters, then hits the floor. Onions, crackers, cereal, and her twelve-pack tumble out. My handbag slips off my shoulder, and I put it back on, grasping the strap with one hand and raising the eggs with the other.

"Mom!"

I'm on fire.

A man's voice interrupts my rage. "Is there a problem here?"

I can't tell whether the woman's face is red or not because everything is red.

A short, low-level clerk with thinning hair steps in my way, but he's too late. I let the eggs go, and he shields his face, but one of the beauties hits him squarely in the forehead and splashes yolk onto the woman.

"What the fuck?" She wipes the goo from her cheeks.

Ahh.

The release feels good.

This is what I wanted when I beat my fists against the window of the black Audi, but the glass didn't break, and the car that caused my anger to return—the car that killed William—got away. It got away with murder, but this woman didn't.

She got what she deserved.

I'm glad my anger is back. I love the release.

She stands there, glaring at me, dripping. Furious.

It's calming to see her this way.

The clerk yells at me to leave.

The heat fades. My vision clears.

Mason yells, "I hate you."

He drops his hot chocolate and runs down the aisle.

I run after him.

CHAPTER NINE

LAUREN

I awake on Saturday morning, one week and a day since William died. I am counting the days because I don't want to forget anything about him, but I know I will. The more time that passes, the less of him I'll have. Already, nothing is the way it used to be. I'm lying on the sofa in the sitting room instead of lying next to him in our bedroom.

My heart is a sunken ship, and I'm drowning.

"William is gone."

Saying this to the ceiling doesn't make it any more real or any less painful.

Every day, I try to jump from denial to acceptance, to do what my father would have done—*accelerate the inevitable*—but the emptiness follows me around like a hungry puppy. My father would have moved on by now. He wrote his last will and testament the day the doctors said he had terminal cancer. Then he went skydiving for the first time. He jumped from denial to acceptance in a single bound.

William is gone.

I've done everything to accelerate the inevitable—met

with lawyers and discussed the will, reviewed our insurance, reviewed the benefits package from TriamSys, made funeral arrangements. The only thing I haven't finished is the guestlist for the funeral. I bought a set of designer cards William would have loved. Black and blue with silver embossing.

But he'll never see them.

William is gone. He's really gone.

I sit up and put my feet on the floor.

The tears come, fighting to escape, but I don't let them.

The clock above the fireplace ticks loudly. It's ten in the morning, but it's dark enough in here to be midnight. I gaze at the two overstuffed leather chairs sitting on the other side of the coffee table and picture William sitting there, his legs crossed. A glass of Cabernet in one hand.

I look away.

Loneliness is an empty chair.

Other than Mason, I have no one. Olivia is a good friend, but we don't spend much time together. She cares about me, and I love her, but she was there when Mason was taken. She saw my anger at its worst. It took years for me to recover, and I did, but she still keeps her distance.

A faint glow drifts in from the hallway, illuminating the carpet. Mason must have left the kitchen light on, though I don't remember hearing him get up. I hope he ate some cereal. He is finally interested in girls, but I'm not equipped to give him the advice he needs. I'm not his father.

I pull my laptop off the coffee table and open the lid. It boots, and the web browser opens, but before I can click on the bookmarks, a window pops up telling me my virus detection software has expired. I fight with the adware for a few minutes, kill some tasks the way William taught me, and navigate to my old anger management website. HeatSinkers.

I haven't been here in years. Fortunately, my login still works. MasonsMadMom. The website hasn't changed much. A silhouette of a couple holding hands before a setting sun still graces the page.

Feeling angry? Need a way out? Click here to answer the 3 Questions, *and we promise you'll feel better. Over 22342 people have been helped by* the 3 Questions. *Click* here *to read answers posted by fellow heatsinkers.*

The mail icon at the top shows twenty-three messages, and my last login was nine years ago. Do I really want to get involved with this again? Maybe I should dig out my old anger management books and read those instead.

No. I need help.

I open the inbox. The messages are old, but I still recognize some heatsinkers—JacksoTally, ReadyToRage02, MaggieO. I abandoned these people when I stopped logging in, but I don't feel bad about it. When my anger came less frequently, I didn't need their help anymore, and that's the point, isn't it? To get better and move on?

I close the inbox and click on the 3 questions link.

1) What happened?
"A woman ran her cart into me at the store."

2) Why did it make you angry?

I think about this. My hip hurt when the cart hit me, but that wasn't what set me off. The woman was on her phone, not watching where she was going, and there was beer in her cart.

I type, "The woman was a drunk."
I don't feel better.

3) Who or what can you forgive?
"The woman."

That's enough. I should be working on the invitation list, but before I can click on the logout button, the thumbs-up icon appears. Someone named florence72 has *liked* my answer to the three questions. I click to see her most recent answers.

1) What happened?
My husband died.

2) Why did it make you angry?
I wasn't ready for him to go.

3) Who or what can you forgive?
God.

Good for her.
She forgave God.
I click on the *like* link.
Her husband probably died of old age. My heart goes out to her. Really. No one is ever ready for their spouse to go, but at the same time, it's not like dying of old age is a surprise.
William was only forty-six.
A window pops up.

florence72 wants to chat. Will you accept? Yes *or* No?

I hesitate. Coming back to HeatSinkers has made me feel

better, but I'm not in the mood for a deep conversation about dead husbands. It's a no.

I open my notes app to make the guestlist. Friends first, then family. The friends list is easy—William didn't have any. I have Olivia, and her name goes at the top. William used to entertain people from work years ago, but I don't remember their names. That was before he switched departments. TriamSys kept him so busy, he didn't have time to socialize with anyone except me.

He always tried to make time for me, but it was never enough.

I'll have to go through his things later and see if there is anyone at TriamSys I should contact.

Now for family. I have no siblings, and my parents are dead. Actually, my mother might be alive, but I wouldn't know. She's probably passed out in an alley somewhere, drunk.

Cancer took my father, but I add him to the list anyway. I won't be sending him a card, but I want him to know I miss him.

With great hesitation, I put William's parents on the list. Nigel and Evelyn Kaine. I should send them a link to HeatSinkers. If ever two people needed to learn the calming effects of forgiveness, it's these two. When I called and told them what happened, Nigel hit me with a barrage of questions. He was worse than the police, and I heard Evelyn yelling in the background—*what did she do? Did she lure him onto the bridge? I bet she did. I bet she planned it.*

They've hated me ever since Ryan took Mason. They blamed me when Ryan started living on the streets. They blamed me when he stopped calling. I don't know if he ever talked to them again, but I do know we never saw him. The only thing he ever did right was honor the restraining order.

I'd like to leave the Kaines off the list, but it's not a choice. They're Mason's grandparents. Things would have been easier if Mason had never known them, but up until high school, Mason went with William to Connecticut for visits twice a year. He always came back with an exaggerated British accent, mocking his grandparent's pretentiousness. I loved it. William hated it. Despite his mockery, Mason always had a good time.

I put their names on the list.

Now, for William's brother.

My finger hovers above the R key, then I press it. The letter appears on the screen. At first, I don't realize I'm holding the key down. A series of Rs stream across the page, hit the edge, wrap, and advance on a new line. I can't take my finger off the keyboard. My hand trembles and my arm heats up. I grasp my wrist and pull, but the Rs keep streaming.

I can't put the name Ryan Kaine on my list. It should be easy to type, but I can't do it. I can't invite him. Not after what he did.

And I can't get angry again.

I shove the computer off my lap and cover my face. My cheeks burn. I don't know if William would have wanted Ryan to come or not, but it doesn't matter now.

Wait.

Of course William wants his brother there, but I don't.

I can't.

Breathe. This too shall pass.

Maybe I don't have to invite Ryan. Maybe Ryan is dead in a gutter somewhere. Worthless alcoholic. Thoughtless, worthless drunk. I *hope* he's dead in an alley. I hope he suffered. Those three nights I spent worried to death about

Mason—all because of him.

The big hand on the clock covers the six. It's 10:30 in the morning already, and I haven't done anything today. The clock's face turns pink, and Ryan might be out there somewhere. Alive. The room turns pink, then red, and Ryan might be a free man, enjoying his life.

I seethe.

In an instant, I'm logged back into HeatSinkers.

Three questions. *What happened? Why did it make you angry? Who or what can you forgive?*

This is all because William died. I'm angry he's gone, but I'm not going to forgive anyone for that. Not God. Not the driver of the black Audi. Not anyone. I'm not a saint like florence72. I'm not ready to answer the three questions about William's death, but if I don't get myself under control . . .

1) What happened?

"I tried to invite my brother-in-law to my husband's funeral."

2) Why did it make you angry?

"Because it reminded me of what Ryan did to Mason."

3) Who or what can you forgive?

"No one. I can forgive no one."

CHAPTER TEN

RYAN

Saturday afternoon, Ryan changes into the middle lane on I-90 right where the freeway becomes a floating bridge over Lake Washington. The high-rise buildings of Seattle vanish behind him, and the shining blue lake reaches north and south. No clouds to dim the open space today. Cruising in his delivery truck, he's making good time. He volunteered for the weekend shift, partly because traffic is lighter, and partly because he needs the extra money.

Mostly because he misses his brother.

But it *is* easy money. Time and a half. And, he's not delivering refrigerators or back-breaking furniture anymore. That stuff is for the guys in his old division. The younger, bigger guys. It took him over two years to convince his manager, Ed, he deserved to work in the valuables department, delivering art, jewelry, legal papers, and tech devices. Packages that sometimes require a signature.

The exit comes up fast, and Ryan glides onto the offramp, taking in the greenery of Mercer Island. He'd love to live here, but his home is downtown Seattle. If he ever had enough money, he supposes he could drive to his AA meetings from here, park near his old apartment, and go to all the usual places. With enough money, Ryan could keep his old apartment. There'd be no more eating at Denny's.

Ryan pictures Juan sitting in Denny's last night, giving in to the craving.

Life could be worse. Ryan's life could be like Juan's. He could be the subject of King Alcohol, shivering in the King's mad realm along with his sponsee. The look in Juan's eyes disturbed Ryan, but as sad as it was to see Juan choose the wrong side of the rock, it also angered Ryan. Juan, with his new job, driving around in that fancy Audi, taking everything AA has given him for granted. With a job like that, Ryan could afford a condo on Mercer Island in no time.

Ah, but resentment is the number one offender. Ryan can't let himself be jealous of Juan, or he'll succumb to the craving. He's got his own path to follow, and it begins with today's deliveries.

The first address leads to a lakefront mansion just off Mercer Way. He rings the buzzer at the wrought iron gate, and a woman's voice asks him to wait. Out of habit, he reaches for his clipboard, then remembers the new SPD Delivery app on his phone. Cost-cutting measures. His manager, Ed, said that from now on, all deliveries are tracked in the app. If everyone follows the preloaded routes, the company will save thousands.

A woman in a green flowing satin robe approaches the gate.

Ryan hands her the package through the bars, and she signs for it. Her fingernails shine like emeralds, and each of her rings has at least one diamond. She doesn't look like she's worked a day in her life.

She leaves, and he opens the app. The previous version didn't show drivers' locations, only tracking numbers and final destinations. His brother's house isn't far away, but Ryan makes a disturbing realization. The app will know if he goes there. This means no more drive-bys hoping to catch a glimpse of Mason growing up. No more chances at accidentally running into William. Accidentally on purpose.

Ryan taps the PACKAGE DELIVERED button for the current address, and the map scrolls to the next stop. A condominium complex.

He starts the truck and takes off. The feminine voice inside his phone spouts directions and leads him away from the large lakefront homes toward the island's center. Toward his brother's house.

Ryan thinks.

He could take a "wrong" turn. He could tell Ed he misheard the navigation system and made a left when he should have made a right. And what is he worried about? Ed manages dozens of drivers. He doesn't have time to monitor everyone's movements. He wouldn't know if Ryan went off-course and drove by William's house.

The condo complex appears to have been recently updated. It's nothing like the old brick apartments downtown. There's a park across the street, and again, Ryan imagines living here. Eating lunches with fellow residents in the clubhouse. Visiting his older brother. Throwing the football with Mason.

Making amends to Lauren.

He delivers a legal-sized envelope to a second-floor unit, and when the man signs, Ryan smells divorce. The man probably got kicked out of his mansion and went to live in one of his extra condos. What a luxury. Ryan walks back to his truck and thinks about how nice it must be to have a condo, one with a functioning heater. He wonders how many places his brother has by now.

William's house is only four blocks away.

Ryan opens the app, taps PACKAGE DELIVERED, and the next address displays.

9112 South 43rd Place.

It's William's house.

Careful what you wish for.

Excitement mixed with dread swirls inside him.

Ryan puts the transmission in drive and hits the gas. There's no signature required for this delivery, and he checks the address again. It *is* William's address. He follows the preloaded route. He must follow it. It's a company mandate. The time limit on the restraining order must have ended by now, and if not, would Lauren and William really file new charges? After all this time?

He scans the side streets for police cars. Because of the restraining order, this neighborhood has always made him anxious. Paranoid. It would be such a weight off his shoulders to be done with it. To be forgiven by his family.

He rounds the corner onto their street and slows down. William might not recognize him at first. Ryan's bloated belly is gone, and a decade of wrinkles have crept onto his face. His black hair is gray on the edges, and his eyes aren't bloodshot anymore. And, he's filled with hope.

If William answers the door, should he shake hands or go in for a hug?

It's been so long.

He parks in front of the house. The lawn struggles to break through a thick blanket of leaves. No one has raked. Or mowed. William is not the type to leave things untended, and with all his money, he must have gardeners. They're obviously not doing their job. Ryan wishes he could help.

The two-story house is not a mansion. It's not like the lakefront homes, but it does take up its share of land, and on Mercer Island, it's easily worth over a million dollars. Maybe two. The gate to the back fence is closed, and the blinds in William's downstairs office are drawn. A Lexus SUV sits in the driveway by the garage, and Ryan has the feeling William isn't there. The SUV is more Lauren's style.

If Lauren answers the door, there won't be a hug.

Ryan grabs the package and steps out of the truck. The box has no advertising print, no Amazon smile, and the return address is Dearborn, Michigan. Ryan holds it with both hands, assuming it's fragile, and strides up the sidewalk. Some people get angry if you walk on their lawns, and Lauren might be watching him from behind those blinds.

He puts the box down at the door. No signature required. No reason to ring the doorbell, other than to let them know a package has arrived.

He lingers.

He hesitates.

He could play it off as a mistake—claim he thought a signature was needed. Claim he didn't know this was William's house, and . . . not only would that be a lie, but the sign reading THE KAINE'S above the door blows this idea out of the water. Sweat accumulates on his brow. Excuses shouldn't be needed to visit his nephew or his brother, but if Lauren answers the door, there will be hell to pay.

But he misses them so much.

Even her.

He raises his hand. Extends his index finger. Attempts to clear his mind so he can press the doorbell, but fails. Flashes of Lauren attacking him, coming at him with her arms flailing, fists flying, a whirlwind of dark red hair and hate. He can still hear her screaming at him outside the courthouse. *Go away. Go away and die. Put yourself out of our misery, you coward!*

It *was* Ryan's fault.

She had every right to want him dead, and he's certain she still does.

He lowers his hand, turns, and foots it back to the truck, keeping his head down and his face away from the windows. Now is not the time for a reunion. With William, maybe, but not Lauren.

He jumps in the cab and starts the engine.

He should have left a note.

He's not a coward, but he should have done something.

If he'd been drunk, he would have rung the doorbell. Nothing would have stopped him. Liquid courage. One shot would have made all the difference in the world, and it's been a long time since he tied one on. The reality is, there's nothing stopping him from getting a ninety-proof mini bottle of schnapps right now—because that's what it would be, of course, if he were to relapse. The hard stuff. No beginner beer. Then, he would take it all the way and get a fifth of Vodka. He would return with no fear, bang on the door, and demand to see Mason.

It's been too long.

If he could clear his mind, nothing would stop him from pulling over at the next convenience store. He could blank out, buy a mini shooter, and drink it. He could. He could make that choice.

Ryan guides the truck onto the floating bridge, leaving Mercer Island. It's beautiful out. The sunshine makes Lake Washington shimmer like no day he can remember. He reaches into his pocket, and he feels around for his sobriety rock, but it's not there.

He gave it to Juan.

There's a rough side and a smooth side. It's his choice, but the rock is gone.

He crosses the bridge and exits I-90.

This is not his neighborhood.

He pulls into a convenience store and hits the brakes.

An ad in the window shows a sale on eighteen packs of beer.

His cell phone vibrates.

You have departed from the preloaded route.

He taps the PACKAGE DELIVERED button and rests his head on the steering wheel.

Next time.

Next time, he'll ring the doorbell.

CHAPTER ELEVEN

LAUREN

I drift into William's office and pause, resting my hand on the credenza. He kept his office like his life—calm and organized.

The way I always wanted to be.

I'm here to finish the guestlist for his funeral. Like it or not, this is my office now, and I'm going to make use of it. I refuse to let it become a shrine. Instead, I'm moving on—accelerating the inevitable.

I should redecorate.

But the flame mahogany credenza came from one of William's relatives in Britain—a family heirloom. It must stay. The books on the shelves behind his desk are ordered by subject—computer technology, history, internet security, philosophy. Mason might want those for school someday. They must stay.

The early evening light shines through the window, showing me the way to his desk. I run my hand over the credenza as I pass. Then, I shove his monitor, keyboard, and mouse out of the way, put my laptop down, and sit.

I won't redecorate, but I will take his desk.

I open my laptop and pull up the guestlist—Olivia, Nigel, Evelyn.

The Rs are still strewn across the bottom of the screen.

Every time I think about adding Ryan, my fingers seize. A minute passes while I stare at the Rs. I've put this off all day. After buying the invitations this afternoon, I purposely lapsed into a daze cleaning the house. The funeral is a week from tomorrow. The invitations need to be sent, but more than that, I need to move on.

I delete the row of Rs.

Across the street, the sun dips behind the neighbor's trees, and the streetlamp comes on. I should pull the blinds and turn on the light, but—no. I need to finish the list.

Who can I add?

William's colleagues at TriamSys?

I don't know them. He never talked about work after switching departments a few years ago. He also never said anything about a card until he was hanging from a bridge.

I picture the black Audi, and my soul begins to burn.

Breath. Think about something else.

The oil paintings above the credenza bring back fond memories. One year, we sailed out of the Mystic Seaport in Connecticut. Another, we camped out in northern California. We didn't enjoy the camping as much as the sailing, but the gigantic redwoods made us realize how small we were, and back then, we were small.

But we were happy. We had time.

The Mystic Seaport painting hangs next to the California Redwoods painting. Like the redwoods, the Atlantic Ocean's enormity kept us in our place. The painting of our home-away-from-home, St. Croix, hangs near the window. During our honeymoon, we paid an artist to stand on a hill overlooking Christiansted and paint the inlet. The white-crested waters in the distance remind me of my spirit animal, the seahorse. It's calming.

It's getting late.

If I can find some of William's colleagues to invite, then I can call the guestlist good for now. I open the bottom desk drawer, and the forensics bag containing his final possessions tumbles forward. I forgot I put it in there. When I came home from the hospital last week, full of rage, I threw it in his desk, swearing to never open it. William's wedding ring looks like a caramel candy through the plastic.

It makes me shudder.

There's a box of business cards by the bag. I flip through them, but none have the TriamSys logo. Then it occurs to me—*the card* could be a business card. I flip through them again, this time checking for handwritten notes, cryptic symbols—anything out of the ordinary.

Nothing.

I shove the box back in the drawer and spy a crumpled sticky.

New guy in R&D - Robert Lang x4896.

It's William's handwriting. I add Robert to the invite list on the outside chance he met William at least once. If nothing else, maybe this Robert can tell me who William worked with. But all I have is his work extension, and it's the weekend. TriamSys is closed.

I need William's personal contact list. I need his phone.

I take a deep breath and open the forensics bag. William's wallet, the cuff links he wore to our anniversary, his wedding ring—I sift through his things, searching for his cell phone like a grave robber. A leaf, still wet from the river, sticks to my hand. Fortunately, his phone fell out of his pocket before he fell off the bridge. It's dry. I plug it into a charger, count to ten, and turn it on.

The screen is locked.

For a moment, I think I can guess the code, completely forgetting the internet security books behind me. I'll have to wait until Monday to call Robert. If only there was another way. Searching for phone numbers on Google never works. It always returns too many misleading results.

I miss the old days when the white pages listed everyone's number.

My eyelids are heavy, but the invitations must go out tomorrow or they won't get there on time.

Every night this week, I woke up and moved to the sitting room sofa. I can't stay asleep in the bedroom without William. Tonight, I think I'll start on the sofa. But first, Mason needs dinner.

And I must finish the guestlist.

Exhaustion washes over me.

William's phone vibrates.

The screen reads CALLER UNKNOWN.

I tap ANSWER.

A voice buzzing like a chainsaw says, "Hello. May I speak with Mr. Kaine?"

"Who is this?" I ask.

"I'm calling on behalf of—"

"If you're selling something, we don't want any."

"Is this Mrs. Kaine?"

The man's voice irritates my ear. It's so strong. So grinding. He breaks into a coughing fit, and I'm forced to hold the phone away.

"How did you get this number?" I ask.

"Mrs. Kaine, please." He coughs again. He must be a

smoker. "I've been trying to reach your husband all day. We have an urgent matter to discuss with—"

"How do you know my husband?"

"I'm sorry, I can't say. Will you please put him on the phone?"

It's got to be a solicitor. If it was a friend, the screen wouldn't read CALLER UNKNOWN. If it was someone from TriamSys, it would show the corporate number. "Look, I don't know what you're selling, but I'm sure it's not urgent. Please take us off your list."

"Mrs. Kaine, wait." He coughs again—a brittle rattling, a hacksaw cutting through metal. "Could you have him call me? I'll give you my number. Please. When can I speak with him?"

"Never." Red skirts my vision. "You can speak to him never. He's dead!"

I mash the hang-up button with my thumb.

00:38 CALL ENDED.

I tap and swipe the lock screen, attempting to bypass it and open William's contacts, but the phone asks for a PIN. I try William's birthday. Our anniversary. Mason's birthday. My birthday combined with William's. Nothing. It's useless.

I see red.

I rage, and—shit.

I should have stayed calm and kept the man on the line. Asked him questions. Maybe he wasn't a solicitor. Maybe he knew something about William's work. The card.

My rage ruined everything.

Again.

My legs tense, and I drop the phone on the desk, stand, and wander over to the credenza.

I place my hands on the lacquered surface and lean forward.

Breathe.

We used to keep the scotch on the credenza. We had to throw it out to keep Ryan from sneaking shots. Worthless alcoholic. Drunk.

The back of my neck burns.

I gaze at the Mystic Seaport painting and pinch my lip. The Connecticut coast. The Atlantic with its seahorses . . . but the seahorse—my seahorse, my spirit animal—swims in St. Croix, not Connecticut. We were snorkeling in the aquamarine waters of St. Croix when I found my spirit animal.

Breathe. This too shall pass.

I picture my seahorse.

Calm, cool, and collected.

Floating in the deep, my seahorse is at peace.

And so am I. Almost.

I return to the desk, sit down, and glance at the sticky note. Robert Lang. I reach into the drawer for the forensics bag, but a framed photograph falls on top of it. I shove the frame aside, and try again, but it falls over again. It's frustrating, and after failing to make the frame stand on end, I take it out.

I wish I hadn't.

It's a photo of William standing outside the King Dome with his arm around Ryan. They're young, and their smiles tell me the Seahawks just won a football game.

William never liked football, but he loved his brother.

I put the frame down and open the other drawer, thinking there may be more photos, but this drawer only contains manila folders stuffed with financial papers—the mortgage for this house, the contract for our condo in St. Croix, auto sales receipts, advertisements for jet skis, brochures promoting the Caribbean.

I flip through the folders until I come across one containing court documents listing Ryan as the defendant. The documents have his phone number.

Before I can stop myself, I punch his digits into my phone. William would want him at the funeral. If I talk to him now, I can tell him about the service and get it over with.

I can accelerate the inevitable.

It rings.

He doesn't answer.

I wait.

I wait, and I wonder if he's still alive.

My imagination takes over, and I see him lying on his back in the blackberry brambles beneath the freeway, surrounded by trash, clutching an empty wine bottle. No. It's an empty vodka bottle, and he has a beard. He hasn't shaved in thirteen years because he can't afford a razor, and he's wearing the Seahawks jersey from the photo, and everything is red, and—

An automated voice comes on. "I'm sorry, but the number you have dialed has been disconnected."

Great. Ryan is gone. He's "disconnected."

Glancing back at the photograph, at William's gentle smile, and Ryan's youthful glow, the air leaves my lungs. I'm a monster. Ryan wasn't always a drunk, and William loved him, and I'm horrible for wishing him dead, and now he's . . . disconnected.

The court documents make a disturbing fluttering sound when I throw them at the ceiling.

Damn you, Ryan Kaine.

I close my eyes.

The backs of my eyelids are bright red.

I know better than to let him make me so angry. Blame causes anger, and I blame Ryan for leaving Mason alone, but the kidnapping wasn't all his fault. It's definitely not his fault William died. It's not my fault either, but it happened.

Dammit.

My mantra. I need my mantra.

Breathe. This too shall pass.

But it doesn't pass. It gets worse.

I need help.

HeatSinkers. The three questions.

What happened?

"Someone ran my husband off a bridge, chasing him for a card. A fucking card."

Why did it make you angry?

"It was for a card. They killed him for a fucking card."

A business card? A greeting card? An index card?

No.

No one uses index cards anymore.

I lean forward, and the chair creaks, and the armrest bangs into the desk as I stand, turn toward the window— toward the painting of St. Croix.

Breathless, I stumble forward, arms outstretched.

William said the card was in St. Croix.

I reach the painting.

I run my hands down each side of the frame.

My fingertips burn, and the felt lining changes color from black to red to black. The water in the center is blue and cool, but the canvas's edges are crimson, and if I can't find out who chased us, who killed my husband, the rage will keep coming.

And coming.

The water *is* cool. I close my eyes, but my seahorse is on

fire.

I've got to get out of here.

Mason hasn't had dinner. He hasn't eaten today. No girl wants a skinny, malnourished punk.

I break away from the painting and rush to the window, and I'm about to close the blinds when I see the bearded old man from the grocery store standing across the street. He's smoking a cigarette and talking on a cell phone.

The sun has gone down. Shadows lope in and out of my neighbor's driveways, hugging the shrubs and fences, but the man stands directly beneath a streetlamp. He stands there in full view, wearing a red baseball cap and staring straight at my house from behind those sunglasses.

He can see me.

I'm certain he can see me.

Slowly, I close the blinds, then rush into the hallway, through the sitting room, and into the foyer.

This ends now.

Accelerate the inevitable.

I fling the front door open and burst onto the walk, but the old man is gone.

CHAPTER TWELVE

MASON

It's a sunny Sunday afternoon outside, but it's always dark in the hallway upstairs when the lights are off.

Mason stands just inside his bedroom, peering out the door.

He listens.

Silence.

His mom never comes upstairs during the day, so he should be okay. He gingerly steps into the corridor and heads for her bedroom. All week, she's been talking about how they need closure. She keeps bringing up the funeral and asking if he's eaten. Asking if he's okay, and he *is* okay. She's so annoying. She offered to let him stay home from school again this week, but he's not going to. He's ready to go back.

He's dying to go back.

Tomorrow, everything is going to change.

At the end of the hall, a shuffling noise comes from inside her bedroom. He halts, turns around, and hoofs it back to his room, closing the door behind him with a gentle click.

She'd better not be packing up his father's things. She

promised she wouldn't do that until he had a chance to see what he wanted.

He presses his ear to the door and listens.

She tromps down the hall.

It sounds like she's in a hurry, but that's nothing new.

He counts to fifty and opens his door.

Now, she's rattling things in the kitchen downstairs, probably making him something to eat, suffering from her delusion that he's anorexic. Maybe she's making a grilled cheese. If so, she won't be back for at least ten minutes.

He rushes down the hall into her bedroom. It always smells funny in here, like dirty laundry mixed with old-people-smell mixed with his father's cologne. But this time, the burnt chocolate scent is almost gone. It's fading away.

Daylight barges in through the window, and he narrows his eyes on the walk-in closet. Forbidden from entering his parent's room at a young age, he imagines himself now as a phantom thief. He deftly prowls into the closet and peruses his father's suits. The immaculate jackets are smooth, and he could see wearing one to a dance. His attire, clean and sophisticated. His date, Garrett, wears a viciously multi-colored suit. Hand in hand, they take the dance floor, and everyone applauds.

But there is no dance, and there is no him and Garrett.

Not yet.

Tomorrow can't come soon enough.

He takes a pair of suit pants off a hanger and holds them up to his waist. As expected, the long pant legs crumple on the floor. His dad stood over six feet tall, but that's okay. Mason can wear his new jeans to school tomorrow. It's time he finally put on the tight-fit denims and let the world see him for who he really is.

His father's dress shirts range in color from black to blue to white. Just because Garrett always wears bright colors doesn't mean Mason should. Garrett can get away with it, and not just because orange fits Garrett's personality, or because he has been out since before puberty, but because people expect it from him. Everyone knows him. They know his dark, wavy hair. His cool gray eyes. They know the way the world stands still when he smiles.

Mason pulls three shirts out of the closet and lays them on the bed. The shirts are too long, but they should fit his shoulders. He can tuck the bottoms in. Back in the closet, he searches for a pair of dress shoes, but they're all too big. He considers shoving a pair of socks into his father's wingtips, but fears it would look ridiculous. It's going to be hard enough coming out without looking like a clown. The jocks would totally get off on teasing a gay clown. Especially Hunter Stalwell—homophobic beef-head.

At the last minute, Mason's grandparents bought him a pair of dress shoes for his cousin's wedding when he was in ninth grade. He still has them, and they fit, but he has no dress socks, so he goes to the dresser.

The ultimate invasion of privacy.

A forbidden trove of parental secrets.

He's the phantom thief again, and before he slides the top drawer open, he glances toward the hallway.

He listens.

Nothing. Not a sound.

Inside the drawer, he searches for a brown pair of socks. His father was fond of blue, black, and white, but there must be a pair of brown in here somewhere. He keeps digging until he comes across a box of condoms.

Lifestyles Ultra Sensitive.

His father isn't going to need these anymore.

Neither is his mother. In one of her angry fits, she declared she will never love again, but it's not true. She says a lot of things when she's mad. If she does start dating though, Mason will move out. He will. He's sixteen.

He doesn't need a new dad.

He needs Garrett.

If things work out tomorrow, these condoms could come in handy. With the right clothes, the right attitude, and now, with protection . . . there's no better time to come out of the closet. He doesn't have to make a big announcement. He just has to be himself.

He'll dress gay.

He'll act gay—because he is gay—and he'll be himself.

For the first time.

And when Garret sees him, and when he asks Garrett out, and Garret says *yes*, the whole world will know Mason is homosexual. Hunter Stalwell and Scott Turner, and the other testosterone monkeys can go screw themselves.

Mason will be free.

Tomorrow.

He takes a black pair of socks from the drawer and shoves them into his pocket.

Her footsteps startle him. She's coming up the stairs.

He grabs the condoms, scoops the shirts off the bed, and rushes into the hall. He's got to make the corner and run for his room before she reaches the top. That way, she'll only see him from the back. Otherwise, he'll be trapped. Caught dead. The phantom thief will be imprisoned forever.

There'll be no tomorrow.

And he'll be forced to endure her rage.

The rage of the dragon.

He rounds the corner, sprints down the hall, and—

"Mason," his mom calls from behind, "wait. What are you doing?"

"Nothing."

"I have something I need to ask you."

His hand slips off the doorknob, and he nearly drops everything. He tries again, but his hand is wrapped up in the clothing, and he can't get a grip.

His mother puts her hand on his shoulder. "What are you—"

Mason turns and deftly slides the condoms behind his back, pinning the box against the door.

She's not touching her lip. That's a good sign, but his throat is dry, and his first attempt at speaking comes out as a crackle. "Mom, I—"

"Oh," she says, taking a step back. "Your father's shirts."

"I'm sorry."

"No. No. It's okay. I meant to ask if you wanted to help me today. I was about to go through his stuff." She casts her eyes down. "I think I'm ready. There's no reason to wait."

"But you promised you'd wait."

"Why didn't you tell me you wanted his shirts?"

"I don't know."

She reaches out, lifts one sleeve, and strokes the material with her fingers. "These aren't your style. Did you want them as a keepsake?"

Mason can't speak. He can't get the words out, and it feels like the box is about to collapse behind his back.

"I only ask because your father's mementos are in the walk-in closet. There's probably something better in there to remember him by."

"You don't know my style." Mason's eyes sting. "You

don't know me."

She raises her arm, and he flinches, but she's not angry. She's—it's unbelievable. She's coming in for a hug.

Mason wants to hug her back, but if he does, the condoms will fall. Instead, he turns his head away, and she stops. When he looks back, she's staring at him, still holding onto the sleeve with one hand, confused. Hurt. He's never seen pain in her eyes like this, but it's not his fault. The phantom thief must not get caught.

She—it can't be. She looks like she is about to cry.

He should tell her now.

He should tell her why he wants the shirts. The condoms.

He should tell her he's gay while he has the chance. While she's not raging.

For the first time in his life, she looks like an ordinary person. Not his mom. Not a dragon. But an actual, everyday, normal person.

"Don't be angry with me," she says. "But I have to ask. Have you had thoughts of . . . suicide?"

And now she looks like one of Mr. Jackson's health class brochures. "No. Can you just leave me alone?"

"Okay, but, later, would you want to help me go through your father's things?"

"No, Mom. Please."

"Alright. I won't throw anything away you might want. I'm starting in the bedroom today, and maybe his office tomorrow. I promise I won't pack it up until you've had a chance to see everything." She puts the sleeve to her face. "I love the way his shirts smell. Don't you?"

"Yes."

She turns to go.

The box of condoms slips. He presses his back against

the door.

She walks down the hall, but not fast enough.

The box crumples. He needs her to move faster, go down the stairs, disappear, but she doesn't.

She stops, puts her hand to her forehead, and turns around. "I almost forgot the reason I came up here. Do you remember your Uncle Ryan?"

"No, not really."

"He's your uncle, on your—he's your dad's brother. I guess you wouldn't remember him, but I was thinking of inviting him to the funeral. Would that be okay with you?"

"Sure." The box slides down the door. "Whatever."

"If you don't want him to come, it's alright. I want to keep the guestlist small."

"I don't remember him, so I don't care."

"Are you sure you don't remember him?"

"Yes. Can you just go?"

Her eyes narrow. "Why aren't you going inside your room?"

"I—"

"Is something wrong?" She walks toward him.

Mason turns, attempts to catch the box, but his hands flail, and the condoms hit the floor.

Wrappers scatter everywhere.

She halts. "Oh, I see."

Mason twists the knob, throws the door open, and drops to his knees. He scoops the condoms and the shirts into a pile. He won't face her. He's not going to say anything. He shoves the pile into his room and crawls in after it, slamming the door shut behind him with his foot.

She doesn't see him for who he is.

But after tomorrow, it won't matter.

CHAPTER THIRTEEN

LAUREN

We keep a stack of collapsed cardboard boxes in the corner of the garage. I grab a roll of gray duct tape off the workbench and begin rebuilding a box. I'm going to pack up William's things in the bedroom this afternoon so I can sleep through the night in my own bed.

The tape screeches when I pull on it.

I wish Mason had wanted to help me pack, but after our run-in earlier, he needs time. Caught stealing condoms by his mother—he must be mortified. He's been acting stranger than usual lately, but with everything that's happened, I can't blame him. He's probably nervous about what the kids will say at school tomorrow.

I'm nervous too.

An old man is stalking me.

I finish taping up the box and grab another.

To be safe, Mason should stay home another week, but I don't want to tell him about the stalker. That would only make him want to stay in his room forever. Yet, I'm surprised he doesn't want to stay home.

Then it dawns on me.

The condoms.

He wants to see his girlfriend.

We've never discussed the birds and the bees, but he's obviously aware of the dangers. William must have had "the talk" with him at some point. Nevertheless, I'm sure he's not having sex. He's probably just curious.

I finish taping up the second box and head upstairs. As I pass Mason's room, I slow down and listen, but hear nothing.

The midday sun creeps into my room. I toss the boxes onto the bed and face the walk-in closet. Everything here is so empty. Without William, an insipid gloom has settled into the walls. The walk-in closet looks like a jail cell.

I lift my chin, grab a box, and march into the closet. I wish I didn't have to do this alone, but I've been taking care of myself since I was nine. Since my mother—worthless alcoholic—left me.

William's shirts cling to the hangers. Blue, black, and white Oxfords all in a row, grouped by color. In one swift motion, I could sweep them into the box. It would only take a second, but William's shirts were a part of him. They *are* part of him.

I take a deep breath. Close my eyes.

All I have to do is thrust the shirts to the left, pull them off the rack, and shove them into the box. It's so easy. It could be, and it should be, done in a single motion. Like ripping off a bandage. The way my father taught me.

In sixth grade, he tried to teach me to accelerate the inevitable. I had gotten into trouble, but it wasn't my fault. My teacher had misread my name and given credit to another student. She told my father I hadn't been doing my homework. When I explained, he believed me. He scheduled a meeting with her, but when we arrived, he made me go in alone. I was only eleven. He said I should have confronted my teacher after the first assignment went missing, that I should have ripped the situation off like a bandage. Accelerated the inevitable.

My father almost let me flunk sixth grade.

I could never do that to Mason, but I almost did.

When he was in sixth grade, he had the opportunity to battle an incompetent teacher after some kids bullied him. They called him gay and ridiculed his looks. When I found out, I told him to fight back, and he did, but his teacher gave him two months' detention. He hadn't done anything wrong. I scheduled a meeting with her, and I remember thinking I should make him attend it alone, but I didn't. I was too angry. Not only was the bullying wrong, but the homosexual accusation stunted his development. The whole thing was ludicrous. The bullies gay-bashed my son, and he wasn't even gay.

Even now, the memory angers me.

Focus.

William's dress shirts are empty. Lifeless. Hanging there like wilted flowers outside a mausoleum. I stroke a sleeve and wonder if Mason's bedroom feels as empty as mine.

Kneeling, I pack William's dress shoes. The black leather reminds me of the theatre. While I'm down here, I scan the floor for anything resembling a card, but see nothing. Not that I know what I'm looking for. He said the card was in St. Croix, but there could be another card in here. A copy, maybe. I run my hand inside each shoe, hoping to find something other than lint, but come up empty-handed.

William's box of mementos—his Kaine memorabilia—sleeps at the back of the closet next to a crumpled pair of slacks. He must have been in a hurry to change clothes for our anniversary dinner last week. It's not like him to leave laundry on the floor.

I check the pockets.

Bingo.

I find a paper with TriamSys letterhead. The blue logo is stylish, but the handwriting is stilted and hurried.

Will, I'm sorry I couldn't say anything during the meeting, but I need you to take your project and put it somewhere safe. Get it out of here. Destroy everything. Your team is on hold for now. The board thinks we've been compromised. If it got out that TriamSys allowed a corporate spy to steal your technology, our reputation would be ruined. Let me know if Robert Lang tries to contact you. I'll explain more on Monday.

-TJ

William didn't tell me his work was on hold. He must not have wanted to upset me on our anniversary. He—I bite back the tears.

Fuck you, TJ.

Breathe.

I picture my spirit animal. My seahorse. He floats weightless in the waves.

Stay focused. Finish packing. Deal with TriamSys later.

The last of William's shoes fits neatly in the box. I lay his slacks over the top and stroke the fine material once before carrying everything to the bed.

Rushing now, I sling the other box into the closet, and—in one swift motion—sweep William's shirts off the rack. I shove them into the box and collapse onto the floor. Hot tears come. I cover my face as if I can hold them back, but it's futile. William's shirts smell like his cologne. Flowery and rugged.

Burnt Chocolate.

I take out a blue Oxford and hold it to my chest.

William was the only person who could hold me together. At times like this, he would wrap his arms around me and *literally* hold me together. Now I have no one but Mason, and it's not his job to hold me. He needs to be held. The pain he must feel . . . but when I tried to hug him earlier, he leaned away. He glared at me like he didn't know who I was.

Like I was a monster.

I take a long, slow breath, pulling air in through William's shirt, then place it back into the box.

Goodbye, William.

But it's not goodbye.

A part of him is here, alive in his box of mementos.

I pull it onto my lap. There's a floppy disk from the 90s inside. It's labeled CS 192, whatever that means. The disk is an actual floppy and makes a warbly sound when I shake it. Whatever's on here is useless. It's not a card.

There's a stack of photos. I avoid them. Instead, I sift through a pile of jewelry and find William's class ring. I don't recognize the other charms. Broaches, bracelets, necklaces— these treasures probably came from long-deceased Kaines. It's curious. I should know who these items belonged to, but I don't. Everything in this box meant something to William, but without him, it's all worthless.

I pick up the photos.

The first one is a picture of me standing outside the Monroe School of Business, wearing my graduation gown, holding a diploma for a degree I never used. The next one is of William and Ryan. They're young. It's from before we met. Before Ryan went off the rails. They're smiling for the camera, and William has his arm around his brother.

It's sad. The restraining order destroyed their relationship.

I'll never forget that day. It was one of the few times I ever saw William cry.

But it wasn't my fault.

Ryan left me with no choice.

Mason would have died in that hotel if we hadn't found him when we did. Locked up alone in a Motel 6 on the edge of Tacoma because Ryan went on a bender. Three days. Mason was missing for three days. When we found him—his face, his little hands, his chest and legs—he was filthy. He was hungry. He could have died. He—

The photo shakes in my hands.

William convinced me not to press charges, but I made sure Ryan was out of our lives for good.

But now, William is gone too, and I'm alone.

If Ryan were here, and if he were sober, would we grieve together?

What a ridiculous thought.

Ryan Kaine deserves to die for what he did. I'm glad he didn't answer when I tried to invite him to the funeral. I'm glad he's "disconnected." I'm glad he's probably dead.

Worthless alcoholic.

I drop the photo into the box.

My arms tense. I can't hold them still. I grab the box, and the jewelry begins to rattle. Ryan would know the meaning behind these trinkets. I can't ask William's parents. They hate me. They blame me for everything. Even Mason's kidnapping. The funeral is in a week, and Ryan doesn't even know about it. Without him, I'll never know why William kept these things. But with him, I might lose Mason again.

I clench the box. My knuckles are going to burst. The

walls close in, and I stand—*breathe*—but I can't stop the box from shaking. My entire body won't stop shaking. Where is William to hold me together?

If Ryan's not dead, he should be.

I've got to breathe.

If Robert Lang drove my husband off the bridge, he needs to die.

My neck throbs.

William's manager, TJ . . . he put William's team on hold. He put William's *life* on hold. Told him to put the project in a safe place. The project. The card. Robert Lang—corporate spy.

The black Audi.

William's last words—*They want the card. It's in St. Croix.*

Damn you, TriamSys.

I hurl the box at the closet and watch it explode against the back wall. Chains, rings, and broaches flash and fall. Photos scatter like confetti. The release comes, and it is good, like surfing on a lightning bolt, then cruising into shore.

The walls fade from red to white, and a thread of spit runs down my chin. The throbbing in my neck slows to an anemic rhythm.

The shaking stops.

I breathe, and I love the release.

CHAPTER FOURTEEN

RYAN

Ryan decides to skip Starbucks on his morning walk to Denny Park. He woke up early, intending to conquer chapter three in his *Java Programming for Dummies* book, but after his code continually failed to compile, the walls closed in. Though a decent cup of coffee would jumpstart his brain, he's down to his last twenty-five dollars. He doesn't get paid until Friday.

It's going to be a long week.

He sits on a bench near the center of Denny Park. Green snippets of grass grow from between the cracks in the concrete slabs. The slabs form a circle around a barren garden plot, and the sky covers itself with a blanket of ash-gray clouds. In the distance, Denny Way and Dexter Avenue thrum with Monday morning traffic, but the noise doesn't bother Ryan. Like the cloud cover, the humming engines dull the city's ambiance. He knows it well. The park is as warm as his apartment today, which isn't saying much.

And to think, yesterday, he was ready to relapse. Ready to risk losing his apartment and become homeless again. He sat outside that convenience store, praying for God to relieve him of the bondage of self, and his prayers were answered. After a moment of clarity, he drove away. Sure, his apartment is freezing, and he can barely afford the rent, and he can't make any progress toward getting a better job—a computer job—but that doesn't mean he should give up. His delivery job is good, not great, but good. He has a lot to be grateful for, yet . . . he doesn't have his brother.

Or his nephew.

Mason.

He's not sure he wants his sister-in-law. It's not that he's afraid of her—and he *is* afraid of her—it's because she's in the way. She always came between him and William. But making amends might change things this time. Like it or not, he needs her back too, but only after his brother forgives him. Without William's forgiveness, he doesn't have a chance at Lauren's.

A woman pushes a cart filled with empty grocery bags along the sidewalk near Denny Way. The wheels squeak. Her shawl matches the clouds, and Ryan wonders if she's ever had a good day in her entire life.

Maybe Lauren has changed. Maybe Ryan doesn't need William's forgiveness first. Thirteen years is a long time, and if Ryan could stay sober for the last eight years, it's possible she became a kinder, gentler human being. He considers returning to their house. Facing the music. Making amends to her before he's tempted to drink over the guilt again.

He didn't mean to leave Mason alone in that hotel.

A cool breeze caresses the trees, and Ryan remembers pulling his lucky blanket around his shoulders in the winter months. He can't continue to close the door on his past. The truth is, he never completed the twelve steps. He never made amends to everyone he harmed because of the restraining order. He wasn't allowed. It's no wonder he ended up outside the convenience store yesterday, but . . .

Is making amends worth getting arrested for violating the order?

To drink is to die, so the question becomes a choice between jail and death.

"Hey, buddy." A man in a soiled orange and blue sweatshirt limps up to Ryan. "Can you spare a dollar? I need a dollar for something to eat." He has a tattered beige blanket with a big blue "H" draped over his shoulders. The "H" stands for Hilton. Hilton Hotel. The graying whiskers on his cheeks grow only where the heat blisters haven't blossomed. He's rack thin. His legs are toothpicks, and Ryan wonders how long the man has lived out here.

"You like the Broncos?" Ryan says.

"Huh?"

"The Broncos," Ryan repeats, pointing at the man's sweatshirt. "You know, we beat them in the Super Bowl."

The man glances down at the snorting horse on his chest. "I don't know. I wear what they give me. Do you have something you can spare? Two dollars, maybe?" He holds out his hand. His quivering skin puts him only a few hours since his last drink. Delirium tremens. Ryan doesn't doubt the man needs money for food, but it's obvious he'll spend it on booze. It's what Ryan would do.

"Look," the man says, "would it help if I was wearing a Seahawks shirt?"

"No." Ryan glances at the path leading out of the park. "I think you know where help is. Things just haven't gotten bad enough for you yet."

The man averts his eyes. "I don't know what you're talking about."

"I know." Ryan takes out his wallet, grabs a five, and hands it over.

"Thank you. You're very kind. You're a good person." He's missing two upper teeth.

"I'm no better than you."

The man tucks the five into his sweatshirt and shuffles toward Denny Way. A chill hits Ryan's neck, and he wishes he had his lucky blanket. The impulse comes from an old, old thought; one he used to experience daily. *Wrap up tight before you pass out, or you'll freeze to death.*

He runs his fingers over the wooden slats on the bench and wonders how many times he slept in this park. Blitzed on booze all day, every day, there's no way of remembering everywhere he passed out when he was homeless. He must have slept right here several times. Not *on* the bench, of course. Under it. When the parks close, the police come out, and the homeless hide. He remembers sometimes sleeping behind the dumpsters near the administration building, waiting for the police to leave.

Those days are a blur. The people on the street—the users, pushers, the high hookers—they all called him "St. Nick" because of his blanket. His grandparents gave him the reindeer covered fleece during his last Christmas in Great Britain. The last Christmas before his family disowned him for taking Mason.

In a way, the people on the street became his family, but he wasn't like them. He told himself it was his choice to be homeless. To be free of family and work. He told himself he could get a job and a place to live whenever he wanted.

The truth?

He was pretending he hadn't lost everything.

The real truth?

He chose to be free of family and work so he could drink whenever he wanted, and he drank because he liked the effect produced by alcohol. It owned him. Missing his brother and his parents, forbidden from watching his nephew grow up—those were merely excuses to drink. The truth is, his family didn't disown him as much as he disowned them. The restraining order gave him every reason to hide away and drink himself to death.

That's the truth, and the truth is unforgiving.

Through the trees, Ryan sees the man in the Broncos sweatshirt hobbling across Denny Way, no doubt heading for a convenience store. He resists the urge to run after him. Take him to the nearest AA meeting. But it would do no good. Until a drunk hits bottom, AA doesn't work, and sadly, some poor souls die before they get the chance to recover. In some miraculous sequence of events, Ryan woke up in the First Light Church parking lot the day he decided to die.

The relentless cycle—drink, pass out, wake, beg, borrow, steal, drink—it had taken its toll. He'd spent a week summoning the courage to kill himself when a man found him passed out in the parking lot. Garage Mike assumed Ryan was there for an AA meeting and took him into the church.

That meeting saved Ryan's life.

Garage Mike introduced Ryan to Stan, and Stan became Ryan's first sponsor. They worked the twelve steps together—most of them—until Stan relapsed and lost his life to the disease. Ironically, Stan committed suicide.

Drink, pass out, beg, and steal.

Some make it, and some don't. Some decide the cyclic nightmare is worse than death and end their own lives. Ryan swore he'd live the program, live in the twelfth step, carry the message, practice the principles the way Stan taught him, but he also decided never to have another sponsor. Too much pain. Ryan nearly drank over Stan's death. After Garage Mike stepped in and helped Ryan make it through the funeral, he decided that was as close as he would ever let someone become his sponsor.

Only his higher power can keep him sober; put him on the path of happy destiny. He inhales the moist morning air. Stands. Spreads his arms. He will make amends to his brother. Then Lauren. Then Mason.

Strolling out of the park, he's lighter. A weight has been lifted. He follows the path to the street and heads for his apartment. He's down to twenty dollars, but a cup of coffee on this chill morning still sounds good.

He trudges up Capitol Hill toward Starbucks, and a young woman sits on a corner with a sign reading, "No Job. No Food. Looking for Kindness. Anything Helps." She stares at the cracks in the sidewalk, glancing up only when Ryan stops. He takes a five-dollar bill from his pocket and puts it on her lap. She smiles. She's too young to have those lines in her face, those chapped lips. Those bulging blue veins in her arms.

Ryan strides past Starbucks, grateful for what he has. Grateful for his life. He goes inside his apartment building and up the stairs. He doesn't have a lot. Not as much as he should have after all these years of sobriety, but he does have a place to live. More so, he has a plan.

He has hope.

There's an envelope taped to his door. It's from the property management office. As he reads, he realizes the chill of the outdoors followed him inside.

He shivers.

Due to market conditions and increased maintenance costs, the building owners have decided to raise the rent. This is a reminder of the notice they sent sixty days ago. Ryan doesn't remember receiving a notice.

Dammit, Carl.

His landlord must not have given it to him. The increase will take effect at the end of his current lease agreement.

His lease is up this month. This week.

His credit cards are maxed.

He's got fifteen dollars left until Friday.

Fifteen dollars isn't going to cut it, but it is enough for a fifth of McCormick's Vodka and two mini shooters.

Stinking thinking.

Nine years ago, he would have already been on his way to the bar.

To numb his fear.

To disappear.

CHAPTER FIFTEEN

LAUREN

I never had nightmares before last week. Never. Sleep had always been a black jump in time from night to morning. There should be a word for what happens now. I fall asleep, but not all the way. I think and dream at the same time in a sleep-limbo.

And it's happening again.

I'm with William, and we're walking hand-in-hand on our anniversary. The black car, that monstrous Audi, hasn't begun to chase us yet, but I know it's coming. I work through different scenarios, trying to avoid the inevitable. Half-awake, half asleep—the car comes, William runs, jumps over the barrier, dangles from the bridge, and I try to save him.

And I fail.

I break out of this *sleep-limbo* and wipe sweat from my forehead. The sitting room sofa hurts my back, and the nightmarish images fade from my mind. If I'd spent more time working out in the basement, I could have pulled William up. If I hadn't let him run away from the car, he wouldn't have fallen over the edge. If I—

I open my eyes and stare at the ceiling.

The clock on the mantle chimes.

It's early Monday morning, and Mason will be leaving for school soon, but I don't want him to go. It doesn't feel safe with that old man out there, somewhere, smoking cigarettes in the rain.

But Mason needs to go somewhere. He's been cooped up in his room for a week. If the sun comes out, we could go to the park. William always took him there to talk, man-to-man. Or, if it's cloudy, we could find a brightly lit restaurant for lunch. Perhaps the club. We could sit in a secluded booth by the kitchen, and I could kill two birds with one stone. I could get him to open up *and* eat. Three birds. We could mail the funeral invitations on the way. To break the ice, I'll ask him who he wants to invite to the funeral. Maybe he'll invite that girl.

Abigail?

Yes, her name was Abigail.

The clock chimes again.

An hour passed in the blink of an eye.

I must have drifted back to sleep.

My eyes won't stay open, and I wonder . . . if I had just held onto William's arms a little longer. If I'd jumped in after him instead of attacking the car. Could I have saved him if my anger hadn't taken over? Beating the driver's side window, steam rolls over the hood, the engine starts—

I'm drifting back to sleep.

No. Not again.

I swing my legs off the sofa and plant my feet on the floor. The empty leather chairs hide in the dim light. Mason's door closes upstairs with a bang. Good. He's awake. He stays up late every night, surfing the web and talking to people on his new cell phone, or on his laptop. I'm not sure which.

It feels good to stand and stretch. I walk over to the fireplace mantle. Our wedding photo is front and center. William had crooked teeth and a beautiful smile. Next to it, there's a picture of Mason kicking his little legs, rising high on a swing. On that rare sunny day, his face glowed. He grinned. He knew joy.

I drag my finger down the photo, cutting through a thick coat of dust.

His door bangs again.

I head down the hall to the kitchen, fastening my robe around my waist. As I pass the stairs, I catch William in the corner of my eye. These hallucinations are driving me crazy, so I continue on, but when I reach the end of the hall, I turn— and there he is.

William.

But it's not him.

Mason stands at the bottom of the stairs. He's wearing one of William's blue Oxford shirts and a pair of new jeans. His hair is combed back. He looks so much like his father it hurts.

I put my hand on my chest.

"What's wrong?" he asks.

"Nothing."

"Okay." He walks past me toward the kitchen, carrying his backpack. He smells like burnt chocolate.

I follow behind him. "Do you want french toast today for something different? I have strawberries I could put on it."

"No time." He takes a nut bar from one of the bereavement baskets. "I don't want to be late."

"You're really going back to school today?"

"Why wouldn't I?"

"I don't know. I wasn't sure you'd want to."

"I'm fine." He pulls a pair of earbuds out of his pocket and holds them up like he's waiting for me to stop talking.

"You look nice."

"Thanks."

"Are you sure you're ready to go back?"

"Yes. Why do you keep asking me that?"

I take the bread out of the pantry. "I thought if you weren't going back—"

"But I *am* going back. I have plans."

"I just thought—if you weren't—we could go to lunch together at the club." I put the loaf down and turn toward him. "Could you do a half-day?"

"No." He rips open the nut bar. "I'd rather die than go to the club."

"Don't use that tone with me. I'm trying to help you."

"I don't need any help."

"We all need help." I take out the griddle and put it on the stove. It bangs hard. I didn't mean to let it slam, but Mason can be so infuriating. "Maybe it's not a good idea for you to go back to school today. I don't like your attitude."

"What? No!"

"Maybe you should wait until after the funeral. Until you've had time to process things."

He holds up his phone. "I promised my friends. I have to go."

"Friends?" I crank up the burner and take a mixing bowl from the cabinet.

"Yes. Friends."

"Are these online friends or actual people?"

"Online friends *are* actual people. You don't understand." He bites into the nut bar.

I go to the refrigerator and take out the eggs and milk. "I'm worried about you, that's all." Glancing over, I see him in William's shirt. He's stunning. "You've been acting strange lately, but—" I resist the urge to pinch my lower lip. "But it's okay. I think you should come with me so we can talk."

He types on his phone. His fingers fly as if he's entering a sequence to deactivate a bomb.

"Did you hear me?"

I wait, but he keeps typing. I put the eggs and milk on the counter. Smoke rises from the griddle. The smell of burning grease fills the kitchen. "Are you listening to me? You know, I didn't have to buy you that phone." I go to him and jerk it out of his hands. He grunts, and before I can read the screen, he snatches it back.

"Who are you chatting with?"

"No one." He twists away and brings the screen close to his face.

"Is it a girl? Do you have a girlfriend?"

"God, no."

"Then, in that case, you can come to lunch with me. Your friends can wait until tomorrow." I reach for the phone again, but he walks around me into the hall.

"Stay away."

"Mason, stop."

"No. You stop." He halts halfway to the front door and glares. "This is all your fault, you—you bitch."

His words sting. He's never called me anything like that before. "Okay. That's it. You're definitely not going anywhere. I—"

"It's all your fault," he yells. "You let him die. You let him fall."

I run at him. The red invades my periphery, and I reach

for him, but he makes it to the door and leaps outside before I can grab onto his shirt. His dad's shirt. "Mason. Stop. It was an accident. I—"

He sprints down the steps. I run after him. My robe flies open, revealing my nightgown to the world. "Get back here."

The driveway, the street, the houses—everything is red.

I close my eyes, put my hand on my chest, and I squeeze, hoping to slow my heart down. Hoping to make the rage go away. I slump forward, lean, and stumble forward. The world won't stop, and I'm still moving forward—eyes closed—faltering.

Breathe. This too shall pass. Breathe. This too shall pass.

I'm at the end of the walk when my eyes open.

Mason is already a block away, stepping into the intersection when a car slams on its brakes. He stops just in time, and the car passes by. It cruises toward me, and it's black, and for a moment, I think it's going to chase me like the Audi did. It feels like I'm half awake, half asleep, but I'm not in a sleep-limbo. I'm half-naked, standing by the road, and someone grabs my hand, but it's another hallucination. William says, *They want the card.* But William isn't here, and this car isn't an Audi, but it has tinted windows, black rims, black door handles—it's all black, except for the silver emblem of a mustang.

It's a Ford Mustang.

As it passes by, I try, but I can't see the driver's face.

The license plate reads IHJ4954.

I look right. A block away, Mason makes it across the intersection in one piece, heading for school.

I look left. The Mustang continues down the street.

I face my house.

Inside, the grease on the griddle burns.

CHAPTER SIXTEEN

LAUREN

Mason left for school an hour ago, and the house has never been emptier. I wish he had stayed so we could've gone to lunch at the club. I'd feel better if he were within eyesight. Especially now, after that black Ford Mustang drove past us.

I stand by the front window and watch for more black cars.

Nothing.

My suspicions started last week when I saw a black car at the grocery store. It was the same day the old man watched us, smoking his cigarette in the rain. Then, I saw another one on my way home, and two more a couple of days after that. The longer I stand here, the more black cars I can remember.

I peer between the curtains for a while longer, but no cars drive past. No Audis. No Mustangs. Nothing.

Am I being paranoid? Black is a common color. Seattle is teaming with black cars. If I tried, I could probably remember seeing one every day of my life. I *am* paranoid.

Then I remember something William always said.

Even paranoid people have enemies.

I close the curtains, go to William's office, close the blinds, then head upstairs. The curtains in the guest bedroom are light blue and hang limply over the paned glass. I go to them and peer outside.

No cars pass by.

I rush into my bedroom.

The curtains here are also drawn. Lifeless. My house suddenly feels like an empty coffin. I shove Mason's words from this morning to the back of my mind, but they keep marching forward. *It's all your fault. You let him die.*

Mason didn't mean to hurt me. We're both suffering, but still, I don't deserve the blame.

The only curtains I haven't closed are in his bedroom.

I pause outside his door.

When he became a teenager, I vowed to respect his privacy. I vowed never to go into his room without him knowing. William could walk in whenever he wanted, but that was different. They bonded the year Mason turned thirteen. I remember moments at the dinner table, the two of them smirking at each other, making inside jokes at my expense.

Mason trusted William.

It's all your fault. You let him die.

Again, I tell myself he didn't mean it, but—I've got to let it go before I get angry. Without William, Mason has no one but me. He has no one to look up to now. His grandfather, Nigel, lives in Connecticut, and my father is dead. The next closest relative is his uncle, Ryan.

Ryan Kaine.

The drunk.

Thinking of that man is like pulling a trigger. The hate makes me want to hang onto Mason's words and use them against him. It wasn't my fault William fell. How dare he blame me.

The door handle to his room feels absurdly cold because my hand is suddenly hot.

I promised I'd never go into his room, but—isn't his safety more important than his privacy? Closing his curtains is for his privacy. I should break my vow and make sure no one can see into his room, right?

No.

I back away.

But, he hurt me this morning, and he stole from me yesterday—not that I'll ever need condoms again—and I don't know what else he's been doing. I don't know who he has been talking to late at night, and my neck throbs.

My palms sweat.

The door turns red.

Everything turns red.

I'm trapped in this abandoned warehouse that used to be a home, and—

I slam my hands against his door, shattering the silence.

Blinded by rage, I slam my hands again.

And again.

I can't breathe, and the red consumes me, and I fall, and—

I'm downstairs now, standing in the sitting room, repeating my mantra. The red fades from my vision, and I can see again. The clock above the mantle ticks over to nine, and the family photos stare at me like I'm the one haunting them.

Sick of sitting on the sofa, I grab my laptop from off the coffee table and take it into the kitchen. The bereavement baskets remind me William is gone, but at least they're a new addition to the house.

Everything else is old.

Everything else is a reminder.

The bananas in the baskets have turned black. White fuzz grows on the oranges. The potpourri scent overpowers the rotting smell, and it's actually quite pleasant, but I need to throw it all out.

Ugh.

I hate throwing out food.

That, of course, is something that's never bothered Mason.

I picture him this morning, eating that nut bar and blaming me for William's death, and—*stop. Breathe.*

I need to let it go, but I want to find him at school and shove a banana into his mouth, rotten or not.

My hands shake. My lips tighten.

Not again.

I slip the laptop between the baskets and sit at the table.

The screen comes on, and I waste no time logging into HeatSinkers.

Three questions.

1) What happened?

"I tried to invite my son to lunch so we could talk, but he accused me of something bad."

2) Why did it make you angry?

"Because I didn't do anything wrong."

3) Who or what can you forgive?

I leave the third question blank and click the SUBMIT button. The website asks me if I'm sure, and I click YES.

My hands stop shaking.

My breathing relaxes.

I scroll down and read my answers from last Saturday.

1) What happened?

I tried to invite my brother-in-law to my husband's funeral.

2) Why did it make you angry?

Because it reminded me of what Ryan did to us.

3) Who or what can you forgive?

No one. I can forgive no one.

There it is. I'm not so bad. I *can* forgive someone.

I can forgive Mason.

But I'll never forgive Ryan.

A pop-up window tells me florence72 would like to chat. I think back to how she answered the three questions. She forgave God for her husband's death. I hesitate. Getting involved with these people again—it's such a step backward.

I accept and plunge in.

She's handling her anger well today and asks how I'm feeling. I keep it on the surface, tell her I could be better.

MasonsMadMom: I saw your answers to the three questions. I recently lost my husband too.

florence72: I'm sorry to hear that. Mine was cancer.

MasonsMadMom: Mine was an accident.

florence72: Is that what you wanted to talk to your son about at lunch? (I saw your answers too, dear.)

I picture florence72 sitting hunched over a keyboard with

arthritic knuckles, long gray hair, and a gentle gaze.

MasonsMadMom: Yes. He won't talk about his father yet. Or anything.

florence72: It must be hard. How old is he?

MasonsMadMom: He's at the age where he needs a man to talk to. Sixteen.

florence72: I understand. What about relatives? Does he have any older brothers or uncles?

I seethe at the thought of Ryan.

MasonsMadMom: Yes, but it's complicated.

florence72: Ryan?

MasonsMadMom: You saw those questions too.

florence72: Yes. Forgiveness is difficult, but you'll find it. It's the only solution for us rage-a-holics. Have you talked to his uncle?

MasonsMadMom: Not for years. There is no point in talking to someone like him.

florence72: Are you feeling angry now?

MasonsMadMom: Yes.

florence72: It's okay. I understand. I didn't talk to my husband's sister for a long time either because I was afraid I would slap her. After John died, we finally did talk, and I forgave her. Communication heals.

MasonsMadMom: That won't work for me. Ryan is a drunk. Drunks lie and can't remember anything. Talking is a waste of time.

florence72: It sounds like you know a lot about addiction.

The screen turns red.

I don't know where this conversation is going, but it's not helping. My patience grows thin, yet there's something safe about being online. I can write whatever I want. I'll never meet this florence72 in person, so what do I care what she thinks?

MasonsMadMom: You could say I do. My mother was an alcoholic. She lied, then she left.

florence72: I'm sorry that happened. All I know is, forgiveness will set you free. Alcoholics are sick like us. They need help too.

I am not sick like an alcoholic.

I am enraged.

florence72: Maybe if you decide to forgive all alcoholics, then you can forgive your mother. And Ryan.

I hit the ALL-CAPS key.

MasonsMadMom: MY MOTHER NEVER CAME BACK! I HAD TO RAISE MYSELF. HOW CAN I FORGIVE SOMETHING LIKE THAT?

I slam the laptop shut and grasp the edges of the table.

Red explosions distort my vision, and I wish Ryan were dead.

The table shakes.

I pray for him.

I pray, for his sake, he is already dead.

CHAPTER SEVENTEEN

MASON

Mullen High School has always been an egg Mason couldn't crack. White walls, ashen tables, stone-faced teachers, tall windows so clear birds fly into them on sunny days.

But today isn't sunny.

Not yet.

In five minutes, the bell for fourth period will ring, and language arts class will begin. Mrs. Macaby will drone on and on about symbolism and imagery in literature. And Garrett will be there, sitting in the second row. Beautiful Garrett.

Today is the day Mason and Garret begin dating—if everything goes right.

Mason leans against a locker, lifting one foot to roll up his pant leg. The final touch. His new jeans are tight on his ankles, but he manages to cuff both pant legs. He untucks his shirt, and the tails hang down to his knees. It looks like a tunic, so he tucks it back in. The retro-eighties gay look is good, but he's not the flamboyant type. That's Garrett's style. Besides, Mason doesn't want to draw attention to himself. He wants to *be* himself.

He pulls out his cell phone and chooses a different song. His earbuds sing.

"Whatcha doing, gaywad?" Scott Turner has his hat on backward, and that annoying tuft of red hair pops through the hole in the front. Before Mason can respond, Scott smacks him in the forehead and continues strutting toward Mrs. Macaby's classroom. "Nice pants, flamer. Getting ready for a flood?"

Mason ignores him. Looks at his cell phone, then glances up just as Scott enters the classroom. Down the hall, kids open and close locker doors—*clang, clatter, bang.* They disperse, clogging the hallway, trying to get to class before the bell rings.

Scott Turner. What a testosterone monkey. What an asshole. He has no clue.

Mason looks around for Garrett. He's got to be here somewhere.

Cuco's "Lover is a Day" comes on, and Mason taps STOP on his music app. He clutches his folder and joins the fray, squeezing through the crowd into the classroom.

Mrs. Macaby glances down at Mason's pant legs.

She noticed his clothes.

Soon, everyone will notice.

Soon, everyone will know who Mason is.

He sits at the back of the room and watches the door, but Garrett never comes.

Mrs. Macaby lectures on and on about the Great Gatsby. No one cares. At the end of class, the bell rings and Mason races out the door. The hall fills quickly.

"Excuse me," Mason says, weaving through the crowd.

"Watch out," a girl says.

"Sorry."

"Hey," another says. "Get out of my way."

Necks, shoulders, turning and pushing. Scowls and perturbed glances.

"What's your deal, creep?"

Then, like a vision, Mason sees Garrett's orange dress shirt heading for the cafeteria.

Mason stops. He smoothes out his dad's shirt. He ironed it this morning, but it's still wrinkled. When Garrett notices, he'll appreciate the effort. He'll look at Mason like Matt Bomer looked at that guy in *The Normal Heart*, and Mason will ask Garrett out, and Garrett will say yes.

Garrett *will* say yes.

But there'll be too many people in the cafeteria, and though Mason doesn't care who knows he's gay, he does care about getting turned down in front of the entire school.

Up ahead, Garrett strays from the pack, turns, and strides toward the gym, tapping on his phone and shaking his head.

Mason follows.

The hall to the gym is clear, and, risking pit stains, Mason sprints to catch him.

Garrett's hips sway as he speed-walks toward the gym door.

Mason runs right up behind him, then slows to a walk. His heart races.

Ahead, the sounds of basketballs bouncing and jocks bragging echo out of the gym.

No one else is around.

The side door to the parking lot is closed, and there's no one out there either. The hallway is private, but it might be better to go outside.

Mason hesitates, then reaches out, but Garrett turns around. He frowns, then makes eye contact with Mason and smiles. "Hey, what's up?"

"I—"

Garrett's phone vibrates, he looks at it, and the frown returns.

"I'm sorry," Mason says, "I just wanted to know if you would . . . if you wanted to . . . " Garrett pelts the screen with his thumbs. "Is everything okay?"

"No," He says, looking at his phone. "This guy I was dating—he's a hot mess."

Mason takes a step back.

Garret looks up. "Sorry, what were you saying?"

"It's nothing. I just thought maybe"—Mason gazes out the windows into the parking lot—"I thought maybe we could hang out sometime."

Silence.

Mason looks back at Garrett.

Garrett's eyes open wide and focus beyond Mason. "Sorry, I've got to go."

"But—"

Garrett retreats, sidesteps into the gym, and briskly walks along the basketball court, tapping on his phone and stepping over balls without losing his stride.

Mason gazes down at his shoes. His new jeans. His dad's shirt. He can't cry here. Someone will see him. Before he turns to leave, something hits him from behind, launching him forward. He stumbles, stays on his feet, and spins around to see Scott Turner and Hunter Stalwell blocking the hall.

"I told you," Scott says. "See? Look at those pants. He got all gayed up today."

Hunter steps past Scott and grabs Mason by the collar. "What were you doing, fag? Were you trying to ask Garrett on a date? Do you *love* him?"

"Yeah." Scott's freckles match his red hair. "Do you want

him to be your butt buddy?"

Hunter pulls Mason toward the side door by the collar. "Let's go outside."

Scott opens the door.

Mason grabs Hunter's arm with both hands and tries to get away, but he is off-balance, and Hunter's grip is strong. Steadfast. Mason trips over the doorway and falters, crashing onto the sidewalk.

Together, Hunter and Scott lift him up by the armpits and drag him into the parking lot.

"Stop it. Let go." Mason flails and pushes free. Spins around. Tucks his shirt back in.

"Nice pants," Hunter says. "Are you getting ready for a flood?"

"That's what I said." Scott curls his lips. "Who dressed you this morning? Your momma?"

"No," Mason says through clenched teeth.

Hunter steps forward. "Is that right? If your momma didn't do it, then who did? It wasn't your daddy 'cause he's dead, right?"

"Shut up."

"Yeah," Scott chimes in. "Your daddy didn't do it because he's dead."

Hunter puts his hands on Mason's chest and shoves him down.

Mason's head hits a car bumper on his way to kiss the pavement.

Hunter says, "But maybe your daddy taught you how to dress before he jumped off that bridge. Yeah, that's it. Your daddy was probably a fag, too." Mason tries to stand, and Hunter pushes him back down with his foot. "The fruit doesn't fall far from the tree, does it?"

They laugh.

Mason rolls over, gets to his knees, and searches for an escape. For help. The lot is full of cars. His head spins. The kids a few rows away stop talking and start gawking.

"What are we going to do with him?" Scott asks.

Hunter circles. "We should knock some sense into him. I thought you was catholic, Kaine. Don't you Catholics hate fudgepackers?"

Up on one knee, Mason turns his back on Hunter. The cars are packed tight, but there's enough space between those two Subarus to run. From there, he could make it up the hill to lot B. It's only about twenty yards away. If he could dodge the side view mirrors and jump the curb, he could get away.

He stands, steps forward, and —

"Not so fast," Hunter says.

Mason's collar tightens around his throat, and he's jerked back onto the ground.

"Yeah," Scott says. "Not so fast."

Hunter twists Mason's shirt. "We're gonna beat some sense into you now. We're gonna make you a good catholic."

"I'm not catholic," Mason rasps. He grabs Hunter's wrists and pulls, but Hunter hangs on. Mason tries to crawl toward the Subaru, but Hunter won't let him go. A black Ford Mustang comes to a stop up in parking lot B. Its engine lets out three loud *barums* before shutting off.

Hunter glances up at the car.

The Mustang is new and spotless. It can't be more than a year or two old, and—

"Whatcha, doing?" Scott asks.

"Nothing." Hunter retrains his eyes on Mason. "That's a nice car is all."

"Please," Mason says. "You're choking me."

"We always knew you was a fag." Scott says.

"Yeah." Hunter lets go of Mason's shirt. "Ever since grade school."

Mason falls, catches himself on the pavement, and scrapes his palms. He gasps for air.

The cretins circle him. Taunt him.

The Mustang's driver gets out and leans on the fender. A pair of sunglasses hide the driver's eyes, but Mason can tell—he's watching the whole thing. He's wearing a black leather jacket with a silver zipper. His blue jeans are new like Mason's. The sun's rays bounce off the driver's zipper, making it flicker like the fourth of July.

It's brilliant.

The driver just stands there in the upper lot, looking down.

Mason kneels on the ground, looking up.

The driver is tall. His leather boots match his jacket, and his jacket matches his Mustang.

Black.

Immaculate.

Mason's head throbs.

Hunter grabs him by the collar again.

Mason grasps Hunter's arm and pulls, but it's no use.

Hunter raises his fist.

CHAPTER EIGHTEEN

LAUREN

I drive up to the outgoing mailbox and wait for my window to lower. The bushes are wet from this morning's rain, and the sky is gray, as usual. The funeral invitations make a *thud* when they hit the bottom of the mailbox. Sitting here in my SUV at the post office, crossing that off my list, I realize I don't have any plans for this afternoon. Mason refused to come with me to the club for lunch.

I hope his first day back at school is going well.

I'm relieved the funeral arrangements are made. Almost. Everyone I *needed* to invite—William's parents, Olivia—they're all in the maildrop now. Everyone except Ryan and William's coworkers.

I was going to invite William's manager from TriamSys, TJ, and Robert Lang, but then I found that note in William's pants pocket. It was ominous. TJ warned William not to talk to Robert, and the note made it sound like Robert was a corporate spy. I don't want them at William's funeral, but I've got to talk to them about the card. But how? I can't just waltz into TriamSys and start asking questions. They'd have me escorted out by security. I considered contacting TJ and Robert outside of TriamSys, but last night, when I searched Google for their addresses, I didn't find anything.

I also searched for Ryan's address but had to stop. My anger has been flaring up like crazy since William died, and I didn't have the energy to think about Ryan. Whenever I do, I explode. Sometimes I have a red-out. He's like sugar to a diabetic. The Grand Canyon to an agoraphobe. Sunlight to a vampire.

At the same time, it's wrong not to invite him to the funeral if he's alive.

Worthless drunk.

And there it is again—that little hot spot on the back of my neck. To think about Ryan Kaine is to light myself on fire. It's not fair. I hate my condition. I want to forgive him so I can get better, but it's so hard. Florence72 is right; without forgiveness, I'll never be free.

The hot spot grows.

I hate Ryan Kaine.

I wish I'd never posted answers to the three questions on HeatSinkers.

Florence72 may be right, but it won't work for me. I need to find a way to cope without forgiving Ryan. He's unforgivable.

Rather than speeding down 78th Ave like usual, I take it slow and gaze into Mercerdale Park. I've never been one to spend time walking in a park, or strolling along the Sound, but I could change. I could relax, but I don't want to do it alone. Not today.

I hit the accelerator and press the call button on the steering wheel. "Call Olivia."

It rings, but she doesn't pick up.

Oh, well. At least the club serves singles, and other people will be there, unlike home. I can sit at the bar and make a plan. With the funeral arrangements done, I can focus on the card now.

At the next intersection, I take a left and head toward the club.

Mason's words from this morning hit me out of nowhere again. *It's all your fault. You let him die.*

Poor Mason. Acting out. He must know it wasn't my fault.

I brake at a red light. A black car cruises to a stop across the intersection from me, and my heart jumps. I don't think it's an Audi, but I won't know for sure until the traffic clears. Leaning forward, I focus on the driver, catching glimpses through the windows of the passing cars. It's a man. It's hard to tell, but I think he's bald.

The light turns green.

The car is not an Audi, and it's not the Mustang from earlier this morning. It's a Chevy. But it's so similar to the others. Tinted black windows, black wheels, black tires, black on black on black.

We pass by each other in the intersection, and I'm convinced now. These all-black cars *are* following me, and I'm going to find out why.

I pull over in the first driveway I come to, and my cell phone rings.

"Hi, Olivia," I say over Bluetooth. "I know I called you, but I can't talk right now." The Chevy becomes a dot in my rearview mirror before I can turn around.

"Mrs. Kaine, I'm glad you answered."

It's not Olivia.

"Before you make any assumptions, let me—" The caller

breaks into a coughing fit. His voice grates on my eardrums—metal on metal. I adjust the volume down.

Somehow, the solicitor who called William's phone Saturday has gotten *my* number. "Look, I already told you—you can't talk to William. He's—"

"Yes, I'm aware he's dead."

The tires slip on the wet pavement, causing the traction-control to come on as I take off out of the driveway. The Chevy is gone. "Who is this?" I head for the club. The trees along the street blur as I accelerate. "Is this Robert Lang?"

"No." He coughs again. "But I knew your husband. I'm calling because he gave you some information we—I—some information *I* need."

"I don't know what you're talking about." The harder I press on the accelerator, the redder the trees along the roadway become. "I need *you* to tell *me*—"

"Please." He clears his throat, and the speakers buzz like they're going to disintegrate. "I know this must be hard for you, but I'm certain you have what I need. William wouldn't have kept it a secret."

"You didn't know him very well, did you?"

"Well enough to know he told you about the card."

I fly into the club parking lot and hit the brakes. "What's your name? Are you from TriamSys? How did you know him?"

Two elderly ladies, one holding the hand of the other while stepping onto the sidewalk outside the entrance, smile at each other. Their clothing turns red, and my knuckles begin to ache, ruthlessly squeezing the steering wheel.

The man on the other end coughs into the phone.

I grit my teeth. "Are you still there? Dammit. Say something."

"Please, calm down. I only want the card."

"What card?"

William's last words. *They want the card. It's in St. Croix.*

"Don't play dumb, Mrs. Kaine." His voice buzzes.

The older ladies make it inside the club. Vines hang over the entryway, and my empty stomach burns. "What the hell is so important about this card? Did you kill my husband?"

"There are a lot of people who are willing to pay a lot of money, and I'm willing to—"

"I don't need money. I need my husband." I slam my hands on the steering wheel. He's not telling me what I want to know. If I could stay calm, I could negotiate, but he's so smug, and I'm pissed now. Everything is red now.

"I need you to give me the card," he says. "You know where it is, don't you?"

"You son-of-a-bitch," I scream. "When I find you, I'm going to—"

"You're going to give me the card, or you'll never see Mason again."

"You worthless piece of—what?"

"Give me the card"—his voice deepens—"or you'll never see Mason again. I know where he is right now. Taking him would be like picking a strawberry."

Breathe, dammit. Breathe. Breathe.

"Okay," I say. "Wait. I don't know anything about a card. Please." I will my fingers to relax and pull my hands off the steering wheel. "I'm telling the truth. I don't know anything about a card."

"Okay. I will believe you, but that doesn't change anything. You must find the card and give it to me."

I lean forward and look at the sky through the windshield. The clouds are deep, dark, and red. "Fuck you."

"No, Mrs. Kaine, fuck you. Until you find the card, Mason will not be safe. In the meantime, you must bring me William's computer."

"You'll never get into his computer."

"We have ways."

"I'm calling the police."

"We're—I'm monitoring your phone. If you contact anyone regarding my request, I won't just take Mason. I'll kill him."

"When I get my hands on you—"

"Does Mason know how to swim?"

"What?"

"I'm guessing he doesn't. I'm guessing his father never taught him how. William didn't know how to swim either, did he? He really shouldn't have jumped into that river. How long do you think it was before his lungs filled with water?"

"Stop it."

"How long do you think it will take for Mason to drown?"

"I—" a sucking noise, like he's taking a drag on a cigarette, comes through the speakers. I picture the old man from the grocery store smoking in the rain. Smoking outside my house. "I know who you are. I saw you. If you touch Mason, I'm going to—"

"What, Lauren? You're going to what? Throw eggs at me?"

It *is* him. It *is* the old man from the store. "You'd better not do anything. I'll describe you to the police. I'll—"

"And I'll describe Mason to you, right now. He's wearing a slick looking pair of jeans, a fancy, Oxford dress shirt, and he just got out of English class. He's outside in the middle of the school parking lot, and if I didn't know better, I'd say he's about to cry."

CHAPTER NINETEEN

RYAN

It's noon on Monday, and Ryan leans against his delivery truck, waiting inside the SPD warehouse for Gabe to bring a palette of packages. With only fifteen dollars to his name, and payday not until Friday, Ryan considers asking Gabe for a loan so he can cover his rent increase, but it can wait. If he can't figure something out by tomorrow, he'll ask for a loan then.

Everyone is tight on cash these days.

For a moment, he regrets giving money to the homeless man in Denny Park this morning—but only for a moment.

He opens the delivery app and loads today's route—A8: University District. That's good. There are a lot of apartments near the university. Deliveries to apartments take less time, and less time means a better rank in the app. With his rent going up, he needs to impress his manager while he finds somewhere else to live.

He needs a raise.

Gabe's forklift comes rumbling across the warehouse floor at full speed, slipping between the towering shelves. He spins the wheel and heads toward the loading area, bouncing in the seat each time the tires crosse a seam in the concrete. His scraggly black hair pokes out beneath his safety helmet as he wheels the forklift behind Ryan's truck and lowers the palette onto the floor. Plumes of dust escape from beneath the tongs.

"Where's your little helper?" Ryan asks.

Gabe jumps off the forklift and picks up a bin filled with envelopes. "Josiah?"

"Yeah."

"They let him go, man. Cutbacks."

"Cutbacks?" Ryan follows Gabe as he carries the bin to the truck. "What do you mean, cutbacks?"

"Cutbacks. They said the company was losing money. Had to let him go." Gabe heaves the bin into the truck. "Now I got to load all the trucks myself."

"That doesn't make any sense. Josiah was good."

Gabe turns and faces Ryan. "Are you kidding? He helped, but he wasn't good. He dropped shit all the time."

"He had a hard life."

"I know. Meth. But that's no excuse." He picks up another bin. "It doesn't matter. He's gone. They're trying to save money everywhere."

"I was going to ask for a raise."

Gabe laughs. "That's not going to happen, man. They're seriously cutting back. Everywhere."

"Maybe I could take on some extra routes," Ryan mutters.

"Why?"

"My rent went up this morning."

Gabe wipes his forehead. "How long you been working here?"

"Four years."

"Well"—he looks at Ryan concerned— "don't listen to me. Maybe you *can* get a raise. With that much time, maybe you can. What do I know?"

"Let me help." Ryan picks up a bin, and together they finish loading the truck.

Ryan jumps in the cab and opens the delivery app. The first stop is an apartment near Aurora Boulevard. Most of the stops are apartments, just as he'd hoped.

"Kaine?" Ryan's manager appears in the side view mirror. "Kaine, stop. Don't go anywhere."

It's strange. Ed never leaves his office. He's large and in-charge, walking faster than a man his size should, and he bangs on the side of the truck. "Get out of there. I need to speak with you."

Ryan opens the door and steps out. "Now? I was just about to leave on my route."

Ed's face is red like he was yelling at someone. "Hold off on that. I need to talk to you in my office." He swings his gut away from Ryan and shuffles across the warehouse floor.

Ryan follows.

Ed is the only one in the warehouse with a pair of slacks and a belt, and they're about to burst. The dirty khakis stretch over his pancake-shaped ass, and his neck roll smiles when he walks. This can't be good. Ed never wastes time meeting with drivers, especially when they're supposed to be en route.

He stops just inside the office door, motions for Ryan to have a seat, then sits in his captain's chair on the other side of the desk. Fluorescent lamps highlight the few dark hairs left on his head, and the gray filing cabinets behind him look like they haven't been opened in years. The windowless walls in here have always made Ryan feel like a murder suspect.

Ed glances at his computer monitor, then clasps his hands

and rests them on the desk. "How are things?"

"Fine." Ryan's throat tightens. "Things are fine with work, but this morning I got a letter from my landlord—"

"Wrong." Ed leans back, raises both hands. "Things aren't fine with your work. You missed a delivery yesterday."

"I did?"

"Yes. 9112 South 43rd Place. The recipient called and said they received the notification email, but the package wasn't there. Do you remember delivering it?"

Ryan's mind races. Of course he remembers delivering it. That's his brother's address. He vividly remembers taking the box out of the truck, placing it on the porch, and staring at the doorbell. He didn't ring it, and he practically ran away, fearing Lauren would answer and attack him. "Yes, I delivered it."

"We're not the post office. Our customers pay a premium for our service, and they expect their parcels to be delivered, on time, and to the right address."

"I know. I—"

"You marked it as 'Package Delivered' in the app, but are you sure you left it where they would find it?"

"Yes, I'm sure, and I know it was the right house. Google it." Ryan points to the monitor. "Pull it up on Google Maps. You'll see. It's a light gray two-story with a detached two-car garage. I left it on the—"

"I don't doubt you know what the house looks like." Ed puts his attention on the computer screen. "Hold on a minute while I pull something up."

"Maybe a porch pirate stole it."

Ed raises a hand dismissively. "Hold on."

Ryan delivered the package. He's certain of it. Someone must have taken it after he left. Of the hundreds of deliveries he's made, this one gets stolen.

He needs a raise.

Stomach acid climbs up his throat.

Suddenly, he doesn't want to be here.

But if he wants a raise, he needs to stay.

He needs to relax.

Ed types something, moves the mouse in a circle, then types something else. He's searching for something. Something bad.

Ryan must relax. He can't let Ed think he's afraid or he'll look guilty, and he's not guilty. He left the package.

Out of nowhere, he imagines himself seated at a table outside a quaint cafe. No. It's a classy restaurant bar, and, as the sun sets on a warm summer's eve, he sips a Gin and Tonic with lime. This is how he used to relax. And—

Drinking is not the answer.

"There it is." Ed points at the screen and looks Ryan in the eye. "Okay. I don't think it was porch pirates. Not in that neighborhood. But you did go to the right house."

"I know."

"Here's the problem. You know that house pretty well, don't you?"

"What do you mean?"

"I searched all the driver's GPS histories to see if we'd had any problems delivering to that address, and I found something pretty interesting. Who lives there, Ryan?"

"I—I don't know. I—"

"According to our records, you've been going off route, driving down 43rd Place, and stopping at that house. You've never had any deliveries there until yesterday. Is this your favorite napping spot or something?"

"No. I don't take naps. I—it's complicated."

Ed turns the monitor toward Ryan. "I think it's simple." The screen displays dates and times with Ryan's name and William's address next to each. Ryan wishes whatever program is on the screen would crash. A *java.lang.NullPointerException* would be great right now. "You went there twice in March, three times in July, twice in August, eight times in September." He turns the monitor toward himself and cocks his head. "Eight times, Ryan? Why?"

"It's complicated. Please, understand. I—"

"I don't have to understand. Look, the business is going through a transition, and well, I wish things were different."

"No. Please. They're raising my rent. I can't afford to be without a job."

"I don't know what to tell you." He averts his eyes. "You've been a great driver. If it were up to me, I'd ignore all the GPS stuff and keep you on, but they're making us cut ten heads this week alone. Tell you what, come back in a few months, and we'll see what we can do."

"I don't have a few months." Ryan searches the room for answers, his eyes darting around, looking for a way out. "I'll be evicted before then."

"Don't you have someone you can stay with?"

"No." Ryan puts his hands on the desk and stands.

He's come too far in sobriety to stay with someone else. Other alcoholics, like Juan when he came in, and other newcomers—they always stay with him.

This isn't right.

If he's going to be homeless, he might as well be drunk. For a split second, Ryan considers drinking so he can start the program over. Then he'd have a reason to ask Garage Mike for a place to stay.

No.

Stinking thinking.

He shakes his head.

What a ridiculous thought.

What a dangerous, ridiculous thought.

Ryan instinctively puts his hand in his pocket and searches for the rock he gave to Juan, but it's not there. Rough side. Smooth side. Choices.

"Right." Ed stands and holds out his hand. "I'll need the keys to your truck."

Ryan reaches into his other pocket and pulls out his keys. His head throbs. He begins to hand the keys to Ed but stops when he realizes they're the wrong set. These are the keys he took from Juan the other night.

"Whoa." Ed points at the large black key fob. "An Audi, huh? And you're telling me you can't afford to rent another place?"

"No." Ryan shoves Juan's keys back into his pocket. "These are a friend's."

"Look, Ryan. I'm really sorry about this."

That's the nicest thing Ed has ever said.

Ryan hands over the keys to his delivery truck.

"Look at it this way"—Ed hangs the keys on a hook—"when packages go undelivered, the company loses money. Eventually, if the company loses enough money, the board will kick the company to the curb, and we'll all be looking for somewhere to live."

"Not just me."

"Right." He smiles. "You got it."

"But I delivered the package."

"Yes, but you wasted company time and gas sitting outside that house, napping."

Ryan's fingers tense. He fights the urge to make a fist. He

wants to punch Ed's fat face, and at the same time, he wants to run.

He wants to relax.

He needs to relax.

He needs a drink.

Gin and Tonic.

No.

He needs a meeting. Drinking only ever made things worse.

Remember. Drinking only ever made things worse.

"You'll get your last paycheck this Friday. Again, buddy, I'm sorry."

Now, after four years, Ed is his *buddy*.

Ryan's fifteen dollars won't make it until Friday, and his credit cards are all past due. The worst three words in the English language are *minimum, payment,* and *due*. And, he's got heating, cell phone, groceries—every bill imaginable, all coming due.

He'll be on the streets in no time.

He needs to relax.

Ed extends his hand, and Ryan shakes it.

"Are you going to be okay?" Ed asks.

"I'll be fine. Thanks for everything."

Ryan heads for the door, dazed.

"Wait a minute." Ed looks at his monitor. Clicks the mouse.

"What is it?"

Ed's eyes run back and forth, scanning the screen. "Oh, it's nothing. Never mind."

Stomach acid burns Ryan's throat, and he swallows.

"Hey," Ed says, "you can keep the shirts."

"What?"

"Your delivery shirts. You can keep them. We're buying new ones next month anyway."

"Thanks a lot."

Ryan leaves.

He strides across the warehouse floor.

The towering shelves overwhelm him.

This isn't happening, but it is. He's got no job, and that means . . . it means he's free. No job. No family.

He pauses next to his truck, lingers, then continues toward the exit. He left nothing in there he cares to keep.

Gabe is busy loading bins into someone else's rig. "Hey, Ryan. Where are you going?"

Ryan continues toward the door. His feet almost drag—almost glide—sliding over the dusty concrete.

Gabe runs up to him. "Aren't you going to make your—" coming eye-to-eye, his face twists in dismay. "Oh, no. Not you too."

"Yep. Me too."

"What are you going to do?"

"I'm going to go sit somewhere nice for a while and relax. Maybe a café. Have a nice life, Gabe."

CHAPTER TWENTY

MASON

Mason is on his hands and knees in the school parking lot. His head throbs and his back aches.

Hunter has his fist raised, ready to strike.

"You think you can knock him out with your fist?" Scott asks.

Mason stares at the ground. The cool, wet pavement does nothing to soothe his scraped palms. He should run before Hunter punches him, but the only way out is between those two Subarus. The man with the silver zipper and the black Ford Mustang still stands in lot B, watching the fight from twenty yards away. Mason should run, but indecision has him frozen. Who is that man?

Hunter lowers his fist and steps in between the Subarus. "Yeah. Why not?"

"I don't think you can knock him out." Scott takes off his cap, smoothes his red hair back, and replaces it. "Your hands aren't hard enough."

Footsteps sound across the pavement.

"Yeah they are." Hunter slams his fist into his palm. "My

knuckles are. Besides, he's a pussy."

"You should kick him until he throws up."

"H-m-m." Hunter circles. "That might work. I don't know."

Mason eyes Hunter's Nikes. He could grab one, twist it, lock the ankle, and pull Hunter to the ground, jujitsu-style, like Yuji Itadori.

Feet suddenly surround Mason—Nikes, Converse, ankle boots—all coming to an abrupt stop, sending dirty rainwater into his face.

"Hey, what are you guys doing?" Abigail says.

Mason's heart sinks. Abigail—his only friend. How embarrassing.

Scott replies, "We're having a coming-out party."

"Yep." Hunter puts his foot on Mason's hip and pushes him over. "Isn't that right, buttmunch?"

"Stop it," Abigail says.

Mason, lying on his side, puts his head between his knees. He never told her he was gay. He never told anyone. Today was supposed to be the day, but he should have confided in Abigail sooner. They've been friends since the beginning of the year, and for her to find out like this . . . for anyone to find out like this—

"What do you call a gay dinosaur?" Scott says.

"What?" Hunter's shoe is within Mason's reach.

"A Mega-sore-ass."

"Shut up," Abigail yells. "Leave him alone."

She steps forward, and Hunter pushes her back.

Mason reaches for Hunter's shoe but misses. He scrambles forward and gets to his feet. His heart races.

More teenagers gather around, forming a thick circle.

Mason's head throbs from where he hit it on the car

bumper when Hunter shoved him down.

Hunter laughs.

Mason makes a fist, takes a swing, but Scott comes at him from the side and punches him in the ribs. Mason stays on his feet, staggers, and considers running, but Hunter's testosterone monkeys step in his way.

"Leave him alone," Abigail pleads.

Mason puts his hand on his ribs and coughs. The pain is excruciating.

"No," Hunter says. "Mullen High already has plenty of fags. They got their own club and everything. We don't need any more homos."

"Yeah," Scott bellows. "We don't need any more homos. Bunch of homos."

"It's not a bunch of homos," Abigail yells. "It's LGBTQ, and they're people just like you."

"Bullshit," Hunter says. "They're not people. They're queers."

Mason touches his forehead and looks at the blood on his fingers.

The kids inside the school stare out the windows.

Mason is a monster on display. A monsutā. A gay monsutā.

He turns, but there's no way out.

Up in lot B, the man in the black leather jacket watches with his hands in his pockets, leaning on his car.

Hunter slams his fist into his palm. "Are you ready, queer?"

Abigail's little brother, Toby, steps forward. He's wearing a Panic! at the Disco shirt and clutching his math book. "Wait. How do you know he's gay?"

"'Cause, he was trying to do it with Garrett in the

hallway," Scott says.

"Just look at him." Hunter waves his hand. "He's always been a fag. Can't you tell?"

Two kids step next to Toby. They're thin and tall.

Abigail leans forward and her face turns red. "Leave him alone. His father died last week for Christ's sake."

"We know . . ." Scott smirks.

Someone in the crowd says, "I heard he killed himself."

"I don't doubt it," Hunter says. "I'd kill myself too if I had a piece of shit faggot for a son."

"His dad jumped off a bridge," says a testosterone monkey. "It was on the internet."

He's wrong. Mason knows the truth—his mom let his father die. She was there. She could have stopped it, but she let him fall. She's the monsutā. The dragon. She—

"Oh, look at him," Hunter says. "He's going to cry."

Mason flies into Hunter, swinging his fists, grabbing at the asshole's crewcut. He tries to knee the jock in the crotch but misses.

Hunter raises both hands and backs away, eyes wide. Grinning.

Mason grabs at his shirt and claws at his face, leaving a scratch. He tries to punch Hunter in the eye, but Scott grabs his arm, and one of the other monkeys helps, and they pull him back.

Hunter wipes his cheek and glares at Mason.

"Come on," Scott yells. "You were right. Use your knuckles. Knock him out. We'll hold him."

Mason looks away and braces himself.

Abigail takes off toward the school.

The hair on Hunter's knuckles is the last thing Mason sees before everything goes black, but his vision returns immediately. It barely hurts. Everything only disappeared for a second. It must be the adrenaline, but—

Wait.

It only seemed like a second.

Hunter is thumbing through Mason's wallet. How did he take it so fast?

Mason tries to reach for it, but Scott and the other monkey still have his arms.

Hunter pulls out a condom and holds it up to the crowd. "Look, everybody. Gayboy here thinks he's gonna get laid."

They laugh.

"What's that for?" says an onlooker. "You can't get dudes pregnant."

"It's for AIDS, dumbass," another answers.

Hunter throws the condom in Mason's face.

"Gross," Scott says. "Was it open? He probably re-uses them."

Flanked by his tall friends, Toby says, "Give the wallet back."

"Or what?" Hunter asks.

"Or—"

Scott looks over his shoulder and lets go of Mason's arm.

Mason wriggles free of the other monkey.

Hunter gazes at the school, then at Toby, then back at the school. He smiles and puts his hand on Mason's shoulder. "Hey, we were just messing with you, buddy. Here, you can have it back." He hands Mason the wallet.

Abigail and Mrs. Macaby march out of the school.

The teens scatter.

Scott and his friends head for his car, and Hunter walks right past Mrs. Macaby.

"Hello, Hunter," Mrs. Macaby says.

He smiles.

Mason reads Abigail's face. She told Mrs. Macaby everything. Soon, everyone will know. Mrs. Macaby will tell the principal, and the principal will talk to Mason's mom, and she'll talk to Mason. He'll have to listen to her breakdown. She'll pinch her lip, turn into a dragon, yell, and explode.

He shoves the condom into his wallet. The path between the Subarus to lot B is clear now, and he could run, but the man with the silver zipper—

The man with the silver zipper is gone.

The black Ford Mustang is gone.

"Mason? What happened?" Mrs. Macaby asks.

"Nothing. We were just kidding around." Abigail furrows her brow. "I'm alright."

Mason hides his scraped-up, bloody palms behind his back.

"Are you sure nothing happened?"

Abigail's eyes plead for Mason to tell the truth.

Scott Turner drives out of the parking lot.

Hunter Stalwell struts into the school.

"I'm sure."

"Come inside, then."

Mason pictures Hunter skipping—parading—up and down the halls, singing about a fag named Mason. "No, go ahead. I'll be there in a minute. I want to stay here for a while because I—"

"You don't have to explain." Mrs. Macaby glances at Abigail. "I understand."

No she doesn't.

"You know, we have a very active LGBTQ club here."

Heat rushes over his face. His forehead aches. "I know."

"I can't do anything about Hunter unless you talk," she

offers.

"It was nothing."

"Mason," Abigail says, "please. You need a bandage." She puts her hand on his shoulder.

Mason shoves it off. "Leave me alone."

He turns away. Faces the school.

Kids are still staring out the windows at him like he's a monster. A monsutā.

But he's not.

He's not a monster.

He's himself.

For the first time in his life, he's himself.

And it's a nightmare.

CHAPTER TWENTY-ONE

LAUREN

Everything is red. The country club's stucco walls, the vines clinging to the gutters, the bushes lining the pathway to the front door—red.

My face is hot, it stings, and I pinch my lower lip until it feels like it's going to burst.

The old man is still on the phone. He coughs again. He laughs. His laughter is mechanized, and it comes through my SUV's speakers like lightning through a metal tube. If I have to listen to him any longer, I'm going to explode. My shoulder blades cramp up, and my empty stomach constricts, and my palms ache. I've been slamming my hands against the steering wheel since he threatened to kill Mason, and I haven't heard a word he's said since.

"If you touch my son, I—" I lose my breath.

My head tips forward and hits the center of the steering wheel.

Click.

I hung up on him. The old man is gone.

I raise my hand to slam the wheel, think better of it, and

put the SUV in drive.

12:30 p.m.

Mason hasn't gone to his next class yet.

How did the old man know Mason just got out of class? Worse—how did he know what Mason was wearing?

The streets are slick. My SUV slides around a corner, then I gun it down a straight-away. I take chances, flying through yellow lights. Red lights. The old man could be at Mullen High right now. He could be walking toward Mason, right now. Extending his hand.

My phone rings and I hit the button.

"Where'd you go, Mrs. Kaine?" The old man's voice is metal scraping metal. "Or, I should ask, where do you think you're going?"

"Go to hell."

"I would, but it's unreasonably warm down there this time of year. How about you go home and get William's things for me? I'll meet you there."

"Never."

"No, you're right. I can't be seen at your—hold on a moment, will you?" His breathing is like sandpaper. "Mrs. Kaine, stop. I wouldn't go to Mullen High right now if I were you. We don't have a deal yet, and I'd hate for you to make me take Mason prematurely."

I slow down. The school is two blocks away.

"If I see your car, you won't see Mason again for a long, long time. Do you understand?"

"Why should I believe you?"

"You might be interested to know, he is standing out in the parking lot right now. He was talking to a teacher, but now, he's alone. Right out in the open. All alone."

Every instinct, every thought, pushes me toward the

school. I want to confront the old man. Find him and crush him with the grill of my SUV, but it's not worth the risk. I turn onto Island Crest Way and fall in behind a line of slow-moving cars heading south toward my neighborhood.

"Are you still there, Mrs. Kaine?"

"What do you want me to do?"

"Good. Very good. Like I said before, I want you to take anything related to your husband's work and pack it nicely in a box—we can't have anything getting damaged—and be sure to put everything in there. His computer, papers, cell phone, anything you come across. Flash drives. Does he own a camera?"

"No. He always used his phone."

"Fine. Then put the box in the biggest black garbage bag you can find and bring it to Denny Park. Oh, and make sure the bag is black. That's very important."

"Why?"

"Because it must match the others. You must leave it in the dumpster next to the administration building where we—where I can pick it up."

"When?"

"I want you to be thorough, so I'll give you some time. Let's say Wednesday at four o'clock? Does that work for you?"

The day after tomorrow. "And if I do this, you'll leave us alone?"

"No. If you *promise* to do this, I won't take Mason right now."

Pulling into my neighborhood, I accidentally swerve and cross the centerline. "You son-of-a-bitch." I slow down and steer back into my lane.

"I love you too."

"Fuck you."

"H-m-m. Maybe I should go introduce myself to Mason right now. Before he goes inside the school. He looks so sad, standing out there. Do you think he'd like to go swimming in the river with me?"

"No. I'll stop. I'll do it. I'll bring you whatever I find."

"That's a good girl. And remember, what I really want is the card. Promise you'll give it to me if you come across it."

"I can't promise you anything. I don't even know what the card is. Do you?"

A *kerthump* sounds on the other end like someone shutting a door.

"Listen, Mrs. Kaine." He speaks softly. "You need to stop lying. There are some very important people with a lot of money who want that card. They have a lot of money and a lot of power, and they'll kill anyone to get it. I'm not a bad person, I'm just doing my job." He sighs. "I've been at this for weeks. If only your husband had cooperated. The question is, are you going to cooperate?"

"You asshole. Murderer."

"I had nothing to do with your husband's death, but I will kill your son if you don't do what I say. Are we clear?"

Red clouds obscure my vision. "Yes."

"Leave the bag by the dumpster in Denny Park at four p.m. on Wednesday. No earlier. No later."

He hangs up just as I pull into my driveway. I take several breaths and relax my shoulders. I don't care about William's computer. I can't even log into it, but if I don't find the card, he'll kill Mason. If I don't find it, I'll never know who was driving that Audi.

My world spirals out of control, and I have no one to help me hold it steady.

I hit the button for the garage door.

Then I hit the call button.

"Call Mason."

The on-call light comes on. "What do you want?"

"Where are you?"

"I'm at school. I—"

"Are you okay?"

"Why wouldn't I be okay? Never mind. I have to go."

"Wait."

Click.

He's okay. He's at the school, and he's okay. The old man kept his word, but he also kept saying "I" when he meant "we." Why did he want me to think he was working alone? Who is he trying to protect?

I pull into the garage and get out. William's tools hang on the pegboard. The hammers catch my eye. The old man wants me to be thorough, to bring *everything*. I'd love to bring the claw-end of a hammer down on his face.

I grab a cardboard box off the bench and go to William's office. *Pack everything nicely*, the old man said. *Be thorough*, he said.

I drop the box onto the floor and pick up William's computer, pulling the wires tight as I raise the monstrosity over my head, intending to throw it down as hard as I can, but I don't. There's no way the old man will be able to hack into William's computer, but if it's damaged, he'll take it out on Mason.

Gently, I put the computer on the floor.

That was close.

Robert Lang's TriamSys phone extension is on the sticky note next to the monitor.

4896.

Using the browser on my cell phone, I find the number to TriamSys and dial.

"If you know the extension of the party you're trying to reach—"

I punch in the number and hit pound.

"This extension is no longer in use. If you would like to try another number—"

My hands tremble. I put the phone down and gaze at the painting of St. Croix. I'm starving. William said the card was in St. Croix, but if I went there, I wouldn't know where to look. I don't know what to look for, but someone at TriamSys does. Robert Lang does.

My hands won't stop shaking.

I need to eat.

There's no reason to panic.

It's one in the afternoon.

Mason is safe. I am safe.

I have time to make a sandwich.

TriamSys isn't going anywhere.

The ocean in the painting is a cool blue, and I'm in control, and this too shall pass.

After a proper lunch, as William would have called it, I'll go to TriamSys.

I'll find Robert Lang.

And I'll find the card.

CHAPTER TWENTY-TWO

MASON

Mason shoves his phone in his pocket and touches the bump on his forehead. Then he carefully explores the spot on his cheek where Hunter hit him. It's tender, but he's okay. His mom called a few minutes ago, and he didn't lie about being okay—but he did lie.

He told her he was at school.

After the fight, he couldn't face going inside. Not with everyone watching him. Judging him. Not with Hunter laughing at him and talking about him, telling everyone he's a fag.

Everyone knows what happened by now.

Mason lost.

Hunter won.

The sidewalk along Island Crest Way widens near the bridge. He walks fast, but not because he's in a hurry to get home, and not because he's angry. He's lighter than air. A great weight has been lifted. Everyone at school knows he's gay.

He exhales.

Soon, everyone in the houses along this road will know. Everyone on Mercer Island will know. His mother will know.

Maybe she already knows.

It's strange that she called to ask if he was okay. She's never done that before. It's like she knew about the fight. Maybe the principal called her, or maybe . . .

He looks around for her SUV.

Did she drive by the school earlier?

He scans the side streets for his mom's Lexus. If she's out here spying on him, she's truly gone insane. The whole world has gone insane. His dad is dead, Hunter and Scott will beat him up tomorrow, and Garrett doesn't want him, yet— everything is okay.

He's not insane. He's finally himself.

In case she is out here, somewhere, he decides to cut through the elementary school. Memories. The playground has the same swings, slide, and jungle gym from when he was little, but it's different now. Smaller. He remembers playing on the equipment. Being free. Things were simpler before puberty. No one cared who liked who. Boys were friends with boys, and girls were friends with girls, and sexual attraction wasn't a thing. But that's not true.

Sex has always been a thing.

They teased him for being different then, and they beat him up for it now.

He's never belonged anywhere.

But they can all go to hell.

He's free.

He could run away.

Why not?

He's sixteen. He's out and he's free.

As he crosses the school parking lot, he raises his arms in

the air. He's about to yell, *I'm free*, when a black Mustang appears.

Mason turns. Puts the car behind him. He heads for the sidewalk, walking briskly. He could run, but why? The guy in the leather jacket who watched him get beat up might not be looking for him. It could be a coincidence. It might not even be him.

The engine stops.

A car door slams.

Mason speeds up.

"Hey, man. Wait."

Mason glances over his shoulder—black leather jacket, silver zipper, sunglasses. It's definitely the same guy from school.

How embarrassing.

He pretends not to hear the man and keeps walking until he enters the child drop-off zone. His mom used to leave him here every morning. *Remember, Mason. Don't talk to strangers.*

"Hey, wait up." The man jogs toward Mason.

He's coming up fast.

It's too late to run.

"It's okay," the man says. "I saw what happened back there."

Mason turns around and covers his forehead.

"Are you okay?" The man stops. Winces. "Whoa, you've got quite the shiner on your cheek." He takes off his sunglasses. He might be too old to be a student, but he's not *too* old. His black hair shines like his car. It's cut tight on the sides in a pompadour fade like Mason has always wanted.

"I'm Trent." He holds out his hand, and his dimples spring to life.

"I'm Mason."

His hand is warm.

"That's a great shirt. I've got one just like it." His silver zipper sparkles in the sunlight.

"Thanks. I—I have to go."

"It gets better."

"What?"

"Better. It gets better."

"What do you mean?"

"Those homophobes, those jerks, they won't be interested in you forever. They'll eventually get bored and leave you alone. Trust me. I know how it is."

"Oh, thanks. I'm—are you, you know . . . "

"Gay?" His jacket is unzipped at the top, exposing the collar of his T-shirt. A teal V-neck frames his Adam's Apple. His chin. His flawless smile. "Yes, I'm gay."

Mason's face warms.

"You should put some ice on that," he says. "It's not bad, but—"

"I will." Mason covers his cheek. "I need to go."

"Wait, I wanted to apologize. I should have done something, but I didn't know what was going on at first. Wow. I wish I'd stood up to my coming-out bullies the way you did."

"I didn't do anything."

"Yes, you did. You stood your ground. You didn't run. I admire that."

"Do you go to school at Mullen?"

"No, I graduated from high school a couple of years ago."

"Oh, sorry. I—"

"It's okay. I look young. I came to talk to the track and field coach to see if he needed any help."

"Like an assistant?"

"Exactly. I run a lot, but I miss being on a team. Do you

run?"

"No. Yes. I do, but not on a team. I work out."

"I thought so. You're in great shape."

"Thanks." Mason's jeans, as tight as they are, would fall off if it weren't for the belt. Maybe his mom is right. He doesn't eat enough, and he hasn't actually worked out in—he's never worked out.

"Don't worry. Like I said, it gets better."

"Sure. Thanks."

"Hey, do you want to get together sometime?"

Mason glances at the Mustang. "I don't know. I—"

"Just to talk. You know, guys like us need to stick together."

"Sure. Okay."

"The track coach couldn't meet me today, but the receptionist woman—"

"Miss Calhoun."

"Yeah. She said to come back Wednesday. Why don't we meet after school?"

"Sure."

"Great." He rattles off his digits, and Mason types them into his phone. "Text me later so we can hook up."

Hook up. It's a date.

"See ya Wednesday."

"See ya."

Trent said he wanted to "get together." To "talk." But Mason knows this is a date.

To hell with Garrett. To hell with Hunter and his testosterone monkeys.

Mason's got a date with a man.

An older man.

A hot, older man with great hair and a killer car.

CHAPTER TWENTY-THREE

LAUREN

The last time I visited TriamSys was for an after-work farewell party that William's team had thrown him. He'd been promoted to a "specialized" department.

That was five years ago.

William never talked about work again. Not until he was hanging from the bridge.

The main office building reflects the trees surrounding the parking lot. Six stories of glass so clean, the reflections are like a mirage. It's as if the building doesn't exist.

The parking spots nearest the entrance have markers for TriamSys guests. I take one, get out, and go to the door. The person ahead of me flashes their badge, but the door swings swiftly behind them. There's no guest access.

I should have called ahead.

There's no receptionist desk inside either. No lobby.

Foreboding storm clouds come in from the north.

I could go to the coffee cart on the other side of the parking lot, act nonchalant, talk to the barista girl about TriamSys—though she likely doesn't know anything—and get a latte, but, as a rule, I don't drink coffee after one in the afternoon.

A gaunt, angular man with generous eyes and a T-shirt reading, I HEART PIZZA, strides up the sidewalk. Despite the sentiment on his shirt, he's skinny, and I doubt he eats more than a slice a day. Judging by his greasy complexion, though, he does eat pizza.

"Hi, my name is Lauren." I hold out my hand.

He's tentative, like he doesn't know how to act around girls, but he grasps my palm anyway.

When he doesn't speak, I ask, "And you are?"

He holds up his badge. "I'm Milton. It was my father's name. I don't like it, but I'm stuck with it." He glances at my blouse, then my waist. "Do you work here?"

"No, I—my husband works here. I mean, he used to. Did you know William Kaine?"

"*The* William Kaine?"

"How many are there?"

"Only one, I think, but you're Mrs. Kaine? You're so lucky." He lowers his head. "I'm sorry. That came out wrong." A chilly breeze blows between us. "When I saw the email, I was—we were all shocked."

"Yes, it was sudden. You didn't happen to work with him, did you?"

"No, but I was about to. Starting next week. I'm really sorry about what happened. When we found out we couldn't believe it." A man in a black leather jacket and sunglasses walks up to the coffee cart, distracting me. "It's such a tragic thing, I don't understand how something like that can happen to someone like him, but I guess you know what happened, right? You were there, right?"

Milton's questions pull me back into the conversation.

"I'm sorry. I was where?"

"No, I'm sorry. I get excited and ramble. I didn't mean to pry."

"It's okay. Can you tell me what William was working on?"

Something flashes, blinding me for an instant. The man at the coffee cart turns, cup in hand, and his black leather jacket is open at the top. The sun reflects off his zipper and again, I'm blinded for a second. He looks like a modern-day Fonzie, but taller.

"Sure, I could tell you, but then I'd have to kill you."

"You'd have to what?"

"No. No, It's okay. I'm kidding." He raises his palm. "I was only kidding."

I put my hand on my chest. "Listen, do people at TriamSys use cards for anything?"

Milton's forehead creases, and he looks at me like I'm speaking a different language. "Do you mean, like keycards?"

"Maybe. No. More like index cards. I don't know."

"My current team uses index cards all the time. We write user stories on them. It's old school, but it works."

A white van meanders across the parking lot, blocking my view of the Fonz.

"A user story tells us the requirements. It's how we know what code to write."

"I know what a user story is. William used to bring stacks of them home a long time ago."

"Then his team might still use them." He glances up at a security camera. "Or maybe not."

"Why?"

"I don't know. I'm not on his team yet, but anything they do is confidential, so . . . I don't know whether they use cards or not."

The information the old man wants could be on an index card, but there weren't any in William's office. None that I saw. Yet, I missed seeing his badge, so I could have missed seeing an index card. Milton's badge shows him grinning like a lottery winner. "What are you going to be working on?"

He frowns. "I don't know."

"You don't know? You must know what William's team does if you're about to join them, right?"

"I don't know." He raises his eyebrows, nods toward the camera. "I can't say."

Milton is worthless. "Could you let me in, then? I'd like to get William's belongings and talk to his manager, TJ."

"I could, but then I'd have to kill—"

"I know. I know. You'd have to kill me." He beams like it's the funniest joke in the world. "Just let me in, okay?"

The blood drains from his face, and he gazes up at the building. "I can't do that. Security."

My anger wells up and I shove it down. "Please? Can't you sign me in as a guest or something?"

"I'm sorry. I have to get to work."

"Wait." I grab his arm, and he winces. "Do you know Robert Lang?"

He pulls his arm away. "No."

"Are you sure? You do work here, don't you?"

"Yes, I do, but—"

"I thought TriamSys only hired smart people."

"They do." His face reddens.

"Then why don't you know anything?"

"I do."

"Robert Lang. Who is he? What does he look like? Did he work with William?"

"He got canned last month, okay? I didn't know him because he was in upper management somewhere, and he got in a fight with a vice president over leaking some information or something." Milton starts to shake. "I really have to get to work. I'm sorry about what happened to your husband, but—" He waves his badge, and the door unlatches.

I want to shove him inside, knock him onto the floor, and make him tell me everything he knows, but he's a low-level grunt. He's not worth getting angry over.

Employees cluster around the coffee cart, blocking my view of the man in the leather jacket, but when they disperse, the man is gone.

Inside, Milton waits for the elevator, staring at me like I'm a corporate spy.

The storm clouds let go as I cross the parking lot on my way to the coffee cart.

The rain is cold. Freezing.

The barista smiles at me as if I wasn't suddenly drenched.

"What can I get you?"

"You just sold some coffee to a man in a leather jacket. Which way did he go?"

She looks as vacant as her pale green apron.

A car behind me revs its engine—*barum, barum, barum*—and there he is. Fonzie is pulling out of the lot in a Ford Mustang.

The Ford Mustang. The license plate starts with IHJ.

I run to my SUV, jump inside, and race to the exit, but I didn't see which way he went.

The rain beats down on my windshield relentlessly.

The wipers can't keep up.

I've seen that Mustang twice now.

Next time, it won't get away.

CHAPTER TWENTY-FOUR

RYAN

Ryan sits in a chair near the back of the basement, saving the seats up front for newcomers. The last light of day seeps into the First Light Church, and sure enough, a newcomer wanders through the door.

New to Ryan, anyway.

The newcomer sports a clean-shaven face, a light blue button-down shirt, and a pair of clean, dark blue jeans. He walks upright, not to say alcoholics are Neanderthals, but often, first-timers come in slouched, head hanging low, almost crawling. Either this man has recovered at another meeting, or he's young enough that his body is still holding together. Alcoholism knows no race, age, denomination, or wealth status. It's an equal opportunity employer.

Ryan looks around for Juan and doesn't see him. It's no surprise. He knew Juan lied about wanting to start over when they met at Denny's. Juan is a binge drinker. Once he starts, days fly by before he stops. Binge drinkers hit their lows fast, sometimes so low, they die before they can find their way back into the rooms.

Ryan closes his eyes and prays for the alcoholic who still suffers.

The seats are arranged in rows before a small lectern. Sunday School posters hang on the walls. Most, if not all, of the fluorescent lights need replacing. Some flicker. Others are out. Thankfully, plenty of light shines in through the basement windows.

Todd, a big burly guy in a red flannel shirt, sits in the corner. His head is down like he's praying. He's not a newcomer, but he's only been coming to this meeting for about six months.

All the Mikes are here. In Ryan's experience, men named Mike are ten times more likely to suffer from alcoholism. Garage Mike sits in his usual spot beneath the "Twelve Steps" poster that Margaret always hangs before the meetings, and the other Mikes sit throughout the room, desperately random. Golfer Mike, Mikey C, and Mac—whose real name is Mike. They all have fewer years of sobriety than Garage Mike. He has over thirty. He's an old-timer like Warren M. and Alan C. They like to sit near the front, near the newcomers, where they can impart their wisdom.

Ryan feels in his pocket for Juan's car keys. He wonders if the Audi is still parked outside the Squire, or if Juan's company towed it. Ryan had hoped to see Juan tonight and trade the keys for the rock he gave him—smooth side, rough side.

Ryan wants the rock back. He needs it. After the rent increase, and losing his job this morning, he spent the afternoon fantasizing about drinking a Gin and Tonic. It doesn't matter how many years of sobriety someone has, it's always one day at a time.

"Hey, Ryan." Joe sits next to him. Joe's been coming to

this meeting as long as Ryan can remember. "You're not looking like yourself tonight. You okay?"

Margaret stands, walks to the door, closes it, and turns toward the lectern. She signed up to chair the meeting tonight. It's a tough one. Nights are hard because everyone is tired and edgy, and Mondays are hard because they come after the weekend. Drinkers struggle on the weekend.

"Ryan?" Joe says, prompting him to respond.

Margaret goes to the newcomer and whispers in his ear. It's standard procedure. She's asking if this is his first meeting so she can make sure to have a twenty-four-hour chip ready. Silver.

The man smiles and shakes his head no. He's not a newcomer, after all.

"Ryan. Where's Juan?"

Margaret stands behind the lectern, welcomes everyone, and reads the meeting preamble.

"I was going to ask you," Ryan whispers. "Did you come to the meeting yesterday?"

"Yeah, he wasn't here. He promised to help me move my couch after the meeting, but he didn't show up."

"I wouldn't count on seeing him anytime soon."

"Oh."

"If we are to recover," Margaret says, "we must feel free to say what is on our minds and in our hearts. Therefore, who you see here, what you hear here, when you leave here, let it stay here. Now, let's go around the room and introduce ourselves, beginning on my left."

"Hi, I'm Josey, and I'm an alcoholic."

"Hi, Josey," the others say in unison.

"Hi, everyone. I'm Mikey C, and I'm an alcoholic."

"Hi, Mikey C," the group says.

Ryan pays close attention when the new person speaks, making sure to get his name.

"Hi, I'm Steve, and I'm an alcoholic."

Steve.

It's good to immediately memorize an alcoholic's name. Most drunks have burned so many bridges, they feel like no one cares. Remembering someone's name can mean a lot. It can keep them from drinking. "Hi, I'm Ryan, and I'm an alcoholic."

The introductions continue until everyone has spoken.

Margaret scans the room, "If this is your first meeting since your last drink, please raise your hand."

Todd raises his hand. "My name is Todd, and I'm an—I'm sorry, everyone." His hand falls, he casts his head down. His beard folds over his flannel shirt, and he weeps. "I relapsed. Again. I just said, 'Fuck it,' and drank. I'm sorry, I let you all down."

"It's okay, Todd," Margaret says. "Let us lift you up."

"Welcome back," Joe says.

Garage Mike chimes in. "A case of the fuck-its, huh? It's alright. You're always welcome back. We don't shoot our wounded."

Todd had two months clean, maybe more, but from what he's shared in past meetings, he's never strung together enough days to get a year. He's a chronic relapser.

Margaret hands Todd a silver chip and gives him a hug before returning to the lectern. "The meeting is open." She looks around. "Would anyone like to share their experience, strength, and hope?"

Ryan goes to the lectern. "My name is Ryan, and I'm an alcoholic."

"Hi, Ryan." Their voices blend into one.

"I had a rough go of it today. I lost my job."

Concerned looks, a few murmurs. Garage Mike narrows his gaze on Ryan, listening intently.

"But I didn't drink over it. Thank God for this meeting and for everyone here. I'm really blessed I found this group, but, I don't know. Things are getting worse instead of better right now. I have to update my LinkedIn and start over. Find a new job, fast. It's so embarrassing." He stares straight ahead, gazing between the seats. "When my boss told me I was fired, it brought up all those old feelings. The old me would have gone straight to the convenience store." Ryan clasps his hands, lets out a nervous laugh. "There's an episode of *The Family Guy* where the main character—what's his name?"

"Peter," Joe says.

"Right. Peter Griffin. He says, 'Let's go drink until we can't feel feelings anymore.'" A few laughs, mostly from newer members. "That was me. Shove the emotions down and drink everything away. I would have been off to the races if it weren't for AA. My boss wouldn't let me explain, he spied on me, and—it's a long story, but it wasn't my fault."

Garage Mike harrumphs.

Ryan says, "I don't know. Maybe it was my fault. I certainly had a part to play in it. If I'm not careful, I'm going to have to do a fourth step. Take a moral inventory and write down where I was to blame."

Garage Mike's powder blue eyes remain unblinking.

"I mean, I *am* going to do a fourth step."

Several old-timers nod in agreement.

"The truth is, my heart hasn't been in driving delivery trucks for a long time, if ever. I've been trying to change careers, become a computer programmer like my brother, and that's, well, it's how I got fired." Ryan wipes his palms on his pants. "I have to be honest. I got fired because I kept driving by my brother's house instead of making my deliveries. We haven't talked in years and those of you who've heard my story know why. It's a lot to do with my drinking, and I just thought if I could 'accidentally' run into him, he could help me learn to write code."

The basement windows darken as if a cloud passed in between the meeting and the setting sun.

"I feel selfish now, wanting the things my brother has. His house on Mercer Island. His car."

"How did they know about your deliveries?" Joe asks.

Margaret glares at Joe for cross-talking.

Ryan holds up his phone. "They made us put an app on here to track everything. They looked up my route history, and—it's a long story."

"I hate those things," Garage Mike grumbles.

Margaret grimaces at him.

"The good news is, I didn't drink today. Once I realized I was getting resentful toward my boss, I worked on letting it go. Like the book says, resentment is the number one offender."

More nods from the group.

"The other good news is, I'll have more time to work on learning computer programming. It's probably for the best, but I realized something else. I did the twelve steps eight years ago when I first came in, but I didn't do them all the way. Because of a restraining order." He looks around the room. "Yeah, some of you know about restraining orders, don't you?" A few people crack a smile. "Because of this restraining order, I was never allowed to talk to my brother or make amends. I've been carrying the weight of what I did with me everywhere I go, and even though I'm sober, I'm not happy, joyous, and free."

Steve leans forward, gazes at Ryan, his warm brown eyes as intense as Garage Mike's powder blues. Ryan recommits the new person's name to memory. *The well-dressed guy in blue is Steve.*

"I only hope William and his family can find it in their hearts to forgive me. I've missed out on being an uncle to my nephew. Mason is already sixteen, and—" Ryan's throat constricts, his eyes well up "—and that's all I have. I'm Ryan, and I'm an alcoholic."

"Thanks for sharing, Ryan," Margaret says. "Who's next?"

Ryan takes his seat.

If he's to stay sober, he's got to make amends.

Restraining order or not, it's clear to him now.

He's got to make amends.

CHAPTER TWENTY-FIVE

LAUREN

Shadows bury William's desk in darkness. I reach inside his office and switch on the light before entering. His bookcase reflects in the window next to our painting of St. Croix, obscuring my view of the street.

I need to stop obsessing on the black cars, checking the driveway every few minutes, replaying the night William died, comparing the Audi that chased us to the Mustang I saw at TriamSys this afternoon.

The cardboard box from the garage lies on the floor where I left it. The old man wants William's computer, his phone, and anything else I can find *packed up nicely*. I should be like my father and take care of this now. Accelerate the inevitable. The old man wants me at Denny Park tomorrow at four because . . . he's planning to do something to me. Or, he wants me away from Mercer Island so someone can kidnap Mason.

Or both.

I'll be there, but I'm only leaving William's computer. If I find the card, I'm keeping it. It's my only leverage.

William's desk chair is the most comfortable seat in the house. I sit down and rummage through his drawers, looking for index cards. I'm still angry at that pock-marked geek, Milton. He wouldn't let me inside TriamSys, and he told me nothing useful about Robert Lang, except that he'd been fired. If Lang isn't at TriamSys anymore, where is he?

I finish searching the desk—no cards of any kind—and slam it shut. The *bang* rattles the office door. Mason is upstairs in his room. If he heard the drawer, he'll think I'm angry, but I'm not.

I'm not angry, and I'm going to stay this way.

On the outside chance William used an index card as a bookmark, I flip through the internet related titles on his bookshelf, hoping something falls out.

Nothing.

Mason's feet sound on the stairs.

"Mason? Can you come here?"

"No. I'm getting something to eat."

"Please?"

"Not now. I'm fine." It sounds as if he's smiling. As if he actually *is* fine. "Don't worry about me." His voice trails off toward the kitchen.

He says he's fine, but he doesn't know about the old man. He doesn't know about the black Mustang. And I don't know how to tell him. He's in no shape to deal with this information. I've got to take care of the old man myself.

Wednesday at four.

At the window, I cup my hands on the glass to see through the reflection. No parked cars. No smoking man under the streetlamp. No sign of anything, just like earlier. Just like every moment since I returned home.

Mason's shadow crosses the hall. "Mason. Come here,

please."

He approaches, stopping shy of the doorway. A shadow cuts across him at an angle that hides his face. He's still wearing William's Oxford, and he's holding a chicken leg and a bag of Doritos. "What's up?"

"How was your day? You weren't happy when I got home."

"Sorry. I'm fine now."

"Did something happen at school?"

He shifts, edges backward. "No, not really." He takes a bite. "I'm fine."

"No you're not. Come here."

He hesitates, then steps into the light, and I wince. He's bruised. Someone pummeled my baby. I rush forward. "What happened?" He steps back. "Who did that to you?" The goose egg on his forehead matches the blue-green waters in the St. Croix painting, and the swelling on his cheek looks like a rotten strawberry.

Visions of the old man punching my son paint the room red.

Mason smirks. "It's not that bad. Really, I'm okay." He raises the bag of Doritos. "Here. Want some?"

"Tell me what happened."

"Nothing. I fell down, that's all."

"What really happened?"

He crunches on a Dorito. "Nothing."

"You're not telling the truth." I lean forward. Pinch my lower lip.

"Okay, okay. It's not a big deal." He averts his eyes. "You were right. I shouldn't have gone to school today."

"What?"

"I got in a fight, but"—his eyes light up—"I won."

"Who hit you? Wait. What do you mean you won?"

He takes another bite and wipes his chin. "Yeah. They said Dad killed himself, and I got mad, so I yelled at this kid, and . . ." He lowers his chin. Looks away. Puts on a sheepish grin and lowers his voice. "That kid started it, but I ended it."

"I knew you shouldn't have gone back today. Did you put ice on your face?"

"Yeah."

William's shirt looks good on him, and I see my father in his eyes. The red recedes. "Are you sure you're fine?"

"Yeah." There's that grin again. "Don't worry about me. I didn't get in trouble or anything, but if it's alright, I was thinking I wouldn't go back until after the funeral. The other kids are—they're just mean."

"Who was the fight with?"

He points at the box with his chicken. "What's that for?"

"Oh, it's—"

"Wait. You told me you weren't packing up dad's office."

"I'm not. I was thinking about it, but if you think it's too soon . . ."

He turns, scans the walls, the paintings, the window. "You said I'd get to go through everything and pick out what I wanted."

"You still can." I try to touch his cheek, and he flinches. "It's fine with me if you stay home from school the rest of this week. Who hit you?"

He lowers his head. "Hunter Stalwell. He said Dad killed himself."

"That's not true, you know." I place my fingers beneath his chin and lift.

His eyes well up. "I know. And you didn't kill dad, either. I'm sorry I blamed you, Mom. I'm sorry for what I said. I know it wasn't your fault. I just miss him so much."

"I do too." I hug him, crushing the bag of Doritos between us. "I'm not packing up his things today. You have plenty of time."

He returns the embrace.

It's been so long since he's hugged me like this. I can't remember the last time.

I love him, and I'm going to hold him and protect him. I cup his head and pull him close.

He weeps.

This too shall pass, but I don't want it to.

CHAPTER TWENTY-SIX

MASON

Mason's tongue stings. His palms ache. His arms resist, but he pushes through the tenth push-up and stands, shirtless and out of breath.

He gazes into the mirror.

He's not so bad. He's thin but muscular, and he looks tough with that bruise on his forehead. The scrape on his cheek. He touches it. It smarts. Fucking Hunter. Thankfully, that testosterone monkey doesn't matter anymore.

All that matters is his date with Trent tomorrow.

Mason flexes. His pecs swell, and if he tries hard, he can see a dimple beneath each bicep. Definition. He needs to start lifting weights. Get toned. Sleeping until noon feels great, but he should get up early so he can go to the basement and work out. That's the sort of thing Trent would do. It's what Mason should do right now, but his mom is downstairs, milling around in the kitchen. Making lunch.

The half-eaten bag of Doritos from last night lies on the bed between the pillows. What would Trent think? He is probably a health freak, but maybe not. Maybe he eats anything he wants because he exercises so much. Mason imagines a time when they wake up together, eat chips in bed, then head out on a long run.

Guys like us need to stick together.

Mason twists his upper body, examining himself in the mirror. His ribs stick out too much. His hips protrude like open car doors, and there's that birthmark right below his armpit. The same one his dad has.

Had.

Mason didn't tell Trent he's staying home from school this week. Like a ninja, he's going to sneak into the school tomorrow and pretend he's been there all day. Trent wants to become Mr. Mahone's coaching assistant, and he might have to try out for it. If so, Mr. Mahone will make Trent run. Trent will take off his shirt and sweat. Mason considers going to school early and hiding in the bleachers so he can watch, but—no. That's creepy. He'll wait outside the gym instead, as if he just got out of class.

It's going to be great. Trent will shower after running, put on his retro-leather jacket, slick back his hair, and greet Mason with those deep brown eyes. Trent is clean in a rugged way, and he's interested in Mason, and he's a dream.

He's everything that's right with the world.

He's the future.

Mason holds his hand over the birthmark and tips his head forward until his hair covers the bruise on his forehead. He's not bad looking. Garrett doesn't know what he's missing. Compared to Trent, Garret is a child. A high-schooler. How silly it was, getting all nerved up over Garrett. Trent is so much better, and Mason has Hunter Stalwell to thank. If it hadn't been for Hunter, Trent wouldn't have seen Mason in the parking lot. Trent wouldn't have followed him to the elementary school.

They wouldn't have met.

But they did.

It was like that movie, *Alex Strangelove.*

Mason pictures himself lying on his bed, locked in a kiss with Trent, just like the characters in the movie. Tomorrow, Mason will kiss Trent. He's got to know what it's like. He'll wait, see if Trent makes the first move, and if he doesn't, Mason will go for it.

They'll need to go somewhere private, away from the school.

Away from all those eyes.

Mason takes a comb off his dresser. He can't get his hair to stay down in back. People have always made fun of that. Not people. Children. At least he's not a child anymore. By the time he goes back to school after the funeral next Sunday, he'll have updated his status online to "in a relationship." In a relationship with a man. Trent—tall, sleek, straight fire.

Mason sits on the bed and grabs the Doritos. The chips aren't crisp. Three o'clock tomorrow can't come fast enough. His date is over twenty-four hours away. He should put the Doritos down and go work out in the basement to pass the time, but what good would one workout do?

The chips aren't worth eating. He closes the bag, lies down, and rolls onto his stomach. His head hangs over the edge of the bed.

Tomorrow can't come fast enough.

His Japanese manga book, *Death Note*, is on the floor. Trent is too old to like manga, but maybe not. These books are for everyone, despite what Mason's father used to say. He picks the book up and flips through the pages, looking for a good spot to read. Teru Mikami, one of the main characters, is awesome. Teru's jacket reminds Mason of Trent. His tie would look chill on Trent too. Maybe Trent will wear a tie to prom with Mason, but that's a stupid idea. Grown men don't go to proms, and Trent is all man.

Trent would look chill in a tie, though. Mason imagines looping one of his dad's ties around Trent's neck and pulling him in for a kiss. Mason could wear a tie for their date tomorrow, but depending where they go, it might be overkill.

Oh, shit.

Where are they going? Mason doesn't know because he never texted Trent. Trent doesn't have his digits.

He grabs his phone.

"hi. this is Mason. can't wait for our date. do you like ties?"

Carefully, he deletes that last part. How stupid. Then, he deletes the rest.

"hey trent. this is Mason. cu tomorrow. you got my digits now. peace."

That's not bad, but, *peace*? Really?

Yes. Peace. Peace and ties, and Yaoi—love between men. He replaces *peace* with *Yaoi* and hits send.

Yaoi?

Oh, no. He can't take it back.

Now Trent is going to think he's a weeaboo weirdo.

Mason tosses his phone onto the floor and picks up the manga. He reads, turns the page, reads, turns. Teru wears a tie in every picture. Mason's dad didn't teach him how to tie a tie. He didn't teach him anything, and now he's gone.

Mason turns the pages, reads faster, glances at the pictures, but after a while, he stops, and he can't remember anything he's seen. The pictures are a blur, and he turns the page, and Teru wears a black suit jacket, not a black leather jacket, and Teru's tie is perfectly straight, and Trent is too old for manga. Mason's dad was too old for manga too. Mason's dad never understood, and now he never will.

He died.

He left on purpose.

Hunter was right.

Mason's father left to get away from his piece of shit faggot for a son.

Mason throws the book against the wall, grabs a handful of Doritos, shoves them into his mouth, chokes, and slings the bag at the window. Chips stream through the air. The bag doesn't make it to the window—because Mason is weak—and it explodes against the bookshelf instead. An orange cloud settles over his manga. His insides turn sour. His mother will get pissed when she sees this mess. She'll lose it. Tears burn his swollen cheek, and he stares at his dragon poster. The one with the rainbow scales. The ryū. The real reason his father is dead.

His mother is the dragon.

His dad didn't leave because of him.

He left because of her.

Mason's dad wanted to get away from the ryū so badly, he killed himself, just like Teru in the anime version of *Death Note*. Teru went insane and stabbed himself with a pen. Mason's father lost his mind and jumped off a bridge. His mother drove him to it, and she'll drive Mason to it too if he doesn't do something.

If he doesn't run away.

It's a good thing he hugged her last night and apologized. She doesn't suspect a thing.

He grins.

He's got to leave.

Like a mongoose, he burrows under his covers.
Pulls a pillow up to his chest.
Clutches it and pictures Trent.
A grown man like that, someone with his own car.
His own place.
An apartment. A house. Something. Somewhere.
Somewhere Mason can go to escape the dragon.

CHAPTER TWENTY-SEVEN

LAUREN

I've given up.

I spread a sheet over the sitting room sofa and cover it with a comforter from the guest bedroom. If I'm going to sleep down here every night, I might as well be comfortable. The bedroom became a cold and desolate place after I put William's things in the garage. His office will be the same when I pack up his computer, but I have no choice.

The old man will be waiting at Denny Park tomorrow.

I need a good night's sleep.

I switch off the light.

My laptop is on the coffee table, and I close the lid.

The walls, the mantle, the photos—they're all gone. Consumed by darkness.

I lie back, and I'm so . . . sleep takes over.

I'm sitting in the passenger seat of a black car. We're racing down a winding road lined with palm trees and yellow-flowered casha bushes. I'm in St. Croix. The old man is behind the wheel, and his beard sways whenever he makes a turn. He adjusts the radio, and the song "Born to Be Wild" blares.

I grab the dashboard and look over my shoulder. Mason sits in the backseat between two men with his arms behind his back. They point guns at his head, but he's not scared. He's laughing. Grinning that sheepish grin—the one he had when he took a cookie without permission. He was only three, but I punished him anyway. All he wanted was a cookie, but I saw red, and—

I sit up.

Now my sleeplessness is happening here. My mind has too many things to worry about. An empty box sits in William's office, waiting for his computer. Tomorrow is coming whether I like it or not, but I can't bear to pack it now. What can I do?

The funeral is in five days, and I haven't invited Ryan.

I need to take control of something if I'm to get any sleep.

I open my laptop, browser to LinkedIn, and type Ryan's name into the search box. Forty-three results come up. There's one in Atlanta, another in Philadelphia—Akron, New York, San Antonio. Advertising agents, real estate agents, financial advisors. I add "Seattle" to the search, and the site asks me if I meant, "Ryan Cayne Seattle." I didn't, but I scroll through the results anyway, and there he is.

He's alive.

Or, he was alive when he joined SPD Delivery as a truck driver. His hair, loosely disheveled—like always—hasn't receded, but neither did William's. He still has his facial hair, but it's not as thick and unkempt as before, and his face is thinner. He's not bloated. Strangest of all, he's smiling.

This picture was taken four years ago. He could have relapsed since then. He might still be dead in a gutter somewhere.

I go to Google, hoping to find something more recent. Ads for lawn furniture lurk on every page. The week before our anniversary, William and I discussed getting new furniture. I must have shopped online for weather-proof chairs, tables, or umbrellas, but I don't remember doing it. I remember the conversation, and I—William is gone, and I don't need any damned lawn furniture. I want to move on, but right now, the internet—those "bots"—won't let me forget, and the world is full of Ryan Kaines. Worthless, drunk, Ryan Kaines.

Breathe.

I switch to searching for images, and this leads me to a question and answer website like Quora, except this one is for computer programmers. Ryan has posted hundreds of questions, each displaying his profile picture. His facial hair is gone, but it's definitely him. His last post was two months ago.

Back on LinkedIn, I see he has two computer programming certifications, and he's joined several technology groups. He has a sample website, showing off his skills.

It appears he has gotten his life together.

This is not fair.

Not after what he did to us, but—forgiveness is the path to freedom. The annoying ads for outdoor furniture heat me up, and Ryan is alive and well, and I've gone all day without my temper flaring, and—

This is not fair.

Ryan tried to take everything away from me.

My hands tremble, and I pinch my lip.

Ryan made a mistake years ago.

The path to freedom, for me, is forgiveness.

I click on the MESSAGE button next to Ryan's profile picture, and a box appears, prompting me to "Write a Message."

Breathe. You have to invite him to the funeral. For William. For Mason.

No.

I must invite him for myself. I can't go on living in hate.

My shaky hand accidentally types a lower-case "j."

I hit backspace.

Breathe.

I'm fuming, but it's not too late. There's no red. I can still get some sleep tonight.

I type, "Ryan, I thought you should know. William is dead. He died last week. The funeral is at the Columbia Funeral Home this Sunday at two."

That should do it, but I'm not sure I want to send this. How will I handle it if he shows up? I'll have to make sure he isn't drunk before introducing him to Mason, and if he is, then I'll slap him in the face as hard as I can.

No.

It can't be like that.

That's not forgiveness.

The message box turns red. The ads, the browser, the room—all red.

I delete the message.

As long as I hate Ryan Kaine, my rage will flourish. As long as Ryan Kaine is alive—and by all appearances, he is— I'm doomed.

I type, "I'm sorry to let you know this way, but"—I hit the caps-lock key—"WILLIAM IS DEAD! IT SHOULD HAVE BEEN YOU!!!"

My body quakes, pulsates with each heartbeat, and

revenge wraps around my shoulders, forcing me to hunch over the laptop.

The mouse hovers over the word SEND.

All I have to do is click the button.

Mason says he doesn't remember his uncle, but I'll never forget the day we rescued him. The day we found him running around in his underwear—dirt on his knees, his face. He was so thin, I didn't know when he'd eaten last, and Ryan was nowhere to be found. That's when Mason's eating problems began.

Damn you, Ryan Kaine.

I click SEND and close the laptop.

It slides off the sofa and hits the floor with a *thud.*

I lay back and gaze into the dark.

Red becomes black.

The release arrives, and I savor the moment.

The air is cool.

It's so dark in here, so black, I can't make out the ceiling light fixture, but I know it's up there.

I don't know if Ryan is out there, but if he is, and if he comes to the funeral . . . I'm going to savor the release.

CHAPTER TWENTY-EIGHT

RYAN

Tonight's meeting wasn't very good. Tuesdays are usually better than Mondays, but Ryan didn't share at the lectern. Sharing makes a difference, but it's okay. He's doing well. He's attended two meetings in two days, and he's going to keep coming back. Maybe he'll do ninety meetings in ninety days. Meetings are insurance against the drink.

And yesterday, Ryan used his insurance.

After losing his job, he considered taking a drink—sitting outside a fancy restaurant, sipping a Gin and Tonic, numbing his newborn resentment for SPD Delivery. Forgetting the misery that led him to AA in the first place. But he didn't drink.

Thank God for AA.

The cold, concrete steps lead him out of the First Light Church basement, and he waits at the crosswalk for the light to change.

Ninety in ninety is a good idea.

Besides, he needs to be in the rooms in case Juan shows up. Not only does he need his rock back, he needs to help

Juan. The rent increase, getting fired, the years spent missing William—Ryan's problems are small compared to what Juan might be going through. Freezing somewhere on the side of the road, clutching an empty bottle.

Ryan regrets letting the big man leave Denny's last Saturday.

Garage Mike, Joe, and the new guy—Steve—are engrossed in a conversation across the street. Garage Mike has his cigarette, and he's wearing his brown corduroy jacket. The one that soaks up the rain. Joe's Mariners cap hides his ever-expanding bald spot, and he's squirrely as ever, fidgeting in his pockets. Steve stands a few feet away as if he doesn't appreciate Garage Mike's cigarette smoke. He's wearing a blue dress shirt and jeans like last night.

Margaret comes out of the church. "See you tomorrow, Ryan." She chaired the meeting again because Mac didn't show up. "I hope you find a job soon."

"I'm working on it." Ryan spent the day writing code, fighting off null pointer exceptions. During the meeting, he realized he'd succumbed to one of his character defects. Procrastination. He should have made amends to William today, but he put it off, using his financial woes as an excuse.

The walk sign lights up.

"Keep coming back," Margaret calls after him as he steps into the street.

It stopped raining hours ago, but the pavement is still wet. A torn soda cup from a fast-food joint is trapped against the grate in the gutter. Steve stands near the cup, his arms relaxed, his shoulders back. His hair isn't at all out of place, but he runs his fingers through it anyway.

"Have you met Steve?" Joe asks Ryan.

"No." Ryan extends his hand. "Hi."

"Hi."

They shake, and Ryan attempts to match Steve's grip, squeezing hard in return.

Steve lifts his chin. "You shared in the meeting last night, right?"

"Yeah. I—"

"Where's Juan?" Garage Mike focuses his steely eyes on Ryan.

"I haven't seen him."

Joe jumps in. "He relapsed. Right, Ryan? Binge drinking."

"You haven't seen him?" Garage Mike scowls. "You're his sponsor, aren't you?"

"Yeah."

"Have you called him? Gone to his place?"

"He relapsed. Right, Ryan?" Joe says.

"I haven't been able to get a hold of him." Ryan puts his hand in his pocket, feels for Juan's car keys. "I've been busy looking for a job."

"You should be busy looking for Juan." Garage Mike's voice is jarring. "You should be spending all your newfound free time doing service."

"Ryan took his car keys away," Joe says. "Right, Ryan?"

"That's right."

"But that won't keep him from driving drunk," Joe continues. "I know when I was drinking, it didn't matter. I loved to get behind the wheel. Especially if I needed to get more booze. Know what I mean?"

"Do you think he got in an accident?" Steve asks.

"I hope he's not dead." Joe shakes his head in dismay.

Garage Mike exhales. The smoke hangs in the air, then the breeze takes it away. "It won't be drunk driving that kills him. It'll be his pancreas or suicide. Drunk drivers tend to live through car crashes. They're always so damned relaxed."

"Yeah." Joe gazes at the ground. "I know what you mean. And suicide gets more guys than cirrhosis of the liver. Suicide and those grand mal seizures—they kill us as much as anything."

Ryan thinks of his first sponsor. His only sponsor.

"Speaking of suicide," Garage Mike tips his head forward, "how have you been doing, Ryan?"

"Good. I'm good. Don't worry, I'll find Juan. He's just on a bender. He'll bounce back."

"Not without help." Garage Mike turns to Steve, takes a drag on his cigarette. "And what's your story?"

Ryan hasn't heard Steve share in a meeting yet, and he is curious about Steve, but Garage Mike doesn't have to be such a jerk. Nosy old-timer.

"I've been sober for three years," Steve says.

"Congratulations." Joe grins ear to ear.

"I just moved here from Portland for work, and I'm looking for a new homegroup."

Joe motions toward the church. "Our meeting is the best. You should keep coming back."

"It's been good so far." Steve gazes at the church. "And I gotta to say, it's been a relief. I went two months without a meeting while I moved, and it felt horrible."

Garage Mike turns his attention to Ryan. "AA isn't something you graduate from." He takes a puff. "The work never stops."

"What brought you here?" Joe says. "I'm a prep cook."

"I work in the IT department of a small company."

Joe draws his eyebrows together, confused.

Steve smiles. "IT. You know. Computers and Wi-Fi. Websites."

"Oh," Joe says. "I bet that pays pretty well."

"Not as much as you would think. It's a non-profit company."

"No offense," Garage spews smoke, "but I hate all that tech stuff. Man has taken it too far. The internet is nothing but porn and advertisements."

"And advertisements for porn," Joe quips.

"I don't disagree," Steve says. "That's actually what we do, or what we're trying to do. We're making the internet a better place."

"Do you get paid, working for a non-profit?" Joe asks.

"Most people are volunteers, but I get a salary because of my expertise."

Garage Mike throws his cigarette butt on the sidewalk and crushes it out with his foot. "Good luck with that. I don't think anybody wants their porn taken away." He turns and walks down the street. "See you drunks later."

Joe looks at his watch. "I've gotta go too. I'll see you guys."

Steve takes out his phone.

"So," Ryan says, "you work on websites? Are you a programmer?"

"Yes. That's right."

"I created a website. I've been learning how to program computers."

"Cool." He points at Ryan. "Hey, you mentioned that in the meeting last night, right?"

Steve's a decent guy. He listens. "Yeah. So, does your company need any help? I could use the practice."

"How many websites have you built?"

"Not a lot. I'm just beginning, but I have an example one. You can get to it from my LinkedIn page."

"Sure. I'll check it out. What's your last name so I can find it?"

"It's Kaine. Let me know if you see anything wrong or if it breaks. I really want to get better."

"How long did you say you've been doing this?"

"For a while, but, until I got fired yesterday, I haven't had much time to spend on it."

"Right. Well, we're always looking for volunteers. How much do you know about 'net neutrality'?"

"Oh . . . that's what you meant by making the internet a better place. I think Garage Mike's worried you're going to take his porn away."

Steve laughs. "No, we're not taking anyone's porn away. We're just trying to level the playing field. It's not fair that Big Tech controls the speed of the internet, making their websites load faster than the smaller guys' and placing their ads ahead of everyone else's."

"I've read about that."

"Really? That's great." Steve claps Ryan's shoulder. "Tell you what I'll do. I'll introduce you to my coordinator tomorrow. He's always there on Wednesdays. He'll know if there is anything you can help with. Usually, I keep my AA life separate from work, but if I can help you out—"

"That would be awesome." Ryan glances at the church. "You won't tell them about—"

"Of course not. What we say here, what we hear here, stays here, right?"

"Right."

"What time can I pick you up? How's two o'clock sound?"

"Great."

"What's your address?"

Ryan hesitates. Too many times he's given his address to recovered alcoholics only to find them outside his door after a relapse, looking for a place to stay. It's fine when he's agreed to sponsor them, but the other times—there have been some scary situations. "Let's meet on the corner of Denny and Broadway. By the Starbucks."

"Sure. I understand." Steve glances toward Denny Way. "You like to keep a healthy separation, too."

"Something like that. Look, I really appreciate this."

"Let's see how things work out before you thank me," he says with a smile. "Have a good night."

Ryan is halfway back to his apartment when he remembers Garage Mike's advice. Now that he's lost his job, he *should* spend his time working the twelfth step, but he can't miss this opportunity. Yet, Garage Mike is right. To stay sober, the work never ends. Ryan should spend tomorrow trying to find Juan, or making amends to William, but he's been working the program for years, and what has it gotten him?

Nothing.

No, that's not right.

That's stinking thinking.

Working the program has kept him sober, given him a daily reprieve . . . but not much more.

His apartment is cold, and soon, he won't even have that.

Steve said the net neutrality company pays him for his expertise. If Ryan plays his cards right, he could turn this into a real job. If not, the experience alone would boost his resume.

This is his chance.

He needs to spend every waking moment honing his computer skills.

Saving Juan can wait.

Working on his fourth step—his resentments against SPD Delivery, his boss—can wait.

Making amends to William and Lauren and Mason . . .

It can all wait.

CHAPTER TWENTY-NINE

LAUREN

And there goes my spirit animal, my amber seahorse, fluttering her tiny fins, her long sucker nose pointing away, her curled tail ruddering through the coral, flying through the water like a Chinese dragon.

She leaves me in a flurry of bubbles.

My mouth fills with water, so I spit out the snorkel and swim to the surface. At first, I can't find William, then I see him standing on the shore. His tall, slim body is sunburned. Water runs down his chin, his shoulders, over his ribs, and he waves to me. He hates swimming but, sometimes, he puts on a life jacket and joins in. He knows how much it means. The peace it brings me. I wave back to him, motioning for him to come, but he shakes his head. He loves me, but he doesn't have a life jacket on. He doesn't know how to swim.

William can't swim. He drowned because he couldn't swim.

A wave crashes over my head, and—goodbye, William.

The water rushes away, and I'm standing in his office. My hands are pressed against the wall on either side of our St.

Croix painting, and everything is red. The beach in the painting is empty. William isn't there, and my heart won't slow down. The last thing I knew, I was lying on the sofa in the sitting room about to sleep, and now I want to rip the painting off the wall.

Am I a sleepwalker? Have I become some sort of sleeping rage-walker?

Spinning around, I want to rip all the paintings off all the walls. The books off the shelves. The clock.

It's almost midnight.

I went to sleep on the sitting room sofa around nine, and . . . I must have slept, but now, I'm in the middle of a red-out and I don't know how I got here.

This is new.

Breathe.

A bad dream must have set me off.

And I was doing so well.

Or, maybe I've been repressing. Yesterday, when I didn't attack that Milton kid at TriamSys for not letting me inside, I could have been holding my anger in. I didn't get a release. And today—no. Today was the most peaceful day since William died. There was no repression. I found peace. I found forgiveness. I even invited Ryan to the funeral.

But it didn't free me. I'm still angry.

The message I sent to Ryan—*William is dead. It should have been you*—wasn't exactly forgiveness.

I'm not getting better.

I rush to the sitting room, grab my laptop, and check LinkedIn. Ryan hasn't responded. I click around, but there's no way to take the message back. I could send an apology, but I might lose control again.

I'm not in control now.

Breathe.

I log into HeatSinkers and read other members' answers to the three questions, but nothing rings true. They're angry about the lack of parking spots at Walmart, late payment notices. Stupid things. One person comes close when they write about their eviction notice, but it's not enough. I'm dealing with death, child abduction, and survivor's guilt, all at once. All the time.

Day in, day out.

A window with a bright red flashing border pops-up, telling me viruses have been detected. For $9.99/mo, I can subscribe to a service that will remove them and protect me from future attacks.

It's infuriating.

I drag the ad off to the side so I can see the three questions page on Heatsinkers, but answering them won't help. Trapped until Sunday, there's nothing I can do. Peace won't truly come until I've found the card.

William's last words—*They want the card. It's in St. Croix.*

My father would go to St. Croix tomorrow. No. He'd go tonight. He'd accelerate the inevitable, but I can't. The old man expects William's computer tomorrow. Then, Mason and I have to wait until Sunday for the funeral. But then, we can go to St. Croix.

CHAPTER THIRTY

LAUREN

William was the neat one in the relationship. He kept things clean.

I let things build up.

Sunlight shines through the sliding glass door, exposing the chaos that has become my life. My robe and nightgown are filthy. The kitchen is filthy. It's time to take care of this mess.

I pile the empty casserole dishes onto the griddle in the sink and let them soak. I throw away the empty Mac-n-Cheese boxes. The empty frozen dinner boxes. I wipe down the counters, make them sparkle, but the kitchen table might not be recoverable. Bereavement baskets full of rotten bananas, oranges, and apples cling to the tablecloth. The baskets brought me comfort at first, but now everything is soft and sticky. Even the potpourri is bad.

I grab two black garbage bags from beneath the kitchen sink and shove the baskets into the first one. The other bag is for the old man. I have until four today to give him William's computer. Earlier this morning, I boxed the computer up with its cables and put it in by the pantry. I'm not ready to bag the box, though. William's computer isn't trash.

I sling the bag of baskets over my shoulder and head for the garage, pausing near the stairs to listen for Mason. It's after one in the afternoon, and I haven't seen him yet today, but I'm not worried. He's doing better since he won that fight at school. Yesterday, he ate and exercised like a normal person.

I heave the bag on top of the pile in the garage. William always took care of the trash, so I don't know when the truck comes. He'd hate this pile. The bags block the back door at the end of his obsessively organized workbench, but it's not his workbench anymore. It's Mason's.

I wonder . . . with Mason's change in behavior, maybe he'll want to build something, like a birdhouse, or a hope chest. Maybe a gift for his girlfriend, Abigail.

I head back into the kitchen.

Mason acted like a normal person yesterday, but he also acted a little funny. When I asked why he started working out, he gave me that sheepish grin—the one he always made before getting into the cookie jar as a child—and ran up to his room. Overall, it's been a positive change. Especially his appetite. I should make a late lunch and ask him to come downstairs.

But before he comes down, I've got to bag up William's computer and get it out of here. If Mason sees it, he'll be hurt I didn't give it to him.

I unfold the garbage bag and shake it until the opening appears.

The old man told me to be careful. To pack everything perfectly.

Mason's feet sound on the stairs.

I don't have time.

I step into the hall just as he reaches the bottom. Like last week, he's got his backpack on, and he's wearing one of William's shirts. The chocolatey aroma of William's cologne fills the hallway. "Where are you—"

"What's that for?" he asks.

"Nothing." I wad up the garbage bag. "What's your backpack for?"

He steps to the side, and I counter.

"Can I get by?" he asks.

"Where are you going?" He tries to duck under, and I block him. I smile. "What's the rush?"

He steps back, pulls his earbuds from his pocket, and inserts them. The last time he took off like this, I lost it. I chased him into the street and left the griddle on. "Why don't you come into the sitting room with me and have some lunch? I'll make whatever you want."

He taps on his phone, and his earbuds buzz. "I'm going for a walk. I'll be back later."

"What do you need your backpack for?"

He glances at the garbage bag and puts his hand on my shoulder. "Mom. Really. I have to go." Then he pushes me out of his way and steps into the kitchen.

"Stop. Don't you dare push me."

"What the hell?" he yells, pointing at the box. "You said you'd let me have his stuff."

I force the smile back on my face. "I didn't say you could *have* it. I said—"

"You said you weren't going to pack it up." He opens the pantry door and grabs a box of granola bars, his earbuds blaring.

I raise my voice. "No, I didn't. I said you could—you can

have his tools. Let me show you. In the garage." It's everything I can do to keep smiling. "Please, let me show you."

"Whatever." He shoves the granola bars into his bag, grabs another box, and then pushes his way past me into the hall.

He pushes me hard.

One of his earbuds falls out, and he keeps going.

I can't let him leave. It's not safe out there. The old man's threat rings in my ears.

The hallway turns red. "Mason Kaine. You stop, or—"

"Or what?" he yells.

"Or you're grounded."

He doesn't stop.

I march toward him. "Stop!"

He flings open the front door and turns around. "Remember the rule? You can't ground me unless Dad agrees?"

I wince, and my breath escapes me. I close my eyes.

Red clouds fill my head.

Damn my condition.

Breathe.

His voice jabs at me. "Dad isn't here anymore, so you can't ground me."

I force my eyes open. "If you walk out that door, so help me—"

"Dad isn't here, and you're getting rid of him, piece by piece. You keep putting his stuff in the garage, you—you bitch!" He pivots in the doorway.

I clutch my chest.

Breathe.

The sun hits his face, he squints, and bounds down the

steps.

I chase after him, stopping at the threshold, bracing myself in the doorframe, leaning forward, heaving for air, watching him sprint away. I tell myself to let him go. The old man wants William's computer, not Mason.

He runs onto the sidewalk and disappears around the corner behind the neighbor's bushes.

I close my eyes and see William running from the Audi.

Breathe. This too shall pass.

It does not pass.

I count to ten.

You're overreacting. The cars don't matter. The old man is all that matters.

I try counting seahorses, but they turn into cars, each one chasing Mason.

Barum, barum, barum.

I open my eyes.

A black Ford Mustang barrels down the street, heading in Mason's direction.

CHAPTER THIRTY-ONE

RYAN

Ryan spent all morning on his computer, preparing to meet with Steve's coordinator, Luis Gabaldon, head of the non-profit company promoting net neutrality.

He read five articles on *net neutrality*.

He's ready.

Ryan grips the armrest of Steve's Hyundai as they race through downtown Seattle.

"Hold on." Steve spins the wheel and accelerates into an alley, cruising between the beige cinder-block buildings. Splotches of teal paint show through cracks. The city has ignored this section of town for decades. Hazy factory windows dot the upper floors above the crooked loading bays, and the doors bear insignias of graffiti artists going back to the sixties.

Ryan remembers seeking out such places, looking for dark corners where the police would let him sleep. These buildings aren't the sky-high, charcoal glassed towers where he imagined his first computer job would be, but it's a start.

"We're leasing space on the end," Steve says, slowing

down. "We're on a budget."

The backside of an auto body shop has angled parking on the right, but there's only one spot left. Steve doesn't take it. Instead, he pulls over to the left and parks next to a set of concrete steps leading up to a metal door.

"That's interesting," Ryan says. "All the cars at that body shop are black." The back door to the shop reads TED'S AUTO BODY.

"I think they're fleet cars."

"But they're all different kinds. If a company had a fleet, wouldn't they all be the same? All Fords, or Hondas?"

Steve gets out and points. "The one on the end isn't black."

The green car on the end is dented and faded, while the other cars are new and well taken care of. The green car must belong to the owner or something.

"Come on." Steve opens the door for Ryan. "Mr. Gabaldon is waiting."

Windows carved in the cinder-blocks next to the door face the alley, and it doesn't look like anyone is inside.

"Don't worry," Steve says. "You're going to do fine. Luis doesn't bite."

The inside is not what Ryan expected. The hallway has fresh carpeting and clean, light blue walls. He thought it would be like the warehouse from work—concrete and dust. Steve leads Ryan down the hall into a workroom containing several fold-out tables, each with two computers, two folding chairs, and not much else. Makeshift desks done on the cheap. It makes sense for a non-profit.

The volunteers don't seem to be here.

Ryan's palms begin to sweat.

"This way," Steve says. "Luis is in the back."

"Where is everyone?"

"They're at an event over in Issaquah. Luis wanted everyone to go and make a big show of it."

A cheap wooden desk sits outside an office door bearing the sign, MANAGER, and a massive man in a black suit, white shirt, and black tie sits behind the desk, hammering away on a keyboard, staring at a screen. The man is bald, and his head bears an orange birthmark in the shape of Russia. It makes Ryan think of eighties TV—Mikhail Gorbachev squaring off with Reagan.

"Luis, this is Ryan, the programmer I told you about."

Luis rises and extends his hand. "Luis Gabaldon. Pleasure to meet you."

"Ryan Kaine. Nice to meet you, too." The man's hand is as gigantic as his presence.

Gabaldon sits. "How was the drive over?"

"Fine," Steve says. "No issues."

"Excellent. So, what has Steve told you about the DFF?"

"He said you need volunteers to help—"

"We do. We do. We need a lot of help. We've got to stop these corporate bastards from destroying the internet."

"Right," Steve says, his eyes sparkling like he's in a cult.

"What do you know about net neutrality, Ryan?"

It's go time. "Well, I know large corporations have been battling the FCC in court for a long time, claiming they have the right to limit the speed and quality of service rather than making it the same for everyone. They're wrong, and you're right." He points at Luis. "We need to stop those bastards."

Luis grins, leans back, looks at Steve. "I like this guy."

"I told you," Steve says.

"What does DFF stand for?" Ryan asks.

"Steve should have told you."

Steve smiles and raises his hands, miming, *my bad*.

"DFF stands for Digital Freedom Fighters." Luis glances at the door to the manager's office. "My brother started the organization about ten years ago, but then he let it fall flat on its face, the bum. I've taken over, and we're just getting going again."

"Luis is smarter than his brother," Steve says. "He's got a lot more business sense."

The place smells like glue, not like a craft store, but like the stuff on packing tape. One makeshift desk has a stack of DFF pamphlets, but the walls are barren.

"Tell me, Ryan," Luis leans forward, "what do you do for work?"

"I'm a—I *was* a delivery truck driver, but I build websites on the side."

"You *were* a driver?"

"Yes. They let me go on Monday because of budget cutbacks."

"Do you mind if I ask the name of the company? Was it a big one?"

"No. It was SPD Delivery. They're a small outfit. Special deliveries and courier services."

"I'm sure their online presence suffered at the hands of the bigger delivery companies. You wouldn't know it, but all the big players are paying off the cable and cell phone businesses to get their ads displayed fast and first. It's a crime."

"That's what I've read."

"It's going to be okay, though, because we're on it. We're going to make the internet a fair playing ground for everyone, bit by bit." He leans back, waits. "Get it? Bit by bit? Computers?"

Ryan smiles and nods.

Steve's hair gleams in the fluorescent lighting. "That's a good one, sir."

"And," Luis continues, "we're going to do more than that. Right, Steve?"

"You bet."

"After we've helped the small companies, we're going to help the little people, like you." His eyes gleam as he waits for a response.

Steve says nothing.

Ryan breaks the awkward silence. "That sounds good. I—"

"Steve says you're great with computers. That's why you're here, right? To work—I mean, volunteer. Help us with our websites?"

Here comes the hard part. Luis is about to ask the technical questions. This is where Ryan always bombs. Whether it's his nerves or inexperience, he doesn't know. "Yes, I'd love to help out, but"—he averts his eyes—"I don't have any real-world experience."

Luis laughs. "Spoiler alert; there is no such thing as the real world. Only the internet. Everything is virtual now."

"Another good one," Steve says, laughing.

"I wasn't joking."

"Sorry."

Luis folds his arms. His cufflinks match his suit and tie, pristine black sapphires surrounded by silver. "Don't worry about your lack of experience, Ryan. I'm sure we can work something out. I never turn down free help."

"About that. I'm happy to volunteer, but I'm short on money right now. Would it be possible to get paid at some point?"

"That depends on how quickly you can learn."

Steve leans forward. "Luis. This is the guy I told you about. *The* guy."

"Just a second." Luis types something on his keyboard and hits the enter key. He sits back, reads, raises his hands. "How is it the brother of the great William Kaine doesn't have real-world experience building websites?"

"How did you—why are you asking about my brother?"

Steve puts his hand on Ryan's shoulder. "I told him your situation. I thought it would help."

"But, you said you wouldn't. . ." Steve violated the AA cardinal-rule of meetings: Who you see here, what you hear here, when you leave here, let it stay here. Steve heard all about the restraining order, the homelessness, the guilt and shame. Everything. Then he told Luis.

"Is there a problem?" Luis asks.

"No," Ryan says. "No problem. My brother *is* very talented, but we have a rule. We don't talk shop."

Steve's phone buzzes and he looks at the screen.

Ryan shoots Steve a look. "But you probably already knew that, didn't you?"

"Steve? Are you paying attention?" Luis asks.

"Sorry. What was that?"

"Could you give us some time to talk privately?"

"Sure, I've got to take care of this anyway." Steve stands, makes his way around the tables with his face buried in his phone.

Luis leans forward and whispers, "How would you like to make fifty-thousand dollars in a single week?"

CHAPTER THIRTY-TWO

LAUREN

Barum, barum, barum.

The Mustang's tinted windows hide the driver as he barrels past my house. I'm standing on the front steps in my robe and nightgown, shaking. Bracing myself against the door jamb. The driveway is red. The lawn—overgrown and covered in leaves—is red.

The whole damn neighborhood is red.

Mason lied. He's not going for a short walk. He crammed two boxes of granola bars into his backpack and ran away.

I surge down the steps, dodging the slick leaves.

"Mason!"

My foot lands sideways on the driveway and my slipper flies off. I stumble and go down face-first onto the lawn. The grass is wet. I lift my head. Green blades poke up through patches of orange leaves. It's like the gardeners found out William died and stopped coming.

I take off my other slipper and charge around the neighbor's bushes.

The Mustang sits at the end of our street, waiting at the

stop sign.

Barefoot, I sprint down the sidewalk, filled with rage.

The Mustang's brake lights turn off, and it makes a left turn, disappearing around the corner.

I pound my feet against the pavement.

That car is after my son.

I reach the corner, catch my breath, and focus my rage.

The Mustang is a block away at the next stop sign.

I wave my hands and yell, "Wait, you bastard!"

Farther down, Mason has stopped running. He's casually strolling across the street just two blocks away.

Barum, barum, barum.

"Wait!"

The Mustang pulls into the intersection, and the sound of its engine . . . this is no coincidence. This is the car from TriamSys. The license plate starts with IHJ. The driver was spying on me from the coffee cart, and now he's back in my neighborhood, spying on *us.*

The pavement stings my feet. My robe flies open, exposing my nightgown.

The Mustang slows down behind Mason.

"Mason, run," I yell.

He saunters up to the next intersection, unaware of the Mustang.

Unaware of my screaming.

He's got those damned earbuds in his head.

"Mason!"

He's on the sidewalk. The driver would have to jump the curb to hit him.

I sprint.

The Mustang creeps up behind him.

I'm gaining ground.

No one's taking my son. Not again. No one's going to chase Mason into a river—take him "swimming" like the old man threatened.

The world is red, but I'm focusing my rage.

Mason crosses the street.

The Mustang pulls up to the intersection and stops.

I leave the road, hurdle the sidewalk, and land in the middle of a fairy village. Someone with too much time on their hands has decorated their lawn with ceramic wizards, goblins, dwarfs, and gnomes. A little fence leads the way to a miniature castle, and a tiny sign reads, NONE SHALL PASS.

I grab a gnome. The one with the pointiest hat.

The Mustang's brake lights turn off.

I run after it.

Barum, barum, barum.

I hurl the gnome and it shatters against the back window.

The car's tires screech to a stop and the taillights come on. Bright red.

I reach the back bumper, gasping for air. Everything is bright red.

Ceramic bits tumble down the back window. It's so tinted, I can't see the driver.

The taillights turn off, and the engine revs.

"No, you son-of-a-bitch. You're not going anywhere."

I run up to the driver's side window.

He begins to pull away.

I bang on the glass, but it's no use.

The Mustang takes off, turns the corner, and escapes west down 45th Street, leaving in the opposite direction of Mason.

I did it.

I scared him away.

Out of breath, I lean forward, put my hands on my knees.

A crimson halo suffocates my vision. The tips of my toes turn red with blood. Gnome pieces are scattered everywhere.

The man in the black leather jacket is gone.

I feel some release, and it feels good, but Mason shouldn't have run away from me. He should have listened, and the road is still red.

A block away, he watches as I fasten my robe and brush my hair back. "Mason. You stay right there."

That sheepish little grin crosses his face. It comes and goes in a flash.

He takes an earbud out. "What?"

"Wait right there."

"Jesus Christ, Mom. Put on some clothes." He turns and walks away.

I chase after him. He can't do this to me. Lugging his backpack down the street like he's taking a trip.

My toes scream, and I'm angry I have to run to catch up.

I grasp his shoulder and spin him around. "Don't you ever—"

"You're a psycho." He pushes my arm away.

I want to hit him, and I want to hug him.

The crimson lens through which I see the world darkens, and—no. I can't let myself suffer a red-out. I need to be here.

"I forgive you," I scream.

"You're a psycho!" He shoves me in the shoulder.

I reach for him.

"Get the hell away from me, freak." He pushes my hand away.

"Did you see that car?" I say, leaning, pointing, gasping.

"Leave me alone." He turns and runs.

My eyes close involuntarily.

I can't . . .

I can't do this.

By the time I open my eyes, Mason is gone.

There is no release. Only remorse.

The sun beats down on me.

I should have warned him about the black cars—the old man's phone calls, the Fonz—but there was no time. No reason to worry him. Not until now. If only I'd told him why I packed up William's computer, then he might have stayed home. I need to get to my car and go after him before the Mustang comes back, and—

My head spins.

There's no connection between the Mustang and the old man.

The old man.

Shit. It's after two.

He'll be at Denny Park, waiting for William's computer. I have to be there by four.

I dart into the street and pick up the largest shard of gnome I can find and stow it in my robe.

Today, when I see the old man, I'll get my release.

CHAPTER THIRTY-THREE

MASON

Mason steps behind a car parked along the street. He runs his fingers through his hair and straightens his dad's shirt—burnt chocolate. His dad's cologne smells sweet and rugged, but he put on too much. His earbuds threaten to fall out, so he stuffs them into his pocket.

School hasn't let out, but it's about to.

Mason peers around the car.

Trent leans on the fender of his Mustang in the high school parking lot, his jacket zipper sparkling in the sunlight. He stands with his legs crossed and his flawless black hair gleaming. The weather couldn't be better.

Chest out, back straight—Mason emerges and strides across the street.

Trent waves to him.

The cool October air is invigorating.

Mason has everything he needs in his backpack. He brought a blanket, manga, two boxes of granola bars, and clothes for tomorrow. He's ready.

"You're early," Mason says, holding up his phone. In one

minute, the bell will ring, and everyone will come outside.

"Hey," Trent says, "so are you."

"Yeah. I ducked out of science when they weren't looking." Mason rushes to the passenger door and opens it. "Where are we going?" He slides onto the leather seat. The dashboard is clean like someone just wiped it down, and the new car smell overtakes his cologne.

Trent opens the driver's door. The sun catches his silver zipper, blinding Mason for an instant. "I thought we'd go to the park if that's okay."

"Which park?" Mason glances at the school. "Never mind, it doesn't matter. Let's just go."

"You look great, by the way." He starts the car. "I thought we'd go to the one on the other side of I-90 and sit on the beach."

Mason buckles his seatbelt. "Yeah, sure. Let's go."

"Are you okay?"

"Yeah, I just want to get out of here before anyone comes."

"Right." He reverses out of the parking spot.

Mason puts his hand on the dash and looks at the school. "Your shiner looks better."

Mason doesn't take his eyes off the doors. "My what?"

"The bruise. On your forehead. It's barely noticeable."

Mason touches his face.

Trent pulls onto the street. Hits the gas. "I wouldn't worry about getting in a fight with those guys again. Now that you're out, they'll leave you alone."

"I hope so."

"That's how it was for me. Coming out and being proud about it took all the fun out of it for them."

"I don't know. Hunter is pretty stupid. He might not

stop."

"He will."

They come to a light.

"So," Trent says, "I saw you walking to school right before we met."

"Oh."

"But you said you ducked out of class."

"I'm sorry." Prickly sensations sting Mason's neck. "I wasn't in school today. I didn't go because—"

"I understand. Hunter and the others."

"Yeah. That's why."

Mason watches the apartment buildings stream by as they cruise along Island Crest Way. The apartments sit perched in the hills overlooking the water, surrounded by pine trees, and they have tall, spotless windows tucked inside pristine walls. It'd be great to live in one of those. If they're this nice on the outside, the insides must be magnificent.

"Sorry I didn't pick you up when I saw you, but there was this woman in a bathrobe. She came out of nowhere and threw something at my car."

"She did?" Mason shakes his head. "Oh, God."

"Do you know her?"

"I'm glad you didn't stop. That was my mom. She didn't know I was going on a date. She would have freaked if she saw me get in your car."

"Does she always throw things at people? I wasn't doing anything wrong."

"No. She has mental problems."

"That's too bad."

"Could we talk about something else?"

"Sure."

They approach the I-90 overpass.

Mason can't think of what to say. His mom—half-naked and screaming—throwing something at Trent. Unbelievable. She really has lost her mind. Psycho. He can't go back there.

They stop at the light.

Trent glances at Mason and raises an eyebrow. "What's on your mind?"

Trent's lips are on his mind. It will start with a kiss, and soon, maybe tonight, they'll move in together. Mason's ready.

"Are you okay?" Trent asks. "You seem distracted."

"I'm fine. How did your meeting with the coach go?"

"He wasn't there. I'm going back tomorrow. Hey, I hope the park is okay. Have you been to this one before?"

"Not for a long time. My dad used to take me here."

"To go swimming?"

"No. I never learned how."

"I love beaches. Did your dad swim when you went there?"

"No. He didn't know how either."

"What did you do?"

"We mostly walked around. He read books and I played."

"I saw some trails on the park's website. I want to go running there sometime." The light changes, and he cruises onto the overpass. "Is your dad a runner?"

"No. He doesn't exercise much." Mason sniffs. "He spent all his time working."

"Spent? Is he retired?"

"No. I mean 'spends.'" Mason turns his head away, focuses on the apartments in the distance.

Trent puts his hand on Mason's thigh. "Hey, I brought some beer. It's in the back." Mason's heart races. "I thought we'd sit on the beach and talk. Get to know each other." Trent puts his hand back on the steering wheel.

Beer? Mason never imagined his first time getting drunk would be with beer. His parents—mostly the dragon—always forbade alcohol in the house. Mason always thought his first drink would be a wine cooler, or one of those spritzer things in the movies. "That sounds good."

Trent drives off the overpass, and they cruise into Luther Burbank Park. The trees stand tall, and the bushes are thick. The road narrows and winds.

"What does your dad do?" Trent asks.

"Computer stuff for some big company. He built websites, I think. I don't know."

"Are you guys close?"

"No, not anymore. He—he's never around."

"I thought those web guys worked from home a lot."

"He does, but once his office door is closed, it's like he's not there."

"That's too bad. Doesn't he ever show you what he works on?"

"No, not really."

The road bends to the left, and Trent turns the wheel at the last moment, causing Mason to press up against the door.

"Sorry," Trent says. "I didn't see that one coming." He slows down as they enter the parking lot.

"What else does your dad do?"

"Why are you so interested in my dad?"

Trent sucks in his cheeks. "There's a spot." He pulls into an empty parking space and turns toward Mason. His lips look ready. "I didn't know your dad worked on websites. I've done some stuff with the internet, and—it's just something we have in common." He puts his hand on Mason's thigh, higher this time. Their eyes meet. "I'd like to meet him someday, but right now, I'd rather get to know you."

CHAPTER THIRTY-FOUR

RYAN

Ryan stares at the birthmark on Luis Gabaldon's forehead. It's so pronounced. It's the U.S.S.R.

The empty workroom in the Digital Freedom Fighters office feels emptier without Steve. Ryan glances at the hallway, and a door shuts. Steve must have gone outside to take his call, and Luis must be out of his mind, offering Ryan fifty thousand dollars for one week's work.

Fifty thousand dollars? In one week? For "volunteering?"

"What do you mean?" Ryan asks.

"You're in a unique position," Luis says. "You see, the DFF almost went under because of my brother. He took the wrong approach, wasting money on lobbyists and protest rallies. I'm not like him. My aim is to get deep into the technology. Fight the big guys—Big Tech—on their own turf. The internet. I've researched all the best internet security businesses, and you're key to our mission."

"I am?"

"You and your brother." He rubs his forehead. "I hope it's not a problem, Steve telling me about William. You see,

TriamSys is *the* major player in internet security. I could really use your help."

"I'm not sure what I can do. My brother and I—"

"I'll cut to the chase. You can do the world a huge favor by asking your brother to give us the algorithms he's been working on."

"Algorithms?"

"Yes, I think so." He furrows his brow. "Algorithms might not be the right word. It might be code, or diagrams, or—whatever. I just need you to get his technology for me."

"I can't—"

"Don't you hate all the targeted ads on the web?"

"I—"

"They're not fair to the little guys. Whenever you search for something like 'outdoor bar-b-que,' ads for bar-b-ques suddenly appear everywhere you go. The little bar-b-que guys don't get their ads displayed that way. They don't have a chance. Do you think that's fair?"

"No, I don't, but—"

"With your brother's technology, the DFF can stop it from happening. Big Tech will have to listen to us if we take their ads away."

"Why don't you ask William for it yourself?"

"I did." He looks around. "We did. We tried, but his company is in Big Tech's back pocket. Your brother is a pawn. Think about it. He's a slave to corporate America. You'd be setting him free. Don't you want to set him free?"

"No. William isn't anyone's slave."

Luis lifts his chin. "Okay. I hear you. Let's not waste any more time. Can I trust you, Ryan?"

"Yes."

He grasps Ryan's wrist. "Are you a stand-up guy?" He

glances toward the hall. "Are you an honest man?"

"Yes." Ryan pulls away, but Luis won't let go.

"Don't tell anyone—not even Steve—but if you help me, your first paycheck will be for fifty thousand dollars."

He's serious. Fifty thousand dollars.

Ryan looks toward the hall to see if Steve has returned.

Luis lets go of his wrist.

He scans the empty workroom.

No one came in while they were talking, and there doesn't appear to be any security cameras. The door to the manager's office behind Luis has been closed this entire time.

Fifty thousand dollars.

"Did you hear me?" Luis asks.

"Yes. But . . . I'm not sure what to say. That's a lot of money, but I—"

"And it's easy money."

"You don't understand. When I told you my brother and I don't talk shop, I should have said we don't talk at all. I haven't spoken to him in years."

"I know. Steve told me, and it doesn't matter. I don't care, I just need you to get those algorithms or whatever. I'd do it myself, but the DFF can't draw any more attention. We need to stay anonymous."

"It sounds like stealing."

"No, no. That's the point. You're his brother. You have a reason to be close to him. No one will suspect you."

Ryan stands. "No."

"Wait. That came out wrong." He rises abruptly, sending his office chair backward into the wall. "Please. I'm sure we can work something out."

"I'm not interested."

"I'm not asking you to do anything wrong." He waves his

hand. "Sit down, let me explain."

"I should be going."

"No. Please. Sit. You have nothing to lose by listening, and if we work something out, you'll be fifty thousand richer by the end of next week. I promise."

Rent is due on Friday.

Shit.

Ryan sits. The flimsy plastic chair is hard, and Luis's cheap wooden desk suddenly seems out of place. So does his tie, his suit, and his cufflinks.

Luis sits. "What are we talking here?" He puts his hands out. "What do you want?"

All Ryan wanted was a job. A little money and a lot of experience. "I don't think I can get William's technology." Ryan's throat tightens. "I'm sure it's confidential and—wait. How do you even know it's my brother's technology? TriamSys is a big company."

"I trust you, Ryan," he smiles, "and I'll tell you as long you keep it to yourself. My hope is you'll trust me, too. Do you think that's possible?"

Ryan nods. "Anything's possible."

"One of our volunteers worked at TriamSys. A few months ago, he clued us in on your brother's project, but you're right. It's extremely confidential. They fired our volunteer for asking a few questions, and when he protested, they threatened to kill him."

Nothing about this feels right. Ryan shakes his head, thinking it through.

"If you don't believe me, you can ask your brother. Ask him what happened to Robert Lang."

"This is too much." Ryan stands. "I can't get involved in this."

"You already are. Look, your brother didn't threaten Robert. I'm sure he wants to do the right thing, but he can't. He's too close. If you get his technology for me, you can save him and reap the rewards. It's a win-win for you."

"I'm sorry."

Luis heaves his body up off the chair. Plants his hands on the desk. His bald head turns red. "One *hundred* thousand dollars."

Ryan takes a step back. "No. I told you, my brother and I don't talk. I can't help you."

Luis rolls his shoulders forward, and the desk shakes. "I don't care if you talk, I only care about the technology—one hundred *fifty* thousand dollars."

"No."

Luis straightens his back and puffs his chest out. "I can only offer one hundred fifty thousand. Take it or leave it."

$150,000.

That kind of money would change everything. No more cold nights wishing the heater worked right. No more threat of eviction. No more—

No more sobriety. It's dishonest. It stinks to high heaven. Ryan would have to manipulate, lie, cheat, and steal. All the things he used to do to get booze. All the things that led into that cave of guilt and despair.

Guilt leads to drinking, and drinking leads to death.

"I won't do it."

Luis raises both hands, then slams them on the desk. "Yes, you will!"

Ryan takes another step back. "No, I won't. Leave my brother alone."

Steve strides into the workroom from the hallway. "Everything okay?"

Ryan says nothing as he passes Steve on his way out of the workroom.

"You're making a big mistake," Luis yells.

Ryan marches down the hall. The nerve of that man, that so-called leader of the DFF, asking him to betray his brother. To steal.

"Hey, " Steve says. "Wait."

Ryan charges past the windows. The strange black cars at Ted's Auto Body look ominous. Out of place, like everything else here.

"Hold up."

Ryan bursts through the door, strides past Steve's Hyundai, and turns. There's a mini-mart at the end of the alley, across the main thoroughfare.

On sale. Six-packs for $5.99.

"What happened in there?" Steve asks.

Ryan walks toward the mini-mart, avoiding the sewer grates. He's got fifteen dollars in his pocket. "I didn't get the job."

Steve catches him, grabs his arm. "Really? You're kidding. I'm shocked."

Their eyes meet.

Ryan can usually tell when an alcoholic is lying. He's spent years dealing with dishonest drunks, yet when it comes to Steve, something is off.

Ryan pulls his arm away.

"Where are you going?" Steve asks. "Don't you want a ride?"

"No."

"You're not going to drink over this, are you?"

Ryan stops. Gazes at the mini-mart. "No. Far from it. I'm going to do some service work." He puts his hands in his pockets. He's got his keys, and he's got Juan's keys. "I'm going to find my sponsee and see if he's okay."

"I'm sorry it didn't work out. Let me talk to Luis."

"Don't bother," Ryan calls out as he walks across the street. "I don't want what he has to offer. It's not worth it."

CHAPTER THIRTY-FIVE

MASON

Mason sits in the passenger seat of Trent's Mustang wondering if he should get out first. They're the only ones in the parking lot. This late in the fall, no one else is visiting the park, especially on a weekday. Hope fills Mason's heart. The chances they will make out are greater with no one around.

Trent gets out and spreads his arms. He tilts his head to the side, making his neck crack. His black leather jacket kinks in all the right places.

"Is it okay if I leave my backpack in the car?" Mason asks.

"Sure. It'll be safe here." Trent pops the trunk and retrieves a duffel bag. "Which way?"

"Over here." Mason walks toward an opening in the split rail fence that borders the lot.

Trent joins him, and they stroll down the path toward the beach. Mason remembers the trees being taller when his father used to bring him here, but that was only because he was smaller. An urge to hold Trent's hand strikes him, and he resists. Trent is not his father.

Mason slows down.

Trent walks onto the sand, and his boots sink. Lake Washington ripples near the shore where he drops the duffel bag. "Is here good?"

"Yeah, sure."

Trent sits on the water's edge.

Mason has his nicest jeans on—his only nice jeans. Scuffed from the fight yesterday, but still his nicest. "Do you have a blanket or something?"

Trent unzips the bag. "No. I didn't think of that." He plunks a six-pack of beer onto the sand.

Bud Light. Cans.

Garrett would have rolled his eyes and refused to sit down without a blanket and a bottle of wine.

"I have a blanket in my backpack."

"You do? Why?"

"Never mind." Mason sits next to Trent, facing the water. Not too close to him and not too far away.

"Here." Trent hands him a beer.

"You know I'm not old enough to drink."

"That's okay." He raises an eyebrow. "Wait. You're not going to tell anyone I contributed to the delinquency of a minor, are you?"

"No. I—"

"Just kidding. Here." Trent takes the can back, opens it, and foam runs down the side. It drips onto his jeans, and he lets it soak in.

The beer stings Mason's tongue. The bitterness offends his taste buds, and he swallows to get rid of the flavor, but that just makes his throat burn. He smiles at Trent and raises the can, but his eyes begin to water.

Trent grins and puts his beer to his lips. His Adam's apple moves up and down between his sculpted neck muscles like a man rowing a boat. He finishes it off, crushes the can—"A-h-h."

Mason takes another drink, tries to chug it the way Trent did, and gags.

"Easy there," Trent says.

Mason wipes his mouth.

Trent gazes out over the water. "It's beautiful. You're so lucky to have grown up here."

"It's usually raining."

"I would have spent all my time here if I'd grown up on Mercer. Too bad your dad didn't bring you more often."

The lake does look nice today.

"Where did you grow up?" Mason asks.

"A small town in Kansas. There's hardly any water there, just dust. We had a beach, but not like this. There was no swimming. That's why I got into running."

"It shows," Mason says. "I mean, you look good."

"Thanks." He touches Mason's chin. "You're not so bad yourself."

Mason's face heats up, and his jeans tighten over his crotch. He shifts his weight and crosses his legs.

"Sorry," Trent says, leaning back, planting his hands in the sand. "I didn't mean to embarrass you. But it's obvious you work out. Right?" He looks at Mason's arms. "Yeah, you must."

"A little." Mason takes a drink. "We have a gym in our basement. I lift weights sometimes." A speedboat races across Lake Washington, making waves, and Mason can see every detail—the captain's hair in the wind, the silver racing stripe, the whitewater fantail. Vivid. Brilliant. He holds up the beer can and focuses on a single droplet of condensation before taking another drink. It's almost empty.

Trent opens another can and downs half of it in three glugs. He belches. "You want another one?"

"Sure."

"Do you run?" Trent asks.

"Not much, but I'm planning to do more."

"That's great. Maybe we can go together sometime." He takes a drink. "It would be nice to have a running partner again. My dad set the state record in the one-hundred-yard dash when he was in high school, but, you know, it's not that big a deal because, well . . . *Kansas*."

"What do you mean?"

"Kansas is small. Setting that record was like winning a race in the Special Olympics. Just kind of . . . *special*."

Mason feigns a laugh. "Is he still in Kansas?"

"No. He passed away five years ago."

"Oh. I—"

"No. It's okay. We knew it was coming. He had a rare blood cancer." Trent opens a third beer. "But I miss him."

"I miss my dad, too."

"What?"

The floodgates open.

Mason can't keep up the facade.

It's out now—his dad is dead.

He's dizzy, and his eyes scrunch shut on their own. He drops the beer on his pants and covers his face.

"Hey, what's wrong?"

Mason stands. Turns away. "He's gone. My dad. He— there was an accident."

Trent puts his arms around Mason from behind and pulls him close.

Mason sniffs, sucks in as much air as he can, and wipes his nose before turning. Before burying his face in Trent's chest. He puts his hands on Trent's shoulders and grips the leather.

He sobs.

Trent holds him tight. "When was the accident?"

"A week ago."

"That's not long." His arms are iron-strong. "I didn't know."

Mason lifts his head and searches Trent's eyes—his roasted, nut-brown eyes. He mashes his lips against Trent's, and Trent pushes him away. "Whoa, there, kiddo. Not so fast."

The look on Trent's face sends shock waves.

Mason clambers up the beach, stumbling with each step, desperate to get away.

"Wait, Mason. Let me get the stuff."

Mason's ankles twist awkwardly in the sand, and his stomach bubbles up into his throat, and he's never coming back to this park.

"Mason. Stop. I'm sorry." Trent throws the beer in the bag.

Mason's heart bangs against his sternum. He reaches the ground formation and bends over. Taking that chance—it wasn't worth it. Trent didn't kiss him back. It wasn't like in the movie *Alex Strangelove* at all. It tasted like beer.

He wants to throw up.

"Wait," Trent runs toward him. "You caught me by surprise, that's all."

Mason takes off down the path, sprinting through the trees. It's all over now. He won't be moving in with Trent. He'll have to go back home. Back to the angry psycho. The dragon. Dammit. He should have told Trent his father died from the beginning.

Why doesn't Trent like him?

He reaches the parking lot.

His backpack is locked inside the car.

It's over.

Trent's footsteps come up from behind. "Mason? Are you okay?"

"I just want to go. Can we just go?"

"Sure." He unlocks the doors.

The inside of the car is clean, cold, and black, just like the outside. Just like Trent's jacket. Just like Trent.

Mason avoids eye contact but steals a glance here and there as they cruise down Island Crest Way.

"Do you want me to drop you off at school?"

"No. I—can you take me home?"

"Okay." Trent continues past the turn for school. "I'm really sorry about what happened."

"You probably think I'm a monsutā."

"A monster?" Trent asks.

Mason lifts his head. "You know what a monsutā is?"

"Of course. I don't know Japanese, but I used to read manga a lot. Like I said, there wasn't much to do in Kansas."

Mason is about to tell him to turn left at the next light, but he puts on the left turn signal before Mason can say the words.

They stop.

"Where do you live?" Mason asks.

"Over in Issaquah. I'm sharing a place with a guy from Craigslist. It's okay."

Mason thinks back to their conversation in the elementary school parking lot. They talked about Mason coming out and the fight with Hunter. Mason didn't tell Trent where he lived. He's sure of it, yet Trent makes a right turn onto Mason's street like he's been there before.

"I could show it to you sometime," Trent says. "If you'd want to come over."

"I don't know." His stomach clenches, and he hides a burp.

Trent stops directly in front of Mason's house. The dragon's SUV isn't here unless she parked in the garage. She's either inside making him something to eat, or out yelling at someone. Either way, when Mason gets inside, he's heading straight for his room.

For his manga.

"Again, Mason. I'm sorry about what happened."

"It's okay."

But it's not okay. It's embarrassing. Trent is *sorry about what happened*, but really, he is sorry Mason kissed him. He's sorry he ever asked Mason out.

This is not the way things were supposed to be.

Trent puts his hand on Mason's shoulder. "Do you think we can get together again sometime?"

"I don't know. I suppose." Mason's hand trembles as he reaches for the door handle. "I've got to get inside before my mom comes home."

"Okay. I'll text you. I promise."

CHAPTER THIRTY-SIX

LAUREN

The high school parking lot is empty. I check the bookstore. I go back to the high school. He's gone. I circle through the neighborhood, and my time runs out. William's computer sits in a box on the passenger seat. In my haste to find Mason, I forgot to put the box in a black garbage bag like the old man demanded.

He'll just have to take what he gets.

Accelerating down Island Crest Way toward I-90, I'm still reeling from how Mason treated me. He called me a psycho and took off running to God-knows-where. He had his backpack and William's shirt on, and—why didn't I think of it before? He must have gone to that girl's house. Abigail's.

As usual, the traffic over the bridge into Seattle takes twice as long as it should. After entering downtown, I circle Denny Park twice, but the only space left is dangerously close to a fire hydrant. The last thing I need is a ticket.

But it's almost four o'clock.

There's no time to find another spot.

I grab the box and march across 9th Avenue. The

dumpster is on the other side of the park, past the public square, next to the administration building. I hate the old man for making me do this. I hate his beard, his sunglasses—his sandpaper on glass voice.

I hope he's here somewhere.

The ceramic gnome shard in my front pocket jabs my thigh with every step I take.

It feels good, like a release.

Two technology workers wearing blue badges sit at a yellow table, and two policemen stand over a homeless man on the other side of the square.

A cable flops out of William's box and drags on the ground. I hide behind the nearest maple, put the box down, and peer around the corner while stuffing the cable back in. The homeless man sits on the grass beneath a sycamore next to a dirty tan blanket with an "H" on it. He waves his hands at the cops, talking wildly. His filthy sweatshirt appears to have once been orange and blue, and the horse's head on the front may have once been white. It reminds me of the black Mustang's grille ornament.

I can't put the box in the dumpster. Not with the police there.

But it's almost four o'clock.

One cop takes the man's blanket, and the other motions for him to stand. He has facial hair, but he's not the old man.

My phone buzzes. It's a text from RESTRICTED.

"I told you to put everything in a black garbage bag."

He's here.

The techies at the table are talking. A couple walks down the path toward Dexter Avenue. The old man is nowhere to be seen. The way to the dumpster is clear except for the police and Mr. Tan Blanket.

I text back, "I didn't have time to bag it up."

"it's four. leave the box in the dumpster."

"I can't. There's police here."

"leave it now."

"no."

A separate text from a strange, six-digit number appears. I tap on the notification, and it doesn't open. I tap it again, and my phone freezes.

"You can't do this," Mr. Tan Blanket says. "I have rights." He grabs his blanket from the officer and looks directly at me like he's spotted Bigfoot.

I duck back and look at my phone. The hourglass spins, then an ad listing the best deals on outdoor bar-b-ques pops up. I swipe it away, and a call from RESTRICTED comes in.

"Hello?"

"Mason is wearing a very nice shirt today." The old man's voice crackles. "What's the occasion?"

"Where are you?"

"Don't worry about me. It's Mason you should be worried about.

"Where is he?"

"He's safe. He's on Mercer Island where you left him."

"I don't believe you."

"I've been watching him, and you're not going to believe what he's been doing."

"If you're there now, how did you know I didn't bring a garbage bag?"

"Technology is a wonderful thing. I have cameras. Now, leave the box and go."

"If you can see me, you can see the police."

"I'm on a schedule. Put the—" He hacks and coughs like he's dying. "Put the box in the dumpster now. Don't worry about the police. They won't dig it out."

"No, they'll arrest me for using the park's dumpster. You can wait."

He coughs more, and I feel like he's doing it on purpose. The loud, gravel-crushing noise hurts my ears.

Mr. Tan Blanket raises a fist, feigns a punch, and runs. The police chase him into the trees, away from the dumpster.

"Mrs. Kaine, leave the box now. Don't make me take Mason. Not after the wonderful afternoon he's had."

"Leave him alone." I pin the phone against my ear with my shoulder and pick up the box. "I'm leaving it now."

"You know, I saw you drive by the school earlier, looking for your son, but he wasn't there, was he?"

"Shut up."

"Don't you want to know where he went? What he's been doing?"

I stride past the techies, ignoring their looks. "Go to hell."

"It's so good, I've just got to tell you. He went to the park, the one with a beach. He had quite the afternoon."

"I don't care."

"You should care." His voice buzzes. "You're his mother, aren't you? Don't you want to know?"

"Fine, tell me."

"Not until you leave the box."

"Asshole." The phone slides off my shoulder and hits the ground.

I quicken my step.

The police catch Mr. Tan Blanket and drag him to the ground.

The dumpster smells like a neglected porta-a-potty.

I lower the box into the bin and race back to my phone. The screen is cracked, but the call is still active. "There. I left it. Now leave us alone."

"It doesn't work that way. If I don't find what I'm looking for, I'll be back in touch."

"Where are you?" I say, gritting my teeth.

"If I don't find the card, I'm going to take Mason back to that beach." He coughs into the phone. "I'm going to take him *swimming* if you know what I mean."

I march down the path toward my car. Thankfully, the police and Mr. Tan Blanket are on the other side of the park. "I don't know where the goddamned card is. Leave us alone, or I'll—"

"You'll what?"

The red comes.

I stop walking.

Close my eyes.

The anger wants in, but I can't afford to let it win. Not now. I pinch my lip, but—it can't be stopped. "I'm going to hunt you down. I'm going to find out who killed my husband, and if it's you, I'm going to find your family, and one by—"

"Ha. That's rich."

I let go of my lip and dig my nails into my palms and open my eyes. The trees waver in a red sea. The wind blows. My breath escapes, flies out of my mouth like a tornado, and I—

Breathe.

"Lauren? Are you still there?"

I tell myself to forgive the old man.

Forgive him.

The red fades.

I stride down the path, conflicted.

The shard jabs my thigh.

At the street, a traffic cop puts a parking ticket on my car. It's not parked that close to the fire hydrant, but—trembling, resisting every urge to attack—I hang back.

I forgive her.

She's only doing her job.

"Mrs. Kaine? You still there?"

"Yes."

"Don't you want to know what Mason was doing this afternoon?"

"No."

"You sound so angry. It's not good for you. Maybe you should sit down for this."

"No."

"Have it your way." He clears his throat. "Mason had a wonderful time sitting on the beach with his lover. Kissing and groping. I think they might be having sex. I hope he has some condoms."

"Shut up, you filthy—"

"I'm not the filthy one. Tell me, did you even know he was seeing someone?"

I wait for the cop to put the ticket on my windshield. "Yes. I know all about her." The old man's laughter makes my phone shake. "What's so funny?"

"You don't know your son at all, do you?"

"Yes, I do."

"What's his lover's name?"

"Abigail."

"Oh, no. Definitely not. Adam, or Anthony, maybe. Perhaps, Andrew, but definitely not Abigail."

"What are you saying?"

"I'm saying your son is gay. He spent the afternoon kissing and groping a man on the beach. An older man." He howls with laughter. "You really don't know him at all, do you?"

CHAPTER THIRTY-SEVEN

LAUREN

I wait, and I listen.

Mason hasn't made a noise yet this morning, but it's still early. The sun just came up, casting a light across the foot of my bed. I might have to wait until noon to see him, but that's okay. We need to talk about his love life.

He told me her name was Abigail. Not Adam. Not Anthony.

Abigail.

I slept in my own room last night for the first time since William died. Every other night, I've gone to the sitting room sofa to sleep, but last night was different.

After what the old man told me, everything is different.

Mason isn't who I thought he was.

I tried to talk to him when I got home from the park yesterday, but he refused.

Now, I lie here in bed, and I wait.

And I listen for his door.

Maybe Mason *is* the same. Maybe the old man was lying to me, trying to further manipulate me somehow. I've struggled to connect with Mason for a long time, but he wouldn't have kept something like this from me, would he?

Did William know?

If Mason is homosexual, William would have known. Mason would have told his father. But if so, William would have told me. We didn't have secrets.

They want the card. It's in St. Croix.

My heart drops.

We did have secrets.

There's only one way to know if Mason likes men. Accelerate the inevitable. Rip it off like a bandage. Confront him.

Mason's bedroom door opens, and I race into the hall. "Mason. We need to talk."

"No." He puts his earbuds in and heads for the stairs.

"Where are you going?"

"Out." He speeds down the stairs, out of sight.

I lean over the railing.

The hall below flashes red.

It's not worth chasing after him. Not after yesterday's episode. I can't believe I threw a lawn ornament at that car.

The front door slams shut. He's gone, but he wasn't wearing his father's shirt, and he didn't have his backpack. Still, it doesn't mean he's not meeting someone. Some *man*.

The door to his room is cracked open.

I nudge the knob and peer inside.

His bookshelf is covered with Doritos. The bag lies on the floor, surrounded by broken chips. I shouldn't invade his privacy, but I can't stop myself. His smelly workout clothes burn my nostrils. His comic books are strewn everywhere. I should have come in here sooner. If he is gay, he's not the stereotypically neat gay.

His dragon poster is crooked, and it's not a black or green dragon. It's a rainbow dragon. He chose one whose scales run the LGBTQ gambit from pink to purple. I've seen the parades on TV.

He doesn't have any posters of girls.

I should have known.

His obsession with Japanese culture ... is that a gay thing? I never thought so, and I still don't, but I'm not sure.

I pick up a comic book, and the first page I turn to shows a man's head buried between another man's legs.

Ten Count, Volume 2.

I had no idea these books were X-rated.

One character says to the other, "Why are you hard, Shirotani?"

"Am I, really?" says the other.

I look back at the dragon poster.

He always tells me I don't understand.

When he was in sixth grade, I screamed at his teacher, insisting Mason was straight, but she wouldn't listen. She let the other kids call him gay. At some point, she told me to open my mind, and I stormed out. I remember standing alone, seething. Blinded by rage.

I've been blind all these years.

What else has my anger kept me from seeing?

I assumed the condoms were for a girl. Oh, God. I was so sure he was seeing a *girl.* All the times I've teased him about having a girlfriend pop into my head and stab my heart.

The flames flowing from the dragon's nostrils are bright red. The dragon's eyes are soulless, and I remember a conversation with William. An argument, really. Mason had referred to me as a dragon, and I took it as a compliment. Dragons are strong and fierce. They have conviction. But then, William pointed out that dragons are scary.

I understand now.

Mason is afraid of me.

Whenever the rage comes, I swoop down on his village and burn everything in sight.

Everyone is afraid of me. Olivia.

Everyone.

It's not fair. I never wanted to hurt Mason.

From now on, I'm logging into HeatSinkers every day. I will meditate. Every day. Mason will tell me he's gay when he is ready. I'm not going to force it.

I scuttle down the stairs to the sitting room.

Until I get better, Mason will stay afraid of me. He won't talk to me or he would have by now. But he needs someone to talk to. A family member.

An uncle.

Ryan.

My mind flares at the thought of Ryan Kaine, but there's no one else.

I sit on the sofa and open my laptop.

An offer for low financing on a new Audi pops up, and I imagine the old man's rasping laughter. Somewhere, he's still laughing at me. When he doesn't find anything on William's computer, he'll come for me. And Mason.

My mind flares red again—the old man, smoking, driving the Audi, chasing William over the edge. Was it him?

I grip the laptop, and it begins to shake.

Breathe.

Think.

Who drove the Audi?

The old man?

The man in the leather jacket?

Someone else? Someone from TriamSys. Robert Lang?

Is the old man Robert Lang?

It could have been anyone.

I don't know anything.

The borders of the ad flash red. The screen quakes. I can't relax my grip.

Breathe.

Peace will never come until I forgive Ryan and find out who was driving the black Audi.

I tear one hand away and close the financing offer.

Another ad pops up.

Damn the internet.

I grip the screen.

The laptop feels like it's about to explode. I must let go of it. I must forgive these companies, and let go of it.

The cursor shakes.

To get away from the ad, I open a new tab and search for flights to St. Croix. The options are expensive, but money doesn't matter. Time is my problem. It takes a full day to travel from Seattle to St. Croix. By the time I got to our condo, I'd have to come back for the funeral.

Patience.

Peace.

Forgiveness.

I load LinkedIn. Ryan hasn't responded. I cringe at the message I sent him.

William is dead. It should have been you.

Fortunately, the rest wasn't so horrible. The service is at Columbia Funeral Home on Sunday at two p.m. I hope Ryan can come, but a part of me—a big part—still wishes he were dead.

Stop it.

I wish the service was tonight so I could go to St. Croix tomorrow.

I wish I knew whether Ryan was coming or not. He's had plenty of time to respond.

Maybe he's dead.

No. Stop it. This yearning for him to be lying in a gutter somewhere has haunted me for far too long. I'll never find forgiveness if I keep wishing him dead, but when I think of what he did to Mason . . .

Hating him is a part of me.

I lay back on the sofa and close my eyes.

Let it go. Rewire yourself.

Ryan is alive and well, and he'll be at the funeral. He'll explain how he finally stopped drinking, and I will forgive him.

I will forgive him.

I'll do it for Mason. I'll do it for myself.

Ryan is alive and well, and I'm happy for him.

I'm happy for him.

I'm happy—

CHAPTER THIRTY-EIGHT

RYAN

The first key he tries doesn't fit in the lock. Ryan tries another without looking, and it doesn't fit either. He's bleary-eyed and tired, but he hasn't given up. He will get his Java program to work tonight or die trying. What a life. Another fun-filled Friday night.

He tries the next key only to realize he's using the wrong set. These are Juan's.

It's been a long week.

Ryan sent out twenty-two job applications yesterday—a few for programming, some for driving, and the rest for anything and everything. He doesn't want to think about it. Prep cook. Dishwasher. Hotel maid.

Anything.

He rests his head against the cold apartment door and searches his pockets for his keys. He wants to get inside and go to bed, but he needs to get his code to compile. He's tired of thinking about getting a job, but—who's he kidding? He couldn't even get a job working for free at the DFF. They didn't even want him to volunteer. They didn't want him.

They wanted his brother.

He sticks the key in the deadbolt, turns it, and the door pops open.

"Hey, Ryan. Before you go inside." Carl comes trundling down the hall, hands raised. The indentation on his worn-out T-shirt marks the spot where a doctor cut the cord forty years ago and welcomed a landlord with a double chin and a giant neck-freckle into the world. Carl's earrings would distract from the freckle if they weren't the same color, and Ryan can't help thinking how Carl always shows up at the worst possible time. Like rain on the weekend.

"What it is, Carl?"

"You got any exciting plans for the weekend?"

"Every day is the weekend for me," Ryan mutters.

"What?"

"Nothing." He steps inside his apartment. "What do you want, Carl?"

"I'm going up to visit my parents tomorrow. They're getting older."

"That's great. I don't have any plans."

"Is something wrong?"

Everything is wrong. "No, I'm just tired."

"I haven't seen you around much this week. Were you sick?"

"No, just taking some time off. I'm working on getting a better job. Did you want something?"

"No," he averts his eyes. "Have a good weekend."

"You too."

Ryan's apartment greets him with a cool blast of air. It's not refreshing.

"Hey, Ryan, wait. There is something. Did you see the letter?"

"The rent increase?"

He nods.

"Yeah, I saw it."

"Sorry about that. It wasn't my decision. The owners, you know, they have to keep up with market prices."

"I know. Don't kill the messenger, right?"

"So . . . " He lowers his head. Drags his sneaker across the carpet. "The increase begins at the end of the lease and, since yours is up, I was wondering when you were going to pay. If I could get the money by tomorrow—"

"Goodnight, Carl."

"Just let me know."

Ryan closes the door.

He throws both sets of keys on the counter next to the rent notice.

What a horrible week. He made it without drinking, but only barely. Sure, he went to a meeting every day, but he didn't do everything he could have done to stay sober. The guilt weighs on him like a backpack filled with bricks. Instead of searching for Juan, he searched for a job.

The rent notice haunts him daily. Time has run out.

He picks the letter up and—why this week? The new amount is so ridiculous, he doesn't know whether to laugh or cry.

He'll never be able to afford it.

But that's not true.

He could have $150,000 by next week.

All he has to do is steal from his brother, and he could have any place in the city, but he'd relapse for sure. The guilt would push him over the edge. His load of bricks is already too much.

It's not an option.

He sits at his desk, turns on his computer, and wraps his reindeer blanket around his shoulders.

On LinkedIn, he's a delivery truck driver with computer skills. On all the other job sites, he's anything and everything. He's desperate. The end date of his position with SPD Delivery shows CURRENT as if he didn't lose his job. He still can't believe Ed fired him, but no one needs to know that, do they? He could update the end date to last Monday and add a fake computer programming job.

But that would be dishonest.

He rubs his forehead.

Inventing a fake job—that's totally dishonest.

Leaving SPD Delivery as his current position—somewhat dishonest.

Like guilt, dishonesty fuels the craving. It leads to drinking.

It's so frustrating.

It seems like everything leads to drinking.

Ryan closes Firefox and opens his code editor. The last Java compilation error stares him in the face, but he hasn't given up. Inspiration, followed by an exhilarating moment of clarity, presents him with a solution. He types frantically.

It works.

His code compiles.

He sits back in his chair, suddenly energized. He could do this all night. He could make some real progress. Updating his profile with a job at a fake computer company would feel less like a lie.

His phone buzzes.

Juan is calling.

Finally.

Ryan hesitates.

He called Juan every day this week, and the big man never answered.

He stands. Paces.

The phone vibrates in his hand.

His Java program finally worked, and he could move onto the next tutorial. It's taken him days to get this far. Juan couldn't have worse timing.

"Hey, Juan. I've been trying to reach you. How are you?"

"I'm sorry, man. I'm so sorry. I don't know what I was thinking. I—"

"It's okay. How much have you had to drink today?"

"I'm losing my shit, man." He breathes into the phone. "I tried calling sooner, but it, I—I'm sober."

"Right now?"

"Yeah. I swear, man. I haven't had a drink all day."

"But—"

"I'm sorry, man. I'm so sorry. I'm a waste. I tried calling, but—it's like you said. I got drunk and started losing everything. My girl. My job. My car. I found my phone in my sock."

"Where are you?"

"I don't have anywhere to stay. Denny's, man. I woke up at Denny's this morning, the one we went to. Remember that?"

"Yeah." Ryan can't forget it. He should have done more to stop Juan. Six days. All it took was six days for Juan to go from driving an eighty-thousand-dollar Audi to groveling for help.

"When was that? Last week?" Juan doesn't sound sober.

"Yes."

"I can't remember anything, man. You gotta help me. My girl won't talk to me. I drunk-dialed her, and I called her a cunt."

"Okay. Let's start with—"

"My job is gone too. So is the car. Remember that car? It was sweet."

"Yes. It was nice."

"I sobered up on Tuesday, I think. I went to get the car, but I couldn't get inside. I lost the keys, man, and I—the car was at the Squire, so I went inside, and—"

"You drank."

"The next day, the car was gone, and so was my job."

Ryan glances at the counter. The keys. The rent increase.

"I lost my job because I lost the car because I lost the keys—*Dios*, man. I lost a car. A whole car."

"Did you tell your boss?"

"No. I never went back." A door slams in the background. "I gotta find another job, man. She won't take me back without one."

"Don't worry about getting a job. Money isn't as important as staying sober."

"You're smart. That's why I called you, man. You gotta help me. I don't have anywhere to go."

Ryan sits at his desk, clicks the RUN button on his computer screen, and watches the program execute. It works. He could do so much more if he had time.

Money isn't as important as staying sober.

"Let's meet tomorrow, Juan. How about the Starbucks near my place at ten?"

"I need help tonight, man. Come on, it's Friday. You know what that's like. Friday night is alright by me." He sings. He slurs. "Come on, man. I'm not going to make it."

"Don't go out. Go to a meeting. There's a good one on Capitol Hill at eight."

- "I been there already today. I been to three meetings. They're not working."

"It works if you—"

"Work it. I know, man. I'm trying." A car goes by in the background.

"Did you raise your hand at any of these meetings? Admit you relapsed?"

"No."

"You've got to go back to step one."

"I'm trying. You're still my sponsor, right?"

"I can't have you coming here by yourself if you're drunk. You know the rules."

"I swear, I haven't had a drink all day. Come on, man. It's me, Juan."

"You'll need to have someone come with you. Have you called anyone else?"

"No."

Ryan leans back, gazes at the computer screen. COMPILE SUCCESSFUL. "What about Joe? Or Mike?"

"Garage Mike? No way. My phone is dying, man. Could you call someone for me?"

"It would be better if you did."

"You know what?" Juan says. "I don't think I need to. I'm feeling better."

No one should ever twelve-step an alcoholic alone if they've been drinking. It's too dangerous, but Ryan lost Juan last week, and if he lets him go now, there's no telling what might happen. "Are you sure?"

"Yeah. We can talk *mañana*. I'll meet you. Was it Starbucks?"

"Are you sure? Are you absolutely sure you haven't been drinking, and you're not going to drink tonight?"

"*Sí. Está bien.* I'll see you tomorrow."

Ryan hits the power button on his monitor. "No. Let's talk now. You can come over by yourself, but only for an hour. I've got work to do." He heads to the kitchen. Listens to Juan's breathing. Hears a car drive by in the background. "You still there?"

"Yeah, man. *Gracias.* I'm on my way."

Ryan pours water into the coffee maker and retrieves two cups from the cabinet. It's not that late. He can work on his code until Juan comes, then do what he should have done the second he was fired—help other alcoholics. Helping his sponsee will lighten his load of bricks.

Then, he can pull an all-nighter.

Bang, bang, bang.

That was too fast.

"Hey man, you there?" Juan's voice booms. He bangs on the door again. "Come on, I'm dying out here. I need your help, man. Let me in."

CHAPTER THIRTY-NINE

"Let's be clear," Ryan says, evaluating Juan's posture in the hall, "we have one hour to talk, then you need to go so I can get some work done."

He holds the door to his apartment open, waiting for Juan to respond. The hulking man fills the doorway. His jittery eyes can't seem to focus. Grass stains mar his denim shirt sleeves, and a silver button is missing. His leather vest—the one with the skulls and daggers to match his boots—binds his bloated gut, and his hands shake as if tormented by an evil spirit. "I won't stay long, man. I'm sorry."

Ryan motions toward the couch. "Have a seat."

A stinging rotten wood odor follows Juan into the room, and he plunks down. Sweat beads congregate on his forehead despite the cold air.

Ryan pours two cups of coffee. "It's probably best you drink this black. Sugar's not good for you right now."

"I'm sorry, man. I let you down." He takes the coffee. His hand shakes so bad, half the cup spills before he can get it onto the table. The ceramic bangs against the wood.

Ryan grabs a towel from the kitchen. "Do you know why you're shaking?"

"DTs?"

"Yeah. Not quite." He wipes the table and puts his own cup down.

"I'm sorry, man."

"Don't be. The shakes mean you must have stopped drinking for at least a little while today. That's something."

"But I lied to you." He averts his eyes. "I was drinking downstairs when we were talking on the phone. *Dios*. I don't know what to—I can't stop. If I don't drink again, soon, I'm going to die."

Ryan pulls a kitchen chair over to the coffee table and sits down. He wraps his arms around the back and leans his chin over. "You feel like you're going to die because you've been literally killing your nervous system." He picks up his coffee and takes a drink.

Juan clasps his hands together and squeezes until his fingers turn red. Then purple.

"When you drink all day every day," Ryan continues, "your nerves don't just get numb, they begin to die. Whenever you stop drinking, your nerves wake up and go haywire, trying to live. That's why you can't stop shaking."

"I'm going to die."

"Or worse. You're going to live, but you won't want to. It's not just your nerves that go dead. It's your brain too."

He wipes his nose. "So, I'll be like a vegetable?"

"Not quite. Worse."

"You're smart."

"Only because I stopped drinking before it was too late. If you keep on like this, you'll get wetbrain. You won't be able to remember anything. You won't be able to talk. You won't be able to walk. You'll shuffle down the street, slurring your words. And you won't even be drunk, Juan. You'll be *permanently* drunk without the high. It's worse than death."

"Oh, man." He shakes his head. "I think I have it. I can't remember shit."

"I'm not surprised." Ryan sips his coffee.

"I'm losing my memory. I'm losing everything. I lost a car. A whole car."

"I know. You said that on the phone."

"And my job. I lost my job."

"You said that, too."

"I'm sorry, man. Wetbrain. That's some scary shit." He sucks in a deep breath. "I lost my girl, too. I might as well lose my mind."

"No. You can't drink over her. Listen, I lost my job this week, but I didn't give up. I wanted to. I wanted to crawl inside a bottle and die"—sitting on the patio outside an elegant restaurant, sipping on a Gin and Tonic, taking in the sun—"but I didn't."

"You lost your job, man? Where? At the casino?" He wipes away a smirk. "I'm sorry, man. It's not funny. You got fired?"

"Yes."

"Weren't you there for like—forever? Ten years?"

"Not that many."

"And they fired you? That's wrong, man." He glances at his trembling hands. "I deserved to get fired. I lost a car. A whole car." He looks up. "What did you do?"

"It doesn't matter." Ryan finishes his coffee and stands up.

"Tuesday, man. I didn't drink Tuesday. Not much." He cradles his cup and takes a sip.

Ryan heads to the kitchen.

"I could have kept my job if I hadn't lost those car keys."

Ryan pulls the rent notice over Juan's keys.

Juan's head lolls to the side. "I think I have the wetbrain, man. Everything is a blur. When I couldn't get in the car, I gave up and started drinking. Calling my girl and drinking, and—night and day—it's a blur. The week disappeared. I woke up in a booth at Denny's this morning, man, but it was like I didn't sleep. I was in a daze sitting there. *Dios*. It's wetbrain." He puts his cup down on the table hard. It bangs. It spills. "I need help, man."

"Where have you been staying?"

He glances at the window. "It's cold in here."

"I know."

"I've been sleeping outside. Different places."

"You know what you have to do, right?"

"I know." He shifts his weight, and the couch moves with him. He drones. "I have to go to a meeting and raise my hand. Admit I have a problem."

"That's true, but it's not what I was going to say. You have to have hope."

"That's easy for you, you're—"

"It's never easy for any of us." Ryan strides toward the drunken giant. "I wanted to drink this week, but because of AA, I found enough hope to carry me through the cravings, and guess what? Not only did I stay sober, everything got better. I was offered one hundred and—" Ryan closes his eyes and pinches the bridge of his nose. "By staying sober, I got a chance to volunteer at this place doing my dream job. Computers."

The puffy bags beneath Juan's eyes swell. "I got nothing, man. No hope." He looks around. "No place to stay."

"I'm sorry, Juan. You can't stay here."

The couch slides back when Juan stands. His cheeks shake like his arms. "I got nothing."

"My place is too small, and—"

"I got nothing." He raises his hands, palms up. "I got no reason to live. I—"

"Wait."

"*Está bien*. I'm leaving."

If drunk driving doesn't kill Juan, then his liver will, or his pancreas, or he'll kill himself. "Do you still have the rock I gave you?"

Juan turns toward the door. The veins in the backs of his hands throb.

"Juan, stop," Ryan pleads.

"You want your rock back?" He spins around. His leather vest flies open, and he pulls the rock out of his shirt pocket.

Ryan holds out his hand.

Juan slams the rock into Ryan's palm. "Take it, *pandejo*. It's not worth nothing."

Ryan rubs the rough side with his thumb.

"You got it made, man." Juan's eyes go wild. "This place. That computer. You're rich."

Ryan gazes at his monitor. Getting that code to compile took forever. It was rough, but he did it. But how long will it take for him to learn the rest? Days? Months?

Years?

How long can Juan go on drinking before it kills him? Days? Hours?

Minutes?

"I'll never be sober like you, man." Juan steps back. Grasps the couch back. Steadies himself.

Ryan flips the rock over. He rubs the smooth side.

One hundred fifty thousand dollars.

Luis Gabaldon at the DFF will give Ryan $150,000. Next week.

Next week.

Juan says, "I gotta go, man."

"Wait. You can stay. Let me get you a blanket."

"Really?"

"Yes. Here, take this back." He hands the rock to Juan. "I only wanted to know if you still had it."

Juan pockets the rock. "*Gracias.*"

Ryan pulls his lucky blanket off the desk chair. It will always remind him of Christmas in Britain. It will always smell like the liquor-soaked streets of Seattle.

He hands it to Juan.

"*Navidad?*"

"It was a Christmas present from my parents."

Juan sits on the couch and pulls the blanket up to get a better look at it. "Reindeer. Silver bells."

"Yes. Sorry, it's the best blanket I have."

"I'm not complaining."

With the money from the Digital Freedom Fighters, Ryan could buy a thousand blankets. One hundred and fifty thousand blankets. He could open an addiction counseling center.

He goes to his desk, shoves the computer books aside, and finds his *Big Book*—*the basic text for Alcoholics Anonymous.*

"Here." He hands the book to Juan. "I want you to read 'The Doctor's Opinion' before you go to sleep. And—"

"I don't know, man."

"And read it when you get up tomorrow. If you wake up in the middle of the night, read it. If you have a craving—read it."

The big man nods. Takes the book. Opens it. "*Gracias.*"

"Don't thank me. Thank AA."

"*Sí.*"

"Tomorrow morning, we'll go to a meeting, and you'll raise your hand. Got it?"

"*Sí.*" He lies back, pulls the blanket over his chest, and opens the *Big Book*.

Ryan sits down at his computer.

He hovers his thumb over the power button, but he doesn't turn it on.

"Good night, Ryan."

"Good night, Juan. See you in the morning."

CHAPTER FORTY

LAUREN

I'm standing in the upstairs hall outside Mason's room. Alone.

Again today, he awoke, dressed, and left the house before noon without talking. That's three days in a row, including Thursday, but it doesn't matter. Tomorrow his excursions stop. After the funeral, we're going to St. Croix.

I lift the suitcase onto my bed.

I don't blame him for avoiding me. With so much going on, I'm just not ready to address his sexuality. But that doesn't mean it's okay for him to disappear for hours on end.

Last night, when I asked him what he's been doing, he shrugged me off.

Nothing. Hanging out with friends.

He's lying. His friends should been in school Thursday and Friday, so he couldn't have met them in the morning. And he left again today—Saturday—so unless his friends are older and out of school . . . the chain smoker said he saw Mason with an older man.

I wonder.

Could my teenage son be having sex with an older man?

A stranger he met on the internet? Mason doesn't know how people use each other for sex. He doesn't know what goes through men's minds, but if I try to talk to him, he'll tell me I don't understand. Then he'll call me a dragon and storm off. I must wait for him to bring it up. Coming out to your mom is an important moment, and I'm not going to steal it from him the way the old man stole it from me. Laughing. Cackling. Telling me I didn't know my own son.

I open the door to the walk-in closet and realize, once again, I didn't move all of William's things into the garage. His mementos lie against the back wall where I threw them last week. Old photos, jewelry, family heirlooms, floppy disks from college with the letters "CS" scrawled on them—it hurts to see his life strewn across the floor. It hurts to see his class ring sitting on the photo of him and Ryan.

I see it every time I come in here.

I grab a swathe of blouses and shirts off the rack and take them to the bed. There's no way of knowing how much I'll need, so I throw what I have into the suitcase and head back for more.

I'm not sure why William's class ring bothers me so much. Maybe it's because it belongs with him, not in the closet. I could slip it on his finger tomorrow, but he stopped wearing it twenty-four years ago. He said it was childish.

I grab some skirts and slacks, and I pile everything into the suitcase. Shoes. Socks. Bras. Underwear. What am I missing?

My passport.

The police merely *suggested* I stay close to home when they questioned me. They never said I couldn't leave. Earlier this week, they left a message to let me know the investigation is ongoing. That's it. I wish I knew more, but I don't dare contact them. The old man said he'd kidnap Mason if I did. Or worse. I also haven't been answering the phone. William's parents called a few times, but they're the last people I want to talk to, and for all I know, the old man can listen in. We're not safe.

I'll need Mason's passport, too. It's probably buried somewhere in his room.

Back inside the walk-in closet, I check to see what I'm missing. William's class ring stares up at me like a portal into the past. The blue sapphire looks cheap, and the ring is much too large, but I put it on my finger anyway.

Without thinking, I lower my hand, and the ring tumbles to the floor.

I feel naked.

My wedding ring is at the bottom of Cedar River where it fell the night William died.

His wedding ring is in the forensics bag in his desk.

I can never wear my ring again, but he should wear his.

I need to tell him goodbye.

Tomorrow.

I'll say goodbye tomorrow and put his wedding ring back where it belongs. My in-laws weren't happy when I told them about the service. They wanted a traditional Episcopalian ceremony in the church. No open casket. But I need to see William one last time.

The tears come, and I go to the suitcase. The zipper is stuck. The air is dank. Musty. The suitcase is too full. I push on the lid, but I can't get it shut. There's a sound in the hall, and eerily, it feels like William is with me.

Behind me.

Watching me.

He's about to wrap his arms around me.

"What are you doing?"

I turn and see Mason standing in the doorway. "Nothing. I—"

"Why are you packing?"

He's back early.

"Help me with this, can you?" I grasp the suitcase zipper.

"Where are you going?"

"Do you know where your passport is?" My slacks attempt to escape the suitcase, and I shove them back inside. My face feels flush like I'm angry, but I'm not. The slacks won't stay inside the suitcase. They fall out, and I shove them back in.

Mason presses down on the lid. "It's in my room. What's going on?"

"You had it the last time you went to Connecticut. Do you remember where you put it?"

He backs away. "Mom. You're pinching your lip."

"I'm sorry." I lower my hand. He has William's eyes. William's beautiful eyes, but because of me, they're filled with fear.

I'm a dragon.

Breathe.

He's grown so much. He's a man now—a gay man. "It's okay. Everything is okay. I just got into a rush."

"If you're not going to tell me—"

"No. Wait. I didn't want to worry you. We have to go to the condo."

"Today?"

"No, tomorrow." He looks at the floor, working the news over in his head. "Okay."

"Okay?"

"Sure. Let's go."

"Really? I thought you'd be angry."

"Why?"

"Because of your friends. Isn't that where you've been going every day?"

"Sure, but—wait. Isn't the funeral tomorrow?"

"It is. We're leaving right afterward. Are you sure you're okay with this?"

"I'm great with it. I didn't want to go to school Monday anyway." He averts his eyes and puts on that sheepish grin. Cookie thief. "I'll go look for my passport."

"Sorry I didn't tell you sooner, but you've been gone a lot lately. Where have you been going?"

"Nowhere. Just hanging out with friends."

"Are you sure?"

"Yes."

"Have you been seeing someone?"

"No." He stops in the hall. "I told you. I've been hanging out with friends."

"Okay. Okay."

"Where's my suitcase?"

"It's in the coat closet downstairs."

He heads for the stairs. "How much should I pack?"

"A lot." I pull on the zipper, and it works this time. The case closes.

"When are we coming back?"

"I don't know."

CHAPTER FORTY-ONE

RYAN

Ryan chooses to park in the hardware store's upper lot, but it's a sunny Sunday afternoon, and the lot is packed with cars. There's a lower lot, but it's down a steep hill behind the building, and his Civic's transmission has seen better days.

He cruises across the front of the store, watching out for shoppers while scanning for a place to park. Lawnmowers linked by a chain sit beneath a sign reading SALES & RENTALS DOWNSTAIRS. Renting would save money, but he'd have to fill out a form. Write down his name and number.

He's not going to do that.

There's an empty spot near the back where weeds have broken through the pavement. It's a tight fit. A BMW sits over the line. He drives toward it, but a blue car comes idling down the row, heading for the same spot. Ryan hits the gas and claims the space, but ends up too close to the beamer. He crams the transmission into reverse and gazes in the rearview mirror. He must have bumped it when he got in. Instead of seeing out the rear, he sees his own eyes. When he first went to AA, it took three months—ninety meetings in ninety days—before he could look himself in the eyes.

Thank God for AA.

He adjusts the mirror, reverses, and pulls back into the spot, leaving room for the BMW driver's door to open.

Potting soil borders the store's entryway, and he waits for an elderly man in a lime green golf shirt to exit. Bar-b-que grills begin where the tethered lawnmowers end, and he wonders what it would be like to own a house with a patio. To grill steaks on a Saturday night and kick back with a few beers.

Beers.

Ha.

That's stinking thinking. That's his forgetter sneaking up on him, taunting him with the old, glamorous delusion that he can stop drinking after a couple of beers and go to bed like a normal person.

It never happens that way. Not for alcoholics.

Inside, the far corner is lit up like a solar flare. Fans and light fixtures hang from the ceiling. The center section hosts electrical cables, cords, outlets, and fuses, followed by plumbing.

Ryan spots the sign for painting supplies and heads for it, dodging the other shoppers in the tight aisles. He passes by a beefy man in white coveralls carrying two buckets on his way to the end of the paint aisle. There are three types of customers here: Golf-shirt-wearing retirees, coverall-clad workers, and determined women on a mission.

"Can I help you find something?" asks a twitchy teenager wearing a red shirt embroidered with the store logo.

Ryan takes a dust mask off the shelf. "No. I think I found it."

"Doing some painting?"

"Something like that."

"Okay, let me know if you—"

"Hey, do you have any used lawnmowers for sale?"

"I don't think so, but we rent. You can ask the guy downstairs in the repair department." He points to the other side of the store. "Just go down aisle three, turn the corner, and take the stairs. If he's not there, check out back."

"Thanks."

Ryan waits at the top of the stairs for another golf-shirt wearing old man to pass by. This one's carrying a hummingbird feeder and a pair of gardening gloves. It must be nice to have a lawn. To go outside and listen to the birds before firing up the mower. The scent of freshly cut grass. Ryan could have a lawn. He could use the money from the DFF to move out of his apartment into a house, but it's far more nobler to help other alcoholics.

If he accepts the DFF money, he'll be able to help *a lot* of other alcoholics, not just Juan.

He shakes his head.

Juan disappeared yesterday. Ryan wanted to take Juan to a meeting, but when he woke up, the couch was empty. Juan left in the middle of the night.

The drink has a strong hold on his sponsee.

For now.

Someday, Ryan will be able to give twenty Juans a place to stay, and if one out of ten sticks with the program, this will all be worth it.

The odor of engine oil hovers above the lawn equipment at the bottom of the stairs. The back door is open, and the sun shines over the lower lot. A clerk leans against the counter, reading a magazine. Three men in flannel shirts and overalls mill around the shovels along the opposite wall.

Gardening gloves hang from their belts, and dried mud clings to their boots. Green stains climb up their pant legs like ivy on a statue.

Ryan wishes he'd taken Spanish in high school so he could understand what they're saying.

One man—the older one with the tattered baseball cap and a missing tooth—has a black smear on his forehead. He's the grimiest of the three. Landscaping is a profession where appearance really doesn't matter. Ryan could get behind that.

"Excuse me," Ryan says, approaching the counter.

"How can I help you?" asks the clerk.

"I need a lawnmower."

"Sure." The clerk whips around the counter and sails down an aisle toward the back door. "We've got this riding mower over here. You looking to rent?"

The mower looks like it could cut down a redwood. "That won't fit in my car. Do you have anything smaller?"

"How big is your car?"

"It's a Civic."

"Nope. You'll need a truck."

The landscapers look at Ryan. The man with a missing tooth smiles.

"What about those?" Ryan points at the rusted mowers near the doorway.

"Those are for parts. I don't think we have what you want."

Ryan rubs his chin. He needs something. If not a mower, then—

The shortest landscaper bursts into laughter at something another said. They all laugh, look at Ryan, and head for the back door.

Ryan is wearing a T-shirt he got at an Alice in Chains

concert back in the day. He belongs here as much as they do, but maybe he looks out of place to them.

He feels out of place, and he's afraid they'll remember him.

"Is there something else I can help you with?" The clerk glances at the dust mask in Ryan's hand.

Ryan turns and strolls down the aisle. "I'm not sure."

The clerk follows.

"What are these?"

"Those are leaf blowers."

"I meant, are they for sale?"

"No. Anything with the yellow sticker is for rent. Plus," he cracks a smile, "they're horrible at cutting grass. I thought you wanted a lawnmower?"

"I did." Ryan faces away from the clerk. "But, I have leaves to blow, too. Don't you have one for sale?"

The clerk goes to the end of the aisle, moves a lawnmower aside. "I could sell you this one, but it's not very powerful. It's cordless."

"That's perfect." Ryan beats the clerk to the counter and pulls out his wallet. He has the money from his last paycheck.

His *last* paycheck.

"How much?" Ryan asks.

"What about cutting your lawn?"

"I'll find a mower somewhere else. How much?"

The clerk rings up the blower. "Are you getting that mask, too?"

"Oh, right." He puts it on the counter. "Could I also get a hat?"

"Sure. Which one?"

All the hats, no matter the color, bear the store's logo. "I don't care."

The clerk hands Ryan a white hat.

He creases the bill and pulls it over his brow.

"Anything else?"

"No. How much?"

The clerk punches in a price for the leaf blower and scans the mask. "Doing some painting, too?"

"No. It's for the—there's a lot of dust at my house."

"Dust?" The clerk glances out the window. "There's no dust on Mercer Island." His eyes move over Ryan. "Where's your house?"

"It's not far. I mean, it is. I live on the other side of the mountains. Way past Snoqualmie."

"I see."

Ryan pays, grabs the blower and mask, and leaves out the back door, keeping his head down until he's outside.

Black smoke pours out of a white, backfiring Ford F-150 loaded with rakes, shovels, and weed eaters. The driver backs the truck toward Ryan and hits the brakes when he sees him in the side view mirror. The landscapers sitting in the back of the truck stare at Ryan, and the driver waves his hand out the window.

Ryan moves out of the way. If things don't work out with the DFF, he could see becoming a landscaper. Working outside on a day like today would be nice.

He adjusts his hat and trudges up the hill toward the upper lot. The lane is narrow, bordered by the hardware store on one side and a gray fence on the other. He hopes the landscapers won't be able to describe him later, but what are the chances anyone will ask them? No one knows he came here today. He's never been here before. He didn't use a credit card, and he uninstalled the SPD Delivery app from his phone before he came.

He should have turned his GPS off entirely.

Dammit.

Why didn't he think of that?

He hasn't felt this paranoid since he was an active drunk. Since he was a scofflaw. Stealing to pay for the next round. Hiding in the bushes at night and shuffling down the alleyways during the day. But he shouldn't feel paranoid right now. He hasn't done anything wrong. No one will remember he was here. If the two clerks inside remember him, their stories won't match. One thinks Ryan bought a mask for painting, and the other thinks Ryan lives in eastern Washington.

He stops halfway up the hill and turns around. The landscapers are long gone. The fence is overgrown with weeds. He leans the leaf blower against the building, looks both ways, then goes to the fence.

As much as he hates to do this, he picks up a rock, rips a hand full of grass from the ground, and stains his pant legs. He rubs the rock over his jeans until the threads turn white, and several small holes appear.

A car comes down the hill, and he balls up on the ground. He should have waited to stain his pants until later. With his face pressed against the fence, he holds still. He lies there, pretending to sleep. Trying to look homeless.

After the car passes, he takes off his hat and rubs it in the dirt, making sure to cover the logo. Then, he takes a hand full of mud and smears it on his forehead. The breeze cools his brow.

It's time to get out of here.

The leaf blower barely fits in the trunk, but it *does* fit, and he slams the lid.

The BMW has left, and a black Mercedes has taken its

place.

He adjusts the rearview mirror to see if the dirt on his forehead looks authentic. To see if he looks like the landscapers' leader.

He does, but his eyes . . .

He looks away.

Chills plunder his core and sting his skin.

The cold nights come back to him.

Wandering the streets—drunk and dishonest.

Guilty.

So many times he'd caught his reflection when passing by store windows, and so many times he had run away, stopping only when no one could see him. Hiding beneath overpasses. Burrowing into blackberry bushes. Tunneling into the dark depths of his addiction. Shame knows no sanctuary.

Gripping the steering wheel with both hands, he closes his eyes.

He rests his head on the wheel.

He whispers, "God grant me the serenity to accept the things I cannot change, the courage to change the things I can, and the wisdom to know the difference."

William, forgive me. I must do this. I must do it for the alcoholic who still suffers.

CHAPTER FORTY-TWO

LAUREN

"Will you roll your window up?" I ask.

Mason sits in the passenger seat with his eyes closed, his earbuds in, and his head against the headrest. The cold air blasts his face, but he doesn't seem to care. If I didn't know better, I'd think he was asleep.

"Mason?"

I'm freezing, and we're late for the funeral. If he'd looked for his passport yesterday, then we would have left on time, but it didn't matter because I forgot William's wedding ring anyway. We already had to go back for it, and now we're late.

And I'm freezing.

I grab an earbud wire and jerk it out. "Will you please roll up your window? I'm freezing."

Without a word, Mason takes the earbud, puts it back in his ear, and presses the button. He watches me out of the corner of his eye while the window rises.

"Thank you," I say.

My nerves are on fire. I'm dying to get the funeral over with.

Olivia called this morning. She offered us a ride, but she didn't have time to take us to the airport afterward, so I declined. Our conversation hit a bump when I mentioned how angry I was about William's death. She's always kept her distance, but now she's further away than ever.

I'm a dragon.

The sun is shining, but it's cold outside.

William's parents called five times this morning, but I didn't answer. The invitation clearly had the address and the time. That's all they should need from me. They lost a son, but like wedding days are for the brides, funerals are for widows. I'm the widow. Besides, they're just going to blame me. The last time we spoke, Evelyn insinuated I let William die. If I could sneak into the funeral home, put the ring on William's finger, say goodbye, and slip out without being seen, I would.

The traffic light up ahead turns red. We're fifteen minutes late, and I want to run the light, but I don't. Instead, we sit.

And we wait.

Mason sits up, taps his phone. Takes out his earbuds. With a beard, he'd kind of look like his uncle. I can avoid Evelyn and Nigel, but not Ryan. He never responded to the invitation, so maybe he won't come. But if he does, I'm ready. I meditated on forgiveness all morning. When I see him, I'll make small talk, determine if he is sober, then reintroduce him to Mason.

He'd better be sober.

The shops along Ranier Avenue are closed, and the street is empty, but as we near the funeral home, I spy a black car hiding in the shade. I lean forward. At this distance, it's hard to tell if the car is a Mustang or not.

"Why are we slowing down?" Mason asks.

Trees along the avenue block my view of the funeral home, but I look for the man in the leather jacket anyway.

"Mom?"

"I'm looking to see if your uncle is here."

The black car has four doors, but it doesn't have a mustang emblem. It's a Chevy Impala. Maybe a black car coincidence.

Once we're past the car, I reach into my red Gucci handbag to make sure William's wedding ring is still there.

It is.

Looking through the trees, the parking lot is almost empty, as expected. The car closest to the front door has California plates. It's undoubtedly Nigel and Evelyn's rental car. I don't recognize the other vehicles, and I don't know what Ryan drives these days. It's unlikely his old Honda still runs.

I picture him inside the funeral home, drunk and passed out by William's casket. Anger sparks anew, and I shut it down, remembering what I must do. I must forgive him.

"You're going to miss the entrance," Mason says. "Turn."

"There's another one up ahead right before the light." I slow down. "I'm not sure your uncle came. I really wanted you to meet him."

"Yeah. Me, too."

"Really? You haven't said anything."

"He's dad's brother, right?"

"Yes."

"So, I wanted to meet him. That's all."

I pull into the lot and see a black Toyota parked next to Nigel's rental. There's an open spot on the other side, but I'm wary. Mason cocks his head as I drive past the spot and pull around the building. The parking lot is empty except for three black cars shaded by an elm tree on the far side.

All three cars have tinted windows.

"Why are you stopping here?"

A man in a black suit, white shirt, and black tie rests his jumbo hip on a car's fender, staring at a cell phone. He's bald and must stand over six feet tall. His birthmark makes his head look like a deflated basketball. I didn't invite him, and I certainly didn't invite whoever drove the other cars. One of them is an Audi. These could be William's TriamSys colleagues. They could easily have found out about the funeral by searching for it online. Maybe the big man is Robert Lang.

"Should I get out?" Mason grabs the door handle. "Are you dropping me off here or something?"

Basketball-head looks up, sees me, and pockets his phone. He walks toward us.

"No." I hit the gas and turn toward the exit.

"Where are we going?"

"I want to park on the street so we won't have any problems getting out. Our flight leaves right after the service."

"But there's all these open spots."

"Let's park in behind the funeral home." I drive onto Ranier, then turn up the side street.

I'm not staying for the funeral. After I slip William's ring on his finger, we're getting out of here.

We cruise up the hill and turn down the alley behind the funeral home. The alley has a wood fence on one side and a chain-link fence on the other. It's only wide enough for a single car, and there are no places to park.

Smoke climbs up a rusted metal pole. A man stands beneath the smoke, cigarette in hand. He's wearing sunglasses and a red cap. His beard sways in the wind.

I blink.

I'm not mistaken.

It's him.

Hate climbs up my spine, igniting every vertebra as it goes.

I hit the brakes.

Mason plants his hands on the dashboard. "What the?"

The old man smiles, takes a drag on his cigarette, and tips his cap toward me.

I throw the transmission into reverse, turn the wheel, and back out onto the side street. Basketball-head trudges up the hill behind us. Swinging arms. Hands like anchors. We make eye contact in the rearview mirror.

He stops and unbuttons his suit jacket.

Ahead, the old man saunters toward us. He must not have found what he was looking for on William's computer.

"What's going on?" Mason asks.

I hit the gas, and we lunge backward.

Basketball-head jumps out of the way and falls to the ground.

I spin the wheel, and the front tires go onto the sidewalk. The backup camera shows Basketball-head lying in a heap.

I reverse.

He gets up off the ground, shoves his jacket aside, and reaches into his waistband.

He's got a gun.

"What the hell is going on?" Mason asks, his voice shaking.

I hit the brakes, then shove the transmission into drive, and floor it down the hill.

A gunshot blasts through the air.

He fired at us—he missed—but he fired at us.

At me.

At Mason.

He tried to kill us.

Everything turns red.

I hover my foot over the brake and coast down the hill toward the intersection. That man deserves to die. He deserves to be run down, chased off a bridge, and murdered. I want to watch him drown.

"Mom!" Mason grips the dashboard with both hands.

The SUV shudders as I slam on the brakes and skid to a stop at the light.

"Who was that?" Mason yells.

Basketball-head runs down the sidewalk behind us, pauses, then turns up the street, heading toward the Chevy.

On the hill, the old man steps out of the alley. He strolls toward us like nothing is out of the ordinary.

"I don't know," I say. "No one."

An old truck filled with landscaping equipment crosses the intersection at a pace only a sloth would be proud of, and I blare my horn. The passenger turns his head and gives me the finger.

The old man stops. Pulls out his cell phone.

I blast around the corner and veer into the oncoming lane to pass the truck.

Mason glances over his shoulder.

I floor the accelerator.

Breathe.

"Who *was* that?" Mason asks. "What the hell was that?"

"I can't explain right now."

"Mom," his voice trembles, "you're pinching your lip."

"I know." I tear my eyes off the road for an instant to see if he's okay.

He quakes like a volcano about to explode. "That guy

tried to shoot us!"

"Calm down. It's okay." I'm going well over the speed limit, and it's working. There's no sign of the Chevy.

He grips the armrest.

I flip on the turn signal and wait at the next light.

My surroundings are flooded with red, but I haven't lost control.

"What are we going to do?" he asks. "Who was that guy?"

The light changes, and I take a left. "I'll explain later."

"What about the funeral?"

"We're going to the condo." I check the rearview mirror, and it's clear. "We have to get to the airport."

"No. I want to see Dad."

Red blossoms explode throughout. "We're not going to see him. We're never going to see him." I'm screaming now. I know I'm screaming, but I can't stop the wrath.

"Please." His voice trembles. "Please don't get mad."

William's ring is in my handbag, and those bastards crashed his funeral. Those assholes took the only chance I had to say goodbye and destroyed it, but I—

I've got to calm down.

Breathe. This too shall pass.

It's over.

No one is following us.

"Mom?"

"Yes, what?"

"Why was that guy chasing us?"

"Before your father fell—before the accident, he was working on something important. I don't know what, but it's not safe for us here anymore."

"Are you okay?"

I relax my shoulders.

I inhale. I Exhale.

The red recedes.

"Yes. I'm okay. Everything is going to be okay. We just need to get to St. Croix."

CHAPTER FORTY-THREE

RYAN

Ryan parks across the street from his brother's house. On his way here, passing by all the spotless, manicured lawns, he worried his plan wouldn't work, but he's in luck. William's lawn is overgrown and covered in leaves, just as it was when he attempted to deliver the package last Sunday.

Just as it was before his rent increased.

Before Ed fired him.

What a horrible week.

Ryan takes the dust mask out of the trunk, stretches the elastic band, and positions the cup over his face. He straightens his cap, then lowers the bill over his brow. He looks up and down the street. A car pulls across an intersection two blocks away. No one else is around.

All is quiet in suburbia.

He takes the leaf blower out of the trunk and loops the strap over his shoulder. When he drove by earlier, neither William nor Lauren's cars were parked in the driveway. They're still not there, but that doesn't mean no one's home. If they are, he'll be able to run before they can recognize him in this getup.

He scans the windows. The shutters. The curtains.

No movement.

He stops next to the hedge separating William's property from the neighbor's and flips the leaf blower's power switch.

Nothing happens.

He flips the switch again.

A small red light flashes then fades out.

Enough with this charade.

He carries the blower across the lawn to the cedar fence and glances back across the street. His run-down Civic looks horribly out of place in this neighborhood. He should have rented a truck from somewhere. Landscapers don't drive late-model economy cars. If this takes too long, the neighbors will wonder why his crappy car is parked in front of the Kaine's house.

He's got to hurry.

The latch to the gate is on the other side, so he leans the leaf blower against the fence and reaches over the top to open it. The splintery cedar scrapes his arm. He can't reach the latch from here, and he curses.

It feels like someone is watching him.

The garage blocks his view of the house, and he doesn't know if he's been spotted.

He tells himself no one is home.

He's got to believe no one is home.

He's got to believe he can get in, find William's technology, and get out before anyone sees him.

Carefully, he steps up on the leaf blower, reaches over the fence, and pops the latch. The gate swings open, and he runs to the patio, then presses his back against the wall and slides toward the back door. Not much has changed in the yard. The swimming pool and hot tub are still there. He remembers getting drunk, swimming, then jumping into the hot tub and passing out from the heat.

No.

That's not true.

He passed out, but it wasn't from the heat.

The awning above the sliding glass door catches the sunlight and casts a shadow into the house. He peers inside.

No one is in the dining room.

He takes out a flat head screwdriver and jams it as far as he can into the aluminum door frame. He tugs the screwdriver up toward the lock, and the metal screeches like a train hitting its brakes. He presses his back against the wall, scans the yard, and listens.

Birds chirp, and a light wind convinces a few more leaves to fall.

Again, he tugs, the metal screams, and this time, the lock disengages.

The sliding door opens with a *whoosh*, and he races down the hall, through the family room, and into William's office. He closes the door and leans his back against it.

He waits. Listens. Counts to ten and hears nothing.

No one is home or they'd be making noise.

Unless . . . unless they *are* home and didn't hear him. Lauren could be upstairs, taking an afternoon nap, dead asleep. Mason could have his music turned all the way up.

Ryan's heart bangs inside his chest.

This could have been avoided. If only he'd taken the time to spy on them. Establish their daily routines. Call ahead. He could have come when he knew for sure it was safe.

The expensive scotch William always kept on the family credenza is gone. The bookshelf looks larger than he remembers, and it's holding more books than before. Oil paintings cover the walls, and the blinds are closed.

He rushes to the window and peers between the slats. His car is still across the street. The neighbors might be calling a tow truck by now. Could they be that uppity? Or scared? Could they be calling the police as part of a neighborhood watch program?

He can't see the driveway to know if William or Lauren just arrived, but what if they were already here?

Stop thinking. Get the technology, and get out.

Where is it?

Most of the books behind his brother's desk have titles related to computer networking. A few on Java programming catch Ryan's eye, and he wants to look at them, but there's no time. He scans the shelves looking for something with the TriamSys logo—notebooks, private journals, binders of any kind.

Nothing.

In the desk drawer, he digs for a thumb drive. An SSD hard drive. Anything.

A framed photo falls to one side, and he picks it up. He holds it with both hands. It's a picture of him standing next to William after a Seahawks game.

That was one of the greatest nights of his life.

William kept this picture all these years . . .

He puts the photo back and closes the drawer.

William must have hidden the photo in the drawer so Lauren wouldn't know about it. Otherwise, she would have smashed it. She's always hated Ryan. From the moment they met in college, to the moment he made the biggest mistake of his life, she wanted William to herself. She's a hateful, jealous woman. That's why she tricked Ryan into taking Mason.

That's why she told him she needed a babysitter. That's—

He paces.

Old, stinking-thinking thoughts.

She didn't trick him. He kidnapped Mason.

His resentment is trying to fool him, trying to drive him toward paranoia and blame, and he's running out of time.

Where is the technology?

The credenza is empty, and Lauren *was* out to get him. Not William.

It was her. She schemed and plotted, and she found a way.

Ryan hates her.

The shot glasses and the wine glasses—the Glenfiddich scotch. They're all missing from the credenza. All because of her.

And if he could, right now, would he? Would he get drunk? Because of her?

No.

He goes to the painting of the Caribbean by the window. Puts his hand on the wall. St. Croix. He never got to go there with them. He could have if he'd been able to make amends.

It's all Lauren's fault. She filed the restraining order.

No.

Lauren is Mason's mother, and she had every right to protect her son. Ryan forgave her for the restraining order. *Remember? You forgave her.* And he forgave himself. It was his obsession with alcohol that made him leave Mason alone in that hotel room, not any desire to hurt Mason. Mason probably doesn't even remember it.

Yet, if Lauren hadn't pressed charges—if she hadn't convinced the court Ryan shouldn't be allowed to see his brother or his nephew or her—he could have made amends.

It's all her fault.

No.

He had a part to play.

He's lying to himself, blaming her, and if these lies continue, he'll drink. All alcoholics tell lies, but the worst lies they tell are to themselves.

I'll quit tomorrow.

I don't have a drinking problem.

No one cares about me.

It's my boss's fault. My girlfriend's fault.

My sister-in-law's *fault.*

Ryan rests his hand on the credenza. It belonged to his aunt and uncle, George and Alice. They gave it to William as a college graduation present.

Ryan never graduated from college.

He has never graduated from anything, and the scotch is gone.

He remembers sneaking into William's office—birthday parties, brunches, Christmases—and swigging the twenty-year-old whiskey. Slinking in like a feral dog, ready to defend his drinking with snapping teeth and a raised mane.

When doing his fourth step, he wrote down every time he stole from someone to get a buzz and shared the list with his sponsor. After his sponsor committed suicide, he shared it with Garage Mike. He owned his disease, and he got sober.

Mike told him, *You're only as sick as secrets, and now that you've stopped lying to yourself and others, you have a chance at staying sober.*

Being here now, like this . . . Ryan feels sick again.

The picture of his grandparent's home in Manchester is as gone as the scotch, but the Redwoods painting is still there. The full-length mirror next to the door catches his eye. He's wearing the white hat he bought at the hardware store. Dirt is smeared on his forehead. The dust mask covers his mouth and nose. He's hiding in plain sight.

He makes eye contact with himself and jerks his head away.

No amount of money is worth losing his sobriety.

He rushes out the door and leaves the way he came in, running through the house, sprinting across the back yard. He trips over the leaf blower by the gate, and a black sedan drives by before he can collect himself. He brushes a wet leaf off his shirt, and he's glad the sedan's driver can't see the shame burning behind his mask.

He picks up the leaf blower and jogs to his car.

The driver continues down the road.

He puts the key in the ignition and turns it.

The engine cranks once then starts.

The sedan turns a corner and disappears behind the neighbor's hedge.

Ryan goes the other way.

As far as anyone knows, he was never here.

No one can ever know he was here.

He's got to keep it a secret.

Then he thinks to himself, *You're only as sick as your secrets.*

CHAPTER FORTY-FOUR

LAUREN

St. Croix caresses the roof of our two-bedroom condo with a soft morning rain. I lay back in bed, listening. The air has that lemon-brackish scent I've always associated with the Caribbean, but it's milder than I remember. The dim light coming in through the bedroom window casts a hazy gloom over the off-white walls, the dresser, and William's desk.

It feels like Mason and I brought Seattle with us.

The toilet in the bathroom down the hall flushes, and I imagine William coming into the bedroom, wearing his silk pajamas.

Blue and black silk pajamas.

Mason and I battled to get here. The last two days were hell. The airline delayed our flight on Sunday until almost midnight, then the rental place didn't have a car until the afternoon. We made a quick stop at the grocery store, unpacked, and arrived at the condo completely exhausted.

Then we slept until Tuesday.

Through everything, I kept my cool. In the tense moments, I managed to move on rather than attack. The three questions proved invaluable at the airline counter, the rental car counter, and the grocery store. I really wanted sweet rum bread—a breakfast tradition—but I forgave the clerk for not having any.

I bought day-old bagels instead.

Mason has been eating but not talking. After Basketball-head shot at us, I told him about the old man. The phone calls. The threats to kidnap him if I didn't leave his father's computer in Denny Park.

When I told him about the black Audi that chased William off the bridge, I'm not sure he believed me. I asked if he'd noticed any black cars in our neighborhood, and he said no. When I described the black Ford Mustang, he just made that sheepish grin and wouldn't say anything. I didn't pry because we had just arrived in St. Croix, and I was exhausted.

I'm refreshed now, but I don't want to get out of bed. It's strange being here without William. Racing through the airport yesterday, I stopped at the duty-free shop and purchased a chain necklace. I put his wedding ring on it.

Lying here with the ring on my chest, I gently circle the gold with my finger.

The early years vacationing in St. Croix were the best years of my life. The exotic restaurants. The parades with the Moko Jumbie stilt dancers. The underwater adventures—snorkeling, scuba diving. Chasing rock beauty angelfish through the coral forests. We were alive with youthful curiosity. We met locals, like the rack-thin man who told us the best time to find seahorses was at night. He was right. We went snorkeling at midnight on our anniversary that first year, and that's when I found my spirit animal.

Perhaps, when I go back to Mercer Island, I will go snorkeling in the Cedar River and find my wedding ring, but

I strongly doubt it.

I sit up and stretch. Rub my eyes.

William's office area—a small, two-drawer desk and chair—sits in the corner of the bedroom, and I still resent it. He insisted on setting it up so he could work remotely. As the years went by, he worked more, and we adventured less. I'd always planned on selling that desk when we retired.

Now, I might sell the condo.

Or, I might live here forever, hiding out.

It all depends on whether or not I can find that card.

I put on my slippers and sit at the desk. The computer fan whirs to life when I hit the power button, and I wait for the icons to appear.

A pipe in the ceiling rattles momentarily, and the shower down the hall comes on. Mason doesn't normally take a shower unless he's going somewhere or, until lately, unless he worked out. We're here now, so he can't be going to *hang out with friends*. They're all back in Seattle.

The older man he's seeing is back in Seattle.

The icons flash on the monitor, then a blue screen appears.

Your PC ran into a problem and needs to restart.

A progress bar indicates how long before the computer will restart, but it stops at 21%.

The thing just sits there, doing nothing.

21%

I wait, count to ten, then press the power button. The computer goes through its motions rebooting, flashing the icons, and again, it stops at 21%.

I hate technology.

The top desk drawer has nothing but a sticky pad and some pens inside. The bottom drawer, however, is crammed with papers and file folders. The first folder has a book on Ethernet and corporate topologies with hundreds of diagrams. I throw the folder onto the floor and sift through the others. Our agreement to purchase the condo, insurance papers, brochures for boating adventures, coupons for buy-one-get-one-free drinks—all ancient artifacts of our life here, but nothing about TriamSys. No business letterhead, contact numbers, thumb drives . . . nothing.

Nothing that remotely resembles a "card."

I slam the drawer shut.

The computer clicks over from 21% to 22%, then restarts. Harboring the smallest amount of hope, I wait, and again, the onerous thing stops at 21%.

It's toast.

I place my hands on the desk, close my eyes, and picture the man who told us about the seahorses years ago.

I picture my spirit animal.

The ceiling pipe rattles and the shower shuts off. If Mason thinks he's going somewhere, he's mistaken. We could have been followed. So far, there hasn't been any sign of the old man or Basketball-head, but I'm not letting Mason out of my sight again.

I check the dresser. It's empty except for some summer clothes no one has worn in years. The closet has a few Hawaiian shirts, shorts, shoes—I throw everything on the floor. Search the pockets. Nothing. I look under the bed, behind the curtains, under the nightstand.

Nothing.

The sliding glass door leading out onto the concrete patio is locked. Palm fronds wave with the wind in the distance, and I wish the clouds would go away. Instead, it looks like a storm is rolling in.

The computer beeps.

I sit back down and—21%.

The blue screen turns reddish-purple. The off-white walls turn red.

Breathe. This too shall pass.

But it won't pass permanently. Not until I find the card.

There's nothing under the keyboard, so I slam it back into the sliding tray. The keys rattle, and the damn thing bounces onto the floor beneath the desk. I bend over to retrieve it, and my back hits the tray, causing me to lose my balance. I fall onto my hands and knees beneath the desk, grab the keyboard, and my neck cramps. Across the room, a black triangle sticks out of the molding near the dresser. It looks like the corner of a card.

I crawl.

The rain picks up outside, beating on the sliding glass door.

I reach for the black triangle, and—it is a card. A business card.

It's shiny and slick with white print.

TODD WAXELL
COMPUTER SECURITY SPECIALIST
SECURMONT SYSTEMS, ST. CROIX OFFICE
555-930-9203

CHAPTER FORTY-FIVE

LAUREN

The rain outside hammers the patio so loudly, I'm afraid I won't be able to hear Todd Waxell's voice. My phone has blown up with messages from William's parents, demanding to know why I wasn't at the funeral. I swipe the notifications away and press the receiver to my ear.

I pace back and forth in the bedroom, stepping over the clothes I threw out of the closet earlier.

A man with an older voice answers. "Hello?"

"Is this Todd Waxell?"

"Speaking."

"This is Lauren Kaine. My husband was—"

"William. I know. I'm so glad you called. When I learned what happened—well, I just can't believe it. How are you doing?"

"I'm okay. Listen, the reason I called is, I found your business card, and—did you work with my husband?"

"Yes, in a way. He was a great man. Again, I'm sorry for your loss."

"Thank you."

"I assume you had the service on the mainland? I would have attended if I'd known. When was it?"

"I'm sorry. It was Sunday. I—don't take this the wrong way, but William never mentioned you. How well did you know him?"

"Fairly well. He helped me get my business started. Without your William's help, I would never have gotten the thing off the ground."

"When was the last time you talked to him?"

"Earlier this year. Last spring. I proposed we work on his project together, but TriamSys wouldn't let me sign an NDA, so everything fell apart."

"I don't understand. You *wanted* to sign a non-disclosure agreement?"

"Yes. We wanted to partner with TriamSys badly." He lowers his voice. "Don't tell anyone, but your husband gave me an inkling as to the technology he was working on, and we would have signed anything to be a part of it."

"Can you tell me what it was?"

"I'm sorry, but if you don't know, I'm not sure I can— have you spoken with anyone at TriamSys?"

"No. I mean, yes, but—I don't need the details. What I need is to know where William might have kept it."

"What? The project? Or do you mean the algorithm?"

"I'm not sure—yes. Whatever. Do you know?"

He pauses. He isn't going to tell me anything because he doesn't know. The back of my neck heats up.

"I'm not sure," he says.

"The card. Do you know about the card?"

"Card?"

"Yes. Could the technology be on an index card? Do you know where—"

"No, no. The algorithm wouldn't be written on an index card. It's too large. It would be saved in a file on a hard drive. Or a flash drive."

Breathe.

"But William said it was on a *card*. It must be on a card."

"I don't know what to tell you. I suppose he could have saved it to an SD card, like the one in your phone."

He's useless. "Do you know anything else?"

"No. Sorry I can't be of more help."

"Thanks for trying."

"Listen, Mrs. Kaine. Could we get together some time? I'd love to talk more about William's technology. If he saved it somewhere outside of TriamSys, I could help you make sense of it."

"I don't think so, Mr. Waxell. I don't want to make sense of it. I want to find it. Have a nice day."

The rain outside comes down in sheets whipped by the wind. Back home, we have an umbrella for every time we got caught in an unexpected downpour, but not so here.

I put my cell phone on the bedside table and snatch a plain blue blouse, a pair of slacks, and my Louis Vuitton high-heeled sandals out of my suitcase. I didn't pack a jacket. The only thing in the closet is the safe with our emergency money. William installed it after the first hurricane knocked out the power for a week. I wonder how much he—

Wait.

There's a dark suit hiding in the back. It matches the one William wore on our last night together, and again, I picture him yelling, *They want the card. It's in St. Croix.*

Sadly, the pockets are empty.

I carry my clothes to the bathroom and knock on the door. "Are you still in there?"

The door at the end of the hall opens, and Mason steps out of his room wearing a bathing suit and holding a towel. "No."

"Have you eaten? We've got bagels."

"I'm fine." He walks into the kitchenette.

"If you don't want a bagel, we could stop at the store on the way to the park later and get something else. I thought we could go and talk after the rain stops."

"No, thanks. I'll get something to eat at the beach." He grabs the doorknob.

"You can't go out there now. It's pouring."

He opens the door, and the wind gusts, spraying the floor with water. He shakes his foot. "It's not that bad. It's kind of warm."

Storm clouds tussle over the palm forest to the south. The wind whips. It's practically a tsunami. "Just wait a couple of hours."

"No." He puts his earbuds in and glances at his phone. "I have to leave now."

"What's the rush?"

"Nothing." He squints. "It's okay. I like the rain."

"You'll freeze. Shut the door."

"No. It's warm." He steps outside and holds his hand up. Giant drops pelt him in the face, and his skin turns red. "It's not that bad."

"Stop it." I grab him by the shoulder. "I don't want you going anywhere alone. Especially in this weather."

"Alone?" He stumbles backward across the kitchenette and pushes my hand away. "You don't understand."

"What don't I understand?"

His face contorts. "Screw you." He runs for his bedroom, fuming.

"What don't I understand?"

He turns around. Puts his hand on the doorknob. "You don't understand anything. You don't want me to go *alone*?" His face drips with rage. "You don't know what it's like to be alone. You've always had Dad. I've never had anyone."

I see red. He's not the only one who's alone—William is gone.

I'm alone, and I—

He's right. He *is* alone.

My heart aches for him.

He's been hiding in the closet, alone, since puberty.

He's only human, and I'm *not* a dragon, but I have to keep him safe.

"You're right. I always had your father, but I don't have him anymore. All I have is you." My jaw tightens. "And I'm not letting you out of my sight."

CHAPTER FORTY-SIX

RYAN

Joe waves to Ryan from the parking lot across the street. The meeting at the First Light Church ended twenty minutes ago, and Ryan is just now leaving.

He waves back.

The evening sky is clear, and the air is cool. Refreshing.

Ryan always joins the guys late because he likes to hang out in the hallway downstairs and talk to newcomers. Buy them *Big Books*. Offer to sponsor them if he's up to it.

Joe and Garage Mike always stand across the street so Garage Mike can smoke without getting yelled at by Margaret.

Ryan walks up to the intersection and presses the button to cross. A Chevy Impala with tinted windows drives by, and he thinks nothing of it at first. Then, he remembers all the cars parked outside the auto body shop across from the Digital Freedom Fighters building. The Impala is all black, and it moves down the street slowly as if the driver is lost.

The walk sign lights up, and Ryan crosses over.

Garage Mike cups his hand over his face and lights a cigarette.

"Hey, Ryan, you found a job yet?" Joe asks.

Ryan hesitates. His "landscaping" career was short-lived. He still feels like a thief for breaking into his brother's house.

"When was the last time you shared in a meeting?" Garage Mike eyes Ryan up and down. Puffs on his smoke. The lines in the AA old-timer's face are deep.

"Money's not everything," Ryan says, "but yeah, I'm still looking for a job."

"You gonna be okay?" Garage Mike asks.

Ryan nods.

"Money is what killed Stan," Joe says.

"The drink killed Stan." Garage Mike exhales a smoke cloud.

"That too," Joe says. "But it wouldn't have happened if he hadn't inherited all that moolah from his parents. Once he retired, he didn't have anything to do. That's why he relapsed."

"He had plenty to do. He could have been sponsoring alcoholics and going to meetings, but he chose to take that first drink instead. He got a case of the fuck-its." Garage Mike taps his cigarette and watches the ashes fall. "Money didn't kill him. The disease did."

"No." Joe smiles like a child. "I'm pretty sure it was the rope."

Garage Mike scowls. "Death certificates never tell the truth. It's always end-stage liver disease, or pancreatic cancer, or blunt force trauma to the head—usually from falling down shit-faced on the sidewalk—and far too often, it's suicide."

"It was a rope," Joe repeats.

"Sure," Garage Mike says. "They put suicide on Stan's certificate, but the cause of death should have been *the phenomenon of craving.*"

Ryan says nothing. He's never liked talking about how is first—and last—sponsor died.

A late-model Toyota Prius with an Uber sticker in the window pulls up to the curb, and Steve gets out of the back. His button-down shirt looks ironed, and Ryan wonders how much the DFF pays him.

"Where've you been?" Garage Mike asks.

Steve glances at the Church, then at his watch. "I missed the meeting?"

"Yep."

"You missed it by an hour," Joe says. "Meetings are always an hour-long, but you didn't miss much. On Tuesdays, we read from the *Big Book* or *The Twelve Steps and Twelve Traditions*. You know, the twelve-and-twelve."

"Oh, well." Steve gives Ryan a friendly smile.

"My point," Garage Mike says, "is Ryan is right. Money isn't everything. In fact, it's nothing if you can't stay sober, and you can't stay sober unless you work on it with other alcoholics." He puts his cigarette out on the ground. "Which reminds me," he fixes his powder blues on Ryan, "I haven't seen Juan in a while."

The last time Ryan saw Juan, he lay on his couch, wrapped up in Ryan's lucky red reindeer blanket, reading the *Big Book*. That was four days ago. "I haven't seen him lately, either."

"You're his sponsor, right?"

"Yeah, but he's got to want to get sober."

"That's true, but—" Garage Mike shakes his head. "Ah, what am I telling you for. You know the best thing a sponsor can do for a sponsee is to stay sober."

"Yep," Joe agrees.

Steve puts his hand on Ryan's shoulder. "Hey, Ryan. I'm glad I caught you here. Are you still looking for a job?"

"No offense," Ryan brushes Steve's hand away, "but I'm not interested in working for your *non-profit*."

"Hear me out. We really need your help."

"I know, but—no thanks."

Joe says, "Why not, Ryan?"

"Listen," Steve continues, "Luis won't stop asking about you. I'm not sure what you told him in the interview, but he's really interested in having you work with us. There's a new opening for a driver. Weren't you a truck driver before?"

"Yeah, but—"

"He made special deliveries," Joe adds.

"This is a little different. Sometimes, you'll make special deliveries, but most of the time you'll be driving around important people. You know, contributors to the cause. Picking them up at the airport. That kind of thing. Luis owns a lot of really nice cars, and he'll let you use them anytime you want."

Ryan puts his hand in his pocket and grasps the key he took from Juan. He strokes the Audi symbol with his thumb. "Do you think Juan was working for you guys?"

Garage Mike raises his eyebrows.

"You mean, your sponsee?" Steve asks.

"Yeah. He had a job as a driver like that, but he lost it last week."

"I don't know. He might have. I don't hang around with the drivers, but I could ask Luis for you."

"Never mind. It doesn't matter." Ryan pulls his hand out of his pocket. "I'm not interested in working there."

"Why not?" Joe asks. "It sounds like it's right up your alley. Driving and all."

"It's not that, it's the place. It's just not right for me."

Joe cocks his head like a confused dog.

Garage Mike says, "Well, gents. I'm taking off. You have a goodnight and, Ryan, why don't you give Juan a call?" He steps off the curb and looks both ways.

"Sure. I'll do that."

"See ya, Mike," Joe says. "What's wrong with working for a non-profit, Ryan?"

"Yeah," Steve says. "What's wrong with it?"

"You can tell Luis no amount of money is worth what he asked me to do."

"Ha," Joe says. His eyes light up. "What did he ask you to do?"

"Joe," Steve says, "can you let me talk to Ryan alone?"

Ryan eyes Steve. "There's nothing to talk about."

"Sure, sure." Joe puts his hands in his pockets like he's cold. "Hey, I'll see you guys later."

"You don't have to go, Joe." Ryan stares at Steve.

"No, it's okay." Joe grins. "I'll let you guys talk business."

Steve waits until Joe is out of earshot, then takes a step closer to Ryan. "Tell me the truth. What did Luis ask you to do?"

Ryan tries to read him, but it's hard. He seems to genuinely not know about the $150,000 offer Luis made for William's technology. There's nothing about Steve—not his hair, his clothes, his bold attitude—that makes him seem like a charitable volunteer. He always has an air about him like he's the one running the show, but if that were true, he'd know about the money. "Why don't you ask him yourself?"

Steve smirks and cocks his head to the side like Ryan suggested he grow wings and fly to the moon.

"Never mind," Ryan turns to go. "You can tell Luis I want nothing to do with him."

Steve grabs Ryan's arm, pulls him back, and they come

face to face. "Luis isn't going to like that."

Ryan jerks away, surprised by the change in Steve's demeanor. He steps off the curb. Backs away. "Just tell him the timing isn't right."

"Wait, there's something else."

Ryan hesitates.

"Come back. I won't bite." Steve runs his fingers through his hair. Squares his shoulders.

Ryan steps onto the curb. "What is it?"

"Luis wanted me to ask if you found anything blowing leaves over on Mercer Island the other day. What did he mean by that?"

Ryan's neck tenses. The car driving by William's house when he was leaving must have seen him. "You tell Luis, I'm not interested. Got it?"

Steve casts his eyes down and shakes his head. "That's the wrong answer."

Ryan marches across the street toward the church.

Margaret comes up the basement stairs, carrying a stack of twelve-and-twelve books. She greets him with a solemn smile that says, *I know what you're going through. We're all in this together.*

He shimmies down the steps and grabs a *Big Book* off the shelf.

He resents Steve for showing up outside and coercing him to work for the DFF.

He resents Luis for spying on him.

The answer is no. Ryan will not steal from his brother.

He *accepts* that he cannot change Luis's desire for William's technology.

But what does he have the *courage* to change?

Ryan opens the *Big Book* to "Working with Others."

He has the courage to change Juan's life—maybe save him—if he can find him.

But does he have the courage to violate the restraining order and make amends to his brother?

With Luis spying on him, and Steve coercing him, he's got no choice.

He must warn William.

He must find the courage to make amends.

CHAPTER FORTY-SEVEN

MASON

Mason slams the door to his bedroom as hard as he can. It feels good. The doors in the condo are cheap, and the noise reverberates off the walls in a most satisfying way.

He feels strong.

His mother doesn't understand, and she never will. On the way here, she told him a lame story about his father. About how much Mason reminds her of his dad when he wears his dad's shirts, and how he is the man of the house now.

But she treats him like a five-year-old.

He wipes the rainwater from his face and presses his back against the door, listening. Is she coming after him? Is she serious about not letting him out of her sight? Why come to St. Croix if he's grounded the whole time?

He's a man now. He has needs. He's not a five-year-old. He's been eating more and working out, and he looks good. Too good to stay inside.

He slings his towel onto the bed and drops to the floor.

One. Two. Three . . .

He pumps out twenty push-ups and stands. He grips the

backs of his arms. Blood pulses through his body, and he's an impenetrable wall, but his stomach grumbles. A bagel sounds good, but there's no way he's going out there while she's still there.

Dragon.

She's so concerned about the rain, saying he'll freeze. It's as if she thinks the rain will make him melt, but she's the one who would melt. She's the witch, locking him up inside her castle. She's probably afraid those guys from the funeral are out there, but she won't say it. All that stuff about an old man—she never tells the truth. No one has followed them. They're safe.

The second the rain stops, he's leaving. She can't keep him prisoner without a good reason. If she insists on blaming the weather, then he'll go somewhere indoors. A bar or a club. She can't keep him locked up forever.

He goes to the window. Unlatches it. Opens it. Spreads his arms out wide. The torrential rain envelopes him. Stings his chest. The air smells fresh, not rotten like Mercer Island. The lawn extends out to the path encircling the gated condo complex. There's nothing stopping him from climbing out the window and running to the path, then to the gate.

Nothing but the rain.

He closes the window. Picks up his towel and dries off.

She'd come looking for him at the beach, but she wouldn't think of going to a club. Little kids don't go to clubs. He could find an all-ages place, or maybe St. Croix is like Europe. Maybe there's no drinking age. He could leave late tonight and come back early tomorrow morning.

She would never have to know.

He opens his suitcase, pulls out the condoms he stole, and slips two into his wallet. His bed squeaks when he sits on the edge, and he can't resist bouncing a couple times while he opens Firefox on his phone. He types "gay bars St. Croix" into the search box.

Waiting for site to connect.

His new phone is actually slower than his old one. His father always optimized his phones for him, making them faster by removing the extra apps and ads. That won't ever happen again.

Waiting for site to connect.

His mom is going to regret grounding him.

Treating him like a child.

He clicks on the first search result, and the ads on the next page load first. Apparently, there is a government program that could save him a ton on a new mortgage. Mason doesn't have a mortgage.

Before he can read about the first bar, a notification pops up.

It's a text from Trent.

Swipe left—delete the message, and Trent goes back to being out of his life.

Swipe right—read the message, and . . .

The last time they saw each other, they sat in Trent's Mustang in front of Mason's house. Mason was so embarrassed by his failed attempt to make out with Trent, he just wanted to leave. Trent asked if he would go out on a second date, and Mason said yes, but Trent never texted.

Until now.

Mason never texted Trent, either. Mason had cried about

his father on the date, and the kiss had been horrible. Trent tasted like beer. Mason decided he could do better, so he started running and going to the gym every day. It made him strong, and it made him better looking. He told his mom he was hanging with friends so she'd leave him alone. Otherwise, she would have insisted on coming.

Mason is hot now, but Trent—his hair, his jacket, his car—he's hot too.

He flips back to Firefox, the page auto-refreshes, and a new ad tells him to lower his student loan interest rates. Mason doesn't have a student loan.

A bar called the Buckotora allows all ages during the week. It looks more like a restaurant for tourists than a club, but it says there's a dance floor. He wanted to find a flashy techno club with strobe lights, but the Buckotora could work. He reads through the other listings for a while, but doesn't find anything better.

He jumps off the bed. Stands at the window.

Anything is better than staying here with the dragon.

He closes the browser and reads the message from Trent.

"sry I didn't text sooner. wanted 2 give u space."

Space? That's so grown up.

Black clouds move across the sky.

Another text from Trent appears.

"r u there?"

"yes."

"how r u?"

"fight with mom."

"she know we went out?"

"no. doesn't know I'm gay. won't let me leave."

"not cool. it will get better."

"maybe."

"miss u. want to meet?"

"can't leave."

"u sure?"

"not in WA."

"me neither."

"where r u?"

The sun peeks over the clouds, and the rain stops.

"missed u. followed u."

"?"

"I'm in st croix."

CHAPTER FORTY-EIGHT

LAUREN

Cruising toward the ocean, the horizon reminds me of the painting in William's office back home. The ocean. The ferry to the Hotel on the Cay island. It ought to remind me—the artist sat right over there on that hill when she painted it.

Mason and I pull into the parking lot between the historic Fort Christiansvaern and Jackson Park. He opens his door and gets out, clutching his beach bag. I promised to take him to the beach if we could talk. I'm not sure, but this could be the big talk. We need to connect. Before we left the condo, he calmed down and apologized for slamming his door.

I scan the parking lot. The road. The boardwalk.

There's no sign of the old man or Basketball-head.

I grab my handbag and make sure the rental car is locked.

The park is the same as when William and I first toured the fort. The Danish customs house runs along the road between the parking lot and the boardwalk. There's a gazebo on the other side of the house. William and I first stood there on our honeymoon over twenty-two years ago.

Twenty-two years and two weeks ago, now.

I run my finger along the chain beneath my blouse until I feel William's wedding ring.

The clouds from this morning have lightened up, but they're still there. Mason walks ahead, running his hand along the sand-colored walls of the customs house. He has a bounce in his step. He recovered from his outburst so quickly this morning.

I wish I could do that.

I wish I could relax, but I can't stop looking over my shoulder.

I worry the old man will show up.

I worry about the future.

Relax.

It's so beautiful here. The palm trees sway. The old buildings tell no tales. The locals smile. If worse comes to worst, I could sell our house in Washington and open a tourist shop selling knick-knacks—finally put my business degree to use—and forget about the old man and the black cars. Hide out here forever.

"Shit." Mason runs his hands in and out of his pocket.

"Excuse me?"

"I forgot my phone. We have to go back for it."

"But we just got here."

"Mom."

"Can't you go without it for a little while?"

His eyes panic. "No. I need it."

"You'll just have to wait until we're done talking."

We turn the corner.

"But I need to check something. Now." He stops. I know this look.

"Here," I pull my phone out of my red Gucci handbag. "Can you check it on mine?"

"Yeah."

I type in my pin code and hand it to him. "Over here." We sit at a picnic table in the middle of the park.

Mason taps on my phone.

"Can we talk now?"

He glances up, and his eyes widen at something behind me.

I turn to see a young man wearing a skimpy red Speedo and carrying a beach towel with the Corona beer logo. How cute. Beyond the man, the customs house runs along the road, and—

Barum, barum, barum.

The tail end of a black car disappears behind the house. I couldn't tell what kind of car it was. "Did you see that?"

"No." Mason says without taking his eyes off my phone.

I watch the house, waiting for the car to appear at the opposite end, but it doesn't.

My phone rings. "Who is it?"

"I don't know," he says.

I snatch it out of his hands.

"Hey."

The phone reads RESTRICTED. "Stay right there."

It's the old man. I know it. I just know it. He's calling me from that black car on the other side of the customs house. I'm going to catch him.

I tap ANSWER. "Hello?"

"Welcome to St. Croix, Mrs. Kaine." His gravelly voice is unmistakable.

"Where are you?" I round the corner. Everything turns red.

"Your time is up. I know you have the card."

There is a blue car and a silver mini-van, but no black car.

It must have turned up the street.

He says, "It's time I took Mason for a swim."

Click.

I can't breathe. I stop, bend over. Red flashes consume me. I put my hands on my knees.

Breathe.

My eyes want to close, but I won't let them. I tip my head back and open them wide, and the man in the black leather jacket stands at the far end of the boardwalk, leaning against a palm tree.

My throat constricts.

They followed us. The old man has sent the Fonz for Mason, and my eyes . . . I can't keep them from closing.

Breathe. This too shall pass.

My seahorse swims in a sea of red.

Time passes.

I can't move.

Bent over, standing in the crimson darkness of my disease, time passes.

My windpipe opens, and air trickles into my lungs.

At first, I'm vaguely aware of the park, then everything clears in a rush.

The man in the black leather jacket is gone.

Stumbling around the customs building, I'm still repeating, *this too shall pass.*

And it did pass.

The picnic table is vacant.

And Mason is gone.

CHAPTER FORTY-NINE

LAUREN

Jackson Park spins around me.

Mason's not at the picnic table.

The man in the leather jacket isn't leaning against a palm tree.

The trees, the fort, the customs house, the boardwalk—everything's spinning.

It's happening all over again. Mason's gone.

I run to the table. Images of the last time I lost him flash through my mind. He was only three. He was trapped in that rundown hotel room for days, starving. Left all alone while Ryan was out on a bender.

My stomach lurches. It's like I'm on a bender.

Mason's beach bag is gone, but my cell phone is on the picnic table. I shove it in my pocket. The last time Mason disappeared, I stayed home and wasted precious minutes calling the police for help, answering their questions for what seemed like an eternity. I'm not going to make that mistake again.

I spin in a circle, feverishly searching for him.

The black car the Fonz parked behind the customs building isn't there. The shops at the end of the boardwalk block my view of the beach. Cars are scattered throughout the parking lot—but none are black. Two young men in shorts and tank tops, and a redheaded woman in a batik sarong, skip down the boardwalk, laughing and holding hands. I run between them and shove their arms out of my way. The boardwalk angles to the left, and my sandal catches on a raised plank. I fall down, screaming, "Mason!"

Lying on my back, I throw my sandals toward the shops so I won't trip again.

Someone yells, "Eh, eh."

I stand and feel for William's wedding ring hanging from the chain beneath my blouse to make sure it's still there.

It is.

A T-shirt salesman with a handcart glares at me, waving a sandal. His nostrils flare.

I run.

"Hey," the salesman says, "don't you want soulye, mumu?"

The shops and restaurants fly by, and the dock at the end is filled with people lined up to board the ferry. Across the bay, the Hotel Cay happily sits on its little island while tourists play on its shore. The ferry blows its horn and pulls away from the dock, leaving a line of disappointed passengers to wait for the next trip.

"Mason!"

Everyone turns and looks at me.

I take off toward the beach, but a well-endowed older woman grabs me by the arm. "Are you okay, lady-man?"

"No. I lost my son."

"Well, den—"

"Someone took my son. Have you seen a boy?"

"He a chile?"

"No, he's sixteen. He's got dark brown hair and—"

"I seen a man and boy get on de ferry."

"When? What was the man wearing?"

"He had one of den red shirts with parrots."

"Did you see a man in a black jacket?"

"No, but I seen a group of yo adolesan milling up Queen's Cross," the woman says, pointing at Queen's Cross street.

The boardwalk fades from dark brown to amber to dirty pink. I blink. Please no. I can't afford another red-out. Not this soon. I run toward Queen's Cross. My bare feet scream when I leave the boardwalk and hit the pavement.

"Mason!"

Shoppers stroll beneath the awnings on both sides, pausing to gaze into the arched shop windows. I look back and forth, turning my head, frantically searching for some sign of Mason, but there's only travel agencies and bright yellow and purple painted gift stores. A bar that doesn't open until six tonight. A breakfast place featuring Vietnamese iced-coffee.

The sidewalk is crowded, so I stay in the middle of the road.

"Mason!"

At the cross street, I stop, and my soles flare. I limp over to the sidewalk. A policeman wearing dark blue shorts and a matching cap sticks a ticket under the windshield wiper of a tiny car parked on the curb.

I go to him and grab him by the arm. "You have to help me."

"Hold on, miss." He grips his billy club, but he doesn't

pull it out. I let go of his arm, and his gentle smile does nothing to comfort me. "What is de trouble?"

"My son is missing. You have to—"

"Hold on. Hold on." He raises his hand and motions for me to back away. "Gimme some space. Now, what be de trouble?"

"My son is gone."

"And where did he go?"

I bite my lip. His island accent. That smile. I'm wasting my time. "I don't know. He's gone. That's the trouble."

"Okay." He pulls out a pen, tests it on a pad of paper, licks the tip, and tries again. "When did your chile vanish?"

"He's not a child. He's sixteen, and—just now. He was in the park, and there was a man, and—"

"Sixteen." He writes on his pad. "When was your son at the park?"

I grit my teeth. "Just now. You have to help me."

"How old did you say?" He purses his lips. "Sixteen?"

Nothing would satisfy me more than shoving that pad down his throat. My lower lip hurts, so I let go of it and pinch my necklace instead. William's ring is more soothing anyway.

"Did you check the boardwalk, lady-man?"

"Of course, I checked the boardwalk. He's not only missing. Someone took him."

"That man, supposing." He writes on the pad.

"Yes. Yes."

"And he's sixteen?"

"Yes."

"Old enough to drive?"

"Yes."

"And someone took him? Took him like a chile?"

"Yes. Are you going to do something, or not?" My body

quakes.

"You okay, lady-man?"

"I'm fine."

He rolls his eyes. "Boys that age have their fun in St. Croix. He's not missing. He's living. Dis is a fun place." He gazes at the boardwalk. "If your chile doesn't come back dis evening, you come to de station tomorrow." He holds out a business card. "Ask for me."

I rage.

I seethe.

The whites of his eyes turn red. His mocking teeth turn red. The black freckles on his cheekbones go auburn, and I raise my hand to smack him.

He steps back, raises his hands, grinning. "Hey now, lady-man, relax. Dem young men always do dis. De girls in bikinis drive 'em crazy. Your son be fine."

"No. He's—" I feel faint. I lower my hand.

"You should enjoy your time here too, like your chile. Go to de parade tonight. Dance with the Moko Jumbies. Come see me tomorrow if he hasn't come back."

"No. I—" I'm going to kill him if I can get my hands on him. Everything is red. I reach for his throat.

"Or"—he scowls, narrows his eyes, and lowers his voice—"you can come to de station with me now."

I bend over, put my hands on my knees, and close my eyes.

Where's my seahorse?

My mantra?

Breathe.

Three questions . . .

One, what happened? Two, what triggered my anger? Three, who can I forgive?

"Lady-man? Why don't you come with me now?" He grasps my wrist, but I'm not going to the station.

I pull, but he doesn't let go.

Then I remember what the old man said would happen if I went to the police. I've got to break free.

Wrath wells inside me, and I let it build, and I wrench my arm away.

When I open my eyes, I'm sprinting.

The officer is yelling, but I'm already gone, halfway up the street.

My feet scream in pain.

My chest heaves for air.

My eyes search the crimson red road. The bloodshot buildings. The scarlet sky.

"Mason!"

CHAPTER FIFTY

RYAN

Ryan steps into the hall and pulls the door closed, trapping the cold inside his apartment. He'd like to leave the door open while he's gone, let the heat in, but the hallway smells like rotting leaves. He types "TriamSys" into the maps app on his phone and taps the DIRECTIONS button.

It's not far.

Whether his brother forgives him or not doesn't matter as much as warning him about the Digital Freedom Fighters. The way Steve coerced Ryan to work for Luis Gabaldon today after the AA meeting was—he searches for the right word . . . "sinister."

It was dark, disturbing, and sinister.

If Luis is willing to pay Ryan $150,000 for the technology, what is he willing to pay others? What is he willing to do?

Ryan doesn't need the money. He *wants* the money, but he doesn't need it. Not more than he needs his sobriety. The only way to remove the temptation is to warn William about the DFF. He can't worry about the restraining order anymore. William is in danger. He only hopes Lauren doesn't kill him when she finds out.

He locks his door and, like a bad rash, his landlord is back. "Hey, Ryan. Hi."

"Hi, Carl."

Carl stares nervously at the floor. Says nothing.

"Is there something you wanted?" Ryan asks.

"Did you have a—how was your weekend?"

"It's Tuesday, Carl." Ryan walks past him on his way to the stairs.

"I know, but I didn't see you yesterday, and—" He trundles up behind Ryan. "I had a great weekend."

"That's great, Carl. I'll see you later."

Carl blocks the stairs. Raises his hands. "Okay. Wait. I'll just come out and say it."

"Say what?"

"I know you lost your job, and there's this nice couple just starting out, you know, and they need a place to live, so—"

"You gave my apartment away?"

"No, no. Nothing like that. I just need to know if you're going to make the rent or not."

"You're unbelievable."

"I'm trying to help you. If you can't make the rent, I'll make sure you get your full deposit back as long as you move out by this weekend."

"Why wouldn't I get my deposit back?"

Carl reaches behind his back and pulls up his pants with one hand while wiping his forehead with the other. "Your overdue, and you've been overdue too many times. And . . ." He looks away.

"And what?"

"And the owners know you broke the heater."

"Good-bye, Carl." Ryan steps around him and hits the stairs, taking the steps two at a time.

"Ryan," Carl yells into the stairwell. "Please, don't make me kick you out."

He bursts onto the street and jogs to his car. Carl was only doing his job. Ryan will need to do a fourth step later for being so short with him. The truth is, Ryan *has* been past due on his rent several times. He'll need to find somewhere else to live by Friday.

If things work out, maybe he can stay at his brother's for a while.

The maps app beeps because of an accident on I-5 and reroutes him onto 12th Avenue. It will take longer to go through all the stoplights now, but he has plenty of time to make it to TriamSys before five. When he gets there, he'll start with a quick apology and then ask William for the technology.

No.

That won't work.

The amends will take several days, if not years. He's got to tell William about the DFF immediately. Then the groveling can begin.

He turns left onto Ranier Avenue and heads toward the onramp to I-90.

A black Audi with heavily tinted windows appears in the rearview mirror. It's high-end. An A8. He adjusts the mirror to get a better look and accidentally aims it at himself. His eyes are bloodshot from lack of sleep. Long nights battling the guilt from choosing money over Juan. But today, he can look at himself in the mirror. The battle is over. He's doing the right thing.

He moves the mirror back into place, but he can't see the Audi's driver through the glare on the windshield. He thinks of the black car he saw when leaving William's house Sunday, and the black Chevy Impala he saw after the meeting today, and all the strange black cars parked across the alley from the DFF last week.

Ted's Auto Body.

The fleet of black cars.

The DFF must own those cars.

Steve is a liar.

Ryan takes the next right, and heads back to 12th Avenue. He doesn't want the Audi to know he's on his way to see William. He turns left onto 12th Avenue and slows down. A lot. The Audi stays right behind him. Any normal car would have pulled into the outside lane and driven past, but not this one. It's the DFF for sure.

Right before the next intersection, Ryan floors it. The Civic's engine rattles like it's out of oil. He gets some distance and puts a car between him and the Audi before pulling into the left turn lane for Dearborn Street. The light is red, and the Audi is two cars back. He's never had someone follow him like this before. In the movies, cars speed through the streets and run red lights in situations like this, but in the real world, it would only attract the police. Besides, speeding is illegal. It's dishonest.

Sobriety demands honesty.

But how dishonest is speeding?

The left turn light flashes a green arrow, and Ryan breaks the rules. He presses on the accelerator and drives straight into the middle of the intersection, honking his horn. An oncoming car attempting to turn left brakes. Ryan swerves, missing a head-on collision by inches. He speeds down 12th Avenue and checks his mirror.

The Audi is gone.

He lost him.

Passing over I-90, Ryan glances down, wishing he'd somehow made the onramp.

"Rerouting . . . " says the maps app feminine voice.

Ryan veers right to stay on 12th Avenue, passing by Rizal park. The Audi still isn't in his mirror, and he relaxes. He slows down to the speed limit. Gazes into the park. It will take longer to get back to I-90 without doing a U-turn, but his arms are shaking. The DFF might still be following him. Maybe they're tracking him. His old company, SPD Delivery, tracked him, and it cost him his job.

He pulls over and shuts the engine off.

His nerves are shot. He needs to calm down before talking to William.

A path runs through the park, passing by a bench. The city removed most benches downtown a few years ago to discourage people from turning them into homes. It will eventually happen here. The homeless problem isn't going away any time soon. In the distance, beyond the bench, hidden carelessly in the bushes, a makeshift tent flutters in the wind. It wouldn't be noticeable from here if it weren't for a bright red blanket hanging from one end.

Ryan wonders where he'll be staying this time next week. Maybe here. The thought makes him smile. Not likely. He has friends. He has AA. He can humble himself to ask for help.

William might forgive him sooner than he thinks.

The wind catches hold of the red blanket and drags it across the field.

Ryan leans forward, peering over the dashboard.

He gets out, crosses over the path, strides past the bench, and picks up the blanket.

Silver-eyed reindeer, tied together by a golden ribbon,

leaping from rooftops, stare him in the face. His Christmas blanket. The odds of another one like this, out here . . . Juan.

Ryan runs to the bushes. An unzipped sleeping bag and two tattered blankets hang from an orange electric cord tied between two trees.

"Juan, are you in there?"

A leather boot with skulls and daggers sewn in white thread sticks out of one end next to an empty bottle of McCormick's Vodka. The air is intolerably sour like there's an open sewage drain nearby.

Ryan holds his blanket to his chest.

He kicks the boot.

The silver-tipped toe rocks to one side then returns to its original position.

Juan must be passed out.

Ryan opens the tent, and the stench makes him gag. "Jesus, buddy. Have you been peeing in here?"

Juan lies on a sheet marred with mud and grass stains. He's in the fetal position with one leg sticking out straight. His other foot is missing its boot. He's bloated. His hands are clasped over his chest, and dried vomit holds down the grass near his mouth.

His lips are blue.

No.

His lips are black.

His eyes are closed, his face is pale, and his lips are black.

Ryan kneels and touches Juan's cheek.

It's cold.

Too cold.

"No!"

Ryan grabs Juan's wrists and pulls them off his chest.

A rock falls out of Juan's hands, tumbles onto the sheet,

and Ryan pounds on the big man with both fists. "Why, Juan? Why'd you choose the rough side? Why?"

He collapses on Juan, reaches over, and grasps the rock.

Smooth side.

Rough side.

The urine stench changes into something more like rotten cabbage and dog shit.

He stands up, pockets the rock, and sways to the left.

Stomach acid fills his throat, and he fights the urge to puke.

Juan is dead.

This is what happens when a drunk chooses the rough side of the rock.

Ryan swallows, backs away, turns around, rips the sleeping bag off the cord, stumbles forward, and while bending over, he snags his reindeer blanket—and he runs.

This is what happens when a drunk chooses to take that first drink.

It leads to death. It *always* leads to death.

Ryan crosses the park and climbs inside his shitty Civic.

Sooner or later, the disease takes everyone. It's unavoidable.

He wipes his face. He needs to warn William about the DFF. Make amends. Stay sober.

Stay sober.

The best thing a sponsor can do for his sponsee is stay sober.

But what's the point?

He should call the police.

But what's the point?

Another dead homeless man in an overpopulated sea of filth.

He can't believe it, but he can. There is no point. There's no point to life at all.

His sponsee is dead.

Every alcoholic is as good as dead.

He slams his hands on the steering wheel.

Fuck it.

CHAPTER FIFTY-ONE

LAUREN

The smaller board has gold striped notches where it was plugged into the bigger, main board. Pieces of William's computer are scattered throughout. I turn the smaller board over in my hands. Chips and cylinders are soldered to the green surface, each next to a code. A3. T3. H1. H2.

The board is like a card, but it's not *the* card. The card wouldn't be part of a computer that's five years old. I laugh out loud. I'm sitting on the floor with my back against the wall, laughing.

The computer case has dents like I punched it. Maybe I stomped on it. There's a screwdriver and a pile of screws on the carpet, so I must have resorted to opening the computer the right way at some point, but who knows?

My head aches. My feet feel worse. I remember leaving my sandals on the boardwalk and running up the street, searching for Mason. A policeman yelled at me and . . . then it gets hazy.

I stand. I'm in the condo.

Cables, cards, and papers cover the bedroom's carpet.

The keyboard is cracked. The desk drawer is empty. I look at the bottom of my foot. Dried blood sticks to my arch, and there's a gash near my big toe. I remember running back to the park, getting in the rental car and driving around, looking for Mason, but then I must have come back here and lost my mind, tearing William's computer to shreds, looking for the card.

Flashes of leaving the condo, searching for Mason, returning, and leaving again come and go, but there's no order to the events. I've reached a new level. Now, when I red out, I don't pass out, I act out. I run around raging and carrying on like a wounded banshee.

What have I done?

I find my cell phone resting on the dining table. Mason hasn't called or texted, but how could he? He forgot his cell phone, and if he's been kidnapped—if he's tied up somewhere—he wouldn't be able to send messages. I open the web browser and check the history. He used my phone last, sitting in the park, but all he did was read about manga.

How could I have let him out of my sight?

An ad for discounts on trips to St. Croix pops up, and I hit the X to close it. I'm already in St. Croix for God's sake. Then I see the time.

9:00 p.m.

I spent six hours raging and searching for Mason. Searching for the card with nothing to show for it. But I was in a red-out.

Think.

The man in the leather jacket was in the park. He followed us to St. Croix. The old man called, but that doesn't mean he's here. Not yet. I don't know where Mason is, but we've got to leave the island as soon as possible.

I drag my suitcase to the front door and head for his room, but first, I grab my passport off the counter and put it in my suitcase's outer pocket. We've been here two days and his room is already a mess. The carpet by the window is damp, and his clothes are everywhere. I pack his suitcase, keeping an eye out for his passport, then spy his cell phone under the bed.

Privacy be damned, I swipe the screen and enter his birthday for the pin code. The phone unlocks. He's no William. Searches for "gay bars St. Croix" appear. He viewed a place called the Buckotora.

I know it. It's a plain old tourist trap. A bar and grill.

The police officer might have been right. Mason might have run away on his own, looking to meet someone. He was so desperate this morning—*you don't understand what it's like to be alone*—attempting to go to the beach in a torrential downpour.

I find his passport is in the nightstand drawer and drag his suitcase to the front door.

Back in the bedroom, a quick check for any forgotten items yields nothing. Outside the sliding glass door, the wind is picking up. The trees bend toward the lights of downtown Christiansted. The fence in the distance surrounds the condo complex, and I wonder if the Fonz is waiting for me somewhere on the other side.

I picture him, leaning against a tree, relaxed. Watching.

I picture the old man, too. Smoking. Wearing a baseball cap.

In a flash, I'm out the front door with my keys and my handbag on my shoulder, but I'm barefoot. The gashes on my feet erupt. I limp back to the condo, slide my keycard to unlock the door, and retrieve a pair of sneakers from the suitcase.

The road into town isn't well lit, and if a black car were following me, I wouldn't know it was there. So far, I'm alone. The winding road gives way to the straight streets of Christiansted, and I turn onto King.

Almost there.

I hate this rental car. The engine buzzes. The touch screen is confusing. The wheels leave the ground whenever I take a corner. Up ahead, a block past Prince Street, a crowd gathers in the intersection where I need to turn. The Buckotora is on the other side of the blocked intersection.

They're having the Moko Jumbie parade. I've been to it many times. The Moko Jumbie stilt dancers, with their long, flowing robes—red, yellow, orange, black and blue, green and silver—standing high above the crowd. The marching bands. Women wearing flowers in their hair. Drunken vacationers cheering, chanting, "Moko Jumbie. Moko Jumbie." The stilt dancers scaring children with their skeletal masks, then throwing candy.

I turn onto Prince Street and search for a parking spot, but there's nothing left, and a car appears in my rearview mirror. The headlights make it hard to tell, but I think it's black. The side mirror doesn't help. I floor it, the engine whirs, and I wheel into an alley and stop. The word TAXI flashes in the rearview mirror. Whew.

I get out and sprint to the end of the alley. My feet are cold. The gashes must be bleeding into my socks, so I slow to a walk. The night air smells like wilted flowers. Approaching King's Cross Street, I shove my phone into my Gucci handbag and grasp the strap, pulling it tight on my shoulder.

The Buckotora is somewhere on the other side of the street, blocked by a horde of tourists.

I force my way in.

Everyone cheers and turns toward the hill. I'm pushed in that direction and stumble into the middle of the road. Shop lamps cancel out the night sky, making the stars disappear. The crowd splits apart on the hilltop, creating a path down the center for the oncoming parade.

Two Moko Jumbie crest the hill, towering over everyone on their stilts. Their robes trail down to the ground, one black, one white, billowing like silk sails. The Jumbie's masks always remind me of the Day of the Dead celebrations in Mexico. The first Jumbie's mask has colored dots surrounding a smiling skull. The other's mask has orange and aquamarine tulips.

I go against the crowd and spot the sign for the Buckotora glowing above a tan awning four or so shops away. Swimming upstream, I desperately push through the deluge of sweaty vacationers. They shout hurrahs for the Moko Jumbie, and I shout for Mason.

A man grabs my arm. "Wrong way. De Jumbie coming dat way."

I resist and step to one side, then to the other, but I'm constantly blocked. My shoulder hits a teenage girl in the head, and a man pushes me, spinning me around, making me come face-to-face with a Moko Jumbie in a flowing red robe. He leans down close, hanging from his stilts with unimaginable balance, and his mask touches my nose. Black mesh hides his eyes, and he wags his finger left and right, then violently shakes his head.

I scream.

He stands up straight and raises his arms in the air.

Everyone cheers.

I try to run, but someone grabs my arm. "Get out of de

way. De Moko Jumbie!"

"I am," I yell. "Let go of me!"

Breaking free, I turn toward the Buckotora. Somehow, I've floated down the street, past the shops, and I'm directly across the street from it, but the crowd is thick, waiting for the black and white Jumbies to come down the hill. The red Jumbie stutter-steps away. At first, I didn't know where he came from, but then I see more entering from the side streets. Purple and green robes—one is spinning a plate on a stick, and the other juggles fruit.

I start toward the club, but a dance troupe gambols into my way.

The people standing by the Buckotora shout, "Moko!"

The people behind me respond, "Jumbie!"

Through the dancers twirling ribbons, I see him. The man in the leather jacket stands by the Buckotora, holding a beer, gazing at the troupe with a drunken smile. The Fonz. He must have followed Mason. He must know where Mason is.

He sees me.

He raises his beer in a toast.

I freeze.

He tips his head forward and peers over his sunglasses at me.

Sweat runs down my back.

I wait for the dancers to pass.

I'm a thoroughbred waiting for the gun to go off.

The last dancer twirls about, pulling a wide blue ribbon through the air. I duck and charge forward just as Mason comes out of the club. He's unharmed. In fact, he's grinning, holding a drink in a cheap red cup.

I stop.

He walks toward the man—the stalker—and I need to

stop him, to warn him, but before I can, the man puts his beer down and grabs Mason by the chin and looks into his eyes. Mason puts his hands on the man's shoulders, and the man glances at me, then plants his lips on my son's mouth.

They kiss.

It's a deep kiss.

The man puts his hands on Mason's hips, and Mason wraps his arms around the man's neck. His cup falls to the ground.

The black Moko Jumbie stilts in front of me, blocking my view, and I step back. The white Moko Jumbie bends down and motions for me to move farther away, rocking his head from shoulder to shoulder like a freakish marionette. I take another step back, and someone grabs my arm from behind. "I know. I know," I shout. "I'm getting out of the way."

I try to pull free, but they don't let go.

The crowd closes in behind the Moko Jumbies.

I can't see Mason.

Someone grabs my other arm, and I'm swept off my feet, falling backward, but I don't hit the ground. My handbag catches on something, and the strap breaks. I lose it. I kick, but I can't get enough traction to stand. I'm being dragged. Two Jumbie skull masks blot out the sky—one orange, one yellow. I struggle. "Let go of me!"

"Relax, lady. This is just part of the show," the orange Jumbie says with a New York accent.

They're not on stilts.

"Don't resist so much," says the other Jumbie, his eyes hiding behind the black mesh, yellow flowers dancing around his skeletal face, "you'll hurt yourself."

"What be going on?" shouts someone in the crowd.

"Help," I scream. "Mason!"

"She's drunk," the orange Jumbie says. "We've got this under control."

My heels bounce up onto the curb, kicking.

There are legs everywhere, and everyone yells, "Moko!"

Across the street, everyone yells, "Jumbie!"

No one can hear me.

We pass over a sidewalk into an alley, and I twist to see where they're taking me.

A third Moko Jumbie stands next to a black car.

He's wearing a blue robe.

I push, pull, jerk, shake—summon my anger.

The red comes, but their grip is too strong.

The orange Jumbie lied.

This is not part of the show.

CHAPTER FIFTY-TWO

RYAN

Fuck it.

Ryan speeds into the Squire's parking lot. The Civic's rear
end bangs against the curb, and he flies into the closest spot,
cuts the engine, and pulls on the parking brake. Neon BUD
LIGHT, COORS, and HEINEKEN signs glow in the plate-
glass windows. The rearview mirror blocks the OPEN sign,
so he moves it out of the way.

It's lit up.

The tavern is open.

Wide open.

He puts his hand on the door handle and—

What am I doing?

The door handle rattles, and he lets go of it. This is the
seventh bar he's been to since finding Juan dead in the park,
but he hasn't gone inside any of them. He's still sober. At each
joint, he recites every prayer he can remember from the *Big
Book*, pictures his fellow drunks from the meetings, and
eventually drives away. But before he knows it, the reality of
Juan's death and the inevitability of the disease returns, and

he winds up outside the next bar.

Only moments ago, he swore this time would be different. At the Squire, he would let his mind go blank, go inside, have one drink, just one drink, and—

He puts his hand back on the door handle, then looks away.

The reindeer on his lucky blanket stares up at him from the passenger side floor. The blanket's edges are soiled from where Juan must have dragged it through the streets. If he's going to do this, he must forget everything AA has taught him. At the very least, he must blank it all out somehow. Willpower is defenseless against those strange mental blank spots. Seeing Juan dead in the bushes destroyed his will power, so why can't he pull the trigger? Why doesn't his strange mental blank spot come?

Juan went to the Squire all the time. He probably has friends inside, people who would want to know what happened. Ryan owes it to them to go in and have a drink. Tell them what he saw in the park. Just one drink.

No.

Ryan picks up his cell phone.

It weighs a hundred pounds.

The one thing he hasn't done today is call another alcoholic.

He stares at the screen, then thumbs through his contacts and finds Joe's number.

A slim man in a flannel shirt walks into the Squire. That man probably drinks with impunity. That man can probably have just one drink and leave. It's not fair.

Why can't Ryan have just one?

The phone rings.

Maybe, after all this time, Ryan could have just one and

stop.

Joe doesn't answer. Voice mail comes on, and Ryan hangs up.

It wouldn't be just one drink. It would be several.

But he could stop drinking again tomorrow. He could wake up, go straight to a meeting, and raise his hand.

He raises his hand.

Then, he slams it down on the steering wheel.

To drink is to die. He saw that. Today. But it's so futile. Staying sober is so futile.

He reaches into his pocket and rubs the rock's smooth side. A lot of good this thing did Juan. A rock can't stop this. A silver chip, a one-year chip—an eight-year chip—nothing can stop this.

He finds Garage Mike's number in his contact list and hits the call button.

The old-timer answers on the first ring. "Ryan? What's going on?"

Ryan can't speak.

"Are you okay? Probably not if you're calling me this late."

"I'm okay—I mean, I'm *not* okay." His throat aches. He swallows.

"Where are you?"

"I'm in the parking lot of a bar."

"Thought so."

"I don't know how I got here."

"Strange mental blank spot, eh?"

"Yeah."

"Well, the good news is, it's over. You're aware of what's going on. Did you drink today?"

"No."

"And you called me, so you're doing the right things. You're going to be okay."

"I don't think so."

"Listen." Garage Mike pauses. A lighter flicks in the background. "You did the right thing calling me, now do the *next* right thing, and go home. Stop your stinking thinking and just go home. Eat something and get some sleep. Stop thinking."

Ryan's been trying to stop thinking all afternoon, but not so he could go home. "But—"

"But nothing. H.A.L.T.—hungry, angry, lonely, tired. Right now, you're all of these. I can hear it in your voice. Go home, eat, and sleep. Pray to be relieved of whatever you're angry about, and call me again if you're still lonely. Tomorrow, you'll wonder why you ever went to that bar."

"I know about H.A.L.T."

"You don't know about anything. You're an alcoholic. Self-knowledge will fail you. Trust me. I can't tell you how many times I've ended up with my hand on the bottle, arguing with myself about whether I can handle just one drink or not. I've been in the program for over thirty years, and it doesn't matter how much I know. Every once in a while, my mind lies, and if I believe those lies, I'll drink, and if I drink, I'll die. I don't want to see you die, Ryan. Don't make me go to your funeral. Don't make me—"

"I'm starting the car."

"Good."

Ryan puts it in reverse and looks at the mirror. It's cock-eyed from when he moved it to see the open sign, and his reflection makes him shudder.

"Call me before you go to sleep tonight if you want," Garage Mike says.

"Thanks. I will."

Ryan starts to pull out but stops to wait for a car. He adjusts the mirror.

Go home. Eat. Sleep.

The OPEN sign reflects in the car's door.

Go home. Eat. Sleep.

He pulls out behind the car and accelerates. It's an Audi A8 like the one that followed him earlier today. Like the one Juan was driving for the DFF. The one Juan lost.

That was the beginning of the end for Juan.

That was the night Juan relapsed.

Ryan took Juan's keys, and Juan stumbled away. He lost the car. Later, when he found the car, he couldn't unlock it. Then he lost his job. Then he lost his girl.

Then he lost his life.

All because Ryan took his keys.

Go home. Eat. Sleep.

Ryan gains on the Audi. He closes to within a few feet. Black tinted windows. Black body. Black bumper. Streetlamps reflecting in the shiny black roof. Everything—black. The sedan's rear end suddenly lowers, its engine roars, and it takes off as if Ryan were stopped.

As if he were never there.

As if nothing matters.

As if he were dead.

CHAPTER FIFTY-THREE

MASON

For a moment, the crowd is silent. The dancers freeze. The Moko Jumbie stop their march down King's Cross Street, and the parade comes to a halt. Time stands still. The kiss lasts forever. Mason wishes this moment—standing here outside the club, his arms around Trent, Trent's arms around him— would last forever.

Then his heart beats, and the cheering, the dancing, and the march of the Moko Jumbie resumes.

Mason searches Trent's eyes for an answer.

Why did Trent suddenly kiss him out in the open? Their date *had* been going well, but not that well.

He parts his lips, hoping for another kiss, but Trent pulls him close. He rests his head on Trent's shoulder.

Everyone on the other side of the street yells, "Jumbie."

Everyone on this side yells, "Moko."

The crowd is deafening, but he hears someone call his name. It sounds like his mother.

He pushes away from Trent.

"What's wrong?" Trent asks.

Mason doesn't see her. She's taller than most women, and her dark red hair is usually easy to spot. "Nothing. I thought I heard my—"

A black-robed Moko Jumbie steps in front of Mason, leans down, and violently shakes his head. His face is bright white with crooked teeth surrounded by hundreds of colorful dots.

Mason startles, raises his hands, and screams. He stumbles backward into the crowd, falters, and reaches for someone to hang onto.

Trent rushes over and grabs him by the elbow. "Are you okay?"

"Can we go back inside?"

"Sure. I need another beer anyway."

The Buckotora isn't what Mason had hoped for. His dream of a Japanese discotheque with flashy dancers and flashier lights didn't come true. Plain brown tables with benches line the wall across from a long bar with a small dance floor in the back by an old machine that plays music for money. Some song about a hamburger in paradise has already played twice.

Mason sits at their table, and Trent stops at the bar. The place allows all ages, but they don't serve alcohol to minors. Mason's been drinking Diet Coke while Trent is on his third beer. Maybe that's where the kiss came from. Trent is getting drunk. Loosening up. He looks good, leaning on the bar, his jeans stretched tight over his butt.

Trent turns toward Mason and points at the soda fountain.

Mason nods yes.

Tonight's going to be great. If things continue this way, he won't have to sneak back into the condo. He can stay in

Trent's hotel room, and one thing might lead to the other.

"Here." Trent puts Mason's Diet Coke on the table and sits down. "Wow. You should have seen your face when that clown came at you."

"He surprised me, that's all."

"You looked like you thought he was going to kill you."

"Yeah, it's embarrassing."

"Do you have a clown thing?"

"No. They're not clowns. They're Moko Jumbie. When I was little, my parents took me to the parade all the time, and those things gave me nightmares for years."

"Like, recurring nightmares?" He takes a draw on his beer.

"Yeah. There was one where they'd come into my room at night and put me in a bag." Mason sips his soda. "Then they'd beat me with baseball bats."

"That sucks." He glances toward the door. The people on the street are still cheering for the Moko Jumbie. "So, you guys came here a lot?"

"A few times a year. Less when I got older."

Trent takes another drink, swooshes it in his mouth, and swallows. "You said your dad was a computer guy. How'd he get so much time off? Don't those guys work all the time?"

"Yeah, but he had a desk in the condo."

"Oh, so he worked remotely. What websites did he build? I think you told me, but I can't remember."

"I don't think I did. I'm not even sure he built websites. He never talked about work."

"Really? That's strange." He takes a drink.

"Why?"

"Most guys like to talk about what they do. I guess that doesn't apply to geeks." He drains his beer, puts the mug on the table, and Mason watches the suds stream down the inside of the glass. "Are you sure he never talked about it?"

"Yeah. Why do you want to know?"

"Just curious. He totally could have worked on stuff other than websites. There's the cloud with huge servers and security software. Business intelligence and machine learning. Lots of stuff." He glances toward the bar. "Did he ever talk about those things?

"Are you going to get another beer?"

He reaches across the table and takes Mason's hand. "Hey, let's go to your condo."

"No. That's not a good idea."

"Why not?"

"My mom might be there. She's going to be mad I left."

Trent squeezes his hand. "Don't worry. I can handle her."

"*Handle* her?"

"You know. Talk to her. I'll tell her it's all my fault."

"She doesn't know I'm gay."

"She doesn't have to. We're just two guys who met in the park and became friends." He lets go. Leans back. Stretches his arms out wide. Smiles. "And, if she's not there, we could get to know each other better."

That's the discotheque music Mason wanted to hear. "Why don't we go to your hotel room?"

"That's not going to work." Trent lowers his arms.

"Why not?"

Trent's phone vibrates, and he picks it up. His thumbs fly over the screen.

"Did you get a text?" Mason asks.

"Yeah. It's nothing." He lowers the phone and leans over the table. "Look, if you don't want me to come over, then I won't come over."

"No. I—it's my mom. You don't understand."

"No. I think I do." He puts his phone in his pocket. "I come all the way to the Caribbean to see you, hoping to *be* with you, and you don't want me to come over. That's fine."

"But I do."

"You know what?" He stands up—a bit off-balance—and places his hands on the table. "Never mind. You don't want to talk about your dad, I get it. I'm sorry he died. Really, I am, but someday, you're going to have to deal with it. *And* with your mom."

"What? What are you talking about?"

Trent wipes his mouth. Sways to the left. "I got to take a piss." He turns and heads for the men's room. His hips swing loosely as he crosses the dance floor then disappears around the corner.

The cheers die down outside, and people file back into the Buckotora.

Maybe it *would* be easier if Trent came to the condo. Mason wouldn't have to face the dragon alone. If she tried to ground him, he could just leave. Go to Trent's hotel room. If she lost her temper, flew into one of her fits, then Trent *could* handle her.

He's bigger than she is.

If Trent really wants to come to the condo, and if Mason lets him then . . . well, depending on how things go, who knows where the night might lead. It could be like it was for Shirotani in *Ten Count*.

Mason finishes his soda.

The lights come on over the dance floor, and a reggae song plays. People crowd along the bar, waving at the bartenders, shouting their orders. One—a big barrel-chested ape of a man—takes the orders and tells the other, mousy bartender, what to do. The mousy one rushes around, filling mugs and mixing drinks.

"Would you like another Diet Coke?" A waitress in a white apron and flowered smock picks up Mason's cup.

"No, thanks."

"Are you done then?"

Mason glances at the hall leading to the men's bathroom, hoping to see Trent. "I think so."

"Good, because we're going to need the table. Here's your tab."

Mason picks up the bill. Reads the amount.

She stands there, waiting.

"My friend went to the bathroom. We'll pay when he comes back."

"You sure, hon? I just saw him step out the back door." She wrinkles her upper lip. "I think he left."

"What?" Mason stands.

"He went into the alley," she says.

Mason runs toward the dance floor.

"Barry, are you seeing this?"

The ape bartender reaches under the bar. "Yep."

Mason rounds the corner, runs past the men's room, and exits the club. He stops, turns, and slams the steel door shut.

His pockets are empty. He doesn't have a cent.

The light above the door casts a sporadic glow a few feet into the alley. Darkness stretches in both directions. At one end, the parade is winding down. A few stragglers shuffle in the distance. At the other, nothing. The street is empty.

Trent is gone.

The door swings open and hits him in the butt.

"Don't move." Barry has a bat. "You haven't paid."

Mason runs toward the empty street as fast as he can.

CHAPTER FIFTY-FOUR

RYAN

Ryan carries his lucky blanket into his studio apartment and throws it onto the couch.

It's not lucky anymore.

He stands in the center of the room, not knowing what to do. The heater is off. The sink is full of dishes. The kitchen table is empty, the rent notice lies on the counter, and his computer is off. The bookshelf in the corner is half full, and the stack of computer books on his desk leans to the left like it's about to fall over.

Finding a job building websites feels like a figment of his imagination. He placed so much importance on learning, and he put so much time into it, stressing out whenever something got in his way. And for what?

Nothing.

Carl wants him out by the weekend. Having an eviction show up on a background check won't help him get a job. He's exhausted, but he should go online and see if anyone has responded to his job applications. He should log into LinkedIn and do a new search. Apply to a hundred jobs.

But what's the point?

Don't give up. Life must go on.

He sits down at his desk and logs in.

No one has responded to his job applications.

He opens the code editor. The last time he programmed, he got it to work. COMPILATION SUCCESSFUL. Maybe there is some hope.

He hits the F5 key to run his program, the hourglass spins, and the message, *java.lang.NullPointerException* displays.

Ryan is a null pointer.

He swivels in his chair.

He's alone here. Always alone. No family. No mom or dad or brother or nephew or . . . Lauren. Even his psycho-sister-in-law would be better than no one.

No, she wouldn't.

H.A.L.T.

The "L" is for lonely, and it slaps him in the face. He's also hungry, tired, and angry. He's angry God took Juan, and he's so . . . he's so lonely, he's thinking about Lauren of all people.

Eat and sleep. The rest will take care of itself in the morning.

He opens the freezer to grab a microwave dinner and instinctively reaches for the shelf where he used to keep his Vodka.

He jerks his arm away.

Ryan hasn't done anything like that since his first year of sobriety. Not since before the drunk dreams stopped. It took a long time for habits like this to fade. Vodka in the freezer, beer in the fridge, mini shooters in his pocket in case he needed to go out in public.

Vodka is best when it's cold. Ice cold.

He must be more exhausted than he thought.

There's orange juice in the refrigerator and not much else. He could make a screwdriver if he had some Vodka, but he never really liked those. In the end, the orange juice just got in the way.

He closes the refrigerator door and pulls his phone out of his pocket. He's supposed to call Garage Mike before he goes to bed, and he should, but he's hungry, and Juan is dead, and Garage Mike will lecture him if he calls. He already knows everything the old-timer will say. He's been to all the meetings, and he's heard it all a million times. Garage Mike will ask leading questions, and Ryan will give all the correct answers.

What a waste of time.

He doesn't have to call Garage Mike.

There are answers in the *Big Book*, and it isn't annoying.

He goes to the bookshelf, but his *Big Book* isn't there. For a moment, he takes it as a sign. The book has disappeared because he doesn't need it anymore. He's graduated. He can drink with impunity. Nothing bad will happen. He can stop tomorrow.

Lies.

All lies.

Last week, he gave the book to Juan to read before bed.

Again, Ryan's mind tells him sobriety is futile. The disease is going to get him whether he drinks or not. It got Juan. The twenty-four-hour chip didn't work. The rock didn't work. All the meetings didn't work. Juan is dead.

Ryan pulls his reindeer blanket off the couch, but the book isn't there. He pulls the cushions off and reaches into the seam. He searches, running his hand along the back, inside the couch, until his fingers hit something.

It's not the *Big Book*.

He grasps the object and, instantly, he knows what it is. The smooth surface. The slim design, making it easy to carry, undetectable inside a coat pocket or in the outer pocket of a backpack. The red-ridged, screw-off top.

Juan, like any accomplished drunk, hadn't shown up empty-handed last week.

Ryan pulls the bottle out of the couch and holds it up to the light.

Premium Skol Vodka.

375ml.

40% ALC/VOL (80 proof).

It's over half full.

Juan had barely gotten started on it.

He reaches into his pocket and pulls out the rock.

He rubs the smooth side with his thumb and considers pouring the Vodka down the drain, going to bed, and burying this nightmare of a day for once and for all.

He rubs the rough side and imagines the Vodka coursing down his throat. The familiar burn. He imagines the ensuing euphoria. The lighter-than-air-without-a-care euphoria. The Vodka would be better if it had an hour in the freezer, but he's too tired to wait, and he doesn't want to go to bed.

He doesn't want to apply for jobs or look for a new place to live.

He doesn't want to learn how to program computers or make amends to his brother.

He doesn't want to warn his brother about the DFF or steal his brother's technology for $150,000.

It's all futile.

Money doesn't matter. Nothing matters.

He doesn't remember why he ever wanted to do those things.

Life doesn't matter.

It's a zero-sum game.

In the end, we all die.

He tries to come up with a reason to put the bottle down, but he draws a blank.

A strange mental blank.

And he drinks the Vodka.

CHAPTER FIFTY-FIVE

LAUREN

The red clouds dissipate like I'm waking up from a dream. From another red-out, but I'm not.

I'm waking up from a nightmare.

But I'm not.

The nightmare is real.

Mason is gone.

I straighten my leg and my toe hits something. The pain makes me scream, but my voice is muffled. My throat aches, and my head clears.

I've been abducted.

Before the red-out, two Moko Jumbies grabbed me. I'd finally found Mason—he was kissing the Fonz—but the Jumbies dragged me into an alley. A third Jumbie, a giant in a dark blue robe, opened a car door and got into the driver's seat. My world went from black to red to black while I flailed and lashed out, but it was no use. The Jumbie in the yellow robe pulled my hands behind my back and zip-tied my wrists together. The one in orange taped my mouth shut and pulled a hood over my head.

They locked me in the backseat.

I kicked the door until blood ran up my leg.

Then I yelled until I ran out of breath.

Then I passed out.

It feels like morning now. Wednesday.

I can't see anything through the hood.

The glue on the tape is gone from where I tried to lick through it. The zip ties have cut into my wrists. When I get my hands on the yellow Moko Jumbie—what was his name? Frank?

Yes.

The smelly Jumbie with an east coast accent called the other one Frank, but I couldn't hear anything else over my wrath. I should have stayed calm and listened rather than grabbing Frank by the throat and screaming in his masked face.

I slapped him when I should have run.

My new mantra.

I must not let the anger in. I must not let it win.

A chain rattles and wheels squeak.

It sounds like a garage door opening.

They're back.

The rattling stops, and I listen intently. A car engine slowly gets louder, then stops. The chains rattle again, and the wheels squeak. Terror grips me, ripples through me, traveling from my hooded head to my wounded feet, and I hold my breath, but only for a moment.

A car door slams shut. Then another.

I run my toe along the armrest. When they open that door, I'm kicking. I going to kick them and kill them. Kick and kill, and kick and—no.

Breathe. I must not let the anger in.

The door opens.

"There she is," a man says.

I keep still. Play dead.

A second man speaks. "We're going for a little walk, Lauren. Are you going to play nice?" He sounds like the yellow Moko Jumbie—Frank. He's at my feet, and I want to kick, but I resist the urge. I bite my lip.

Clouds enter my mind, rage red, but I can't let the anger in.

I must stop letting it win.

"Did you hear me?" Frank asks. "Are you going to play nice?"

"M-m, h-m."

"What was that?"

Louder this time, forcing more air through my nose. "M-m-m. H-m-m."

"Good."

Hands grab my ankles and pull. I slide across the leather seat, and just when I'm about to fall, they grab my arms and pull me up. If I could see, I'm sure the world would be spinning. My head is light, and it's difficult to stay standing.

They hook their arms into mine, one on each side, and pull me forward. The ties cut into my wrists. I lose my footing, but they don't let me fall. They hold me up by my elbows and drag me across the floor.

"She wasn't this heavy last night, you know?" The man on my right is wearing too much cologne. He reeks of sugar cane and sandalwood, and his accent screams Long Island.

"No, she's the same," Frank says. "We were just pumped up."

I try to get to my feet and fail.

"You should ease up on the pies, lady," says the cologne

man.

Finally, I get both feet planted on the floor and thrust my head to the right, trying to bash cologne man in the face.

I'm not fat.

My head hits nothing but air, and they drop me on my knees. The floor is hard like concrete.

I shouldn't have done that.

My cheek explodes in pain.

He *hit* me.

The stinky son-of-a-bitch *hit* me.

My cheekbone flares up, and the back of my head pounds, and it feels good, like a release. Like an angry, red release.

"You said you'd play nice." Frank's voice is like velvet.

Cologne man jerks my arm. "You gonna play nice?"

I nod yes.

They lift me up, and we walk. The hood blocks my nostrils, making it difficult to breathe. I've got to calm down before the thought of suffocating causes me to panic. The odor of engine oil mixed with bad cologne doesn't help.

"You oughta know something," the cologne man says, jerking my arm. "This is the second time this week somebody bled on my shoes. Now I gotta get another shoeshine."

"You pay for a shoeshine every time there's a little blood?" Frank asks.

"Yeah. So?"

"Why don't you just use a towel to wipe it off before it dries?"

"I don't know. Doesn't feel clean that way."

"Why are you so strange, Tony?"

"There's nothing strange about hygiene."

Tony. Cologne man talks like a "Tony," and he smells like he never showers. Like he thinks he can cover up his body

344

odor with AXE. It's not working.

"Shining your shoes isn't 'hygienic,'" Frank says.

"It is when there's blood on them." Tony jerks my arm, and my wrists writhe in agony. I slip. We stop while I regain my footing. "C'mon, skank. We ain't got all day."

I stand. My back aches from walking bent over.

"Did you find out when we're getting paid?" Frank asks.

"I'm gonna get my shoes shined at the airport."

"When are we getting paid?"

"When we get outta here."

"When's that?"

"I don't know. Depends on whether she talks or not."

They pull me forward, and my foot slams into something solid, making me let out a muffled cry.

"Shut your trap." Tony squeezes my arm and pulls me up.

I want to head butt him, but—

Not yet.

I'll get my chance.

Patience.

I must not let the rage in. I must not let it win.

My foot slips, and I fall again.

"This ain't working," Frank says. "Here. Let's try this."

They flip me over, reach under my armpits, and drag me up a set of stairs backward. My heels bang on the steps. I lift my feet and kick, trying to get a foothold, but it doesn't work. The stairs sound hollow and thrum like they're made of steel.

What will happen if I don't talk? What will they do to me?

We stop.

Tony adjusts his grip.

"C'mon," Frank says. "She's not that heavy. Imagine if she was dead."

"You're right. Keep on kicking, lady. You're actually

helping us."

I let my body go limp like a child refusing to go to bed.

"Nice work, asshole. Now she's—"

"Whatever. We're almost there."

They drag me to the top.

A door creaks open, and my feet bounce over a threshold.

They pull me up straight and spin me around. Hands land on my shoulders, and Tony's woodsy stench penetrates my hood. It sounds like metal scraping against concrete until something hits the backs of my knees.

"Sit," Tony commands.

I sit.

He holds my shoulders against the chair.

Skirtch. Skirtch.

Someone else runs tape across my chest.

Skirtch.

They fasten my ankles to the chair's legs.

I bide my time.

I will kill them.

Someday, I will tie Tony to a chair like this one. I'll use a frayed extension cord, and when I plug it in, he'll light up like the Space Needle. Maybe he's married. Oh God, I hope they're both married. I'll escape and find their wives and rip their hair out, strand by strand, making these thugs watch. The release will feel so good.

"How's your vacation going, Lauren?" The old man's voice buzzes like a chainsaw.

I hold still.

He's here. In this room.

The red comes, but I hold still.

I must not let the anger in. I must not let it win.

"What's wrong?" he rasps. "Not speaking?"

"M-m. M-m."

"Oh, I'm sorry. I forgot. Frank told me he had to tape your mouth shut. You were saying some nasty things to him last night."

When I get my hands free, I'm going to do more than say nasty things.

Tony's woodsy cologne mixes with the old man's cigarette smoke, making me want to gag.

The old man has me now, but—

"Tony, what's that on your shoe," the old man asks.

"It's blood."

"Oh, Lauren. Did you misbehave? Did you lose your temper?"

I . . . hold . . . still.

"Take her hood off, Tony." His voice grates on my every nerve. "And the tape. We need to talk."

"Got it."

"Wait," Frank says.

"And just look at her wrists," the old man continues, "that looks so painful. I'm sorry, Lauren."

"M-m. M-m."

"Take those ties off, too, Tony. She's not the enemy. She's here to help us."

"But, Dennis," Frank says, "you don't understand. She's wild. She's insane."

"I know what she is. Just do it."

He's right. I am insane. I'm going to rip out the old man's throat and light it on fire. I'm going to breathe in the smoke and blow it in Tony's face until he smells better.

"You won't do anything stupid, will you, Lauren?"

The hood comes off.

Tony grabs the tape and rips it from my face, jerking my

head sideways before I can see the old man.

I open my mouth and stretch my jaw.

"Now," the old man says, "let's talk like civilized human beings."

CHAPTER FIFTY-SIX

LAUREN

The light burns my eyes. I strain against the gray duct tape binding my upper body to the chair. The same type of tape holds my ankles to the legs. I've been swallowing blood since the one with the awful cologne, Tony, punched me in the face. If he, or the other one—Frank—had told me where we were headed—to visit the old man—I wouldn't have resisted so much.

I want to see the old man. I want to kill him.

Dennis.

Frank called him *Dennis*.

But I can't see him because of the light. Because my eyes are watering.

I rock forward, and someone pulls my chair back, slamming the legs down. My hands are zip-tied behind my back. The thug on my right is a blurry blob, and a brown, amorphous shape swims in front of me. It's a desk.

"Hold still," Tony says, his voice coming from behind.

Snip.

My hands are free.

I reach for the thug on my right, flailing.

He steps back, just out of reach.

"Relax, Lauren." The old man's chain-rattling voice comes from the desk.

I rub my eyes.

The desk is covered in dust, and a thick, old laptop lies in the center. Dennis sits on the other side with his back to me. It's definitely him. The old man from the grocery store. Gray hair sticks out from beneath his baseball cap—blue this time—and a cigarette dangles from his hand. The smoke rises and mixes with a cloud that hangs from the ceiling the way smog hangs over Mexico City.

There are no doors that I can see from this angle. There are no windows. A single light hangs from a wire in the middle of the ceiling, but it's too weak to reach the corners. Ancient circuit boards, desktop computer enclosures, and cables hide in the shadows beyond the old man.

Beyond *Dennis*.

I glare at the back of his head.

He takes a drag on his cigarette.

Tony's rotten cologne precedes him as steps out from behind me and stands on my left. His face looks like he smells—wooden pits filled with oily pools of rum. Frank stands on my right, his hands clasped over his waist. A stone-cold statue in a white silk shirt. Black palm trees decorate his sides. He's dressed for vacation, but he's not smiling.

I grasp the tape around my chest and pull on it with both hands. "You can't keep me here."

Tony slaps me in the face.

I suck on my cheek and spit blood on his shoe.

He slaps me again.

"That's enough, Tony." More smoke rises above

Dennis's head.

I lean to my right, looking for a mirror or something reflective in the menagerie of equipment beyond him. How did he know it was Tony and not Frank who slapped me?

A green light flashes in the corner of the ceiling above the equipment.

It's a security camera.

"Why am I here? I gave you what you asked for." I say.

Dennis laughs.

"I demand you let me go." I grasp the tape and pull again, hoping Tony doesn't strike me a third time.

Instead, he puts a gun to my head.

"You're in no position to demand anything, Lauren," Dennis responds.

The red comes, and I want to let him have it. I want to rip the tape off, then rip his head off. I—

I must not let the anger in. I must not let it win.

I let go of the tape. "Was it you? Were you driving the Audi? Did you kill my husband?"

"Audi?" He holds his cigarette out to the side, taps it, and lets the ashes fall to the floor. "Tony, please put your gun away. She's not going to try to escape, are you Lauren?"

I grit my teeth. "No."

"Can I pop her if she does?" Tony asks.

"Not unless you want more blood on your shoes," Frank says.

Tony lowers his gun. Stows it in his jacket.

Dennis's voice drones. "We need the card."

"Let me go. I already gave you William's computer."

"And I appreciate that, though it was a challenge. It took the guys a lot longer than I expected to break into it and decrypt the files."

"Then you know more than me. Let me go."

"Stop lying, Lauren."

"Turn around, you coward." I'm in a red tunnel. "Look me in the eyes. I'm telling you the truth."

"Frank, can you come over here?" Statue man marches around the desk, and Dennis hands him a computer tablet. The old bastard was watching me on that thing this entire time. "Please, show her this."

"Why won't you face me?" I ask.

Frank approaches, holding the screen so I can see it. I lean forward, stressing the tape. The screen shows a picture taken from inside William's office back home. It's the painting of St. Croix.

"Do you recognize this?" Dennis asks.

I hesitate.

"Lauren?"

"Yes. That's a picture. I bet you found a lot of pictures."

"We did." He lets out a corroded chuckle. "We had a team of volunteers work through the night looking at all the pictures, but there's something special about this one, isn't there? It's why you're here, isn't it?"

"I'm here because you assholes kidnapped me."

Slap.

"Tony," Dennis says, "please control yourself."

I put my hand on my cheek.

"Lauren," he continues, "what is special about this one?"

"It's a picture of our painting of St. Croix. We had an artist paint it for us after our honeymoon. It's special to us. To William and I."

"Not the painting. The file. What's special about the file?"

I shake my head.

"Stop playing stupid." His voice deepens. "Where's the

card?"

"I don't know."

"Your husband named this image file *sdcard.jpg*. You found it, saw the painting of St. Croix, and that's why you came here. To get the card. The *SD* card."

"I couldn't get into his computer. I've never seen this file before in my life. I don't even know what an 'SD card' is."

"It's one of those things you put in your phone for more pictures, you stupid bitch." Tony raises his hand, glances at Dennis, then lowers it.

Dennis speaks up. "You should have told me about the file, Lauren. I could have paid for your flight. We could have sat next to each other on the plane. We could have avoided all this nastiness."

Tony licks his lips.

Frank is expressionless.

"I don't know where the card is," I say.

"How about Mason?" Dennis asks. "Does he know?"

"No. He doesn't know anything. Leave him alone."

"Oh, I plan to—after I get the card. Besides, I'm not into dudes." He laughs. "But because you lied about finding the file, I'm not sure I can believe you about your son. I think he knows something."

I clench my fists. My jaw tightens.

"How much worse do you want things to get, Lauren? You already lost your husband over this thing. You're not the caring type, are you? You barely know your son."

"Shut up, you—"

"I think it's because you're too angry. Too upset all the time. You didn't even attend your husband's funeral."

I jerk forward. "That's because *you* were there. You and your thugs kept me from saying goodbye. You—you, asshole!"

Frank backs away, walks around the desk, returns the laptop to Dennis.

"Tony, go ahead."

Tony grabs my hair and pulls. My neck bends backward over the top of the chair, exposing my throat. My trachea feels like there's a rock inside it. His face hovers near mine, and the stench of rotten rum makes me gag. I reach for his eyeballs, but he pulls out a knife and presses the flat side against my throat.

Dennis raises his voice. "Where is the card, Lauren?"

"I—"

"Do you know what happens to people who smoke too much?"

I can't speak. Tony presses the knife hard against my voice box. I can barely breathe.

"They cut a hole in their neck so they can get air easier. It's called a laryngectomy."

"Stop," I rasp.

"What was that?"

Tony relaxes his hold on my hair.

"Stop. I can't breathe."

"That's what I'm talking about," Dennis says. "A laryngectomy so you can breathe. Or . . . you can tell me where the SD card is."

It was never an index card. Or a business card. Why didn't William yell, *The* SD *card is in St. Croix*? He's dead because of a stupid little chip. "Fuck you," I say to the old man. "Even if I knew where it was, I—"

I reach for Tony's eyes again. He moves his head, but not the knife, and I grab his wrist, and I scream at him. He pulls harder on my hair and tilts the blade. The point pierces my throat. Blood streams down my neck, and I hold my arms out like Jesus on the cross.

My hands shake, and the rage comes.

I must not let the rage in. I must not let it win.

If I attack, Tony will cut me deeper. He'll kill me.

I close my eyes.

I must not let the anger in. I must not let it win.

I lower my arms.

Relax my shoulders.

Open my eyes.

There's a ceiling fan behind the light. It's not moving.

"Last chance, Lauren. Are you going to tell us where the card is?"

Tony relaxes his grip on my hair enough for me to nod yes.

"Let her speak."

He pulls the knife away, and I sit up.

"Well?" Dennis asks.

"It's in my condo, but you'll have to take me with you unless you want to break in and search for it yourself."

"Give us the keys," Tony says.

"My condo's in a gated complex. There are no keys. Only keycards. You'll need me to ask for a replacement."

"Why?" Dennis asks. "Where's your keycard?"

"I lost it when your thugs grabbed me last night. It was in my handbag. The one my husband gave me for our—"

"We can break in," Tony says.

"No." Dennis clears his throat. His voice sounds like an old tractor going over a bump. "Where is the SD card in the condo?"

I glance at Tony. "It's not in a cell phone, I can tell you that."

Tony pulls out a white handkerchief. "I can make her tell us now if you want." He wipes his knife.

"Those cards are small," Frank says. "We might not be able to find it. Especially if she's lying again."

Tony wipes the blood off my neck and puts the handkerchief back in his jacket. "Let's leave her here while we go—"

"No," Dennis rasps. "We're running out of time. I can't have you two traipsing back and forth, trying to find the card, or worse, getting caught breaking and entering. Take her with you."

"Then what?" Tony asks.

"Bring the card back to me."

"Then what? What about her?"

Dennis twiddles his cigarette between his fingers. A smoke tendril spirals toward the ceiling. "Then you can do whatever you want with her. Consider it a bonus."

Frank glances down at Tony's shoes.

Tony looks at me, spreads his lips, and licks his teeth.

I put my hand on my chest and feel for William's wedding ring.

It's still there, hiding beneath my blouse, and suddenly . . . I'm not angry.

I'm ready.

CHAPTER FIFTY-SEVEN

RYAN

The throbbing begins in the base of Ryan's neck and works its way up into his skull where it beats on his brain, every pulse forcing him to close his eyes, every step toward the kitchen an onslaught of gut-wrenching pain.

He opens the freezer to get some ice for his head and squints at the incandescent light hiding behind the frost.

A Vodka bottle lies nestled between a bag of peas and the ice tray. He picks the bottle up, not remembering when he put it there, or when he bought it, or why it's half empty—or is it half full? He swirls the bottle and watches the Vodka wash up the sides. The motion makes him dizzy, but if this is all he drank, that's not so bad. After eight sober years, it makes sense he would have a horrendous hangover.

Then he glimpses his computer desk.

Beer cans everywhere. Bent and crushed. Not a six-pack—no—he must have bought twelve. His Java programming books lie in a heap on the floor. An empty whiskey bottle shadows his coffee cup on the desk, and he remembers mixing the two. He needed caffeine to stay awake so he could drink more.

He always wants more.

Eight sober years.

Gone.

It's as if he never stopped drinking.

After finding Juan's Vodka in the couch last night, he drank it. That much is clear, but everything after that plays like a damaged film. He was off to the races. He went to the convenience store where he used to buy all his booze and saw Pradeep. Pradeep—his old friend. Pradeep told Ryan he'd missed seeing him.

It felt so good to be missed.

Ryan had only wanted a six-pack. That's not much. He only wanted to keep the Vodka buzz going until bedtime, but then he bought the beer *and* the whiskey. And why wouldn't he? He'd already started drinking, and tomorrow he would have to quit again, so why not get the whiskey?

So he did.

Then he sat at his computer and played Texas Hold'em with new online friends. The minutes flew by. He won some, lost some. They didn't judge him. They didn't make him feel guilty for not helping alcoholics. For not saving Juan. For not making amends to his brother.

They played cards.

It was bliss. Mindless bliss.

To make the bliss last, he put on a pot of coffee and used it as a mixer for his whiskey, and when the whiskey was gone, Pradeep was waiting for him with a bottle of Vodka.

This bottle of Vodka.

Ryan swirls the bottle again.

His stomach churns.

His good friend Pradeep was waiting for him with this

bottle of Vodka, and it's still half full. Maybe his addiction has lessened. A true alcoholic would have finished this bottle last night. A true alcoholic wouldn't have had the presence of mind to put it back in the freezer. Maybe he's not really an alcoholic.

Stinking thinking.

Denial.

His forgetter is telling him he's not an alcoholic.

He needs help.

He puts the bottle on the counter and pulls out the ice tray. A lone cube hangs onto a corner spot. It won't come out no matter how hard Ryan twists the tray, and his throat constricts, and his pulse beats the backs of his eyes with blood. He puts the tray down and remembers running into his landlord in the hallway.

Oh, God. Carl. He talked to Carl.

It must have been after midnight.

Carl talked about visiting his grandmother in New Jersey.

Ryan talked about the rent. He told Carl he wasn't moving out. That he would have the money by next week. He—did he?

Yes.

He told Carl about the $150,000.

Oh, God.

He rubs his eyes, his head, the back of his neck.

What else did he say? Did he tell Carl about the DFF?

The clock on the stove reads noon.

He kneads the back of his neck, desperately massaging the muscles, but the throbbing won't go away. He should go to the one o'clock Wednesday meeting, but the Vodka bottle sits on the counter, half full. He still feels last night's remnants coursing through his system.

He takes the bottle over to his desk and puts it down next to his rock.

The rough side is up.

Juan is dead.

Nothing matters, but—he's got to try.

He opens Firefox and browses to the AA website. It's been years since he went to the one o'clock meeting. Maybe they don't do it anymore. With any luck, they don't, and he'll have an excuse. Besides, going to a meeting drunk is like watching a movie with your eyes closed. You can hear what's going on, but it doesn't make any sense.

An ad for leaf blowers pops up, and he closes it. He's not a landscaper. He's not a truck driver, and he'll never be a computer programmer.

He's a drunk.

The one o'clock meeting has moved across town. He can't walk there in time, and he's probably too drunk to drive. He could lose his license or worse. Jail. He's not going back to jail. Once is enough. He should never have been sent there in the first place. That was all Lauren's fault.

Lauren.

Mason.

His brother.

Now that he's drinking again, William will hate him. He'll never be able to make amends, so why try?

More stinking thinking.

Don't give up. Do the next right thing. Call another alcoholic. Don't take that first drink.

But he did take that first drink.

The guilt impales him. AA has ruined his drinking career. There's nothing worse than a head full of AA and a belly full of beer. He should have finished the bottle last night so he wouldn't be tempted now.

Life is full of should-haves.

He should have called Garage Mike and asked for help.

He should have poured the Vodka in the toilet before going to bed. But he didn't. It's like he planned this. It's like he saved some to get rid of his hangover this morning.

Old habits never die.

It's like he never stopped drinking.

He opens the bottle. Sniffs the lid. Licks the rim.

It burns going down, and his hangover eases.

A screwdriver sounds good. He walks to the kitchen, empties the Vodka into a 7-Eleven Big Gulp cup, tops it off with a dash of orange juice, then returns to his computer.

The minutes fly by.

When he's up twenty-thousand dollars, playing his fake Texas Hold'em card game with his fake online friends, he's overcome with loneliness. Then he loses a big hand, and his cup is almost empty. He has no reason to stay here.

He's lonely.

He misses his friend at the convenience store.

He misses his brother too, but he misses his friend more.

He misses Pradeep.

CHAPTER FIFTY-EIGHT

LAUREN

The tape around my wrists closes off the blood flow to my hands. They tingle, yet I'm glad those thugs didn't bind my wrists with a zip tie like last night. This is much more pleasant.

"Stop wiggling," Tony says. He reeks of rotten wood. He must have put on more cologne when I wasn't looking.

"Is this the place?" Frank asks, slowing the car down.

Spindly bushes reach through a black iron fence surrounding my condo complex. "Yes. The main gate is still a ways off, but if you follow the fence, you'll get there." We're miles from town. My phone is in my red Gucci bag somewhere in the streets of Christiansted, probably smashed to pieces.

"You must be loaded," Tony says. "This place is nice."

"Not really."

The countryside whizzes by. I keep an eye out for Mason. All night, I worried he didn't make it back to the condo after the parade, but now, I'm hoping he didn't.

God, Tony stinks.

I'm sitting next to him in the back seat right behind Frank.

I press up against the door, trying to keep my distance. He sits in the middle, leaning forward between the front seats, so he can talk to Frank.

Frank hits the gas, and we fly around a corner.

Palm trees and yellow-flowered casha bushes run alongside the road.

"When are you going to take the tape off my wrists?" I ask.

"I'm not," Tony says.

Frank accelerates up a hill. "As long as you're in the car, the tape stays on."

"The gate is locked. You'll have to let me out to talk into the intercom."

"No," Tony says.

"They have cameras. They'll see the tape."

Frank slows down, turns onto the narrow drive leading up to the gate. The peach-colored condo units, with their flat-top roofs, are stacked across the hilltop.

"No they won't," Frank says. "You can lean out the window." He hits the button, and my window lowers.

At first, the air feels good on my face, then my bruised cheek stings, and my cracked lips burn. "They won't be able to hear me."

"Then yell," Tony grumbles.

Frank angles the car close to the intercom and stops.

"Welcome to Questa Verde," Tony says.

"What?" Frank puts the transmission in park.

"The sign. It says, 'Welcome to Questa Verde.'"

I stick my head out the window, and Tony grabs my arm, pulls me back inside. Breathes into my ear. "One wrong word, and Frank will shoot you." His breath is toxic. "But he'll only hit your shoulder." His teeth haven't been brushed in ages.

"Then we'll play Christmas. I'll carve you up like a ham. Won't that be fun?" He brandishes a knife, keeping it low by his crotch.

For just a moment, I see the flicker of an abused child in his eyes.

I nod.

His oily skin glistens and turns red.

The inside of the car turns red.

I must not let the anger in. I must not let it win.

I stick my head back outside. "Anyone there?" The salty air hasn't been kind to the intercom. Rust covers the white wire mesh. "Hello?"

"How can I help you?" A man asks. The mesh vibrates with his voice.

"This is Mrs. Kaine in unit 106. I forgot my keycard. Can you buzz me in?"

"Mrs. *Who?*"

"Kaine."

"I'm sorry. Did you say 'Lane?'"

I turn to Tony. "See?"

"Yell louder." He shoves me toward the window.

"No. This is Mrs. Kaine. Unit 106."

"Can you get closer to the speaker? If you're making a delivery, the service entrance is on the other side."

I lean out farther, careful not to let my lips touch the rust. "Open the gate, please. This is Mrs. Kaine in unit 106. I left my keycard inside, and—can you please open the—"

The speaker crackles. "Are you okay?"

I glance up. A security camera hangs from a pole "I'm fine. I was riding a bicycle and, well, I haven't ridden one in years. I had a crash."

The speaker crackles, and I can't make out what he's

saying.

"Can I please get in? I need some Ibuprofen. My head is killing me."

"O-k-k-kay." The speaker crackles, and it reminds me of Dennis's chainsaw voice. "Someone will meet you at 106 in a few minutes."

The gate opens, and we cruise inside.

"It's to the right." Mason had better not be in the condo. The thought of Tony putting his knife to my son's throat terrifies me. Our luggage and passports are by the front door, but there won't be time to take them with us. We'll need to run first and sneak back later.

Tony puts his knife away and leans forward between the seats. "What's the plan? They're sending someone to the door. What are we going to do about them?"

"Nothing," Frank says. "I'm not getting out."

"Why not?"

"I don't want to be seen. Look around. There are cameras everywhere. If something goes wrong, I'm not going down. There's no way I'm going back to prison."

"You're right."

"That's it up ahead," I say.

He parks on the other side of the lot, away from the building. Away from the cameras near my unit.

Tony sits back, pulls out his gun, and licks his teeth.

Frank eyes me in the rearview mirror. "Lauren, listen. I'll have my gun on you the entire time. Don't do anything stupid. When the attendant comes, you thank him for coming. When he opens the door for you, you thank him for opening the door. Is it customary to tip at this place?"

"Yes," I say.

"Tony, give her five dollars."

"Why do I—" Frank shoots him a look. "Never mind." He pulls out a five and hands it to me.

"Thanks," I say.

"Don't thank me. I'm just paying it forward. You're going to play Christmas with me later. You're my bonus."

I feel sick.

"After you're inside," Frank says, "you've got five minutes to get the card and come back. Got it?"

"What if she runs out the back door?"

"She won't because you'll be there."

"No way. I don't want to be seen."

"Do you have any better ideas?"

Tony gazes at the condo. Frowns. "No."

"Just stay away from the cameras." Frank turns off the child locks. "You'll be alright. Go now before the attendant comes."

Tony opens the back door and gives me a parting wink.

Frank says, "Remember. You've got five minutes to get the card and come back. You understand?"

"Yes."

"If you don't, it'll be playtime with Tony. Maybe not today. Maybe not tomorrow. But it will happen. Dennis will have him kill your son first. Then he'll come for you."

"You son-of-bitch," I say under my breath.

A young man with light ebony skin, white shorts, and a white, short-sleeved button-down shirt walks toward the condo with a keycard in his hand and bounce in his step. His eyes are as relaxed as a pair of empty hammocks, and he moves as if he's listening to music, but he's not wearing headphones.

I step out of the car, and Frank rolls his window partway down.

His gun is barely detectable behind the tinted glass.

I walk across the lot, waving to the attendant.

"Mrs. Kaine?" the attendant says.

"Yes."

He reaches toward my cheek. "You got a hurt on you."

"Yes." I cover my face and look down. "I crashed on a bicycle."

"So sorry." He swipes the keycard in the lock. "It don't look like a bicycle crash, though."

I grab the handle and step inside.

"It looks like you lost a fight." He puts his hand on the door jamb.

Frank leans out the window, gun in hand.

"Thank you for letting me in. Have a nice day."

The attendant looks up to the sky. "It is a nice day today."

"Yes, well, I—oh." I pull out the five dollars and hand it to him.

"Nicer day, now. You take care of that bruise, okay?"

"I will. Thank you." I close the door and lock it.

The luggage is where I left it next to the dining table.

"Mason? Are you here?"

For the first time since we bought this place, I wish we'd paid for telephone service. The kitchen phone only connects to the condo's office.

I dial.

"Questa Verde. Main office."

"I need the police. Now. I'm in 106."

"What's the problem?"

"Can you transfer me to the police?"

"I don't know if this phone can do transfers. Let me see."

"What's wrong with you?"

"Hold on."

The line clicks and goes dead. "Are you still there?"

I check the clock on the stove. At least a minute has passed. Maybe two.

"Mason?"

I rush into his room. His phone isn't there. He must have come back.

I check the bathroom, then my bedroom.

He's not here.

Computer parts litter the floor, and I remember my episode. I trip over a power cord on my way to the other side, stumble and catch myself on the sliding glass door. It's locked. Outside, beyond the patio, beyond the lawn, Tony stands in the bushes, waiting for Christmas.

I run to the walk-in closet and punch the code into the safe. William put enough money in here to outlast a nuclear winter. I take a bundle of hundreds and glance in the mirror. My face will be scarred forever.

Knock. Knock. Knock.

"Lauren?"

It hasn't been five minutes.

I race to the kitchen and pick up the phone. "Hello? Are you there?"

"Come on out," Frank yells. "It's time to go."

"Yes," the woman says, "I'm here. I'm sorry, it's my first day at work and they didn't show me how to transfer calls."

Bang, bang, bang.

"Call the police. Unit 106."

I drop the phone and open my suitcase's outer pocket.

"Lauren," Frank yells. "Don't make me break the door down."

"Just a minute." I grab the passports.

"You don't have a minute."

My suitcase weighs a ton, but I manage to heave it onto the dining table and position it so the handle faces the door.

"Open up now, or I'm coming in."

Maybe he's bluffing. He didn't want to be seen. What changed?

I peer into the peephole. He's got one hand in his jacket pocket, and he bangs on the door with the other, startling me.

"Hold on," I say.

My heart races.

The anger comes, and I welcome it in.

Bang, bang—crack!

The front door flies open.

I turn away.

"Stop," Frank commands.

He pulls out his gun.

I grab the suitcase and lean back like an Olympic hammer tosser.

He aims.

I swing.

Everything is red, and I connect.

His gun goes flying.

He's knocked off balance and stumbles toward the oven.

I'm out the door, running. I make it to the other side of the lot before he fires. The back window of the car next to me shatters, and I duck down between it and the fence, but I don't stop moving. I crawl.

"Tony, let's go." he yells.

I creep behind the next car over, then the next, keeping my profile low.

He bounds down the steps and stops, looking back and forth.

I hold my breath.

When he pulls out his phone, I make a break for the service entrance, and I don't look back.

The service gate opens to let a truck in just as I get there, and I run across the road into the forest. There are sirens in the distance. I fight my way through the foliage, pulling on slick branches and stepping on uncertain clumps of weeds and vines.

Either I lost Frank and Tony, or they didn't come after me.

My car is in downtown Christiansted near the Buckotora, where I left it last night. Or, it's been towed. It doesn't matter. I don't have my keys, and I've got to stay off the streets.

I've got to find Mason.

The forest clears, and a shack sits on the other side of a dirt road.

There's a bicycle out front.

It's been years since I've ridden a bicycle.

CHAPTER FIFTY-NINE

MASON

Mason stands on the top of the hill at the corner of King's Cross and Queen Street, wondering if his mom's car is still at Jackson park. It wasn't at the condo last night, and it wasn't there this morning. Far away, a lone sailboat floats in the bay, a white fleck on the blue horizon.

His legs ache from walking. He should have taken an Uber, but he has no money. Trent stiffed him with the bill at the Buckotora last night, and when he couldn't pay, he ran. Then he wandered around Christiansted not knowing what to do before giving in and going back to face his mother's wrath.

The wrath of the dragon.

But she wasn't at the condo.

Like Trent, she abandoned him.

Like his father, she's gone.

The airport is on the other side of the island, miles away. If she went to the airport, she's probably on a plane already. Could she have left? Could she have become so angry with him for running away that she flew back to Washington alone?

If anyone could get that mad, it would be her.

He checks his phone for messages. Nothing new. The most recent texts came yesterday afternoon, and they're all from her. Worried, angry texts. The last one is an incoherent jumble of numbers and letters. Then she stopped texting.

She abandoned him.

No.

This is his fault. He's just like Trent. And his father.

He abandoned *her*.

He types, "so sorry. where are you?" and hits the SEND button.

A moment passes with no response. No flashing "dragon is typing" notification.

She's not going to reply. She's gone.

He trudges down the hill toward the park. Toward the ocean.

Alone.

Pressure builds in his head. He doesn't want to cry, but it's all too much. Everything is too much.

If her car is at the park, then what? Where'd she go? Did the bald man from the funeral come? Did he kill her?

If her car isn't at the park, then . . . did she leave? Did she leave him here to survive on his own? Sink or swim?

Sink or swim.

He crosses the intersection at the bottom of the hill and continues down Queen Street toward the park. His eyes burn as they fill with tears. The road runs past the parking lot, ending at the bay. There's nothing to stop him from going for a swim. He could keep walking straight ahead, off the pavement, onto the sand, and into the water. Into the blue depths of the Atlantic. Walking until his feet leave the ocean floor, and he floats, and his head goes under, and he is no more.

Sink or swim?

He never learned how to swim.

"Mason!"

He's never seen his mother on a bicycle before, either, but there she is, coming down the hill at high speed on an old fat-tire bike. She looks ridiculous.

He wants to laugh, but that might make her mad.

She's coming fast.

"Mason, wait."

She takes a hand off the handlebars and waves at him, nearly crashing into a power pole. The bike wobbles out of control, and her feet leave the pedals. She holds her legs away from the frame while the pedals spin.

He covers his face and turns away so she can't see him smile. She looks so ridiculous.

"Mason. Stop right there."

She's yelling at him. As stupid as she looks, she must be livid with him for running away. He glances over his shoulder. Her face is red, and—it's kind of messed up.

The bicycle tips over, and she jumps off, landing on her feet, letting the frame slide into the curb. She sprints toward him faster than he thought possible.

He's petrified.

It's too late to run.

She raises her hands.

Her face is cut and bruised like she got in a fight.

She's going to hit him. Slap him, beat him—

He shields himself, crouches down, and she barrels into him. They roll onto the ground. "Mason. Oh, God. Mason, you're okay." She grips his shoulders and smiles at him. There's a gash on her forehead, her cheek is purple, and her left eye is almost swollen shut. "You're okay."

"I'm sorry. I—"

"It's okay." She pulls him to her chest. "I'm just glad you're safe."

He hugs her back, and like a Japanese tsunami, tears flood his eyes. "Mom, I'm gay."

"I know," she says.

"No. I'm *really* gay."

She grasps him by the shoulders. Looks into his eyes. "And I'm your mother. And I love you."

"Aren't you angry?"

"No."

"But I ran away, and I'm—"

"I'm not angry." She strokes his cheek. Wipes away a tear. "I'm so sorry for all the times I yelled at you. Embarrassed you. I'm trying. I'm—" She takes a deep breath. "I'm not letting the anger win anymore. I'm not going to let it in. Not anymore."

CHAPTER SIXTY

LAUREN

"This way."

I take Mason's hand and pull him into an alley. We run. I'd love to find a breakfast place, sit down, drink a latte, and talk to him, but if Frank's threat holds true, the old man has someone looking for us right now. I don't know if the police arrived at the condo in time to arrest Frank and Tony, but I'm not going to risk it. The Questa Verde office girl might not have called the police like I asked.

"Where's your car?" Mason asks.

"I lost my keys."

"Where?"

"Come on." We stop at the end of the alley, and I peer down the street. "My keys were in my handbag with my phone. I lost it last night. I—" I scrunch my face, holding back the tears. In this moment, losing that bag is like losing William all over again, and—I bite my lip.

"Are you okay? What happened to your face?"

"It's nothing." I wipe my eyes. "Your father gave me that bag for our twentieth anniversary. It was a Gucci." I grasp

William's wedding ring through my blouse. "I promised myself I would carry it with me forever."

"I'm sorry."

I sniff back the tears. "It's okay. It was unrealistic. Come on. We don't have time."

"But what happened to your face?"

We scurry across the street into the next alley. I want to get off this island, but Dennis might have men at the airport. From the beginning, he said he would take Mason if I contacted the police. He most certainly has his thugs watching the police station. I can't believe I talked to that policeman yesterday when Mason disappeared. How stupid.

I lead Mason behind the buildings parallel to King's Cross, keeping out of sight until we reach the edge of Christiansted. Large plots of land covered in reckless shrubs surround dilapidated shacks on either side of the road.

"Mom, wait."

"Over here. Hurry."

"Wait." His eyes plead, and he starts to limp. "Can't we stop for a minute?"

"No, we have to keep moving."

"Why?"

I grab his hand and pull. "The Moko Jumbie are after us."

His eyes bulge with terror. "What?"

I shouldn't have said that.

We run across a dirt driveway and down into a shallow culvert thick with brush. I tell him how Dennis's thugs were dressed up as Moko Jumbie. How they put a hood over my head and locked me up overnight. How Dennis interrogated me, asking about William's technology, and how a horrific smelling man named Tony punched me in the face.

We approach Christiansted Bypass, the main road to

town, and stand near a Maho tree, waiting for the traffic to clear. Recovery Hill and miles of unspoiled island forest await us on the other side.

I check my pocket for the passports and the emergency money. Everything is still there.

"I've always been afraid of the Moko Jumbie," Mason says.

"I know." I grab his hand. "C'mon, it's clear."

We run over the four-lane highway and down a short incline to the mouth of a dirt road. "Hurry." A military green water tower lies at the end of the road, and we rush to the other side. "Let me see your phone."

He glances at the screen before handing it over. "There's a signal."

"Oh, no. That means they can track us." I head for the trees.

"Mom, the condo isn't that way."

"I know. We're not going to the condo."

"What are we going to do?"

"We're sleeping out here tonight."

"Why?"

"Because we can't go to the airport. The old man will be looking for us there. If he doesn't find us by tomorrow, he'll give up. Then we can go to the airport and get the hell out of here."

He stumbles, his foot gets caught in a bramble, and I grab his arm.

"I'm alright," he says.

His phone has completely lost its signal now, but I don't feel safe. We continue on, hiking through the hills. The afternoon sun beats down. We forge our way through thickets of reeds and flower bushes bearing thorns.

"Did your father ever talk about a card?" I ask.

Mason wipes sweat from his brow. "What kind of card?"

"An SD card. He said his technology was on a card."

"He put a bigger one in my phone one time to make it faster." He puts his hand in his pocket. "I wonder if there's one in my new phone. It's kind of slow."

"I'm sorry he's not here to fix it for you."

"It's not your fault." He stops walking. Looks me in the eyes. "You didn't make him fall, right?"

"Of course not. I tried to save him."

His eyes puff up. "I'm sorry. I'm so sorry. I—"

"What?"

"I blamed you. I was going to run away because—"

"Why?"

"You're always so angry." He sniffs. "I thought Dad jumped to get away from you."

I take his hand. "Mason, I understand. I'm so sorry. I never wanted to hurt you, but . . . I'm sick. My anger has gotten out of control since your father passed. I never—I should have told you about the old man sooner. You could have helped me."

He turns away. "I'm sorry."

"You have nothing to be sorry for."

"But I ran away, and they took you and beat you up because of me." He raises his voice. "I'm sorry."

I put my hand on his shoulder. "Then I forgive you. Can you forgive me?"

"Yeah." He wipes his face. "Let's just go."

We walk hand in hand. Never have I felt so close to him. So whole. So in control of myself. Forgiveness is the key.

"Mason, I want you to tell me something."

"What?"

"I know you've been seeing a man." The words sound strange coming out of my mouth—Mason with a man. But hearing myself say it out loud makes it feel natural, like something I've always known. "Who is he?"

"I would have told you sooner, but I didn't know how you'd take it. Me being gay."

"I haven't always shown it because of my—you know, condition, but I love you. I love you so much. You're my son, and I'll always love you, no matter who you are."

He steps over a fallen palm. "Stop it." His face reddens. "You're embarrassing me."

"And I'll always protect you but, I need to know who that man is."

"It doesn't matter." He swallows hard. "It's over."

"I saw him at your father's work last week."

"Trent?"

"His name is Trent?"

"Yeah."

"Trent who?"

"I don't know—wait. Dalrymple, I think. Why does it matter?"

"I think he's been spying on me. He keeps driving by our house."

"Yeah, but that's because we were dating, or . . . okay. We had *one* date before you and I came here."

"Did you tell him where we were going?"

"No. He just knew. He—" Mason stops walking, leans forward. Puts his hand on his head. "No. No, no."

"What is it?"

"He asked about Dad. About Dad's work. He was obsessed with it. And his car, it's—"

"Black. I know."

Mason's upper lip twists. "He was using me."

The familiar red flare shoots across my vision. I will get even with this man for hurting my son. "That's what I was afraid of when I saw you kissing last night."

"What? You saw us kiss? You were *spying* on me?"

"No. I was protecting you, but then you looked so happy, and then the Moko Jumbie grabbed me."

He gazes at my face—at my cheek—and sighs. "It's okay. You were right." He walks away. "Trent used me. I can't believe he is one of them."

I catch up. "What did he ask you about?"

"He said he was into the internet and wanted to know if Dad built websites. I didn't know."

"Did he ask about the card?"

"The SD card?"

"Yes."

He rubs his chin. "No. I don't think so. He mentioned the cloud and a bunch of other stuff."

"Have you heard from him since last night? Has he texted you?"

"No. It's over. I deleted his number."

"Oh." A small clearing opens up ahead. "That's probably for the best." My feet, throat, and cheek throb. I check Mason's phone. Still no signal. "This is far enough."

We cross the clearing and stop at the base of an ancient kapok tree. The venerable giant's roots climb out of the ground and hold its thick mast upright. The branchless trunk stretches into the sky, blooming into a wide-leafed canopy, keeping the forest floor drenched in shadow. I find a space in between the roots for Mason and me.

I collapse onto the ground, sitting with my legs crossed.

Mason sits close by my side.

"Are we sleeping here?" he asks.

"I think so."

"Does your face hurt?"

"I'm okay."

"Did you hit them back? I bet you lost your temper big time."

"Not as much as you would think." A breeze ruffles the leaves high above us. "I'm not letting my anger win anymore. I'm using it to my advantage."

"It's your *ki*."

"My what?"

"Nothing. It's a manga thing."

"No, tell me." My eyelids are heavy.

"It's from *Dragon Ball*. *Ki* is the life force that flows through everyone. It's super powerful. Some characters train for years to harness its energy so they can use it against their enemies, like you with your anger, but if they mess up, it can be really bad."

"It's not easy." I lie back against the tree. "I have to stop letting it in." I close my eyes. "I have to stop letting it win."

"What?"

"Get some sleep. We have a big day tomorrow."

CHAPTER SIXTY-ONE

RYAN

Ryan drifts toward his regular meeting at the First Light Church. After drinking the day away, he feels no pain. Seattle's skyline swallowed the sun an hour ago, and a dismal mist hangs in the air. It's refreshing out, but he may have overdone it. He sees two First Light Churches, one overlapping the other. He closes his right eye, and now there is one church. He opens his right eye and closes his left. The church pops to the right like magic.

Double-vision is a pain in the ass.

He can't read the time on his phone, but he knows he's late for the meeting. Taking that hot bath before leaving home made him late, but it was so luxurious. He was warm, inside and out.

He blinks until there is one church. One phone. One time. One more chance.

He walks around the corner of the church and crouches in the shadows by a basement window. The window filters the light coming from everyone's experience, strength, and hope.

Ryan has experience. If he can talk to Steve, he'll have

hope. Strength? Not so much. He questions why he ever started going to AA. It's so good to be free. To be himself. To drink with impunity. The only problem is, if he doesn't stay drunk, the freedom dies.

Wait.

How much money does he have left?

He reaches into his jacket pocket and feels around for his wallet. His hand comes out with a mini shooter. Peppermint schnapps. The little bottle feels good in his fist.

The basement window muffles the chairperson's voice, and the frosted coating hides her face. He listens for Steve. Between the ringing in his ears and the breeze, he can't make out anyone's words.

He waits.

People take turns sharing, but Steve never speaks.

Where is Steve? Ryan needs to talk to him about Luis. Reopen . . . what's the word?

Negotiate.

He needs to negotiate with Luis and the DFF.

He needs money.

But he's sick. He needs to stop drinking.

It's not too late. He could still go inside and raise his hand. It couldn't have been more than fifteen minutes since he knelt by the window, but—his phone shows five minutes until the top of the hour. He's been crouched out here for over forty minutes.

Time flies when you're having fun.

He didn't want to raise his hand anyway. Not tonight. He can stop drinking tomorrow.

The pleasant *pop* of the schnapps cap coming off the cute little bottle ignites his saliva glands, and he sucks it down. The minty sting is hot and cold at the same time.

Inside, the recovering alcoholics speak in unison. They end the meeting with the serenity prayer—*God grant me the serenity to . . .*

Ryan runs across the street to the parking lot. The keys inside his jeans pocket jab his thigh. He's got his keys, and he has Juan's. He might as well throw Juan's keys away. The big man is never coming back.

Hiding behind a Park-n-Ride sign, he peers around the edge, and two churches peer back at him. He shakes his head, blinks, closes one eye, then the other.

One by one, members of his homegroup appear at the top of the stairs. He watches carefully, but Steve doesn't come out.

Ryan wanted advice on negotiating with Luis. For an advance on the $150,000, Ryan will talk to his brother. He'll get William's technology. At least, that's what he wants Luis to think. Ryan doesn't plan on stealing from his brother, he just wants an advance. Ten thousand dollars ought to do it. He'd settle for five.

Something. Anything.

His mouth is dry.

He needs a drink.

Ryan stands, fishes in his pocket for another mini shooter, and downs it. Fuel for the road. He ambles onto the sidewalk, heading toward Denny Park. The DFF warehouse is several blocks beyond the park, near Queen Anne Hill, but he'll make it. When the schnapps hits, he'll be flying. The park is closed this time of night, but it's the shortest route. Shadows crisscross the path leading to the administration building.

"Hey, buddy. Where are you going?"

The police.

Ryan is drunk, and he's not supposed to be here.

Drunk in public.

His adrenaline spikes, but he doesn't run. There's no point. He's tried that before, long ago, and they always caught him. "I'm sorry, officer. I know. I'll go."

"No, wait." A silhouette limps out from behind a tree. "Don't go."

"What do you want?"

A man carrying a beige blanket with a blue "H" on it steps into the light. "I thought that was you." He's wearing an orange and blue sweatshirt. The Denver Broncos. He's rack thin, and Ryan remembers seeing him before.

"I don't have any money," Ryan says.

"I don't want your money. I want to thank you." He puts his hand on Ryan's shoulder.

Ryan jerks back, surprised. The homeless man came up on him so fast, he didn't realize how close he was. Ryan stumbles sideways and falls down.

"Hey, I'm sorry, buddy." The man offers his hand. "I didn't mean for you to—" His eyes lock on Ryan's.

Ryan sees two homeless men now, one overlapping the other.

"I didn't mean for you to fall."

Ryan takes his hand. Wobbles to standing.

"Looks like you've had a few," the man says.

Ryan slurs. "I don't have any money."

"Here." The man reaches under his blanket and pulls out a five-dollar bill. "I wanted to pay you back. I've been sober for over a week after what you told me. I've been going to those meetings, and—thank you. Thank you for not judging me. You saved my life."

Ryan snatches the bill out of the man's hand and shoves it into his pocket.

"You look cold," the man says. "Do you want to borrow my blanket?"

Ryan stares at the blue "H."

"Here," the man says, "Take it. It's lucky."

CHAPTER SIXTY-TWO

LAUREN

The St. Croix airport has always reminded me of a black and white movie from the fifties. A time before flat-screens and jet bridges. A time when airplanes pulled up outside, and people boarded like they were getting on a bus.

Mason boards ahead of me, and we take our seats.

When we get home, we're grabbing our things and running. Dennis won't stop until he gets the card. Maybe we'll go to Canada. Or Alaska.

The cabin fan blows air in my face, drying out my eyes. I reach up and turn it off.

"It's my fault." Mason flips his tray table down and puts his cell phone down. "I should never have dated Trent."

"Has he texted you?"

"No. He went dark. What are we going to do when we get home?"

"I don't know."

His face scrunches. "Why are they doing this?"

"We'll figure something out."

"But you said they were going to kidnap me."

"Only if I went to the police, and I'm not doing that. The police would separate us, and I'm not letting you out of my sight again. I lost you once when you were little, and I'm not—"

"What? You *lost* me?"

I can't look at him. If I look at him and think about Ryan, I'll lose it.

But it's too late.

My mouth feels dry. My throat tightens. Like a frantic cat, I glance around the cabin, looking for the red wave that always arrives with thoughts of Ryan Kaine. That worthless alcoholic. He stole my son, but—no. That's not the truth.

That's not what happened.

I turn to Mason. "When you were three, I asked your Uncle Ryan to babysit you. He was my last resort. Your father and I had been fighting for weeks, and my friends—I'd been fighting with them too. My anger—" I cover my eyes.

"It's okay, Mom."

"My anger was out of control, and I was afraid I might— oh, God—I was afraid I might hurt you. I didn't want your father to know. He was at work, and I was so angry at the world that I—it doesn't matter. I asked your uncle to come watch you for a while, and he took you out for ice cream or something. Do you remember that?"

"No, but it doesn't sound like you lost me."

"No. I guess I didn't."

I feel a release. Not the satisfying, rage-release I love so much, but a soothing release. A weight off my shoulders. Ryan is a sick man, a worthless alcoholic, but he didn't kidnap Mason. And now that my secret is out, I feel released.

But—Ryan did leave Mason alone when he went on a bender. I'll never forget Mason standing there holding a half-eaten piece of jerky an officer gave him, wearing dirty underwear. His hair matted to his head, and his feet black from running around shoeless.

The red comes.

I pinch my lip.

Breathe. Don't let it in. Don't let it win.

"Are you okay, Mom? You're pinching your—"

I stop pinching and start rubbing. "I'm fine. There was something stuck to my mouth." My head clears. Mason doesn't need to know Ryan left him alone. Ryan's addiction has fueled my fire for thirteen years. I don't need to pour that gas on my son. I don't need to pour it on myself anymore, either.

"If you didn't lose me," he says, "then we can go to the police. You can let me out of your sight for a while."

"No. If we do that, the old man will send someone to kill us. We'd eventually have to leave the police station, and that would be it. Our only chance is to run away."

An Alaskan blizzard swirls around me, freezing my future. I don't want to go to Alaska. Mason wouldn't want to either.

"Not if we find the card," he says.

I put my hand on my forehead. "I searched everywhere."

"Could it be at home?"

"No. I searched everywhere there, too, but—you're right. I wasn't specifically looking for the card then because I thought it was in St. Croix. I was trying to find out what kind of card it was. I could try again."

"Did you look in his computer? I'm sure it had an SD slot."

"If the card was in there, the old man would have found it. All he found was an image of a painting from your father's office."

Sdcard.jpg.

A flight attendant rattles off the pre-flight announcements. "At this time, make sure your seat backs and tray tables are in their full upright position."

"Mason."

"Yeah, I know." He puts his tray up.

"Everything's going to be okay."

"How?"

"I know where the card is."

CHAPTER SIXTY-THREE

RYAN

Ryan's old routine comes back like the flu. Beg, borrow, and steal. There's comfort in having a schedule. At night, he saves enough booze for the next day to ward off the hangover. In the morning, he searches for his next drink. He searches for *money* for his next drink. He sits on the sidewalk. In the park. At the bus stop. He holds a cardboard sign.

Out of work. Need money for food. Veteran. God Bless you. Anything helps.

He accepts donations with a smile and a thank you.

Then he buys liquor.

Only the strongest.

Drink.

Drink more.

Save some to get tomorrow started and pass out.

Wake up and start over again.

Beg, borrow, and steal.

But the begging will end.

Tonight.

Standing beneath a streetlamp, he gazes at the maps app

on his phone. Closes one eye. Then the other. Counts to ten, then opens both eyes at once. He reads the street name just before his double vision resets.

His heavy head makes him sway to the left.

The street name on his phone matches the street sign above.

He's in the right place.

The Digital Freedom Fighters office is right around the corner. Down the alley. Across from that auto body shop. Ted's Auto Body. He couldn't remember the name until a few moments ago, which is why it's taken him three days to find it. The DFF. Or was it two days?

Yes. It's been two days. Tonight is Friday night. Time to party.

His head is light in a good way.

He's found the DFF.

He's at the height of his buzz, and when he gets that advance from Luis, he'll have the money keep the party going.

The way God intended.

He walks around the corner and heads into the alley, staying close to the right side. The side backing Ted's Auto Body. A wet wind whips through the corridor, and he wishes he'd brought his blanket. His new lucky blanket. The one with the Hilton "H" on it.

The black cars at the body shop are gone. He vaguely remembers his discussion with Steve. Some sort of company fleet cars. Maybe a bunch of companies or, no. Steve is a liar. The black cars belong to the DFF.

But who cares?

The cars are their business, and they're all gone except for the old green one by the back door. Ryan stops behind it, ducks down, and unscrews the top off his last mini shooter.

Goldschläger. Liquid courage from Switzerland.

The burn goes down good. So good, he wants to scream, *Woo hoo!*

Across the alleyway, two men in blue coveralls exit the DFF office carrying a desk. They maneuver around a car and walk up the ramp into a delivery truck. It's a nice truck. Nicer than any Ryan ever drove. It's a Mercedes. He misses his job, but he'll never need to work again. Not after Luis gives him an advance. Is ten thousand too much to ask for?

His heart thumps erratically, and he pounds on his chest to make it stop. This happens sometimes. Sweat pours off his brow, and he takes a deep breath. It will pass. He's had too much, too fast.

Like they say in AA, this too shall pass.

And it does.

He wipes his brow and attempts to straighten his shirt. It shouldn't matter how he looks. He's the brother of the great William Kaine. This isn't a job interview. It's a negotiation. He's not doing anything wrong. If Luis won't give him an advance, maybe he *will* steal William's technology. His brother probably wants the DFF to have it, anyway. For all Ryan knows, William's company is the evil one, holding his brother hostage. Threatening to withhold his paycheck.

Having a job is being held hostage by a paycheck.

Ryan is grateful he's free.

The movers exit the building with another desk. "I'm glad this is the last of it," says the man in front.

"Me too. I can't wait to get home and tie one on."

They load the desk into the truck.

Ryan comes out from behind the car, pretending to walk somewhere other than the DFF office.

The mover's drive past him down the alley, then he turns

around. He can't help swaying as he walks back. If Luis and Steve knew how drunk he was right now, they'd take advantage of him for sure. He does his best to steady his steps as he moves along the windows.

Violent butterflies swoop inside his stomach as he enters the office. No one's there. The lights are off. The hall to the workroom runs along the windows, and he can see his way courtesy of Ted's security lamps shining in from across the alley.

All is quiet, but someone must be here. There was a car parked right outside the front door. An Audi. The kind he is going to buy when he gets the money. Hopefully, it belongs to Luis, and the negotiations won't take long.

He needs a drink.

Ryan pauses at the end of the hall, takes a breath, then marches inside the workroom. The desks are gone. Is the DFF moving? Maybe they're getting new desks tomorrow. The sign reading MANAGER is still on the door on the other side of the workroom, but that is all. Even Luis's desk is gone.

Ryan blinks his eyes.

The tables, chairs, computers—everything is gone.

He can't believe it. They're shutting the place down. He—

Voices come from the manager's office.

Hope.

Experience, strength, and hope.

He belches and strides toward the office door.

Luis might be in there. That's hope.

"I understand," a man says, his voice like stainless steel. "I'll let Tony know. He's standing right here. We'll be on our way soon."

Ryan leans against the wall. That's not Luis's voice. It's not Steve.

"Well?" another man asks.

"Hold on a second," the steel voice says.

"C'mon, tell me what he said." This man is younger. He sounds agitated. Rough. He has a New York accent.

"Tony," the steel voice booms, "shut the fuck up. Give me a minute to process this."

"Relax. What's the big deal?"

"Mr. Gabaldon isn't happy. He sent Dennis over to the Kaine's to fix this mess once and for all. Apparently, he's already in their house."

"Why does he get to do it?"

"Because he's the one who screwed up."

"That's crap. I wanted to play Christmas with her. What are *we* supposed to do?"

"We're on cleanup."

"You're kidding, right? He gets to have all the fun, and we have to clean up after him?"

"Yep. He's supposed to help, but there's going to be a lot of blood. Gabaldon said it's too much for one man to do."

"That's not fair."

Ryan moves away from the door. His soggy brain chews on the conversation.

. . . sent Dennis over to the Kaine's . . . already in their house . . . a lot of blood . . .

William. Mason. Lauren.

He's got to warn them.

He heads for the hallway. His feet refuse to cooperate, and he drifts to the right.

Go slow, be quiet.

He's the one who screwed up, the steel voice had said.

That's crap, said the New Yorker.

Run.

The workroom shifts to the right. Ryan compensates, leans left, guides his ship toward the hallway.

"Hey!"

"Stop!"

The voices sound as if they're coming from underwater.

Ryan enters the hall. Flies past the windows.

Footsteps echo from the workroom.

"Come back here," the New Yorker yells.

Ryan rounds the corner and bursts outside.

The men appear in the windows, running toward the door.

The New Yorker pulls out a gun.

The green car is still parked across the alley at Ted's Auto Body. The nearest dumpster is a few feet from the car.

The Audi is parked right in front of Ryan.

He runs down the steps and glances over his shoulder.

The men stop inside the building. The New Yorker raises his gun and yells something.

Ryan ducks down and pulls on the door handle. It's unlocked.

He pauses.

Nothing happens.

The door opens easily, and he crawls into the driver's seat.

The New Yorker must be waiting for him to lift his head. No wires hang beneath the dash, and it doesn't matter because he has no idea how to hotwire a car. But maybe he doesn't need to know how.

He pulls out his keys and searches for the one he took from Juan.

It fits in the ignition.

This must be the Audi Juan left outside the Squire that night.

He starts the engine.

Keeping his head down, he puts his foot on the brake and the transmission in reverse. Then, he slowly rises.

The office window explodes. A shot rings out. Ryan's head screams in pain, but it's only from the sound. Glass fragments from the window dance on the hood, but the windshield is okay.

The bullet missed.

He mashes the accelerator to the floor and spins the wheel. The car backs out, rocks to one side, and narrowly misses the green car. He hits the brakes and slides to a stop by the dumpster. The alley stretches out before him, but he sees two alleys, each pointing in slightly different directions.

The men come running out of the building.

The New Yorker raises his gun, but the other man makes him lower it.

Ryan closes his left eye.

The two alleys become one.

The New Yorker shoves the other man away and takes aim.

Ryan puts the car in gear.

He's got to warn his family.

A gunshot rings out as he exits the alley and barrels onto the main thoroughfare.

CHAPTER SIXTY-FOUR

LAUREN

Driving past Mason's elementary school on the way home from the airport, I remember waiting in the car line to pick him up. He loved the swings and playing in the mud at the base of that old maple tree. He was so little then. So innocent.

He's asleep in the passenger seat. It's almost nine o'clock. I'd love to go home and fall asleep too, but I've got to make sure I'm right about the card. It's got to be in William's office.

I check the rearview mirror again, and there's no one following us. Dennis and his thugs weren't there when we landed in Seattle. Because we spent the night in the forest, they could have come back yesterday.

As I pull onto our street and cruise toward the driveway, I silently rehearse the plan. Once I get the card, Mason and I are going to a random hotel. Dennis will eventually call Mason's phone. We're sure Trent works for Dennis, so Dennis will have gotten Mason's number from him. When Dennis calls, I'll suggest we meet to handover the card.

Then, I'll leave Mason with Olivia.

I spent the flight convincing myself it was okay to let him

out of my sight.

There's no other way.

Right before the meeting, I'll call the police. When Dennis shows up, I'll refuse to give him the card. He'll threaten me, order Tony to attack me, but it won't matter. The police will arrive, and it will all be over.

My heart jumps.

There's a car parked in front of our house. It's so white, it glows in the dark. The windows are heavily tinted, and I've never seen this kind of car before. The body is long, but it's not a limousine. It has a hatch, but I wouldn't call it a hatchback or a wagon. It looks fast. As I drive past, I see it's a Mercedes.

I pull into the driveway and glance in the rearview mirror.

The Mercedes glows.

It's not too late to back out, but without the card, I have nothing.

The garage door opens, and I drive inside. Mason sleeps peacefully with one earbud in and the other on his chest. The garage door closes. I quietly get out and close the driver's side door. He'll be safe here. This should only take a minute.

I enter the hallway and head for William's office. It's dark, but I know my way, so I don't bother with the light, and—

Coughing comes from the sitting room.

I stop. Put my hand on the wall.

My face flares. How dare he invade my home.

The rage comes, but I don't let it in.

I must not let it win.

I back down the hall toward the garage, one step at a time.

The cough comes again.

Dennis is here.

In *my* house.

I slip into the garage.

Thank God I left Mason asleep in the SUV.

The white car out front seems too obvious to be Dennis's. It must be a coincidence, but I don't want to risk it. Tony and Frank might be in that car, and if I leave, they'll follow me. Chase me down and torture me until I tell them where the card is.

Then they'll kill me.

Then they'll kill Mason.

The anger comes, and I let it in, but I'm *not* going to let it win.

I'm going to use it.

The dim light from the garage door illuminates the workbench. Screwdrivers, pliers, tape, wrenches, and—I pull a hammer off the pegboard.

My chest thumps.

I enter the hallway—hammer raised—and feel my way to the adjoining corridor.

The coughing has stopped.

I peer around the corner, toward the stairway. Toward the sitting room. The lights are off.

I let my anger build.

He's in the dark. He's sitting in the dark in *my* house.

The rage feels good.

This is going to be the release of all releases.

I hear him move and tighten my grip on the hammer.

The darkness turns red.

My jaw tightens.

The light switch at the end of the hall is on the left.

I hold the hammer in my right.

One step, then another.

He's here for the card, and if he gets it, he'll kill me. I

assume he brought a gun, but I have a hammer, and he doesn't know I'm coming. If he had heard the garage door over his coughing, he would have left the sitting room.

But he didn't.

I take another step forward.

And another.

I turn sideways, put my back against the wall. Feel for the light switch.

Breathe.

I need to see him to hit him.

He's only a few feet away.

My fingers find the switch.

"Hello, Lauren," he says. "Long time, no see."

I switch on the light.

CHAPTER SIXTY-FIVE

RYAN

Ryan's foot slips off the gas. The car coasts into an intersection. His head lolls to the left, and a big pink elephant spraying water on its back smiles down at him. The sign for the Elephant Super Car Wash looms overhead.

He knows where he is and where he must go.

The men from the DFF are on cleanup. *Lots of blood.* There's a killer in his brother's house, and—

Ryan sits up. Presses on the accelerator and exits the intersection as if he hadn't just passed out.

Man, he's drunk.

And tired.

But he's got to warn his family.

He turns left at the next light. His dry eyes ache. They fog over. The world is a tilt-a-whirl.

He blinks, shakes his head, and everything clears up.

He can do this.

He needs a second wind, that's all.

The engine purrs. This car has so much more power than his Honda. He tests the acceleration, then pulls his foot off the gas.

The police.

He can't forget about the police. If he gets caught driving drunk, they'll take his license away. Send him to jail. He checks the rearview mirror, and no one is tailing him. No police. No digital freedom fighters. Of course—he laughs to himself—he took the DFF's car. To follow him, those guys would have had to take that old green car, and it couldn't keep up with this baby.

He guns the engine.

He hits the brakes.

He looks around for the police and sees none.

Where is the freeway?

Where is he?

Up ahead, a road passes under the one he's on, but he doesn't know if it's I-5 or I-90. He needs to get on I-90, then take the exit onto Mercer Island. The street signs are a blur. He slows down, trying to decide whether to take the next on-ramp, and a semi-truck blares past him, scaring him into the next lane over.

He grips the wheel. Holds it steady. Drives over the freeway and stops at a red light.

Pine Street.

He's at Pine and Boren. That was I-5 he passed over. The way to I-90 is clear in his mind now, and he turns left. When he gets to 12th Avenue, he'll turn right. He repeats this to himself—*turn right at 12th, turn right at 12th*—and he reads every street sign out loud as he cruises through the intersections.

It works. Drinking and driving isn't so hard if you concentrate.

12th Avenue.

He turns right, heads for Ranier Avenue, then I-90. He's got this. The police aren't following him. No green cars have followed him. No black cars, either, but he's not completely sure about that. Unless there's a streetlight, all the cars look black, but he's feeling better. More awake.

The stereo system in this thing is unbelievable. A local station blares Nirvana. It takes him back to his twenties. Back to when he was invincible.

He's invincible now.

He will always be invincible, as long as he can get drunk.

The next song plays.

He sings along.

Six songs later, he's still singing, but he's getting thirsty. The unnerving feeling his buzz is about to end throws him into a frenzy. He needs a mini shooter. A pint of Vodka. Something.

He needs to find an exit.

A great green sign reads EXIT 4—RENTON.

Renton?

He's on the 405.

How did he get on the 405?

He's got to warn William. Dammit. He slams his hand against the steering wheel. An entire island. Mercer Island. He's so wasted, he missed all of Mercer Island, and worse, his buzz is fading.

It's fading fast.

He needs some wake-me-up juice.

The radio blares Soundgarden.

He takes the next exit and pulls into the first convenience store he sees. He'll have to backtrack up I-405 to get to his brother's house, and he'll never stay awake that long without another buzz. Some peppermint schnapps. A can of double-shot espresso would help too.

He pulls out his wallet, leafs through it, and—it's empty. He could have sworn he had five dollars left, but it's gone. It's happening to him—wetbrain. Because he's drinking again, he's starting to lose things, just like Juan.

He promises God he'll stop drinking tomorrow if he can have a drink tonight.

God tells him to look in the glove compartment.

He pops it open and finds nothing but the proof of insurance and a gun.

The sign in the convenience store window reads, BLUE MOON SPECIAL 12-PACK BOTTLES.

Beg, borrow, and . . . steal.

No.

Armed robbery for a bottle of Vodka? It's not worth it. He'll get caught and go to prison for sure.

He closes the glove compartment. Pulls out of the parking lot.

His eyes close, and he jerks them open.

He needs to find somewhere to pass out.

His family will be okay. Maybe the wealthy Kaines aren't home.

Ryan did his best to warn them.

He cruises down the road, looking for a dark place to pull over. A laundromat. A sub sandwich shop. Martin's drycleaners. He glances down a side street and sees a couple walking hand-in-hand. Straight ahead, the boulevard dances in the light of restaurants and bars, so he takes the next right into suburbia.

His eyes begin to close again.

He swerves, counters, and makes another right turn.

A police cruiser sits in front of a small blue house. The

cop probably lives there, but Ryan can't risk it. He takes another right at the next stop sign, and again, he sees a couple walking hand-in-hand.

The couple passes beneath a streetlamp.

Ryan squints.

The woman is carrying a red handbag, and the man has on a dark blue shirt. The kind his brother wears. The man is tall. Thin.

Ryan blinks.

It's him. It's his brother William.

It's William and Lauren, walking hand-in-hand.

They're not home. They're safe.

Now's his chance.

He hits the gas, and the awesome Audi lunges forward.

He can make amends. What better amends could there be than saving his brother's life?

The car veers to the right, and Ryan's vision blurs. Tears flood his eyes, and his stomach revolts. He pulls the car straight with the road, but he can't keep his eyes from closing.

The engines revs.

His head hits the steering wheel, and his eyes pop open.

William and Lauren are running ahead of the car.

The car is swerving.

Now, two Williams and two Laurens are running ahead of the car.

Get off the gas.

His foot doesn't listen.

He's got to warn his brother. The DFF. Lots of blood.

His hands slip off the steering wheel, and he falls back against the seat, eyes half-open. The car jerks to the right, veers toward William, and there's something coming. Something gray. William leaps, his blue shirt disappears behind the blurry gray blob, and—

Ryan lacks the strength to get his eyes open. He's half-awake, coming out of a deep, deep sleep. Blood and gunpowder—no. It's talcum powder. He rubs his eyes, and it's something *like* talcum powder. It's white, and it's all over him. His nose is bleeding, and he feels like someone punched him in the face, and the engine isn't running anymore.

He's stopped.

Consciousness arrives, and with it comes reality. He crashed the car, and the airbag deployed. He shoves the bag out of his way, and the crinkling noise makes him cringe.

Steam rises over the hood.

Lauren is standing on a bridge, bent over a concrete barrier, screaming.

William is gone.

If the police come, they'll lock Ryan away forever.

He turns the key, and the dome light flashes. The headlights flash.

He can't go back to jail.

He's got to—he can't stay awake.

His eyes close, but he turns the key anyway, and this time, the engine starts.

His foot finds the gas pedal.

Vroom.

But the car goes nowhere.

Stay awake. One last push.

Ryan sits up straight. Opens his eyes. Grips the gear shift lever.

Lauren marches toward the car, her auburn hair trailing in the wind. Fire in her eyes. Hands balled in fists.

He pulls on the lever, and the gears grind.

She pounds against the driver's side window.

He pumps the gas. Pulls harder on the transmission, but it's stuck in neutral, and it's going nowhere.

Blood from her knuckles streams down the tinted glass.

He should tell her about the DFF. Help her. Help his brother. Mason. Make amends.

"Open the door, you bastard! I'm going to kill you."

The transmission hooks, and the car lurches backward.

His foot slips off the gas and onto the brake.

Now it's a hit-and-run. He's not only going to jail, he's going to be executed.

Lauren is screaming.

By the grace of God, Ryan eases the transmission into drive, and the car moves forward.

He drives away.

CHAPTER SIXTY-SIX

LAUREN

I flip the switch, and the light from the hallway surges into the sitting room.

I charge in, my hammer raised, blind with rage.

The old man dies tonight.

"Hello, Lauren."

I try to stop, but my momentum forces me to take two more steps.

I'm stunned.

My eyes must be lying.

It's not him. It's not the old man—Dennis—and it's not Tony, or Frank, or any other thug.

"Long time, no see."

Ryan Kaine stands slouched, one hand on the sofa, leaning toward the mantle. A gun dangles from his hand, and he coughs. His head lolls to the side. He wipes his mouth and attempts to stand up straight, but leans back too far, recovers his balance, then sways toward me. "How've you been? I've missed you."

The room reeks of alcohol.

I slowly lower the hammer.

"Thanks," he says, "for the invite on LinkedIn. I was there at his funeral. You" —a sad smile breaks through his scruff— "always had a way with words."

William is dead. It should have been you.

"Ryan. What are you—"

"It was a wonderful service," he exclaims. "Why weren't you there? You sent me the invit—the invit—the invitation, but then you didn't show."

"Why are you here?"

"You didn't have to tell me William was dead. I saw it on the internet." He scrunches his face. The webwork of veins on his cheeks turns red. "What was that? Two? Three weeks ago?"

His grip on the gun tightens.

"I'm sorry about the message," I say.

"Don't be."

"Please, put the gun down."

His eyes go to the photos above the mantle. He blinks slowly. "I didn't mean to, but I . . . ah, fuck me. I was drunk again. I'm so sorry."

"The gun. Can you—"

"You have to believe me. I didn't mean to." He waves the gun in the air. "I was trying to warn you."

I step back. "About what?"

He lowers the gun, and his lips tremble.

I could hit him. He's so drunk, I could attack and beat him senseless before he knew what happened, but I must not let my anger in. I must not let it win.

"I'm so sorry," he sobs.

"Warn me about what, Ryan?"

"They were going to kill William." His eyes go wild. "Ha!

I did it *for* them. Isn't that ironic? It's—oh, God. What have I done?"

"What are you talking about?"

He sobs. He slurs. "These guys, they wanted William's tech-stuff. They said he was in your house. They gave up on getting his stuff. They were going to kill you guys. I tried to get here to warn you. Really. But they tried to kill me and— ah—I fucked up. I'm a drunk."

"What the hell are you saying?"

"I did it, Lauren. I stole one of their cars, and I'm so sorry. I was trying to warn you, but I passed out and crashed into the bridge."

"You—"

"I did it. I killed William."

I raise the hammer. "You? You were in the Audi?"

"Yes," he cries.

It hits me like a meteor.

Ryan.

Three weeks ago, drunk Ryan killed my William.

"Do you work for them?" I yell. "Tell me, dammit. Do you know who they are?"

"Yes. No. I don't know. I almost worked for them. They're freedom fighters. Some tech geeks. They wanted me to steal, but I wouldn't do it." He slurs. "I wouldn't. Ah. I can't go home anymore. They're following me. They won't leave me alone. I've been living on the streets since the crash. I can't take it anymore." He wipes his forehead. "What's it been since William died? Two? Three weeks?"

My jaw tightens. "You worthless asshole. Put the gun down."

"You're right. I'm worthless. I suck at computers." He looks up at the ceiling. "I killed my own brother. I—my drinking killed him. I crashed that car and then—"

"And then you left me there. You just left me there."

"I was scared." He pivots slightly, standing on one foot. "The police were coming, so I ditched the car. I was going to sober up and turn myself in, promise, but the car was gone the next day. They must have found it. Fixed it. They own a body shop."

"And you didn't sober up, did you?"

He lowers his chin. "No. I can't."

I tighten my grip on the hammer.

He stares at the floor. "It's a living hell."

I take a step forward.

He raises his head. "I couldn't go back to jail."

"Jail is too good for you."

"I know." He raises the gun.

I stop.

"I don't deserve to live. I—I killed my brother." The gun shakes in his hand.

"And now you're going kill me?"

He sways and looks at the gun as if he's surprised it's there. "It's not me, it's the disease. The rough side keeps getting me. I'm obsessed." He turns the gun around. Holds it by the barrel. "I can't go on living like this. Here." He thrusts the grip at me. "Take it."

I hesitate.

"Take it." His body quakes.

I drop the hammer, snatch the gun, and point it at him. It weighs more than I thought it would.

He falls to his knees. Tilts his head back. Closes his eyes. "Please. Shoot me."

This man.

This *monster*.

He ruined my life.

Because of him, Mason has no father.

No future.

I'm alone.

An atom bomb goes off inside my chest.

A mushroom cloud fills my head.

And everything turns red.

Blood red.

Crimson.

"Do it," he pleads.

He grabs the barrel and puts the muzzle between his eyes.

I hold onto the grip with both hands.

"Do it," he says. "Pull the trigger."

My brain burns.

My heart aches.

I slide my finger up and down the trigger.

The metal is cool.

He lets go of the barrel and holds his arms out wide. "What are you waiting for, Lauren? I left your three-year-old son alone in a hotel room to die. I murdered your husband. Aren't you angry with me?"

CHAPTER SIXTY-SEVEN

MASON

Someone is yelling. Mason wakes up. Shifts in his seat. Why isn't his music playing? The yelling comes again, and he wonders why the flight attendant doesn't tell everyone to shut up.

But he's not on the airplane anymore.

Right.

The plane landed, his phone went dead, and he fell asleep in the front seat of the SUV. His mom must have gone inside the house without him.

He opens the door and hears more yelling. It's coming from inside the house, and it sounds like a man is shouting, *shoot me*, over and over.

Who's here?

He goes behind the SUV and looks out the garage window. A strange white car is parked across the street.

Louder now, he hears his mom yell, but he can't make out her words. The garage moves in slow motion as he races toward the door. He sends the door banging against the wall and rushes into the hallway.

"Shoot me!" yells a man's voice.

He sprints into the sitting room, and—

His mother has a gun pointed at a stranger's head.

The stranger is on his knees.

Her face is red and twisted.

Mason shouts as loud as he can. "Mom, stop!"

She turns her head—fire in her eyes. The dragon is alive.

"No," the man says. "Shoot me. You have to shoot me."

She keeps her gaze on Mason and takes a step back, but she doesn't lower the gun. The look in her eyes—she's not in there. The monsutā has taken over.

The white car outside. The old man. "Mom, don't do it. Let's find the card and get out of here like you said."

"He's not one of them," she growls.

"What do you mean?"

"This is your uncle. Ryan." Her eyes ablaze.

"Hi, Mason," the man says. His cheeks are swollen, reddish-purple, and he smells like the Buckotora—but his forehead, the curves around his eyes . . . he looks like Mason's father.

"Mom?"

She narrows her gaze. Aims the gun at Ryan's face.

Mason moves across the floor like a ninja.

Ryan closes his eyes. "Please. Do it."

Mason comes up behind his mom and gently puts his hands on her shoulders. "You don't have to do this."

She's trembling.

Mason tries to hold her still.

She's afraid.

"No," Ryan says. "You *do* have to do this. Please. Pull the trigger. I don't have the will to do it myself."

"He deserves to die," she says.

Mason puts his lips to her ear.

"Mom," he whispers. "You don't have to let the anger in. You don't have to let it win."

CHAPTER SIXTY-EIGHT

LAUREN

Ryan Kaine—the source of all my anger, rage, hate, and pain—kneels on my floor, in *my* house, and begs me to kill him.

He begs me.

The room glows like Mars on fire, and—the release. I want to feel the release.

My shoulders were shaking, but now they won't move.

Something has a hold of me.

Mason.

He whispers in my ear, "You must not let the anger in. You must not let it win."

"Do it," Ryan yells.

He begs. He pleads.

My trigger finger tenses.

"Please," he sobs. "Do it."

"You must not let it win," Mason says.

I lower the gun.

"No," Ryan says. "What are you doing?"

"I won't let it in."

The red melts away, but Ryan's face stays the same. Weak and wet with tears. Worthless.

"That's it?" he asks. "You won't?"

"I won't."

Mason takes his hands off my shoulders.

Ryan moans. His breath is flammable. He drops to the floor and crawls toward the sofa.

"Wait." I train the gun on him again.

"Huh?"

"If you don't work for them, where did you get that car?"

"What car?"

"There's a white car out front. Where'd you get it?"

"That's not mine. I sold my car to buy booze. I haven't driven since—oh, God. Not since I crashed into the bridge. That was like, what? Two? Three weeks ago?"

"I saw it," Mason says. "It's still out there."

Ryan climbs onto the sofa.

"Stop," I say.

He doesn't listen. Lies on his back.

"Mom, put the gun down. Please? Let's call the police."

Ryan blubbers, spewing spit when he speaks. "No. I don't want to go back to jail." He tips his head toward Mason. "I'm sorry I left you. Can you forgive me?"

"Sure," Mason says. "I forgive you. Mom, can you forgive him? Please? Can you forgive him and put the gun down?"

"No," Ryan says. "Shoot me." Tears flow. "Shoot me. I can't go on living like this."

"Stop it!" I scream. "Stop it. I'm not killing anyone." I step between him and the coffee table and put the gun down. "What you did, Ryan—it's unforgivable, but I'm not going to put you out of your misery. You have to go on living, suffering like everyone else."

"But, you *want* to kill me," he says. "You have to."

"No, I don't. But you have to tell us whose car is outside."

"Car? I don't have a—I used to have a truck. I got fired."

"Whose car is outside?"

"I don't know." He shifts his hips, and his back pops. "I slept in William's office last night. Where were you guys?"

"St. Croix," Mason says.

"Oh." He closes his eyes. "I always wanted to go there."

I nudge him with my knee. "What do you know about them?"

He folds his arms over his chest. "They wanted me to steal from William." He moans. "Do you have anything to drink? To make a drink. I couldn't find anything. The whiskey is gone."

"Was it a card? Did they want you to steal a card?"

"An SD card," Mason adds.

"Something. Yeah. Whatever William was working on. I didn't do it, but I . . . hey"—he rolls toward us, opens one eye— "if you know where it is, we could make a lot of money."

"Mom, we don't have time for this."

"You're right." I stride down the hall to William's office.

Dennis found a picture of the St. Croix painting on William's computer.

Sdcard.jpg.

I stand where William must have stood to take the picture, searching the painting for clues.

Mason stands in the doorway behind me.

I grab the painting by the frame and jerk it off the wall.

"Mom, calm down. It's—"

"I am calm."

I put the painting on the desk and study it. The colors.

The brush strokes. There must be something here. A clue of some kind. There must be a message scratched somewhere on the surface. In the ocean. On the beach. Something.

Mason joins me.

"Do you see anything?" I ask.

"No."

"Think. Your father said it was *in* St. Croix."

Mason flips the painting over. He undoes the clasps, and when he pulls the canvas out of the frame, a black chip flies across the room and lands by the doorway. He picks it up, faces me, and smiles, pinching an SD card between his thumb and forefinger. "I found it."

"You sure did, kid," a voice buzzes from the hall.

The old man steps into the doorway.

His baseball cap is yellow.

His sunglasses are black.

He points his gun at the back of Mason's head and says, "Hello, Lauren. How was your trip?"

CHAPTER SIXTY-NINE

LAUREN

Dennis stands in the hall wearing a white T-shirt, a black leather jacket, and his beard doesn't look right. It's crooked. He's pointing a gun at the back of Mason's head and his chainsaw voice rattles my nerves. "Don't move, kid."

Mason hasn't seen the gun yet.

"Quick, come here," I say, motioning with my hands.

Confused, Mason steps toward me.

Dennis reaches for him but misses.

I wrap my arms around Mason and glare at the old man. "Go to hell, asshole."

Dennis glances at the SD card in Mason's hand, then aims the gun at me.

"Trent?" Mason says.

"No." The old man rips his beard off. He pulls out his cell phone and, keeping the gun raised with one hand, taps the screen with his thumb. His grating, chainsaw voice ceases, and he says, "Sorry it didn't work out between us, kid, but I'm not a fag."

"You *are* Trent," Mason says.

"You son-of-bitch," I say.

"Now, now, Lauren." He puts his cell phone back in his pocket. "Is that any way to talk to your son's lover?"

"It can't be." Mason sucks in a quick breath.

Dennis holds out his hand. "Now, give me the card."

"Don't do it." I pull Mason closer. "He'll shoot us the second you hand it to him." I spared Ryan, but I will kill this man. This *Trent*, or *Dennis,* or whoever the hell he is. I will kill him.

My rage comes, and I let it in, but I won't let it win.

"You people are unbelievable." Dennis takes off his sunglasses and hooks them on his shirt. "I tried to do it the nice way, but you people—shit." He takes his cap off and slings it at the window. "I worked my ass off to blend into your lives, to get a hold of the card as peacefully as possible, but you wouldn't have it, would you? You had to act like you didn't know where it was. Christ. Just hand it over, kid."

Mason puts the SD card in his pocket. His face is cast in iron. I've never seen him like this.

"As peacefully as possible?" I ask, buying some time. Ryan is passed out on the sofa in the sitting room. If he wakes, he could help us.

I raise my voice. "You call having your thugs beat me up 'peaceful?'"

He shakes his head. "That wasn't my fault. If only your husband had let me join his team, none of this would've happened. But no"—he takes a step forward—"he had to get me fired."

"You're Robert Lang."

He nods. "I'm a lot of people. It's what I do." Pride decorates his eyes. "Look, I'm sorry Tony beat you up, but you kept lying about the card. My boss isn't as forgiving as I am." He points the gun at Mason. "At this point, it's you or me, kid, so give me the card, and I won't shoot you in the face."

My skin heats up, every pore an angry bonfire. A pit of bubbling oil. "I'm going to kill you."

"Oh, really?" he says. "How? Are you going to throw another gnome at me?" He grins. "You've got some real anger problems. When you threw those eggs at that woman in the store, I lost it. I laughed so hard, my beard almost fell off."

"I don't get it," Mason says. "You—we went on a date. You're Trent. I told you about my dad. Did you—did you run him off the bridge?"

"No. That drunk sleeping in your living room did that. Asshole. His relapse really messed things up. I was going to take the card that night, but after he killed William, we had to come up with a new plan. I had to stop screwing around, pretending to be in AA, and put on a beard. I thought if I threatened kidnapping, you'd give me the card, but no. I doubled down, turned gay, but that didn't work either." He looks at Mason. "You were my last chance, kid. Now here's your last chance." He holds out his hand. "Give me the card."

Footsteps, followed by a *thud,* comes from the hallway.

Dennis backs into the corridor.

"Steve?" Ryan's voice is ragged. "Hey, Steve, is that you? What are you doing here?"

Dennis turns and points the gun down the hall. "Stop right there."

"Don't," Ryan yells. "Wait. Yeah—do. Shoot me. C'mon, shoot me."

Mason lunges forward, crashes into Dennis, and pushes him up against the wall. I follow, my hands outstretched.

Ryan yells, "Yeah, Steve. C'mon. Do it. Shoot me."

Mason knees Dennis in the crotch just as I reach the hallway.

Dennis doubles over, and Mason runs toward Ryan.

I attack. I tear into Dennis, clawing at him, trying to take him down, but he's too strong. I try to grab the gun, but—

A flash.

A boom.

Mason goes down.

The most brilliant shade of red I've ever seen consumes me. My arms go on auto-pilot. My fists fly, sometimes hitting something hard—the wall maybe—and sometimes hitting something soft. His face, I hope. The fury coursing through my body knows no bounds.

My muscles burn.

My throat constricts.

I want to go to Mason, but I can't because my wrath wants this man dead. It wants a release.

Dennis yells. He calls me names. His voice sounds garbled as if it's tumbling in a cement mixer, yet he's right in front of me. I'm hitting him. I'm hitting the wall. I'm—

I'm suffocating.

His face bleeds through the red. Comes into focus. His hands—he's got me by the neck. He's choking me. I grasp his wrists, and he shoves me to the floor. His gun is lying right there, and I reach for it, but he kicks me in the head and snatches it up.

I roll against the wall.

He runs down the hall.

I struggle to rise, to follow him, but the walls are red. The carpet, the ceiling—everything is still red.

The rage won. I let it in, and it won.

Mason and Ryan are gone, and Dennis is getting away.

He shot my son.

I sprint after him.

My ankle twists as I round the corner, and I hobble into the sitting room, out of breath.

Ryan lies belly down on the floor with his arms wrapped around Dennis's leg.

"Let go of me," Dennis yells.

"No," Ryan says, "you'll have to shoot me."

"Fine." Dennis leans down and puts the muzzle against Ryan's neck.

I roar.

Dennis looks up.

I hit him at full speed, and we crash onto the coffee table, rolling—chest to chest—falling onto the floor. His gun bounces toward the sofa. I come out on top, straddling him, but he wraps his hands around my throat and squeezes. He pushes on my neck, forcing me to sit up straight. The photographs on the mantle are a blur. He tightens his grip, and I struggle to breathe.

Crimson clouds overtake the mantle.

I must not let it in, but the clouds thicken.

I must not let my anger win. I must not—

My mantra fails.

I flail.

Grab his wrists.

Pry his hands off my neck.

I scream, "I forgive you!"

He slaps me hard, connecting with my jaw.

"I forgive you!"

I slip sideways, catch myself on the carpet, and my palm burns, but my rage cools. "I forgive you." Still straddling him, I slide back on top. The red clouds thin out, and the hammer from the garage is lying right there, just above his shoulder.

I lean forward, reaching for it.

He grasps my hair and pulls my head back.

I lean harder. "I forgive you for stalking me. I forgive you for abducting me. I—"

"Why are you saying that?"

"Forgiveness is freedom."

"What?"

I grasp the hammer and hit his head with a glancing blow.

He covers his face.

I bring the hammer down again and hit his hands.

He reaches for my throat.

I swing the hammer as hard as I can, and it strikes him in the forehead, dead on. His eyes roll back, his head lolls to the side, and his hands fall from my neck. "I forgive you for breaking my son's heart."

"I don't forgive him," Ryan says.

I stand. "Mason, where are you?"

Ryan looms over Dennis, wavering, holding a gun.

"Where'd Mason go?" I ask.

Ryan doesn't answer.

"Mom. Over here." Mason limps into the sitting room.

I run to him. "Are you hurt?"

His pant leg is soaked with blood. "I got shot in the calf."

I wrap my arms around him.

"Mom, let go." He pushes me away. "Look."

Ryan falls to his knees and presses the gun's muzzle against Dennis's nose. His lips quiver. His forearms flex.

"Stop!" I yell.

Ryan's eyes are filled with crazy. "No—he—the DFF. They ruined my life." The gun trembles. "They killed Juan. I drank because of them. Juan is dead because of them."

"Stop, Ryan. You don't want to do this."

"Yes, I do."

"They'll send you to jail. It's over. Look, he's out. Just put the gun down."

"It's not over. He's still breathing." Ryan slips off his knees, catches himself, and repositions the gun over Dennis's face. "He shot my nephew."

"I'm okay," Mason says. "Please."

I cross the room and hold out my hand. "Give me the gun."

He shakes his head.

"Ryan. Look at me."

His eyes jitter. "It doesn't matter if I shoot him or not. You're going to send me back to jail anyway. You hate me."

I kneel and put my hand on his arm. "I don't hate you."

"Yeah, you do. I took Mason."

"You didn't take him. You—"

"What?"

"It was my fault. I should never have asked you to babysit. I—you're right, I hated you, but I hated everyone. I was angry at everyone because—I'm sick." The air leaves the room, and I breathe the truth. "You went to jail because of me, but it wasn't all your fault."

He lowers the gun. "But I left him alone in that hotel, right? I'm shit. He could have died because of me. I'm a piece of—"

"No, you're not. It was my fault as much as yours." A release comes like a flowing river, carrying my rage away, drowning my judgments. Making me one with everything and everyone. One with William. One with Mason.

One with Ryan.

Ryan Kaine and I . . . we're one and the same. Driven by

our addictions.

Mason is bleeding. He needs me now, but so does Ryan. "You're not a piece of shit. You're like me. We—people like us—we lose control sometimes. It's not our fault."

"What are you saying?"

"You didn't mean to leave Mason alone, did you? That wasn't your intention, was it?"

"What about William?" he asks. "I—oh, God. I killed my brother." He raises the gun. Points it at his head.

Red flares shoot across my vision. "Did you want to kill him? Did you want your brother dead? That wasn't your intention, was it?"

"No." He trembles. "Of course not, but there's no way I can ever make amends for that. I'm doomed."

"I forgive you, Ryan."

He shakes his head in disbelief.

"I forgive you for leaving Mason alone, and I forgive you for what happened to William."

Chills pour over my back, and I'm free.

He closes his eyes. Swallows. Tears stream into his scruff. He lowers the gun. He lowers his head. Wipes his cheeks.

Carefully, I take the pistol out of his hand, and I point it at Dennis.

Blood runs down Dennis's forehead, drips, and pools on the carpet. His chest moves up and down. His eyes are closed, but he could wake up at any moment.

"Ryan, I need your help. We've got to get Mason to a hospital, but we can't leave this asshole lying here."

"Steve?"

"Yeah, Steve. He's got a phone in his pocket.

Ryan retrieves the phone. "It's locked."

"Give it to me."

I tap on the EMERGENCY button.

Ryan stands. Stumbles over to the sofa. Sits down.

"911. What's your emergency?"

"There's been a shooting. My son is shot. Please, send someone—"

"Are you in a safe place? Can you stay where you are?"

"Yes."

"Someone is on their way. Stay calm. Can you do that?"

"Yes. I can. I can stay calm."

EPILOGUE

LAUREN

The landscapers didn't come today because of the rain. I thought it was an excuse, but now I understand. I'm standing in the kitchen, watching unusually large drops splatter off my new lawn furniture, and I miss William. This time of year is so depressing. Not just because of the holidays, but because of the darkness.

The shortest day of the year has only eight hours of sun.

Less when it's raining.

I finish slicing a banana, pour milk over Mason's cereal, and walk down the hall toward the sitting room. He's in his office talking to Ryan. As always, his voice reminds me of William. I still see William once in a while, standing in the mirror, coming down the stairs. These hallucinations might never cease.

Thankfully, though, the red is gone.

I haven't had a red-out since the night they arrested Dennis Dalrymple. AKA Trent Jenson. AKA Steve Hendricks. AKA Robert Lang.

An out-of-work actor turned professional corporate spy.

The police arrested Dennis right here in the sitting room.

And there it is—a red flash.

What's with me today?

I woke up missing William more than usual.

'Tis the season, I guess.

All morning, I've been rehashing what happened, turning it over in my head, switching the blame from Dennis to Basketball-head to Ryan. Forgiving them set me free, but forgiveness isn't a door that will stay closed. Today, the door is opening, and it's letting my anger in.

I work every day to forgive everyone, again and again.

I carry Mason's breakfast to his office. He sits behind William's old desk with Ryan at his side. They're working on our startup business. Rain pummels the window next to the painting of St. Croix, and I shiver just thinking about the cold.

"See?" Ryan points at the screen. "You can copy and paste this part into the main program. That should work."

"Mom, come look at this," Mason says.

I don't see anything on the screen except gibberish and semicolons. "Why do you make the background black with blue letters? Isn't it harder to read that way?"

"Not that," Mason says. "Look at what Ryan got."

Ryan lowers his chin. "She doesn't want to see it."

"Show her."

"What is it?" I ask.

Ryan reaches into his pocket.

I place the cereal bowl on the desk, careful not to let it spill.

"It's not a big deal," Ryan says.

"Didn't we have any strawberries?" Mason asks.

"No."

Ryan holds up a green chip.

Mason grabs it out of his hand. "It's for ninety days. He's been sober for ninety days. Isn't that great?"

Mason's words tumble inside my head like cement in a mixer. I don't like to think about Ryan's drinking. Forgiving him set me free—forgiving Dennis set me free—but sometimes, when I picture Ryan behind the wheel of that Audi . . . it's triggering. "I'm not sure what to say. I—"

"Here." Mason hands me the chip.

Ryan looks at me.

Our eyes connect.

He's a different man. He has spent so much time with Mason at the computer, deciphering William's algorithm for our startup. He has done everything one could do to fill the void, and I'm grateful, but forgiveness is one thing. Trust is another. To this day, I haven't left Mason alone with Ryan for more than an hour or two.

I turn the chip over.

TO THINE OWN SELF BE TRUE.

Ryan has been true. He has recovered.

"Congratulations," I say. "This is great. Did you tell your parents?"

"No, not yet. Have you talked to them?"

"No, not since before the funeral." I look at the painting of the Mystic Seaport. It hangs above the Kaine family credenza.

"Don't worry," Ryan says. "They'll come around. They just need time to heal."

Mason points at the screen. "Right there?"

Ryan nods.

It's exciting. We're starting a business selling the best adware blocker known to man. I brushed up on my degree, read a book on marketing, and wrote a business case. With our software, there'll be no more pop-ups selling lawn furniture, low-interest-rate mortgages, or anything else. The best part is, websites can't detect our blocker and force users to turn it off because it doesn't actually block anything. It intercepts ad content and replaces it with inspirational quotes, news headlines, or funny sayings—*when life gives you lemons, squirt someone in the eye.*

We're going to make millions.

Seeing Ryan working side-by-side with Mason, one would never know he once lived on the streets. A miracle after only three months.

Yet, he relapsed once before. He could do it again.

"Here." I hand the chip back to Ryan. "William would have been proud of you." I put my hand on Mason's shoulder. "Both of you."

Mason types something. "There. How's that?"

"You did it," Ryan says.

"I'll leave you geeks alone."

I walk into the sitting room, pick up my laptop, and nestle on the sofa. The heavy rain outside makes me happy to have a warm, dry place to rest. I'm grateful to have never been homeless. Ryan has ninety days . . . but what if he starts drinking again?

I've forgiven but not forgotten.

Ryan had no intention of hurting William. I said nothing to the police and let the case turn cold. Mason needs his uncle, but if Ryan relapsed, it would devastate him. Sure, Mason's made friends, joined the LGBTQ group at school, and started dating someone named Garrett, but he's still vulnerable. Losing Ryan would be like losing his father all over again.

I don't want to spend Christmas without William.

It's not fair.

Another red flash, and I open my laptop.

I touch William's wedding ring. It hangs from the chain around my neck, always.

Williams' death is Dennis's fault.

I hate him.

He deserves the death penalty.

Breathe.

There's no reason for me to be angry about him anymore.

Breathe.

The lawyers said he'll get life in prison without parole. His basketball headed boss, Luis Gabaldon, went to jail too. Luis operated four non-profit companies like the Digital Freedom Fighters, using each one as a cover for his industrial espionage business. He hired con men like Dennis to steal technology from one company and sell it to another, and thugs like Tony and Frank to make sure the deals went through. Tony and Frank were arrested in St. Croix for breaking into my condo and trashing the place. No one ever asked who really tore up William's computer, and I never said.

Everyone went to jail, but that doesn't make me feel better.

William is still gone.

At least his legacy will live on.

Someday, Mason will be the CEO of our business. A confident, intelligent Kaine. Fortunately, TriamSys wanted nothing to do with the DFF scandal. As a security company, they were embarrassed to have "Robert Lang" listed as a former employee. William's manager, TJ, refused to take the SD card back. He said William's project had been so top secret, he didn't even know what was on the card, and he didn't want to know.

His loss was our gain.

William's algorithm is the magic behind intercepting online ads and replacing them.

I open the laptop, and a message pops onto the screen, declaring half-off on all Christmas tree ornaments. It's ridiculous. I clear the ad, log into HeatSinkers, and click on the three questions.

1) What happened?

My fingers tremble over the keys. I haven't done this for a long time. For it to work, I must be honest. The events leading to William's death began the day I asked Ryan to babysit Mason. If I hadn't done that, there would never have been restraining order. Ryan would have been in our lives all those years, and he wouldn't have relapsed.

He wouldn't have stolen the Audi.

William wouldn't have died.

It was all my fault.

I type, "My husband died because of my anger disorder. I can't stop blaming myself."

2) Why did it make you angry?
"I woke up in an empty bed again this morning."

3) Who or what can you forgive?

I slam the laptop shut.

It's not about forgiveness.

It's about letting go. I need to let him go.

I need to get out of here.

Fresh air.

I don't care how hard it's raining.

Laughing comes from the office. They're so good together. It's time I trusted Ryan.

In the garage, I hit the button, the garage door opens, and I grab a shovel. The rain is coming down hard. The gutter at the end of the driveway rages like a river. I slide the shovel into the back of my SUV and jump in the driver's seat.

Who or what can you forgive?

The windshield wipers can't keep the neighborhood from blurring. The houses, the lawns, the hedges, the rough-sawn cedar fences—everything is tinted red. This shouldn't be happening. I forgave everyone. Everyone. I even forgave my mother for leaving me to raise myself.

It's not fair.

There's no one else left to forgive.

I cruise onto the freeway, wipers on high speed. The floating bridge is slippery, and Lake Washington welcomes the downpour, pulling the deluge into its depths without remorse. I press on the accelerator, and my four-wheel-drive glides over the wet pavement. My heart races with the engine around every curve, and the tires slip when I take the exit for Bellevue, but I don't slow down.

I fly through the streets.

Brake, turn, accelerate.

Rage, burn—*I must not let the anger in.*

The long, narrow drive into the cemetery ends in a "T," and I take a left. Then a right. Then I leave the gravel path and rumble over someone's grave before sliding to a stop. The rain drenches me before I can get the shovel and run to William's resting place.

WILLIAM KAINE - BELOVED HUSBAND AND FATHER.

I stab the earth.

I sling clumps of sodden grass over my shoulder.

I drop to my knees, grasp William's wedding ring, and pull.

The chain breaks.

I hold the ring up to the sky.

The red rain comes down. Melts the mud. Fills the hole I dug.

I drop his ring into the hole and cover it with dirt.

William. I love you. I will always love you.

The wind blasts.

I wrap my arms around myself.

I shake. I suffer. I seethe.

I see red.

Across the cemetery, a massive statue bears the Lord's Prayer.

". . . forgive us our trespasses, as we forgive those who trespass against us . . ."

The rain dies.

I read the prayer again.

Time passes.

I read it again.

The red recedes.

William, please forgive me my trespasses, as I forgive those who trespass against me. As I find a way to forgive myself.

AUTHOR'S NOTE

Thank you so much for reading *The Resentment*. I am grateful for the time you spent with Lauren, Ryan, and Mason, and I am thrilled to have shared this story with you.

The idea for this story began one day when I looked at my wife and asked myself, "What's the worst that could happen?" An image of her dangling from a bridge popped into my head, but I knew it could get worse. I pictured myself holding onto her arms, keeping her from falling into the raging river below. But, it had to get worse. I would have to drop her. We lived near Seattle at the time, and one day, I saw a woman screaming at a barista in Starbucks. Her face turned red, and she slammed her hands on the counter, and that was it. Lauren was born.

Once I got to know Lauren, Mason, and Ryan, I realized they, like everyone, grapple with obtaining social acceptance of their concerns—anger, addiction, sexual orientation. I wanted to see how they would react to the mystery surrounding William's death and whether they could come to a loving understanding of each other despite years of resentment. I was both surprised and gratified by the ending. I hope you were too.

Thank you again for reading *The Resentment*. Please feel free to connect with me on my website at www.topaine.com, on Twitter @TOPaine, or on my Facebook author page: www.facebook.com/TOPaineAuthor.

Warm regards,

T. O.

ACKNOWLEDGMENTS

First and foremost, I thank all of the fearless readers out there. You make the literary world a wonderful place for us all. Without you, this book is a tree falling in the woods, not making a sound.

Thank you to all the early editors, critiquers, and reviewers. Elena Hartwell Taylor for development, encouragement, and kindness. Robert Dugoni for development, motivation, and exemplar.

Thank you to my family and friends. Dad for always telling me to "be good and pack the bacon." Mom for always telling me to "just do the best you can." Jess Caudill for always knowing right from wrong and the bravery to act in kind. Kim, Jade, and River – my reasons for being. My reasons for trudging the Road of Happy Destiny.

And finally, thanks to everyone who has suffered at the hands of obsession, denial, and circumstance, and lived to share their experience, strength, and hope.

ABOUT THE AUTHOR

T.O. Paine holds a master's degree in information systems, and when he is not writing, you can find him running or cycling through the mountains of Colorado, USA. He has run over thirty marathons, ridden over twenty 100-mile cycling events, and completed an IRONMAN.

T.O. resides with his wife, two children, and a Boston terrier who stares at himself in the mirror, questioning his existence.

Made in United States
Orlando, FL
19 June 2022

18959592R00269